THE PROPERTY PEOPLE

Michael Hillier

Published by KSF Publishing

All characters in this publication are fictitious and resemblance to real persons, living or dead, is purely coincidental. Many of the locations mentioned are real but fictional licence has been taken with some of the details.

To my late wife Sue.

Inspiration, researcher, critic, editor and best friend

1 - October 1953

John Tucker staggered to the top of the steps with a bagful of books over his shoulder and several more in his arms. He fished in his pocket for the key and fiddled with the lock to open the door before he realised it was already unlocked.

"Damn Ambrose - forgotten to lock up again."

He swung the door open, dropped the bag of books in the lobby, and headed for the kitchenette to make a cup of tea. Then he came to a sudden halt.

A beautiful young girl was sitting in the only comfortable chair in the flat.

"What are you doing here?"

Her expression was somewhere between horror and contempt. "I might ask you the same question."

He noticed her voice was attractive, melodious yet perfectly correct in intonation, as if she had been trained for the stage. It made John realise that she was more mature than she had at first seemed.

"These are my rooms." He was annoyingly aware that his voice had a tone of explanation, almost of apology.

"They most certainly are not. This is Ambrose Stacey's place."

"You know Ambrose?"

It wasn't surprising. Ambrose seemed to know every beautiful girl in Cambridge. This was obviously his latest – and by far the best.

"Know him? I happen to be his sister - for my sins."

"His sister? Ambrose has a sister?" John was aware that he sounded like a half-wit.

"Some people *do* have sisters."

"I'm sorry. I expected you to be much younger."

"I am still under twenty-one."

5

John was saved from further apologies by the arrival of Ambrose, sweeping into the rooms in his usual proprietorial way. He stopped just inside the door and gazed from one to the other.

"Ah, I see you've met. Tucker - this is my little sister. She's up here for the Freshers' Ball. Shall you be going?"

"Can't afford it."

"No – well . . . Alison, this is Tucker. He shares my rooms."

"Hello," said John.

The girl ignored him. "You didn't tell me you shared rooms," she accused.

"No choice, m'dear. Pater keeps me on such short rations that I can't afford anything better." His voice took on an exaggeratedly upper-class tone. "It's all very well for you in your plush finishing school in Geneva."

"But to share with –." She inspected John distastefully.

"They're building a new residential block in the meadows across the river. I've put my name down for one of those but they won't be ready till the spring."

"Couldn't you find someone more suitable?"

"Oh, Tucker's more than suitable. He's bloody good at doing my prep for me."

John was starting to feel angry. "She's not changing in here, is she? And you know she can't *stay* here. It's against the rules . . ."

"Don't worry. I'll be taking her across to the guest rooms in a minute."

Alison had risen elegantly to her feet. "You're taking me *now,* Ambrose." She looked John straight in the eye and he could see nothing but icy distaste in her gaze. "Your room-mate's manners match his dress sense."

She swept from the room leaving even Ambrose looking slightly alarmed. He picked up her suitcase from beside the armchair, tut-tutted at John, and followed her down the steps.

"Not a very good start," John muttered to himself. "But then - I don't expect I shall ever see her again."

He closed the door and started to tidy up the place which had been left in its usual mess by Ambrose when he got up earlier.

2

It was mid-morning two days later when there came a knock. Fortunately John didn´t have a lecture this morning and he was working on his own. He opened the door to find one of the college servants standing there, puffing and blowing from his climb up the steps.

"Them stairs'll be the death of me," the old boy complained. "You John Tucker?"

"Yes."

"Message from Professor Coggins. Will you go to his room straightaway?" He handed John a piece of paper.

"Did he say what it was about?"

The man shook his head. "Wouldn't tell me that, would he?" He turned and started to stumble back down the steps.

John read the message and saw it was urgent. He quickly brushed his hair, straightened his tie and rushed out. One didn´t hang about when you received an urgent request from the senior professor in the faculty. A few minutes later he was going up the stairs in the third quad three at a time. He hurried halfway along the right-hand corridor to Old Coggy's office. He paused for just a moment outside the big ornate door to take a breath.

John swallowed. "I wonder what the hell is the matter?" he muttered to himself.

He looked up and down the empty corridor. The oak panelling glowed softly in the dim light which was reflected from the ceiling onto the deep green carpet. There was no sense of hurry here, no indication of the bright October sunshine outside. In here it always seemed the same - day or night, winter or summer. Time didn't seem to intrude. Standing alone in the antique silence, John could believe that nothing had changed in the last five hundred years, except occasionally the names on the door labels. But he couldn't pause to think about that.

He returned his attention to the door in front of him – "D.M.Coggins, Senior Physics Lecturer". This ascetic, uncommunicative sixty-year-old held John's future in his hands. A critical remark on a paper could condemn the student to hours of concentrated study. A bad report from the professor could affect the level of the degree he received.

So the summons he had received ten minutes ago was all the more peculiar. It was the kind of peremptory call usually reserved for students who had consistently failed to turn in their work on time, or who had been reported for trying to deflower one of the chambermaids. With a strange sense of misgiving, John raised his hand and knocked.

Almost at once the green "Enter" light glowed. That was strange in itself. Was old Coggy waiting for him? He gulped, pressed down on the ornate lever and pushed.

The door swished over the deep pile carpet as it swung open and John blinked in the sudden brightness of the room after the dim corridor outside. Professor Coggins was one of the fortunate few who had his offices on the first floor overlooking the Backs and the bright morning sunlight was streaming in through the high windows. John smiled inwardly as he reflected that it was unlikely the old boy ever turned round to look at one of the most beautiful panoramas in Cambridge.

Now the professor was sitting at his desk with his back to the view. He rose to face John as the door whispered shut behind him - a slight, stooping, grey-haired figure, prematurely withered by lack of exposure to daylight.

"Come in, Tucker." His voice sighed like the wind in a pine forest and John's stomach began to shrivel.

Coggins seemed to study the sensitive, brown eyes of the lad who stood in front of him for a moment. "I'm afraid I've got bad news for you, Tucker. I've had a phone call from your mother. Apparently your father's condition has suddenly worsened. I expect you realise what that means?"

So *that* was the reason for the summons. John's mind leaped back to the last holiday he had spent at home. His dad had seemed to be better this summer. He had been able to sit out in the garden on warm days and the sun had apparently helped his lungs. John had even dared to hope that the man was going to triumph over the disease which had dogged him since he was caught in the ship-fire which had caused his early discharge from the navy. But John had also accepted that he was likely to get worse in the short, damp days of autumn.

Coggins cleared his throat. “I gather your father has been ill for some time.” He paused as though expecting John to take over the conversation. “Is that right?”

“Yes sir.”

“However your mother is obviously very worried. I understand he’s taken a serious turn for the worse. She said something about him going into a coma. You must go back to be with her.”

John didn’t doubt that the request was serious. His mother hated even going out to the telephone. She had become good at coping without her son. She knew how important this final year was to him. She wouldn’t have dragged him home in the middle of term unless she thought it was essential.

The professor was still talking. “You’d better go straight away. What further lectures have you got this week?”

“Just one, sir. Applied Statics. Tomorrow morning.”

Coggins made a note on his pad. “Forget that. I’ll tell them what’s happened and get the notes sent to you. What time is the next train?”

“Er - I think there’s one at twelve fifteen.”

The old man glanced at his watch. “Then you’d better hurry. That’s less than half an hour. Can you get a lift to the station?”

“I’ll ask my room-mate, Ambrose Stacey.”

“Oh - him.” Coggins looked down his nose. “Comes from down your way, doesn’t he?”

“My father used to be the Estate Manager for the Staceys before he was taken ill. We still live in an estate house.” John didn’t know why he felt the need to tell his tutor about it.

“Hmm. Young Stacey may come from a splendid family. I don’t know about that. But he could benefit from a little more application to his studies.”

John hardly heard the comment. He looked past the professor and through the large, high window. In the garden the world was bright and the autumn sun dappled the yellow leaves of the plane trees across the river. But now the sunlight seemed less cheerful, the view less beautiful. He had a premonition that none of this luxury was for him. He was being dragged away from his future. His thoughts went back to the depressing atmosphere of sickness in Riversmeet - the house in Devon which looked out across the bleak, wide-open, winter estuary.

"Well," said Coggins, "you'd better get a move on."

John looked up to see that the old boy was regarding him quizzically.

"Is there anything you want?"

"No, sir. Thank you very much." John turned to go.

"Oh - and Tucker."

"Yes sir?"

The grey eyes seemed to have softened just a little. "Get back as soon as you reasonably can, won't you?"

"Of course, sir."

"I have been thinking about putting you forward for a Ph.D. - subject to results of course. I could do with a bright young assistant in the department."

"Thank you, sir."

As he hurried back to his rooms, he felt the warm glow resulting from the old man's commendation. A research position in his department could be the first step on the ladder to a bright academic future. For a few seconds John allowed himself to luxuriate in the dreams of being a rising star in research physics – publishing papers, giving lectures. He would have to learn about public speaking . . .

Then he dragged himself back to earth. He must get packed. He must reach home as quickly as possible. His immediate worry was how he could get to the station in time. If he missed this train he wouldn't be back tonight. He would have to spend the dark hours trying to sleep on a hard seat at Waterloo station. A whole day would be lost. He owed it to his mother to make sure that she spent as little time as possible on her own when her husband was so seriously ill.

3

When John got back to their rooms, Ambrose had returned and was flat out on the settee with his feet hanging over the end. That was his normal position at this time of day. John knew the fellow´s routine - struggle out of bed at eight forty-five, swallow a quick prairie oyster, rush down to register for the lecture, then slide out after twenty minutes when he wasn't under scrutiny. After that he would come straight back here to catch up on the sleep he'd missed last night.

Yet, despite this, Ambrose would somehow manage to pick up a two-two in Politics with Economics. That would be all the qualifications he would need to assure a brilliant future for himself, either in the City or the West End. Ambrose was a young man with all the right connections. It was a very different matter for John.

A strange quirk of fate had selected them to share rooms for their final year. Although they lived within a few miles of each other, the two of them had nothing in common. Ambrose was a true scion of the nobility. Son of a baronet, he had the looks and the personality to go with it. He was clever enough, but idle. He led the life of a typical young gentleman at Cambridge - a social whirl of girl-chasing, hard-drinking parties where life began at 9 p.m. and finished in the small hours. In the afternoon there might be a workout on the river or in the gym but most of the daytime was spent sleeping off last night's hangover. Their activities were officially frowned upon by the authorities, but their fees were needed more than their academic prowess.

He reached down and shook the recumbent Ambrose by the shoulder. He had to do it three times before there was a groan and the watery blue eyes opened.

"What? Oh, my God, it's you again, Tucker. What the bloody hell do you want this time?"

"Look, Ambrose. I've got to rush home. My - my father's ill. The train goes in twenty minutes. Is there any chance you could run me to the station?"

"Not a hope. I'm nearly out of petrol." He rolled over and fell asleep again.

John took a deep breath and tried a second time. "Ambrose - it's important. I'll buy you some petrol. It´s important I catch the twelve fifteen."

"You'd better start running then," he said without opening his eyes. "You'll make it. You're fit enough."

John swallowed his mounting desperation. "It's a mile and a half to the station. I'll never get there on foot, carrying my case."

There was still no response. But he couldn't give up. He had to persuade his room-mate to help him, even if the fellow was going to make him crawl to do it.

"Please listen, Ambrose. My father's very ill. My mother spoke direct to Old Coggy on the phone. He's in a coma. He may not last the night. The twelve-fifteen is the last train which gets me to London in time to get across to Waterloo for the connection to Exeter. If I miss it, I won't get back till tomorrow afternoon. It may be too late by then."

Ambrose rolled back to look at him. "You creep. Do you never let up?" He stretched. "All right. I'll take you, but you'll have to pay me a pound for my running costs."

"You owe me thirty bob already for the prep I did for you last week."

"That's it then." Ambrose sat up. "It'll cost you thirty shillings. Petrol's getting expensive. Is that a deal?"

John glowered at him. "All right."

"Good. Better get moving then. Don't want to be late, do you?"

John went into his bedroom and looked round. He pulled down his father's battered suitcase from the top of the wardrobe and threw some clothes and a few other essentials into it. He selected a handful of books from the shelf and put those on top of the clothes.

"That's right. Don't forget to keep up the study." Ambrose was leaning against the door jamb. "Got to make sure you keep in Old Coggy's good books."

John didn't respond. He didn't mind being ragged. Ambrose wasn't so bad when he'd had a chance to wake up slowly. The fellow just felt he had to put on an act all the time, to keep asserting how superior he was, and how boring people were who had to work to get good results.

"Tell me, John. Why do creeps like you always put themselves in a position where someone can take them for a ride? I can get one over on you any time I like, can't I?" He shook his head. "You're going to have to learn, little Johnny, that you've got to be a whole lot tougher with people if you're going to get anywhere in this world. It isn't enough just to be a clever dick. You've got to be ruthless as well."

For the moment John ignored him as he picked up his case. Later he remembered the advice. "OK. I'm ready. Thanks for putting yourself out, Ambrose."

"That's all right. What would you do without me, young Johnny? Sometimes I think I'm just like a second father to you." Ambrose patted him on the shoulder and smiled indulgently as he led the way down the stairs.

4

Even after a half-mile walk from the station through the soft Devon drizzle, John could still taste the sooty, wet, adventurous flavour of the railway on his clothes. He'd been rushing all day, but as he got nearer home his pace slowed involuntarily. A sense of grim foreboding gripped him - a feeling that he was going to find that it would be too late when he got there.

At the end of the Strand he paused and took a breath. A keen breeze was coming off the river, carrying the occasional squall in its belly. He remembered these south-westerly winds from the past. Nothing could escape the penetrating damp which such weather brought. But he could already see Riversmeet. He only had to go the last hundred yards.

At the gate he paused and looked up at the double-fronted house. The building was dark and blinkered. There were no curtains in the windows at the front and it gave the impression that the place was unoccupied. The last feeble street light was a long way behind him. But the wet house seemed to gleam in some unknown light source, looming larger than its three stories. John had heard that it had once been the home of a prominent local smuggler. In this weather it looked an ideal haunt for such a man.

His shoes bit grittily on the three York stone steps leading up to the front door. He had to rattle around with his key to get the lock to turn. His mother could not have failed to hear him, but she didn't come out to switch on the light and let him in. That wasn't her way. He crossed the echoing hall and pushed open the large kitchen door. For a minute he stood there, blinking in the light and trying to adjust his eyes.

Mrs Tucker was standing at the sink. She was a small, stooping woman whose youthful prettiness had long since faded. John had known that she would be in the kitchen, busying herself with some non-essential chore. She always did that when there was a crisis. She seemed unable to cope with an emotional problem unless her hands were busy.

She didn't offer him a welcome kiss. "John, I'm glad you got here tonight. The doctor said he'd send someone to stay with me, but I didn't want that."

He crossed to her and gave her a peck on the cheek. He noticed the dry, thin feel of her skin against his own damp face. But she was too immersed in her own feelings to respond.

"Is he still - ?" He couldn't ask her if his dad had died yet. "Can I go and see him?"

"Of course you can. You won't disturb him. In fact you won't get any response at all from him. But I'll stay here if you don't mind. I don't like it when he's in this state."

John returned through the hall. In the back sitting room the heavy velvet curtains were drawn tight across the windows. A single table lamp tried ineffectively to lighten the gloom. His father's bed had been in here for most of the last two years since his illness had worsened. John had almost forgotten what it had been like when it was used as a lounge.

Gingerly he approached the low couch. He was appalled by what he saw. It was barely a month since he had returned to university, yet in that time his father seemed to have lost several stone in weight. He lay there in a deep sleep with the covers just below his chin. But, even though it was only his head which was visible, John could see how thin he was. It was as though his flesh had been burned up by the disease.

The face was like a death mask. The eyes were shut. The muscles had shrunk. The dry, brittle skin appeared to be moulded over nothing but bone and sinew. It had turned a pale, creamy yellow with darker random blotches and was shaded with the stubble of a half-shaved beard. His temple was etched across by a dark, rambling vein. The only sign of life in his body was the movement of his chest. It heaved and collapsed in a slow rhythm as the breath rattled in his throat. Nothing else moved. Not a muscle twitched. Not a movement flickered across his face. He was in a deep coma. John knew, with a sinking heart, that his father would never speak to him again.

Now he understood what his mother had been going through in the last month. This quick sight of the man was enough for John. He suddenly wanted desperately to be away from the sickly smell and the atmosphere of approaching death. He looked round the room. There was a low fire in the grate, and the place seemed uncomfortably hot. The clock on the mantelpiece had a soft, menacing tick. It was measuring the count-down to disaster. John felt the hair on his neck tingle. He couldn't wait to get back to the kitchen.

The relief as he walked into the fresh smell of peeled potatoes was overwhelming. He saw that his mother had collapsed onto one of the bentwood chairs beside the kitchen table. She continued looking at the floor as John approached her. Somehow he felt as though she had mentally been there in the sitting room with them. Perhaps even now she didn't know that he had returned.

John forced himself to speak. "What does the doctor say?"

"Oh! Doctor Morton's been here an awful lot. He only left at about seven this evening. He said –." She paused. "He said he won't last another day."

"I've never seen him like this before. He seems to have got an awful lot worse all of a sudden."

His mother looked up at him for the first time. "We knew it would come to this sooner or later." She dropped her eyes again to the floor. "But somehow it doesn't make it any easier."

"Mother, I'm sorry I wasn't here sooner." The guilt was speaking for him. "If I had been, I might have been able to be more help."

She patted his hand. "You came as soon as I called. I didn't want to bring you back - until I knew there was no alternative."

Something about the tone of her voice was ominous. It made him wonder if there was a deeper meaning to her words. But he shook his head. Now was not the time to bother her.

"Is there anything I can do, now that I'm here?"

"Not tonight. Doctor Morton says your father's deeply unconscious. He doesn't feel any pain. We just have to wait." She looked at him and smiled bleakly. "And how are you? How's Cambridge?" It was as though she was forcing herself to find something to say to him.

"Cambridge is OK. In fact it's good. The studies are going well." He sat down opposite her, trying to think of things she would like to hear. “And there are lots of things happening in the evenings. Ambrose Stacey is a lively room-mate.”

“Well! Wasn’t that lucky - you two being picked out of the hat together? I hope you get on well with him. It doesn’t do any harm to cultivate people who can be useful to you in the future.”

John didn’t want his mother to get the wrong impression. “Actually we haven’t got a lot in common. But I did manage to bribe him into giving me a lift to catch the train.”

“Oh. Wasn’t that nice of him? I think that’s really good of him, to put himself out like that when he didn’t need to.”

John thought of the way he had to crawl to get the fellow to help him, but he didn’t bother to correct her.

“We must invite him round at Christmas,” she said.

“Er - I don't know about that, mum . . .”

“I’ve told you before, John, you must put some effort into getting on with the right people. It’s not enough just to be clever.”

“But our backgrounds are so different . . .”

“You sound just like your father. He was always saying things like that.” She seemed to get some spirit for the first time since he had arrived home. “I don’t know why it was, but he would never have anything to do with the Staceys – socially, I mean. Of course, he has worked for them for the whole of our married life, except during the war.”

“Did he ever tell you what he had against them?”

She looked round at him rather too sharply. “He would never tell me anything about it. There must have been some sort of a quarrel. But I’m sure it wasn’t your father’s fault. He’s done a lot for them in his time. You should remind young Ambrose of that when you have the chance to have a serious chat with him – in a nice sort of way, of course.”

“Yes.” He sighed. “Well, we’ll have to see what happens.”

“Perhaps you and Ambrose could patch things up between the two families,” she seemed to be musing to herself.

John decided to talk about something else. “At least Old Coggy’s pleased with me. He even hinted there might be a chance of staying on after my degree. You know - doing research and going for a Ph.D.”

"Oh, I don't know about that. I don't think I like the idea of you as one of those dry old professors."

"Oh, mother," he complained, "You're making me into something middle-aged when I'm only twenty-two."

"Well, like it or not, you've got to start thinking about getting a job very soon. You can't be a student for the rest of your life. You've got to earn your own living. And when it comes to finding a good job it's important to have the right contacts. I'm sure that people like Ambrose Stacey will end up with good jobs."

John snorted. "I don't think he'll get much of a degree."

"That doesn't matter. All that matters is that he's been to Cambridge. It opens the door to so many possibilities. That's why your father was so anxious for *you* to go. He always felt his career had been held back because he had to leave school at fourteen. *He* had to study at home in the evenings to get his qualifications. That's why he was prepared to move heaven and earth to get you the best possible education. He was adamant that you wouldn't be held back like he was. It's no good you hanging around at university after everyone else has left and got themselves proper jobs."

John had heard her say the same sort of thing a dozen times before.

"Mother, the purpose of education isn't only to get you a good job. The pursuit of knowledge is much more important than that. How do you think all the new inventions are developed?"

"Not by crusty old professors sitting around talking rubbish, I'm sure. Now, I must go and settle your father for the night. You'd better go to bed. You'll be tired after your journey."

John gave up. "OK. Can I help with anything?"

"No. I've been doing it on my own until now. I've got my own routine. You go and get some rest. I'll need you to be fresh for tomorrow."

As he made his way up the staircase, he noticed (almost for the first time) the threadbare carpet beneath his feet. In the corner of his bedroom was the wide metal-framed bed that sagged in the middle. Stretched across the windows were the unlined curtains with the faded prints of sailing ships. Nothing had changed since the summer - in fact, since he had gone to senior school. For the first time he saw the poverty and the shabbiness of the place.

He tossed his suitcase down on the broken armchair. He opened it only to get his pyjamas out. Unpacking could be done in the morning. When he came back from the bathroom, he shivered in the pervasive damp. The house had no central heating and the room felt cold and uncared for. Although the bed was freshly made, the sheets felt clammy and slightly sticky when he climbed between them. He thrashed about for more than an hour, trying to get warm and comfortable. It was a long time before he struggled off to sleep.

5

John’s mother was already at the stove when he reached the kitchen at seven o’clock the next morning. He had the fleeting impression that she had been there all night, but he said nothing to her about that. Now the breakfast table was set for one. He remembered that his mother never allowed herself to sit down and eat breakfast with her men-folk.

"How is he this morning?"

“There's no change." She concentrated on boiling the eggs. "Doctor Morton said that, when the time comes, it will all be over suddenly. Until then we just have to wait."

“Can’t we do anything at all?”

“No. Just wait.”

Waiting didn’t come easily to John. “Is there anything you want me to help you with?”

She shook her head. It seemed as though she had cut herself off from him. Perhaps it was her form of defence. But John felt that he couldn’t just sit here in this stifling atmosphere waiting for something to happen. He wanted to be out in the live world.

“I thought I might go for a walk if you don’t mind.”

She glanced at him and nodded. "You could do with some fresh air. That college life makes you look all pasty."

His mother thought Cambridge was a den of iniquity without any kind of healthy activity. John had decided long ago that it was a waste of time trying to convince her otherwise.

They talked a little of everyday things as he ate his breakfast. But, as soon as he decently could, he escaped into the fresh air and left her alone to the cooking, the cleaning and the worrying. The autumn morning was bright and sparkling. A fresh wind drove scudding clouds across the sky. Later it might turn to rain, but John didn't let that worry him. He turned up the collar of his windcheater and strode out with the breeze on his right cheek.

His mind was in a turmoil. Logically his father seemed unlikely to survive more than a few days. He remembered the gasping heave of the man’s chest as he struggled to get his next lungful of oxygen. There was no hope of recovery. John had a nasty feeling that everything in his life was about to change.

Almost without thinking, he took one of his old walks. He followed the footpath to the confluence of the rivers. Then he turned onto the track which climbed the gentle ridge behind the houses. This brought him out onto the main road where it dropped sharply down the hill to cross the flat valley of the meandering tributary on a raised embankment. But he kept going north until he reached the public footpath which crossed Home Park.

He had always liked Stacey Court. The balustraded roofs of the gracious building were just visible from here above the banks of dark, shiny rhododendron and laurel. They were flanked each side by an ancient, massive cedar of Lebanon. But he most enjoyed walking across the well-cropped grass in the park, passing beneath the irregularly-spaced trees which were now betraying the signs of autumn gold around the edges of their leaves. The ordered lines of the hoop-iron railings, rusting gently, were broken only by the creaking latch-gates. They seemed to have stood here for ever, carefully regulating the pattern of the landscape. Everything was in its place. Everything was neatly organised. It appealed to his orderly mind.

John realised his future was changing. The rest of his life was going to take place without his dad – the person he'd relied on most of all as he was growing up. Soon *he* would become the head of the house. He'd have to look after his mum. He suspected that she would want him to come home at the end of his degree in Cambridge. He would have to talk to her seriously about that. He believed there was no future for him in Devon. The county was known as the graveyard of ambition. Everything important happened in London or Cambridge or Oxford. But he knew his mother would never agree to leave the area where she had spent the whole of her life until now. They would have to try and sort out something between them.

At the far side of the Home Park the path plunged into the woods. At first they were ancient, open woodlands but soon they gave way to dense plantations of black, close-marching conifers. The footpath went up the centre of a broad, grassy ride. John knew all the short cuts through these woods. After half an hour he turned along a narrow path where the sun hadn't yet climbed high enough to dispel the dark mistiness which lingered from the night. The short spiky branches of the trees reached out at him from close on both sides and it was a relief to suddenly break out into a clearing.

Too late, he froze when he saw there was a couple already there. They were no more than twenty feet from him. The noise of his crashing through the undergrowth had caused them to spring apart and for a moment they stood transfixed, staring at him as though he was some terrible apparition. John wasn’t quite sure what they had been doing the moment before he arrived, but the man had now blushed a bright red and the woman was straightening her clothes.

He realised he knew them both by sight. The man was a local gentleman farmer called Ralph Trenchard. And the woman was none other than Alison Stacey, the girl he had last seen a few days ago in his rooms at college. She must have travelled back immediately after the Freshers’ Ball to make this tryst. John was struck again by her beauty, even with the angry flush which now coloured her cheeks.

The man was the first to recover. He turned to the girl and gave a little bow. "It's been nice meeting you, Alison. You must call on us some time. Give me a ring to arrange it."

He turned and made for his horse which was cropping the grass nearby. With a graceful movement he pulled himself into the saddle, raised his hand in salute and wheeled away out of the clearing. It seemed to John that he went with undue haste.

"Ralph -." Alison's hand was outstretched. She stayed frozen in that attitude until he’d disappeared. John couldn't prevent his upper lip from curling in contempt.

The girl seemed to become aware of him after a while. She rounded on him. "What are you grinning at?"

John's sneer disappeared. "I'm not grinning," he said quietly.

"What are you doing here anyway? Don't you know this is private land?"

“As far as I'm aware," said John, "I'm on a public footpath."

"No, you're not.” Her beautiful face was distorted by anger. “The public footpath follows the main ride. In future you had better keep to that. I'll tell George to put you in your place if he comes across you in the private part of the woods in future."

"It would appear that Ralph Trenchard had made the same mistake." The ghost of a smile hovered around John's face.

“You insolent -." In three brisk strides she was in front of him, her riding crop lifted to strike.

John raised his hands to protect himself. As the crop descended he caught hold of it and pulled it away from her. His action was a little too violent. Taken off balance, she lost her footing and fell in the bracken.

"I'm sorry." Horrified at the result of his action, John bent down to help her to her feet. "I didn't mean . . ."

"You lout." She struck him full across the face. "You bloody great, violent prick. So you think you can go around assaulting ladies, do you? You bloody coward."

John gasped with surprise, more shocked by her language than the attack. The girl leaped unaided to her feet. There were tears streaming down her face.

“Get out of here," she screamed at him. "You'd better get out fast, you little shit. There'll be someone coming to give you a hiding in a quarter of an hour if there's still any sign of you around. That'll teach you to attack a lady. Do you hear me?" She stumbled towards her horse.

"Here. Wait a minute . . ."

"Don't you dare come near me!" She dragged herself into the saddle, swung the horse round and urged it out of the clearing at a gallop. The thudding of the hooves faded into the distance.

"Phew." John looked round the clearing at the flattened bracken and the grass churned up by the horses' hooves. It was only a couple of minutes since he’d stumbled into the place. Now a major incident seemed to have been caused by his clumsiness.

She had said she was sending someone “to teach him a lesson”. Pride made him feel like staying to face them, but there was really little point. Probably she would have cooled off by the time she got back to the house. Besides, the walk was ruined for him now. After a moment’s hesitation he turned and started back along the narrow path. He was feeling hot with embarrassment. Had the incident really been his fault?

Absentmindedly he raised his hand to scratch a tickle on his cheek. He felt the sticky sensation and looked down at his hand. He pulled out his handkerchief and dabbed at his face. There was blood on the white cotton. Her nails had actually drawn blood.

It was then he felt the first stirring of anger. He couldn't believe that he had been to blame for this foolish scene. She had over-reacted. She had behaved with typical upper-class arrogance and without any justification - just because he'd stumbled across her in a compromising position with a married man. And what was the point? He had seen almost nothing and certainly didn't intend to spread stories about them that he couldn´t substantiate, even if he wished.

The more he thought about it, the more unreasonable he thought she was. He vowed that next time they met he would be ready for her. He would tell her exactly what he thought of spoiled upper-class girls who lacked self-control. That thought made him feel better as he emerged from the woods into the sunshine.

It wasn't until he was half-way home that he realised he was still carrying her riding crop.

6

In fact Alison was in a towering rage when she got back to the house. She swung into the stable-yard and skidded to a halt in front of a startled Mary. She leaped from the saddle and flung the reins at the stable-girl, then rushed into the house without another word. She entered through the back door which took her straight into the kitchen. Annie was frying breakfast.

"Where's George?" she demanded.

"George?" asked the cook innocently. "Do you mean George Hayter?"

"Of course I do."

"Bless you, my dear. I ain't seen 'im in six month - since 'e retired. Got a cottage down in Fore Street. Pretty little place, it is."

"Retired?" Alison gawped at her. "Well, who's the gamekeeper now?"

Cook shook her head infuriatingly. "Oh no, my lovely. We 'aven't 'ad no proper gamekeeper since afore the war. George was a sort of 'andyman for 'is last ten year. 'E only did a bit of gamekeepin' when the master 'ad visitors what wanted to go shootin' in the woods."

"So now," shouted Alison, working herself into a fine old temper, "that means anyone can just walk through our estates and do what they want, can they?"

"What *is* the matter with ′ee, my dear? Somethin's got you proper riled up," Annie tut-tutted.

But Alison had already gone.

She went straight to the breakfast room. As she'd guessed, her father was still there. He took one look at her flushed face and sparkling eyes and bent again over his bowl of porridge. He didn't feel ready for teenage tantrums.

"Morning, my dear."

Alison stood squarely in front of him across the breakfast table. "Daddy, don't we have anyone to look after the estates any longer?"

"Pardon?" He raised his bloodhound eyes to look at her. She thought he looked just like an overweight version of one of his dogs.

"Daddy, you know we used to have a gamekeeper to check there was nobody lurking around the place. Don't we have anyone like that any more?"

He shook his head sadly. "My dear, that was a long time ago. We can't afford people like that nowadays. They cost *far* too much money."

"So that means anyone can just walk anywhere they like and do anything they like on our land, does it?" Her chest was rising and falling with emotion.

He tried to calm her down. "Well, not exactly. If we think there's a problem somewhere, I will call Constable Harrington. He *is* here to protect private property, after all. Why? Have you seen anyone committing damage?"

"Not damage – no. But some young man came barging out of a side path through the woods and frightened my horse and landed me in the bracken." She indicated the damp patch on her breeches. "And when I told him to get out, he said he had a perfect right to be there. He was most obnoxious."

Sir Oswald looked startled. "Did he molest you in some way?"

"Not bloody likely. It was more a case of my molesting him - with my crop."

"Oh, dear. He won't make a complaint, will he?" Her father's voice took on a worried tone. "One has to be most careful these days."

Her fists slammed down on the table and made the plates bounce. "Goddammit, father, he was trespassing on our land."

"Alison." Sir Oswald took in a deep breath and composed himself in the way he imagined a landowner might. "I do wish you would behave in a more ladylike fashion. Why am I spending all this money on a finishing school, if you're going to go about talking like a guttersnipe? Thank goodness you're off to Switzerland again on Sunday."

Alison nodded. "I see. So whenever I'm out riding in future, I'm likely to have strange characters popping up all over the place to disturb my ride." She planted her hands on her hips in a way that reminded him so much of the way her mother used to look when she was roused.

"Not all over the place - no. But there are long-standing public rights of way through the park and the woods which we can't do anything about. You'll just have to keep away from them if you don't want to see anybody."

"How do I find out where these public routes are?"

"Oh, don't ask me. I don't know where they go." He scratched his forehead. "I would tell you to ask the estate manager. But Tucker's replacement (I've forgotten his name) resigned in the spring. I suppose I'm going to have to find someone else now." Stacey didn't like to be reminded of all the responsibilities which went with owning a large estate.

"Oh – Tucker!" Her eyes rose in recognition. "I remember the name now – Tucker. That's who it was."

"Who what was?"

"The man who disturbed me."

Her father shook his head. "Oh, no. Can't possibly be. The man's been bedridden for months. It couldn't have been Tucker."

Alison sighed theatrically. "Not the father. It was the son." Her temper started to work vindictively on her quarry. "I met him the other day in Ambrose's rooms - tall and arrogant and thinks he's good-looking. What's his Christian name?"

"Oh yes, I do believe Tucker had a son." Sir Oswald shook his head again. "Damned if I can remember his name though. I thought he was away at university somewhere."

"Well, he's *not* - not today anyway." She had a sudden thought. "Tell me, daddy, does his father live in an estate house?"

The old man nodded lugubriously. "I'm afraid so. They live at Riversmeet."

"Riversmeet? But daddy, that's huge. It's almost grand. How can you let a bloody employee live somewhere as smart as that? *And* he's not working for you any more."

"I know." Stacey ran his hands through his hair. "That family are like a ball and chain that your grandfather shackled round my ankle. It's all most frustrating. I want to get rid of the place. I've even had an offer for it. But the problem is that your grandfather gave Tucker the use of it for the rest of his life. He maintained that the chap did something special for him - saved him a lot of money or something. I've asked about ending the arrangement." He shook his head again. "But the lawyers have looked at the lease and they say there's nothing we can do about it."

"And meanwhile his damned son goes around frightening my horses and thumbing his nose at the Staceys. Oh, I can't stand it." Alison stamped her foot in frustration.

He nodded sympathetically. "Of course the man's has been seriously ill for a couple of years and I understand he is not expected to live long."

"And when he dies - can you then kick them out?"

"Kick them out?" Stacey examined the innuendoes of the words carefully in his mind. "Of course the mother and son can't expect to continue to occupy a great big house on their own. I'm afraid they'll have to move into one of the smaller cottages."

"But daddy, surely you're not expected to carry on looking after them when the father dies – especially if neither of them is working for you."

Stacey shuffled in his seat. "Well, one feels one has a duty . . ."

"Duty nothing. That's absolute rubbish. I tell you the man is living off us and treating us with contempt at the same time. You don't owe him anything. Let him find a job and get a house of his own to keep his mother comfortable." Alison was coming to realise that she was about to start on a crusade.

"Oh," said Sir Oswald hopefully, "do you really think so?"

"You bet I do. The little whippersnapper can stand on his own feet for a change. Let's see how he feels about *that*. Maybe *that'll* cut him down to size."

"Well, I suppose we don't owe anything to Tucker's family. They've done all right out of us for a long time." Sir Oswald shrugged and raised his eyebrows. He stared down at the half-empty porridge bowl and decided he'd had enough. He pushed it away from him and leaned back in his chair. Looking up at Alison he suddenly had the feeling that perhaps he was looking at the power and the direction which had been lacking in his life since his dear wife's death.

"That's settled then," said Alison. "Now daddy - you haven't given me a reply yet to the question I asked you last night."

"Really? What was that, my dear?" He swallowed, knowing full well what was coming.

"You know what it is. I want a rise in my allowance." Alison posed dramatically. "Daddy, I think I'm almost the poorest person going to St Theresa's."

Stacey pulled a face. "I've already told you, my dear, money is very tight at the moment."

"What about the money mummy left for me? I was told there would be plenty to get me through until I was married."

He shook his head. "I'm sorry, my dear. I'm afraid your mother didn't know very much about these things. I don't think she'd even *heard* about inflation. At the moment I'm finding it very difficult to make ends meet. I don't actually get anything myself from the trust fund. You know how these American lawyers have tied things up. So I just haven't got anything extra to give you at the moment."

"What if you sell this Riversmeet place?"

"Ah." His expression softened. "Now of course that *would* be a help."

A demonic smile spread across Alison's beautiful features. "Then leave it to me. I'll get *you* Riversmeet and you can give *me* ten pounds a week increase in my allowance. Is that a bargain?"

Stacey nodded reluctantly. "Well - yes, I suppose it is."

"Of course, I will need you to write a short note to your solicitors. I'll prepare a draft for you." She clenched her teeth. "Look out, John Tucker. I think I'm going to enjoy this."

7

The first thing John saw when he turned the corner of the Strand towards Riversmeet was Doctor Morton's black Rover pulled up outside the gate. Something must have happened. It was too early for a routine visit. His mother must have called the doctor, and that meant a crisis. It made John feel guilty. He should have been here for her to turn to. Hopefully it wasn't too late. He hurried round to the back and entered by the kitchen door.

As he arrived his mother rose from where she had been sitting at the table to confront him with a white face. "Oh, John. It's your father. Doctor Morton's here."

"I saw the car outside. What´s happened, mum?" He looked at her nervously-twisting hands. He knew that he ought to offer her some sort of comfort but he had the strangest feeling she would cringe if he approached her.

He tried to think of something helpful to say. "Don't worry, mum. You said that it's happened several times before."

She shook her head. "Not like this time." She was looking down at her hands as if to attempt to still them. "John, I -. I think he's already dead."

John's heart seemed to stop. His mother had never talked like this on the previous occasions. Always before she had seemed unwilling to accept her husband's true condition, as though believing he had some kind of immortality.

"You can't give up that easily," protested John, but he was aware his voice lacked conviction.

"I'm sure of it." She paused as though gathering strength to carry on. "This attack was much worse than the others. He didn't seem to be able to breathe at all. I didn't want to leave him - not even to go to the telephone half way up the Strand. But finally I had to. And then, when I got back, he had fallen out of bed onto the floor and his face seemed to be turning blue." She broke down in sobs.

Somewhat hesitantly John put his arms round her.

"John - I wasn't strong enough to pick him up. I think he died then."

"Did you try to make him start breathing? Press his chest or anything."

She raised a distraught, tear-streaked face to him. "I just seemed to go to pieces. All I was able to do was to take him in my arms and pray for him to be all right. If I hadn't been so useless, he would probably still be alive."

He patted her shoulder feebly. "That´s rubbish, mum. For all we know he is all right. You mustn't blame yourself, whatever happens. It wasn't any fault of yours. You did all you could."

But John couldn't excuse *himself*. He should have been here. He shouldn't have escaped for his walk when she needed him. He shouldn't have tried to ignore the reality of his father's condition. If he had been at home, he could have helped her. After all, that was why she had sent for him to come back from Cambridge.

"Doctor Morton was very quick getting here. I helped him to get David on to the bed. Then he gave him artificial respiration while I went to telephone for an ambulance. It should be here any minute now." She subsided on to her chair again.

John had become aware that he had been too wrapped up in his own life, centred on the university and his friends up there. Perhaps he should have been doing more to help his parents. He ought to have considered them, instead of enjoying himself in Cambridge, or going off on his cycling holiday in the summer with Rosemary and the others. He felt full of guilt.

His reverie was broken by the hall door opening. The massive frame of Doctor Morton appeared, stooping in the doorway. He seemed to dwarf the furniture around him. He shook his large, grey head.

"I'm sorry, Mrs Tucker. I'm afraid your husband has passed away. There was nothing I could do to save him. I think he was already deceased when I got here."

John's mother seemed to crumple back onto the kitchen chair. She appeared very small and frail as she looked down at the hands which she had been clasping so tightly to keep them still.

"What was the cause?" asked John.

"It was another stroke - far worse than the last one. We knew there would always be the risk of it happening again."

"I kept him downstairs." She spoke so quietly that she almost seemed to be musing to herself. "I kept him quiet. He only had to call to get whatever he wanted. I was always nearby." She sounded as though she was apologising.

"That´s quite right," said the doctor. "You couldn't have done any more, Mrs Tucker. It was just his constitution, I'm afraid. He had become very weak from the previous attacks."

John nodded. All this was quite true. There was nothing more to be said. It was one of the things you had to accept in life. "Well," he said, "thank you for doing your best for him."

There seemed to be a very long silence. Doctor Morton cleared his throat. "I've - er - tidied up in there and pulled the covers over the - um - over your husband's face. There's nothing more I can do here. The ambulance will take his body away for tests to confirm my diagnosis."

"Should I go with them?" asked John.

"I wouldn't advise it. They will let me know if they find out anything important."

His mother looked up. "I would prefer you to stay here, John."

"Of course I will, mum."

"Would you like me to arrange for someone to come round and talk to you, Mrs Tucker?"

"No." She shook her head. "No, thank you. John and I will be all right."

"Shall I ask Mr Hardwood to make the arrangements for the funeral?"

She could only nod, biting her lip to retain her composure.

"Yes please," said John. "Thank you very much for your help."

The doctor scratched his cheek. "Is there somewhere I can wash my hands?"

"Show Doctor Morton to the bathroom, John."

As they reached the foot of the stairs they heard the ambulance draw up outside. John directed the doctor to the bathroom. Then he went to open the front door. It seemed as though the last of his childhood slipped away as he showed the men into the back living room.

The rest of the day seemed to be filled with frantic activity. His mother insisted on cleaning out the sitting room. Then he had to go and get various things for her from the shops. When the multitude of chores was finished it was already getting dark. John went into the kitchen and found his mother was sitting back in the same position that she had occupied when he got back from his walk.

She looked up at him. "I've been thinking, John. Would you run a message for me? I promised Sarah Grant that I would help her with the Bring and Buy stall on Saturday. But I can't face that just now."

How could she think about a Bring and Buy stall when her husband had just died?

"That sort of thing doesn't matter, mother. Mrs Grant will cope without you. Shouldn't I stay here with *you*?"

She forced a little smile. "Oh, don't worry about me. I'll be all right for an hour or so. There are lots of things I've got to do. I'll just scribble a quick note for you."

So John didn't protest too much. In any case he wanted some time on his own. He had to try and come to terms with what had happened. His father's death was going to make a big difference to him. Now he had to become the man in the family. His mother wouldn't understand much about finances and things like that.

What was he going to do about Cambridge? He would have to write to Professor Coggins to tell him he needed to take a couple of weeks off to deal with the arrangements here. For the next few days there would be a lot happening - the funeral, relatives and family friends coming, all kinds of people to talk to.

He had a strange, uncomfortable feeling that something outside his control was happening to his life, disorganising it, subtly changing it. But at that moment he had no idea how completely it was going to be transformed.

8

"Sarah - where's my bow tie?"

"I expect it's where you put it when you last took it off, dear."

Sarah was damned if she was going to let her husband order her around. She had made it clear to Reggie Grant right from the beginning that she would only marry him as an equal. Of course, she hadn't told him it was also because he was too much of a bore to put up with on any other basis. Long before he proposed, she had realised that his commanding height of six feet four and his upright guardsman's deportment disguised a dismal IQ and an unshakeable chauvinism. These almost, but not quite, negated the attractions of his comfortable income and his lovely old house.

"Ah, here it is." Reggie finished ferreting around at the back of the top drawer and emerged triumphant with the tie in his hand. "I say, my dear, would you mind awfully tying it for me? You know I'm no good at that sort of thing."

"Reggie, I'm only too pleased to do these little things for you when you ask nicely. Give it to me." She reached up and started doing the simple chore which every actor quickly learns to do with his eyes shut.

He squinted down at her. "Sarah, I do wish you were coming with me. Tonight *is* a Ladies Night, you know, and I *am* president this year."

She sighed. "Reggie - we've been through this a dozen times before. I've consistently told you that I can't imagine anything more boring than spending the whole evening listening to your golfing friends telling me how they struck their five iron to the eighteenth, or whatever."

"It won't be as bad as all that. Most of them will have their wives there."

"And most of the wives will be as boring as their husbands." She hadn't realised when they married that most of Reggie's friends were even worse than he was.

"There's dancing after dinner," he smirked.

"The dancing skills of your golfing friends are on a par with their conversation. Furthermore, they aren't exactly restrained when they've had a few drinks. Last time two of them made grabs at my tits while we were dancing."

"What?" Reggie pretended to be shocked. "I don't believe it."

Sarah stood back and eyed him coldly. "You know damn well that they did. I told you at the time, but you did nothing about it. Since then you've kept pretending that you were too drunk to understand."

"But Sarah," he wheedled, "these are old friends of mine. And that low-cut dress of yours *was* extremely fetching."

"I wouldn't have minded so much if there had been some finesse about it. But I was grabbed and squeezed as if they were trying to get the juice out of an orange. I felt like a cow at an auction. That chap Hobson was particularly unpleasant."

"Oh - Bunty." Reggie attempted to pass it off with a smile. "He always plays the silly ass when he's had too much whisky."

"Well," said Sarah pointedly, "he won't play it with me any more. I warned him the first time. Then, when he tried it again, I put my knee into his balls. You may have noticed he sat out the rest of the dancing."

"My God!" The expression on Reggie's face looked as though he'd just received the same treatment. It made her feel better.

"Well, get along now." She removed a speck of invisible dust from his lapel. "Have a good evening and make my apologies to your friends. I'll see you in the morning if you're sober enough."

"But what do I *say* to them all?"

"Goodness knows. You ought to be good at it by now." She smirked benignly. "Good night, darling."

He slunk out and Sarah began to luxuriate in the thought that she had a whole night to herself. Later in the evening she would see if the new television set would come up with a picture. There was an interesting play on. Perhaps she would be able to see the whole thing without interruption this time. Sarah found television very intriguing. She believed it was going to be *the* future for actors. If she had remained on the stage she would have tried to get into television. But giving up professional acting was her half of the bargain with Reggie, when she had decided to go for security.

She heard the purr of the Armstrong Siddeley′s engine and crossed to the window to watch it nose down the gravel drive and disappear between the laurel bushes, which shielded the house from the road. Now she was alone. The experience held no problems for her. There were a dozen books waiting for her to read. She loved books. She had read English at St Hilda's when her father had insisted she had a "proper qualification" before he would let her indulge her passion for the stage. She smiled to herself. Poor daddy - what would he have thought of her now?

She gave herself a shake. Here she was talking as though he had existed decades ago, when he had been dead less than six months. Nestling in her dressing-table drawer was the letter from the solicitor which told her she had inherited more than thirty thousand pounds. It was a fortune. Now she could be as independent as she chose. She must find something useful and valuable to do with the money. She had to find an investment that would give her satisfaction as well as a good return.

As she looked down a young man came into view, walking straight up the drive towards the front door. Something made her pull back from the window, although he didn't look up. He wouldn't have seen her if he had, standing as she was in an unlit upstairs room in the autumn evening. But she recognised *him*. It was Mary Tucker's son, a good-looking boy who was clever enough to get to Cambridge. She studied the slim well-muscled body, only a couple of inches shorter than Reggie's, but not much more than half his weight. He was moving with a lithe grace which was completely different to her husband's ponderous, lumbering presence. Sarah smiled to herself as the doorbell rang and she made her way down the stairs.

9

"Mother asked me to bring you a note."

Sarah Grant's look was cool and appraising and slightly unnerving.

"Come in." She turned and preceded him into the hall, leaving him to close the front door behind him.

"We'll go upstairs, John. It's quieter up there." She didn't even deign to look at him this time.

He obediently followed the plump rounded buttocks as they undulated up the wide staircase. Her slacks were tight enough around her bottom to let him see the outline of her underpants. The sight was vaguely exciting, like the rich-scented, almost animal smell that she trailed behind her. He found himself wondering whether he ought to notice such things about a married woman nearly fifteen years his senior.

She passed along the balustraded landing and down a short corridor, pushing the door casually open at the end. She seemed to assume he would follow. John came to an abrupt halt just inside the door.

He supposed this must be what they called a lady's boudoir. There was a small sofa and a couple of circular armchairs. In front of him was a bay window through which the last of the evening sun was streaming. The window must overlook the lawn at the side of the house. To his left an ornate writing desk stood in front of another window which gave a view of the front drive. Opposite that window a pair of double doors stood open. They led into a large room where he could see a double bed covered in some shiny fabric.

"Close the door, there's a dear," said Sarah. "It's getting chilly."

John regained his senses as she turned back to face him.

"Would you like a drink?"

On the trolley by the door there was a jug of real orange juice with ice cubes floating in it. It seemed to him like the peak of luxury.

"Could I have some of that fruit juice, please?"

"Help yourself. Want some gin in it?"

"Oh - no. thanks."

"Do me a gin-and-it, will you?"

He clumsily prepared the drinks while she took the letter to the bay window. She tore open the envelope and took out the single sheet of paper. There was a moment's silence and then she burst out, "Oh, my God!"

John was advancing towards her with her drink and found himself suddenly transfixed. The setting sun was almost straight behind her profile, illuminating her fair, curly hair in a halo of light. Her loose blouse seemed to be transparent in the brightness. It gave the illusion of her being almost naked from the waist up. He noticed she had large breasts. It was a vision which stayed with him for many days afterwards.

She reached out for the drink and took a large swallow. "This is an awful shock. I was very fond of your father."

John didn't know how to reply. He sipped his drink and gazed at the vision.

"I knew he was ill, but -." Sarah looked directly at him and John felt as guilty as a peeping Tom. "What about your mother? Is she all right? How is she taking it?"

"Well." He shook his head. "I think she's all right now. But she was very shaken at first. You see - when she came back from telephoning the doctor, she found him on the floor. Unfortunately, I´d gone out for a walk, and she couldn't get him back on the bed by herself."

"Oh, that must have been a dreadful experience for her."

"When she told me about it, I thought for a while that she was going to break down. However, by the time the ambulance had left, she seemed to have got herself under control. But she was very anxious that I should come and tell you that she doesn't feel able to do the Bring and Buy stall."

Sarah waved a dismissive hand. She seemed to muse to herself, "Of course she had known it was coming for a long time, but that doesn't make it any easier when it actually happens."

John still couldn't tear his gaze away from her. He was certain that she must be aware of his transfixed stare. But the sunlight, which was streaming into his eyes, seemed to hold him imprisoned. Her body swam in it, as if in a warm pool.

"John, do you think there's anything I can do to help?"

"What?" He was startled by her direct question. "Oh! Well I don't know really. I'll tell her you asked, shall I?"

"Yes, please." Sarah arched her body and put her head back as she took another large mouthful of gin. He found the sight absolutely magnificent.

"And what about you, John?"

"Me?" Was she about to make him some kind of offer? "What do you mean?"

"I *do* understand how you feel, you know. My own father died about six months ago. So I understand what a hole it leaves in your life. How are you going to cope now that he's no longer around?"

"Er - well, I suppose I'll go back to Cambridge after the funeral. I think I may have the chance of a postgrad place."

"No. I mean how will you deal emotionally with your father's death?"

John noticed she wasn't afraid to use words like "death."

"I - I don't know really. Of course, I shall miss him a lot. But he's been ill for a long time. I've almost forgotten what it was like when he was well. We used to do a lot of things together, before I went to university."

Her question brought the good memories flooding back - the walks in the country; learning about birds; trips to football matches; days at the beach digging canals and making dams; his dad laughing at things that amused him until there were tears streaming down his face; making model buildings for the railway layout; doing puzzles in front of the winter fire. John thought he must make sure he didn´t forget those things.

"I suppose we had begun to grow apart," he admitted, "what with me being away at Cambridge and things like that."

She was watching him closely. "I expect you'll feel the loss later. It'll hit you from time to time." She smiled in a strange way. "If you ever want to talk to someone, John, don't forget that you can always come here."

She moved out of the sun to look into his eyes and the spell was broken. Now she was just an ordinary woman. She was quite short really. Her forehead scarcely came up to his chin. He could smell her again, but now it seemed to be the faint, sickly odour of make-up and perspiration mingling with the rich scent of the gin. For a moment he found it almost revolting.

The sun slipped out of sight behind the trees across the garden and the room turned suddenly darker. John took a swig at his orange. "I should be getting back," he announced.

"Oh, there's no hurry. Your mother will want to be on her own for a while in order to get to know herself again. You can sit and talk to me and unwind. You'll feel better for it."

Her restless hand slid up his back as she guided him to the window seat. She sat on the sofa facing him, her legs crossed. Her face and most of her body were lost in shadow.

"You said you were going back to Cambridge. Don't you think that perhaps your mother will need you here?"

"I haven't really considered it." John shook his head. "I don't think my being in Cambridge would be a problem. I could always get home in a few hours if she wanted me."

"You're getting on well at university, are you?"

"I've been told I ought to get a first."

"What are you reading?" She *really* sounded as if she was interested.

"The subject's called Physics of Structures. I suppose it's not much good to anyone outside university."

"Physics of Structures - does that include buildings?"

John considered. "Well, I suppose it could - from a theoretical point of view."

"Are you interested in buildings?"

What a funny question, he thought. But he said, "I used to be. When dad was well, he and I used to discuss that sort of thing. Of course he was *very* interested, being an estate manager. And I agree that it must be great to conceive a building on paper and see it turn into the real thing."

Sarah stroked her throat thoughtfully. "Would you be interested in surveying? You know – doing the sort of thing that Reggie does?"

"I don't know anything about it." Her questions puzzled him.

"If you're ever looking for a job in that line, I'm sure he could find a place for you."

"Oh. Thank you very much." He couldn't think why she'd suddenly brought up the idea of a job.

As if reading his mind, she said, "You'll have to find a job some day, you know. Of course, you wouldn't have to stay in that field. But with your degree you would be able to get a professional qualification in two years. It would be a good start, and you could move on to other things."

John found it difficult to be enthusiastic about it, but he was careful to be polite. "Yes, I can see the possibilities. Perhaps I could speak to you again when I´ve finished my degree."

"Of course you can. I told you that you must come round any time you want to discuss anything, and I meant it. I'm serious, John."

"That's very nice of you." He felt a sensation of genuine warmth towards her. "I'm very grateful."

"Oh, you don't need to be," said Sarah dismissively. "One day perhaps you'll do something for me in return."

Her remark took the edge off his pleasure. He had been basking in the illusion that this woman was interested in offering friendship because she liked him. Was it just a calculated arrangement as far as she was concerned? He was reminded again that she was fifteen years his senior and there was an unbridgeable gulf between them.

Sarah stood up sharply and broke into his introspection. She crossed to the door and switched on the light. "Come on. Let's have another drink. We can toast your future. Try one of these. It won't do you any harm."

She poured him the same as herself, effortlessly overcoming his objections. John sipped it carefully, sitting on the edge of his seat. The spirit bit at the back of his throat and moistened his eyes. She stood in front of him, balancing on the balls of her feet as she inspected him.

"I think you'd make a good estate agent. You've got the personality and the looks. You'd have no trouble in persuading the ladies that they liked a house once *you'd* shown them round. It's the wives who make the decisions on these things, you know. They persuade their husbands afterwards. I keep telling Reggie that."

John looked up at her. This was a world he'd had little experience of. Something about it seemed vaguely enticing. He wondered if he might even enjoy a career in business. Incautiously he took an over-large gulp of gin-and-it and started to cough.

Sarah giggled. "You do look awkward on that narrow seat, John. Come and sit on the settee. It's far more comfortable."

He took another sip of his drink and rose to his feet. "Really I should be going now. Mother will be expecting me back. I should be with her."

"Rubbish. It's still early. She won't notice if you take another half an hour. I said I wanted to talk to you."

Now she was standing very close to him. She rested her hand on the bare forearm that held his drink and he felt an electric thrill run through his body. For a moment he wasn′t even able to speak.

At that moment the door swung open and Mr Grant walked in. John jerked round. He saw a large man in his forties who gave the impression of being older than he really was. The bulging stomach suggested he enjoyed his food and drink overmuch. His tobacco-coloured, receding hair was cut short. At first sight he seemed pompous. But his expression was neutral.

"Er - hmm. I was halfway to the golf club when I realised I'd forgotten my wallet. I left the car out on the road in case you were sleeping."

It was a new experience for John to be caught in a married woman's boudoir by the husband. He felt himself blush scarlet to the roots of his hair. But Sarah seemed not in the least embarrassed, as she casually removed her hand from his arm and turned to face her husband.

"Reggie, isn't it dreadful. John's just brought a note from Mary to tell me that David died this morning. Poor Mary. It must be a terrible shock for her."

"Oh - oh dear." Grant sounded more embarrassed than distressed. "How sad. I'm very sorry, my boy."

John nodded and cleared his throat.

"John and I have been talking about his future. He thinks he's going to get a first at Cambridge. I said I thought you might well be able to find a place for a bright young man like that. He'd make a good trainee, wouldn't he? You could do with someone with a well-trained mind, now that the business is expanding."

"What? Oh, well, it's worth thinking about it." Grant turned to John. "Mind you, the pay would be quite low to start with. You see, you wouldn't be a lot of use to us for the first couple of years, while you were training."

John heard himself saying. "Well, I appreciate that I would have to start at the bottom."

"All the more incentive to work hard," said Sarah.

"That's right. Well - I'll give it some thought." Reggie Grant turned to leave the room.

"Why doesn't John come to see you next Saturday morning?" suggested Sarah. "You can show him what's involved in the work."

Grant looked a bit startled. "Saturday? I'll be playing golf on Saturday."

"When then?"

"Er - well – I suppose the following Saturday. We haven't got a tournament that week. We won't be too busy if you come early - say about nine o'clock."

John felt that the conversation was getting out of his control. "Wouldn't that be a bit premature," he said. "I won't finish at Cambridge until next June."

"OK." Grant gave half a shrug. "Please yourself."

John was aware that he'd sounded ungrateful. He felt as if he was being manipulated and was powerless to stop it. But he also realised he would be thought rude if it appeared that he wasn't interested. "I'm, sorry," he said. "I meant -."

Sarah stepped in to save him. "I think it would be a very good idea if you went, John. It doesn't commit either of you to a final decision. But it may be quite a useful connection for you. Good jobs aren't that easy to come by."

"Yes. Thank you. I'd like to." He stuttered. "I'll be there promptly at nine."

“Very good.” Mr Grant stopped in the doorway. “Oh, and give your mother our condolences. Tell her to let us know if there’s anything we can do.” He disappeared down the corridor.

“Tell her I’ll come to see her tomorrow,” said Sarah as she shepherded John towards the door, her hand resting gently (almost conspiratorially) in the small of his back.

At the front door she stopped. “Well.” Her voice was almost playful. “It looks as though we'll be seeing more of each other.”

John took a deep breath and nodded as he made his way down the steps. He could feel his heart thudding more strongly than it should have done. It had been a strange half-hour in more ways than one.

10

Alison decided she owed herself a taxi ride home from the solicitor. She was basking in the satisfying glow of success. Mr Silverstone had assured her that John bloody Tucker would be getting a letter giving him his marching orders within the week. That would teach him what his correct place was in future.

As she got home, her pleasure was slightly spoiled by finding her elder brother's car at the front door. He came down the steps as she got out.

"Why - hello, little sister."

"Ambrose! What on earth are you doing here?" Why did the sudden meeting with her brother make her feel guilty?

"I might ask you the same," he said in his lazy voice. "Aren't you supposed to be in your fancy convent place in Geneva or wherever it is, doing elocution classes and lessons in deportment?" He minced around in a little circle on the gravel.

Alison ignored him. He always belittled her, and she wasn't going to let him get under her skin today. "I go back on Monday. What are you doing home again? You were only here the weekend before last."

"Yes. Well - I've got to talk to pater about my allowance." Ambrose rocked his shoulders in an unconscious swagger. "Cambridge is getting so bloody expensive these days. I've scarcely got enough to keep mind and body together."

She sniffed. "I can tell you that you won't have any luck with him - not yet at any rate. I tried a couple of days ago and I got absolutely nowhere."

Ambrose nodded to himself. "The old bugger does seem to be pretty tight at present. I wonder what he's doing with all that money from the estate. He keeps on saying he hasn't got anything, but he must have a lot of rent and stuff coming in."

"*I've* found a way to bring some money in." Alison raised her head proudly. "I've arranged to get the Tuckers booted out of Riversmeet and daddy's going to sell it. Then he's promised me an increase"

"Wait a minute." Her brother was suddenly alert. "Is that *John* Tucker?"

"That's right. Ghastly man. It's about time he got cut down to size."

"Oh - I don't know about that." For some strange reason Ambrose seemed to want to stand up for him. "John Tucker's all right. I suppose some people might find him a bit wet. He spends most of his time studying. But he's no problem to me. As you know, he's my room-mate at Trinity, and I don't have any trouble with him. He's a bit out of sorts at the moment because his father's ill."

"His father's dying," said Alison defiantly. "For all we know he may be dead by now. It's for that reason that we can get them out."

Ambrose looked at her carefully. "That comment makes you sound a bit of a barbarian, little sister. What has this fellow done to get you so steamed up?"

"That's nothing to do with it." She tossed her head. "I simply want some justice. The Tuckers have been living off us for ages now. Daddy says his father hasn't done a day's work for more than two years. We can't afford to carry them for the rest of their lives. The son will just have to go out and do some work and support himself for a change."

"Wait a minute." Her brother was suddenly struck by a problem. "If you're going to make John Tucker go out to work, that means he won't be able to finish his degree."

"So what!" Alison rounded on him. "I don't think that people like that should be educated to such a high level. It only encourages them to believe they're better than they really are. That's probably why he has learnt to behave like a pig."

"Do you realise," demanded Ambrose, "that your action may have lost me the best chap I've ever had for doing my private work since I went up to Cambridge?"

"So what about that?" she sneered. "If you want him around that much to do your work for you, then you'd better pay for him yourself out of your own allowance. I expect you'll soon be able to. When Riversmeet's sold, you'll probably be able to get an increase out of daddy as well. You can donate it to your friend John Tucker. Will that suit you?" She turned on her heel and walked into the house with a satisfied swing of her hips.

Ambrose followed her more slowly, scratching his head. He wasn't sure that this was such a good idea at all. What on earth had Tucker done to get under Alison's skin like that? Perhaps he ought to look into it.

11

On the morning after the funeral John was down late for breakfast. His mother was sitting at the kitchen table. Her face was white. She was staring down at her trembling hands, as though in a state of shock. John took the seat opposite her. He was surprised to see her in such a state. She'd kept herself well under control the previous day.

"What's the matter, mum? I thought yesterday went quite well."

She didn't respond so he tried again. "As you said last night, we have to start planning for the future. You said we mustn't forget dad, but we've got to make a new life without him. I've thought about it and I agree with you."

"This came in the post." Her voice was flat.

She pushed a letter across the table to him and John picked it up. It was from a firm of solicitors. He started to read:

> *We act for Stacey Estates. We have been asked by our client to write to you to remind you that Riversmeet House, which you currently occupy rent-free, is a property of which Stacey Estates needs the use for the efficient running of the estate. As such, our clients can no longer afford to allow you to remain in occupation of the property.*
>
> *We therefore request that you make arrangements to find yourselves a more suitable residence so that Riversmeet House may be released for other purposes. We feel a suitable date for your vacation of the House would be 30th November, which gives you several weeks to obtain a suitable dwelling for yourselves. Of course, our clients would deal sympathetically with any request which you might choose to make to them for assistance with your move.*
>
> *Please acknowledge receipt of this letter and confirm the property will be vacated by the date requested.*

John found he was struggling for words to express his fury. "My God! They don't waste much time, do they? Dad worked all his life for these people. They paid him a pittance because he had an estate house. Then, the minute he dies, they throw you on the scrapheap because the Tuckers are no further use to them. I tell you, I've never heard of a clan like the bloody Staceys."

"You mustn't talk like that, John," she reproved him. She was obviously near to tears. "Your father and I discussed this during the summer. We knew the place was far too big for us, especially when you were away at Cambridge. We agreed that something had to be done some time soon. But it was -. It was a shock to actually receive the letter."

"I should damn well think it was. We've lived in this house for twenty years. Then they turn round and boot us out with only a month's notice as soon as dad dies."

"John! Please don't take that attitude. It's perfectly reasonable for Sir Oswald Stacey to want his house back. Your father hasn't done any work for two years. Of course, he will need the place for the new estate manager."

"At the very least I would have expected him to call round and explain it to you himself. Then he should have given you a decent period to find somewhere else. But to have a solicitor's letter turn up the day after the funeral is pretty insensitive, even by the Staceys' dismal standards."

His mother shook his head. "You don't understand, John. Your head is filled with these theories you get fed at Cambridge. The world is a hard place. Sir Oswald has to make sure the estate is working efficiently, or he'll be in trouble himself. He can't go around handing out gifts any more. Riversmeet House is worth a lot of money to him. The place has always been more than *we* really needed. It's just that your father liked it and Sir Bertram (he was Oswald's father) got it cheap and let him have it for the rest of his life in gratitude for what your father did."

"What exactly did father do that caused a Stacey to be so uncharacteristically generous?"

"Oh, it's a long and complicated story and I don't really

understand it. I believe your father had a cousin in America who was something in banking. He told your father that, when the stock market began to fall, he thought the same thing might happen in England. Of course, no-one knew how bad it was going to be. When your father told Sir Bertram about it, he decided to sell a lot of his shares. Then, when the crash came, he was able to get back in again with a considerable profit. Property also became very cheap as a consequence and he put some of the profits into buying places like Riversmeet House. So that's how we came to be here."

"So he wasn't as generous as all that," said John. "If he'd made so much money out of dad's good advice, you'd have thought he'd have *given* the place to him."

His mother shook her head. "The aristocracy don't hang on to their wealth by giving it away. You should remember that in the future. I think it was very good of Sir Bertram to let us have the place for the rest of your father's life. He obviously realised how much the place meant to him."

"What I don't understand is why dad didn't buy the house himself, if it was so cheap and he liked it so much?"

"Oh, we would never have had enough money to buy a place like this. You see, your father didn't have a degree or anything like that and, although he did qualify, he had to do it by correspondence classes after he had started to work for the Staceys. That's why he never earned very much."

"I see. He was paid a low wage throughout his working life and it was partly made up to him by being given the use of a nice house. So he was never able to save up for his own place, and now we're thrown out on our ear because of the greed of other people." He took a deep breath. "I tell you mother, I think this whole thing stinks. In future I'll make sure that *I'm* never put in a position like this."

"Hush, son. Don't be so unreasonable. As I said, the place is far too big for us. It costs an awful lot to heat and to keep comfortable. In any case, I don't want to stay here any longer without your father. I would far sooner have a cosy little cottage in the village where the shops are just round the corner and I can have friends who call in to see how I am when they're passing."

"Well," he conceded, "I suppose there might be some advantages in that for you. You'll be on your own for most of the year. But I've grown up here. It will be a big wrench for me to leave the views and the smell of the salt water as the tide comes in." He thought of the time he'd spent looking across the mist-covered estuary that very morning.

"It'll be difficult for me as well, John. We'd been married twenty-three years last month - only two short of our silver wedding. And we've lived here for all but the first few of those years. But if I can move on without regrets, so must you."

"We won't have a home any more," he mused. "Think of all the things that have happened to us here, mum - all the memories."

His mother put her head on one side. "Oh, I don't know. Perhaps there are too many memories for me to live with."

"And I don't like the way it's been handled. How could anyone do that to you just a few days after the death of your husband? It all seems so unfair."

"I'm afraid you're going to have to face the fact, John, that life *is* unfair." She shrugged. "It seems unfair to lose your father when he was still a comparatively young man. But at least I've got you." She reached out and patted his hand. "I haven't thanked you for being here when I needed you."

That made him feel guilty. "Oh, don't worry about that. In any case I don't feel that I've helped very much." He got up to try and shake off the feeling of self-consciousness. He realised he hadn't been much comfort to her so far. He must try and think of things which he could say to make her happy. "I tell you what - would you like me to get you a cup of tea?"

"Oh, yes please." She gave him her first little smile. "Don't forget to warm the pot before you put the tea in."

That was typical, thought John, as he filled the kettle. These little details were so important to her. You'd think the world ran on little details. Even when her husband had just been buried and she'd been thrown out of her house, she couldn't forget little details like warming the tea-pot. Now she had no-one but him to organise, and that would only be for a few more weeks.

"Why don't we sit somewhere more comfortable?" He

persuaded her to get up and go into the dining room. He sat her in the fireside chair and placed the small coffee table beside it. He switched on the electric fire.

"Just for comfort," he said to her.

"Only one bar, mind. We're going to have to be careful now."

"You can rely on me, mum." John grinned and went back to the kitchen.

When he returned with the tray of tea she was still sitting deep in thought. He poured out a cup for her. He added just half a spoonful of sugar, unstirred as she liked it. It was surprising she could taste it at all.

"John." She suddenly seemed to come to a decision. "Sit down here."

He brought his cup over and sat on the stool by her feet. He had often done the same thing as a boy when she had read fairy tales to him or told him stories of her youth. She took a couple of delicate little sips of the scalding hot tea, wiping her lips with her tongue.

"John - I've been thinking." She refused to look at him. "There are a couple of things that you and I must sort out."

"Like what?"

"Well," she said, "firstly there's the question of money. We've got to be able to pay our own way now, you know."

John found this serious line of talk disconcerting. "Oh - we'll get by, mum. You don't need to worry yourself about that at the moment."

"No. We *must* talk about it now. I'll feel better if I'm concentrating my mind on something practical. And these things just have to be faced. What you may not realise is that your father has only been on half pay for the last year. Money was starting to get very difficult during the summer. Fifty pounds a month isn't a lot to keep the three of us, and now that's gone. But your father wanted to do his best for you. He was very keen to see that you were given the best possible start in life, seeing that you're a clever lad. We cashed in his life insurance to pay your expenses at Cambridge." She looked sadly at him. "But that money ran out in the summer. Now there's nothing left."

It was the first time his mother had discussed anything like this with him and John felt rather out of his depth. Surely the government would see that she got some income. "Won't you have a pension or anything like that?"

She shook her head. "No. I'm not old enough. And we haven't got anything put aside for a rainy day any longer. There was no spare money for savings. We had planned to start saving when you had finished at Cambridge. But your dad's illness put an end to that." There was no disguising the bitterness in her voice.

"Isn't there any money coming in at all?"

"I'm under fifty, so the government says I'm young enough to earn my own keep. I'll have to find myself a job."

John wrestled with the idea. "What sort of job?"

"Well, I suppose I can always go back to being a typist." She tossed her head. "I used to be very quick at shorthand, you know. I was secretary to the Managing Director at Cameron's before I met your father."

John thought about it. As she said, the world seemed unfair. His mother hadn't worked since he was born. It wouldn't be easy for her after all this time.

"In any case," she continued, "we'll have to get the money from somewhere. Even though we'll move to a cottage, we'll still have to pay rent on that."

"There was something in the letter." John picked it up and read it again. "It seems to suggest that the Staceys might be willing to help you out for a while."

His mother smiled and patted his shoulder. "No. I wouldn't dream of it. We couldn't expect Sir Oswald Stacey to help with the rent."

"I agree that we don't want any charity from the Staceys." John snorted. "But what about renting one of the smaller estate cottages? That ought to be cheap."

"Oh, Sir Oswald wouldn't do that. The estate cottages are for the workers on the estate."

"But he owns half the cottages in the village as well," he pointed out. "Surely the man could let us have one of those at a low rent."

She shook her head. "You've got to understand, John, that

Sir Oswald relies on those properties for his living. They are his main source of income."

"But he's got hundreds of them."

"Oh, no. Not hundreds. Anyway, I'm sure he'd never agree to let places out at a reduced rent. Once he did that, everybody would be finding reasons for him to give *them* reductions as well. He has to run the estate as a business you know." She straightened her shoulders. "No - we'll have to pay a proper rent for the place we get."

"Well," he said, trying to look on the bright side. "You can get somewhere small, because I shall only be here during the holidays."

His mother looked down again at her hands. John sensed that something unpleasant was coming. It was as though she was trying to work out the best way of putting it.

"That's the other thing I wanted to talk to you about, John. I've been trying to screw up the courage to mention it since you got back last week. I'm afraid that I'm not going to be able to afford to keep you at university any longer."

"You won't need to, mum. I've got a scholarship."

"Ah, but that only pays for your tuition fees. *We've* had to pay for your clothes and food and lodgings. I wouldn't be able to afford that any longer."

"Then I'll have to find some other way of getting the money." He cast around in his mind. "Perhaps we could borrow some money and I could pay it back when I'm earning. And I could get a holiday job to help."

"Oh, that wouldn't be nearly enough. You don't realise how expensive it is to live in a place like Cambridge. Besides, that's one thing your father insisted on. We've never let ourselves get into debt." She smiled bleakly. "No, John. I'm afraid your dad and I had already decided that you wouldn't be able to finish your degree. He was supposed to talk to you about it during the summer holidays. But he was feeling better and was foolishly optimistic about getting back to work. Otherwise we knew we couldn't afford to keep you there after Christmas. Even his half-pay was going to come to an end in December."

"But - just at this stage -. I've only got until next June. There's a real chance I might get a first. That's an important qualification." It had never really crossed John's mind before that his father's death might prevent him from completing his education. "I've worked hard these last three and a half years, mum. If I leave now, I'll feel as though I'm letting them down at Trinity."

His mother looked up at him and there were tears in her eyes. "I'm sorry John, but I'm afraid that can't be helped. They'll just have to understand. I'm as upset about it as you are. My mind has gone round and round in circles thinking about it. But I just can't see any other way out."

John shook his head. He could tell she was close to breaking down. He couldn't push her any further. He knew in his bones that he was defeated already. This was devastating. Why should it happen to him now, of all times? Somehow, he felt that his mother had never really been keen on his going to university. She believed young men should get proper, safe jobs when they left school. But he couldn't possibly accuse her of that at the moment.

"Have you also thought," she enquired, "that I will need you here? Life is going to be very difficult for me. I'll need help around the house. I've already explained that money will be short. I won't be able to earn very much. I'll need you to bring home some money to help me with the food and the rent. I'm sorry, but I'm afraid you'll just have to get a full-time job, John."

"What sort of job would I get?"

"You're clever enough to do all sorts of things." She smiled, sensing that she was winning. "I was discussing it with Sarah Grant at the funeral. She said her husband is looking for bright young trainees and she's sure you'd be the right kind of person for that sort of job. In fact, she said you'd already arranged to go and see Reginald on Saturday - so you must have been thinking about it."

He felt the trap closing round him. These women seemed to have it all sewn up. He hadn't previously regarded the proposed interview as a serious attempt to get work. However, he couldn't back out now, without seeming rude and ungrateful to the Grants and inconsiderate towards his mother. Yet he didn't want to be stuck in some rural backwater for the rest of his life. He felt that if he took on a local job now he would never get free again. Somehow, he had to make one more try for the sake of the rest of his life.

He looked at her pleadingly. "I've never much fancied an office job. They're so routine. I'd really prefer something where I could stretch my brain a bit."

"Oh, all you youngsters talk like that. But it's the office jobs that have a future. They're safe and secure. Your father was always very aware of security after living through the depression. Things were very hard in those days. Once he got a safe job with Stacey Estates, he hung on to it."

"And a fat lot of good it did him. Look where we are now." John tossed his head petulantly, then instantly regretted it as he saw his mother's face pucker. "I'm sorry, mum. I'm sorry," he blurted out. "Here, let me pour you another cup of tea."

She forced a little smile through the tears. "John, I'm afraid you're just going to have to start growing up. There are plenty of other young men of your age who have been earning a living for several years. They've all had a less fortunate start than you, but they're doing well, just the same. Your father and I have done our very best to give you a first class education. But I'm afraid we didn't have enough money to finish it. Now that's come to an end. Things have got to change. You've got to stop taking from others and start repaying them."

"OK, mum. I'm seeing Mr Grant on Saturday." John capitulated. "As you say - it'll do me good. If I don't have any luck with him, I'll start applying for other jobs next week." He tried to grin. "In any case, I was only thinking the other day that I'd had enough of studying."

His mother sipped her tea. She looked calmer now. Soon she started talking about her plans for a new cottage. But John found it difficult to listen to her. All *he* could think about was the life he was going to have to leave behind in Cambridge, and what the people there would think. He would never get away from South Devon now. The rest of the world would go on without him. Truly this was the end of his carefree youth.

12

The rain which had been dourly threatening all morning finally crept across the city just before noon. It began as a slow, insistent drizzle which turned the pavements grey and greasy. But gradually it increased until its wet, cold fingers had insinuated their way into every smallest corner. John knew it wouldn't let up until long after nightfall. He abandoned his plans to stay in town and made for the Central Station before his clothes became soaked.

The station was quiet. It seemed as though most people had already made for home before the autumn gloom turned to premature night. The local train stood ready at the branch line platform despite the fact that it was twenty minutes before the scheduled departure. John chose an empty compartment and sat on the soot-smelling seat. He gazed morosely through the rain that trickled down the grimy window, across the silent Saturday sidings and up to the prison on the hill. The thought crossed his mind that this miserable weather was an aspect of the holiday coast which the posters forgot to mention.

John's mood matched the dismal scene exactly. The happy autumn sunshine of Cambridge already seemed years away. The loving, everlasting summer holidays with Rosemary and their friends had been part of a different world. He had left his youth behind. Somehow he couldn´t take any pleasure from the fact that, only two hours ago, Mr Grant had given him a job, or that on Monday week he would start earning a regular salary for the first time in his life. He still yearned for that other world which had died with his father. He promised himself, that as soon as he had been able to save up enough, he would go back to finish his degree. He would write to Old Coggy to explain what his plans were and hope that they could keep a place open for him next year or the one after.

There came the double click of the carriage door opening. In his present unsociable mood, he didn't welcome sharing a compartment with anyone. He looked up at the person who entered. The chap's dark hair was trimmed to a tight crew-cut.

His eyes were a sparkling blue. John almost laughed aloud.

"Why - it's Sammie. Sammie Joslin."

"Well, I never . . . Hello, John." The short, stocky young man came over and sat opposite him. "It must be at least a year since I last saw you. I thought you were still at Cambridge."

"You know that my dad died, Sammie?"

"Yes, I was sorry to hear about that." He didn't need to say any more. There was no embarrassment. The eyes didn't slide away from his face.

John smiled wryly. "Well, that means I shan't be going back to Cambridge. Mum and I decided we couldn't afford it any longer. We've run out of money while my father was ill. To stay on and finish my degree would only have made things worse. We've got no capital to speak of, you see. And – well, she needs me here"

"Blimey. That's a bit of a shock. What're you going to do now?"

"I've just been offered a job by Grants, the estate agents. My mother knows Mrs Grant, and her husband has been very helpful. But he's only going to pay me five pounds a week. I won't save much doing that job."

"It's no good complaining," said Sammie. "When I started as an apprentice carpenter, I only got seventeen and six. And my parents were lucky they didn't have to pay for my indentures. Even now I only get just over six quid and I still have to stand all the insults and things."

John was intrigued. "Insults? What insults?"

"Oh, you know. They keep on about how funny it is – a chippie with a posh accent. And they call me the boss's favourite and things like that." Sammie grimaced. "I don't really fit in with the other blokes. They don't understand why someone with my education, actually likes to do things with his hands. I've had to stand up and fight for myself once or twice, when I needed to. But I keep quiet about it most of the time. I've wanted the training, you see. You can't really complain if they're giving you a good training."

"If I'd finished my degree I'd be able to get three or four times what Grants are paying," said John darkly.

"Are you going to take the job?"

He nodded. “I haven’t got much choice really. We need the money.”

“Does that mean you'll be coming back here to live permanently?”

“That’s right. Perhaps we’ll be able to see something of each other from time to time.” John grinned at his old school-friend, pleased to see the cheerful face again. “What are you doing these days?”

“I’m in the last year of my apprenticeship,” said Sammie. “That means that very soon Barkers won’t be able to order me around as they want. I’ll easily be able to pick up another job if they don’t pay me enough. There are plenty of opportunities nowadays for carpenters.”

“I meant, what’s going on socially. What do you do in the evenings?”

Sammie pulled a face. “Not a lot really. My parents are pretty old now, as you know, and they don’t like me going out much at night. In any case I’ve got lots of private carpentry work for people. I replace their rotten window frames, fit out kitchens, repair roofs, build garages. I even do work for new houses from time to time. I’m doing pretty well out of it. It’s all done for cash and I’ve got quite a bit saved up for the future. I reckon I might build my own place some time.”

“My goodness - you *are* thinking big. I hadn’t thought of you as a self-made businessman.”

Sammie leaned forward enthusiastically, “You can give me some help if you like. I could often do with a second pair of hands and you used to be pretty good at woodwork when you were at school.” He hesitated. “I’d pay you, of course.”

“I must say it’s a thought,” said John. “I could do with getting some extra money from somewhere. If I could save up some money this year, I might be able to get back to Cambridge to finish my degree. I really regret having to break off my studies in the middle of the last year.”

“Well, I can understand that, but learning a trade suits *me* just fine,” said Sammie, “I reckon this sort of work is the way things are going to go in the future. I’ve got so many jobs now that it keeps me busy most of my spare time – evenings and weekends as well. I even have to turn work away sometimes.”

"Don't you do anything else? You used to be keen on cycling. Don't you do that any more?" John grinned. "I remember how you used to flog yourself up all the hills and would never get off. I used to struggle to keep up with you." He could see that his friend still had the same bulging muscles.

"What do you mean? It was you who used to leave *me* behind. You with your posh derailleur gears."

"Do you remember some of the trips we had?"

Sammie nodded. "You bet I do. I often think about our trip to France after you'd finished in the sixth form. What was it? - fourteen hundred miles in less than three weeks?" He shook his head. "But I only use my bike for getting around town nowadays."

"They were good days," said John. "I remember that you never stopped talking. I'm surprised you had the breath to get up some of the hills."

"Come off it. You could talk all right yourself." Sammie punched him playfully on the shoulder.

John felt a rush of warmth towards his old friend. "It's good to see you again, Sammie. I'd like us to meet up again - if you can spare the time, that is."

"Remember our old scouting days?" Sammie went on. "Well, I'm an Assistant Scoutmaster now. I took our troop on a week's camp during the summer. I thought about you then. Remember those camps when we were the patrol leaders and we used to share a tent halfway between the two patrols?"

"Don't I just. And Skip shouted out in the middle of the night, that if you didn't stop talking, we'd be digging out a new lot of latrines in the morning."

Sammie feigned mock horror. "Don't blame it all on me. *You* always seemed to keep your nose clean, just because you were brighter than me."

"Poor old thickie."

The former friendship seemed to settle back on their shoulders as if they'd only been apart a week. John felt a little to blame for the fact that they'd drifted out of touch with each other. Since he'd been at Cambridge, he was aware that he'd hardly given Sammie a thought. Now here was a chance to make amends. He found he was brightening up.

Sammie was talking like he used to in the old days. “My troop’s got a boat now. We were given it for nothing ’cause it was in a bit of a state. So I’ve done it up. You know the shed at the bottom of our garden that opens out onto the back lane. I extended it and put on double doors so that I could get the boat in. The shed′s sixteen feet long and I’ve got it fitted out like a workshop. I’ve run electricity to it - you learn all these things when you’re working for a builder. I’ve picked up some power tools cheap over the years. There’s a lathe and a small bench saw that I can fit up as a planer, so there’s not many jobs I can’t do. And nobody complains about the noise down at the bottom of the garden. I’m in the workshop whenever I’ve got the time. You ought to come and see it.”

John didn’t feel as excited as Sammie about his friend’s preoccupation with carpentry. In his opinion there were more interesting things that a young man of twenty-two could be doing in the evenings and at weekends. But Sammie had never been a great one for the girls. He said, “All right. I’ll call round in a few days, if that’s OK.”

“Of course it is. You’ll be able to see if I’m in the shed ’cause the light’ll be on. You can come in by the back gate. I’ll enjoy showing you round.”

“Have you kept in touch with any of our other old friends?”

“Not really. I’m not the social type, like you. What about you? Are you still going out with Rosie Williams?”

“I only see her in the holidays,” said John. “We had a good time last August, but I haven’t seen her since. She’s up at Sheffield, so we haven’t had a chance to meet up.”

They started an orgy of story-telling and reminiscences. They didn’t pause when the train pulled away from the platform with a jerk. And Sammie was still droning on as they walked home from the station, hardly noticing the gentle rain falling on their bare heads.

John felt hugely cheered up.

13

Alan Hardacre knocked at the door and waited. It was opened by an attractive blonde, dressed in the ubiquitous jumper and slacks of the Sheffield student.

"Oh, hello Alan."

"Hi, Rosie. Are you going to invite me in for a cup of tea?"

"All right." Rosemary Williams pulled the door open wide and showed him into the living room of the flat she shared with two other girl students. "I'll make a new pot. How do you like it?"

"Two sugars."

He followed her shapely figure into the kitchen as she went to boil the kettle. "What are you doing tonight?"

"Oh, I need to stay in and work tonight," she said. "I've got to hand in my Shakespeare essay tomorrow lunchtime."

"Surely they'll give you more time for that. There's a live trio down at the jazz club."

Rosemary turned up her pretty nose. "I don't want to have any more time. Besides I'm not that keen on jazz."

"It's the first time they've been to Sheffield. We ought to give them as much support as possible."

She wondered why he was so keen. Perhaps he had friends in the group. On the other hand, Alan had been trying to get her to go out with him since they got back to university. During the summer, when she'd been with John, he'd kept well away from her. Now he was suddenly all attention again.

"I'm sorry, Alan," she said. "I really don't feel like going out. I'm a bit upset because I've just had a letter from John and it's not very cheerful. His dad has died. They had the funeral last week."

Alan wasn't that easily deflected. "Well, *you* can't help that. He won't expect you to sit around like a nun just because he's got family problems. A night out is just what you need to cheer you up."

"Oh, I don't think so." She poured the boiling water into the pot. "Why don't you take Melanie? I'm sure she'd love to go with you, and I know she likes jazz."

Alan shook his head. "Melanie? No thanks. I'm not interested in Melanie."

"Well," said Rosemary forthrightly, "you oughtn't to be interested in me either."

"Why on earth not?"

She faced him. "Alan, you know jolly well that John and I have been going out together since we were in the sixth form. We spent the whole of last summer hols together. You were there part of the time." She stopped herself from telling him she was John Tucker's girl. That might be too presumptuous.

"So what?" he demanded. "I bet he doesn't stay celibate all term when he's not got you around."

"What *are* you suggesting, Alan Hardacre?"

"Now look here, Rosie," he said in a more placatory tone, "it's not as though I'm asking you to jump into bed with me. I only said, will you come to the jazz? I'm not trying to make any indecent suggestions."

Rosemary couldn't prevent herself from grinning. "No, I suppose you're not. I'm sorry to bite your head off. But I'm afraid that I just don't feel very cheerful tonight." She poured out the two mugs of tea, handed one to Alan and preceded him into the living room.

"Melanie! Jill!" she called out to her flatmates. "There's a fresh pot of tea in the kitchen if you want some."

There was no discernible response.

Rosemary sat down and picked up the letter. "Poor old John, as well as losing his dad, he's been told by his mum that she hasn't got enough money to send him back to Cambridge. They've also had a letter from the Stacey family´s solicitors to say they've got to get out of Riversmeet House and John's got to get a job to help his mother pay the rent on a little cottage in the village. I think that's dreadful."

"Blimey," agreed Alan, "that's going to cut him down to size - chucked out of Cambridge and losing his flashy big house. He may even deign to talk to ordinary people like us from now on."

She rounded on him. "Alan, you know he's not like that at all. He has never refused to talk to anybody, nor has he ever pretended to be the least bit snobbish."

"I don't know about that." Alan shrugged. "He's always had that posh accent and behaved as though he had some sort of right to go to Cambridge. We all know that's the place where the upper classes send their kids. So why should *he* go?"

"You're being ridiculous, Alan. If John's clever enough to go to Cambridge, why shouldn't he try for it? I've never heard such rubbish. I think it's you who's the *inverted* snob, if you think places like that are only for the upper classes."

Alan rocked his shoulders aggressively. "Well, it doesn't matter anymore. It looks as though that dream is over for him. I don't envy you, Rosie. I shouldn't like to be the one who's got to bring that bloke back down to earth."

"I don't understand what you mean." She smoothed back her long, wavy hair. "This is just the time when he needs me most. I want to see if I can help. In fact, I think I'll go home for the carnival weekend. That's only a fortnight away. Maybe I'll be able to be of some comfort to him then."

He shook his head. "Well, don't say that I didn't warn you, Rosie. I think you're going to have problems with John. I'm going to be home as well that weekend, so I'll be around to pick up the pieces if you need me." He downed the rest of his tea and stood up. "Well, I must be on my way. Thanks for the drink. Sorry you won't be joining me tonight."

Rosemary relented a little. "I'm sorry too, but I'm afraid that I just don't feel like it."

"Never mind. Perhaps another time." Alan smiled and his lop-sided face became almost good-looking. "I've got a lot of patience."

14

John turned up at Grant's just after nine o'clock on Monday to start his new career. The premises were impressive. The business occupied the ground floor of a double-fronted building in Cathedral Close and the windows were filled with photographs and drawings of houses. He pushed the door open and crossed the lino-covered floor to the wide, low counter.

A bright, buxom young girl in a white starched blouse and black skirt got up from one of the desks behind the counter and came to greet him. "Hello. Can I help you?"

"I'm John Tucker. I'm starting work here today."

"Oh, really? I don't know -." She broke off and turned to consult a rather severe-looking spinster who was typing at one of the other desks. "What shall I do, Miss Brain?"

"You'd better go and ask Mr Kingley." Miss Brain gave John a neat, economical smile.

The girl bounced off down the corridor at the back of the shop and returned a few minutes later with a short, round, cheerful man in his thirties. His hair was thinning already, and his pink face shone as though it had been polished.

"Hello, John. I'm Bill Kingley." He reached across the counter and they shook hands. "I'm afraid Mr Grant isn't here yet, and he hasn't left me any instructions. I think the best idea is for you to come round here and sit at this empty desk, which will probably be yours anyway. Mr Grant should be in soon if you don't mind waiting a few minutes. Then I expect you'll find out what he's got planned for you. If I give you anything to do, I might be making a mistake."

John sat at the desk as instructed. At that moment another young man, scarcely any older than himself, came into the shop.

"Morning, Jimmy. Late again! If you don't pull your socks up, I'll have to ask Mr Grant to have a word with you." Bill Kingley's smile robbed the comment of some of its menace.

"Sorry, Bill. The bus was late again."

Kingley shook his head. "You'll just have to get an earlier one, Jimmy. Nobody will object if you're here ten minutes early." He shrugged. "Anyway, come and meet John Tucker. He may be helping you with some of your jobs."

As if happy to be relieved of responsibility for the two young men, Bill Kingley returned to his office at the back.

"Hello," said Jimmy. "I must say I could do with a bit of help."

John found himself sitting opposite a ginger-haired youth with a face where spots and freckles fought each other to cover an inadequate area of pink skin. He wasn't impressed by his initial meeting with this other trainee.

"I get told off for being five minutes late," grumbled Jimmy, "but we'll be lucky to see old man Grant turn up before ten o'clock. There are two different sets of rules around this office. It just isn't fair."

John heard a hissing intake of breath from Miss Brain who was sitting behind him, but it was the girl who spoke.

"You know full well, Jimmy Perkins, that he's the owner of the company. That means he can do what he wants. If you're paid to start work at nine o'clock, that's when you've got to start. You can choose your own work-times when you've got your own business."

"Shut up, Janice," said Jimmy. "I bet you feel the same way as me."

"Now that you've *finally arrived*," intervened Miss Brain heavily, "perhaps you'd get on with your work and let Miss Fortescue and I get on with ours."

Jimmy sneered. "Oh, it's Miss Fortescue today, is it?"

"Or else," said Miss Brain heavily, "I can go and fetch Mr Kingley."

"Don't worry. I shan't say another word." Jimmy raised his eyebrows and leered at John across the desk.

"What sort of things do you do?" asked John, anxious to change the subject.

"Oh." Jimmy seemed to have difficulty in raising any enthusiasm about it. "Mostly I keep a record of the rents that are paid. Then I go and collect them when the people fall behind. Grants' have got the job of looking after a lot of the big estates around here. The biggest are the Stacey Estates." He went over to the counter and pulled out a ledger. "People come in and pay their rents or send them in the post and I enter them in one of these big books. Then I write out the receipts on one of these pads. If the farms get two months behind or the houses get two weeks behind, I have to tell Bill Kingley. On Friday mornings - the day after pay-day - I take the receipt book and try to collect any rents that are behind. In fact, some people like to have the rent collected. It saves them the trouble of coming into the office here. I sometimes make twenty calls on a Friday. They often invite me in and give me cups of tea and we have a chat. I like Fridays." He came back and sat down again. "Then on Mondays I have to make a list of the payments and give that and a list of the overdues to Bill. Sometimes he tells me to go out and see the people I didn't manage to see on Friday. But we *know* who the ones are who will give us problems. He deals with them."

"Is that all?" John wasn't enthusiastic about rent-collecting. Mr Grant hadn't mentioned that at the interview. "What do you do the rest of the week?"

"I'm at college on Wednesday and the rest of the time I help out wherever Bill wants me."

"Don't you do any surveying or selling properties?" John didn't like the sound of helping with Jimmy's job.

There was a snort from Janice. "Him? Selling?"

Jimmy leaped back to the attack. "Shut up, Janice. You don't know nothin' about it."

"Be quiet! Both of you," said Miss Brain.

"Yes - of course I do selling and surveying," said Jimmy with a little swagger. "I help with that sort of stuff as well."

Further repartee was suspended when a customer came into the shop to pay her rent. Jimmy was busy for the next five minutes. John looked around the place. In front of the counter were several pin-boards on legs where details of properties for sale or to let were displayed. There were a number of large, blown-up photographs of some of the bigger houses and a couple of architect's drawings of new houses. He noticed, as the day went on, that when prospective customers came in, it was Bill Kingley who would talk to them. He would usually spread out more details of the properties they were interested in, on the counter in front of them.

While Jimmy was busy recording the rent payment and issuing the receipt, John could see that Miss Brain was typing letters from her shorthand pad. So far as he could tell, Janice seemed mainly to be occupied in typing and correcting skins for the duplicating machine. Presumably these were details of the various houses which were for sale. He had to look elsewhere when she caught him looking at her and smiled suggestively and half-turned her body towards him. He didn't want Miss Brain to accuse him of taking Janice´s mind off her work.

As Jimmy finished and the rent-payer left, another man came in. He was in his mid-thirties. He walked past the counter towards the back of the shop, hardly appearing to notice the people there.

"Good morning, Mr Cartwright," said Miss Brain primly.

"Good morning," he mumbled and disappeared down the corridor. His personality seemed to match his dull, grey suit.

Janice turned back to John again. "That's Mr Cartwright," she said, somewhat unnecessarily. "He's Mr Grant's junior partner."

John was interested. "Oh. Does he do the selling?"

"Not really." She seemed vague. "Mr Kingley does that, I think."

"Is Mr Kingley a partner?"

There was another snort from Miss Brain, but it was Jimmy who answered.

"No. He's just the chief clerk. He'll never be a partner because he hasn't got his qualifications. I'll be able to qualify two years after I pass my exams. So I'll probably be a partner before Bill Kingley."

Miss Brain let out a noise which was more like a splutter this time.

"That's *if* you ever pass your exams," said Janice. "You failed last year."

"Well - I'm doin' my retakes, aren't I?" Jimmy rounded on her again. "Everybody knows the first year is the most difficult. It just means I'll take a year longer."

"I can't see Mr Grant ever making *you* a partner, Jimmy Perkins."

"Shut up, Janice," he retorted. "A fat lot you know about it."

"Please be quiet, all of you, and get on with your work," said Miss Brain.

Jimmy and Janice lapsed obediently into silence and John was left to wonder about the complex relationships within the office.

"If Mr Cartwright doesn't sell properties, what does he do?" he murmured to Jimmy.

"I dunno," Jimmy admitted. "I suppose he just sits in his office and thinks, like Mr Grant."

"Don't they go out and look at buildings and meet clients?"

"I don't think so." Jimmy frowned. "I suppose Mr Grant does, when he goes for lunch at the golf club. But I never seen Mr Cartwright go anywhere much."

"Do you ask his advice about what to do?"

"No." He shook his head. "I never done that."

"Who *do* you ask?" John wanted to know.

"Oh," said Jimmy, "I ask Bill Kingley. He knows about everything."

It seemed, from what John was told, that Bill Kingley was the man who ran Grants. John discovered over the next few days that Bill was the one who nearly always met customers first. It was he who was usually asked to show them round the properties they were interested in. He was also the one who got customers to the stage of a sale before he handed them over to one of the partners. John thought it was most unfair that Bill would never get any further in his career because he was unqualified and was now too old to take his exams.

15

Half an hour later Mr Grant turned up. He seemed surprised to see John.

"Oh - forgotten about you," he said. "Of course - you're starting with us today. Is Bill Kingley there?"

Bill's cheerful face appeared in the corridor.

"Ah, here he is." He turned back to John. "Bill, I expect I told you about young John - um -."

"Tucker," John supplied.

"Tucker - that's right. He's our new trainee assistant. He's a clever cocker - so my wife'd have me believe. Went to Cambridge, but couldn't finish the course." He turned to John almost apologetically. "Never mind, young man. If you're that clever, you shouldn't have any trouble with your surveying course at the Tech. Bill will show you round and introduce you to everyone. He'll fill out the forms and tell you where you're sitting - that sort of thing. Do you understand?"

John nodded. "Yes, thank you."

"Good. That's fine." Grant disappeared into his office and shut the door.

Bill winked at him. "You'd better come with me, John. We'll ′fill out the forms′ as he calls it."

John followed him back to his office which was the first on the right down the corridor, opposite Mr Grant's. Bill shepherded him into the little room and closed the door behind him.

"Sit down, John. Well, as I guessed, it'll be me who trains you. I hope you're a bit sharper than young Jimmy." He shook his head. "I'm afraid he's only fit for collecting rents. He'll never make a surveyor."

John grinned. "He told me he has ambitions to be a partner one day."

That made Bill laugh. "He must be dreaming. That'll be the day I finally hand in my notice." He leaned back in his chair. "Mind you, he wouldn't stand much chance, if he was as clever as Einstein. Mr Grant only takes on partners who can afford to pay for the privilege."

"How long have you worked for Grants?"

"All my life, except for my five years' war service. I was trained by the old man. That was Mr Grant's father." Bill wagged a finger at him. "Now, there *was* a surveyor."

John was interested. "What happened to him, then?"

"He died of a heart attack about five years ago." Bill shrugged. "Young Mr Grant had just finished at university. He went to do a late degree after the war. That's where he met Mrs Grant. Everyone was surprised when he came back married."

"She does seem quite a bit younger than him."

Bill nodded sagely. "And a lot more flighty."

"What do you mean?" asked John, despite having a pretty good idea.

The older man gave him a knowing grin. "Gets about a bit, does our Sarah. At least that's what *I've* heard. Not that I blame her. All that Mr Grant seems interested in is playing golf. I suppose I have to go up to the Cranford Club at least twice a week to get him to sign things. That'll probably be part of *your* job. Can you drive?"

"No, I'm sorry. I can't."

"It'd be a good idea if you learned. Young Jimmy seems no good at it and Mr Cartwright isn't interested in even trying. I would find it useful, if someone else could use the pool car."

"Really, Bill?" John was full of enthusiasm. He sat forward on the edge of his chair. "I'd like to have a go."

"All right. I'll teach you, if you like. We'll get you a learner's licence and you can drive me when I've got to go out to do valuations and surveys."

"What would Mr Grant say?"

"Oh, don't worry about that." Bill waved his hand airily. "He won't be interested. He always leaves the details to me." He leaned forward conspiratorially. "I could do with a bit of help with valuations and surveys, now that we've got so much more work coming in." He nodded sagely at him. "If you're any good, young John, I could find you very useful. And you'd do yourself a bit of good at the same time."

So the basis of an excellent working relationship was started that first morning.

16

There was a sharp crack as the firework exploded. The girls nearby squealed and a portion of the crowd eddied and swayed away from the procession in the flickering light of a hundred flaming torches. Then it reformed to continue its role of half-watching, half-participating in the carnival.

The floats rolled past in an irregular column. Some were on lorries and some were on trailers drawn by roaring tractors. They were largely manned by local people, dressed in a variety of costumes from the comic to the openly erotic. In their thinly veiled disguises they were the butts of catcalls, shouts and whistles of appreciation from the crowd, which were often returned in kind from the floats.

In the midst of the crowd, John tightened his arm around Rosemary's slim waist, and she laid her head briefly against his shoulder. He could smell the fresh, clean scent of her hair. Her soft shoulder was pressed into his armpit. Her cold cheek carried the smoky odour of November.

There was an explosion just behind which made them all jump. A couple of people cursed the perpetrators. But fireworks were accepted by everyone at this time of year. They added spice to the carnival procession. And the advantage to John was that it made Rosemary more likely to keep close to him.

"I haven't put my arm round you since the Milton's party," he murmured into her soft scented ear.

She snuggled closer. "Well, now's your chance to make up for lost time."

"I wasn't sure you were going to get home for the carnival."

"I wasn't intending to come back originally." She looked at him seriously. "But then I decided I ought to be here. Now I'm glad I didn't miss it."

"I should hope not," said John. "This weekend is the first time I've seen you since September. Why did you leave it so long before you came back?"

Rosemary couldn't let that go. "You don't seem to realise,

John Tucker, how expensive it is to get home. The fare cost me nearly a week's grant. I can't do that more than once a term. Anyway you could just as easily have come to see *me*. You're earning now."

"Only five pounds a week. That means I'm worse off than you." He broke off to wave and shout at some friends on one of the passing floats, shivering in diaphanous costumes on the back of a lorry. "My bus fares cost nearly ten bob a week and I pay my mum three pounds. That means there's precious little left for luxuries like travelling. Besides - if I *had* come, I wouldn't have had anywhere to stay."

"Oh, we'd find somewhere." She hugged him. "I know things are difficult at present. But don't let's argue. At least we're together this weekend. And I get your letter every Tuesday." She pointed at another sight. "Coo - look at that one."

A great canvas and wood dragon had come into sight. It was painted in garish greens and reds and had a massive head with bright, flashing eyes. From time to time the lower jaw dropped open and red glowing smoke was breathed out into the frosty evening air.

John roared with laughter. "I recognize them. Look underneath it." He pointed to where, beneath the dragon, they could see at least eight pairs of wellington boots marching in unison. "That's Sammie Joslin's boy scout troop. He's been spending all his spare time over the last two or three weeks on making that thing."

As though it had heard him, the dragon suddenly wheeled and charged at them. With shrieks and yells of amusement the crowd parted and pulled back. The torch bearers hastily got out of the way. From inside the dragon came an assortment of roars and growls. At the last minute, before it banged into them, it pulled up and backed away. Then it swung in the opposite direction and charged off to harass the other side of the street.

"They'd better be careful," observed Rosemary. "If it comes up against one of those torches, the whole thing will go up in flame."

John chuckled. "I guess nobody thinks about that until it actually happens."

The fire-breathing dragon moved on down the street and the next float came into view. Rosemary returned to her theme.

"I do love to get your letters. It's very good of you to write regularly once a week. I never expected you to keep it up. Of course, you don't give me any news of what's happening. I get all that sort of thing from mum." She squeezed his hand. "But I like what *you* say much more."

"I've been keeping my best news till I saw you," said John, "so that I could give it to you in person."

"What is it?" she asked excitedly. "Is it about the job?"

"I suppose so - in a way. What's happened, is that I've started to learn to drive. I'm having lessons with Bill Kingley, the chief clerk in the office. If I manage to pass my test during the winter, I may be able to borrow the pool car and come up to visit you next spring."

"Oh John, that's lovely. How did you manage to arrange that?"

"Well, it was Bill's idea. We had to get approval from Mr Grant of course. Mum had a word with Sarah, who suggested to her husband that I would be more useful to him if I learned to drive, and he agreed. So Bill has been letting me drive when we go out on surveys. He says I'm coming on well. He reckons I should be able to take my test soon."

"Oh," said Rosemary, "so it's ´Sarah´ now, is it?"

John looked at her suspiciously. The remark sounded a bit catty. But perhaps he had misheard her in the noise of the band passing.

"Sarah Grant's the one who really got me the job. She used to be friendly with my mum and dad. It was Sarah who suggested me to her husband. It's about the best sort of job I can expect, now I've had to pull out of Cambridge." He didn't try to keep the bitterness out of his voice.

Rosemary turned back from watching the retreating back of the bass drummer. "I *know*, John. It's so unfair that you can't finish your degree. You were getting on so well."

"It's those bloody Staceys that did it." John scowled. "If they'd only been willing to wait a year before they booted us out of Riversmeet, I might have been able to persuade mum to let me continue at Cambridge until next June."

"Of course – you're moving, aren't you? Have you and your mum found a new place to live?"

"Yes. We're going to rent a little cottage in Orchard Street, but it seems ever so dark and poky after all the space we have always had at Riversmeet and the lovely wide views."

Rosemary laid a hand on his arm. "Poor John. You've had a tough time recently. But you'll bounce back. I know how strong you are." She stopped and pointed. "Oh look, there's Susan Plowright on the back of that lorry. Coo - hasn't she come on?"

"Wow." John's eyes opened wide. "Not wearing much, is she?"

"I haven't seen her since the fifth form. I wonder what she's doing now."

"Susan? Oh, she's in the typing pool at County Hall. She's been there for three years."

"You seem to know a lot about her," Rosemary said suspiciously.

"Yes. I see her on the bus sometimes. She sat beside me coming home the other evening."

"Oh – I see. I think I'll have to keep a closer eye on you in future, John Tucker. You appear to be making friends with them all." Rosemary seemed to move slightly away from him.

"I can't exactly refuse to talk to her, can I? Anyway, there's not much you can do in twenty minutes on the top deck of a bus," he pointed out.

"Except make arrangements for later in the evening."

"What a daft idea." John decided the best form of defence was attack. "In any case - what about you and Alan Hardacre? We all know what he's like. I bet he's been trying to get you to go out with him. I notice you've both been keeping pretty quiet about what's going on at Sheffield, but you turned up together on the train last night."

Rosemary sighed. "Of course we did. We were coming the same way. Don't be silly, John. We're on different courses."

"But there are socials and dances in the evenings and at weekends. I bet you see him then."

"Of course I do sometimes." She tossed her head but kept looking away from him. "And why shouldn't I?"

"There you are then. It's just the same for you. I bet all sorts of things are going on behind my back that I don't know about."

She turned to face him. "John - what are you suggesting? Take that back. How dare you make such accusations?"

"You're very defensive all of a sudden, aren't you?" he sneered.

"I am not being in the *least* defensive. I just don't like you making accusations like that." She was facing him now, hands on hips, legs astride. "I especially don't like them when they're quite unjustified."

"There must be something in it, for you to make such a fuss about it."

"I am *not* making a fuss. It's you who's making the fuss." Then suddenly she shrugged and turned away. "Well, if you want to go around thinking things like that, then there's nothing more to be said."

"I see. So that's it then. You're going to walk away and pretend there's nothing to it." John could hardly believe he was hearing his own voice. Suddenly the evening had turned bitter with this silly row.

While they had been arguing the carnival had passed them by. Even the band that brought up the end of the procession was now disappearing round the corner, trailing hundreds of scattered followers as the crowds along the pavements broke up. Now they were standing there alone, squaring up to each other like a couple of warring cats. His mouth felt dry. There didn't seem to be a way out of the impasse. And the fun had gone out of everything. The exciting evening which had stretched before them now seemed dull and purposeless.

Rosemary tried to patch things up. "Let's forget this silly quarrel, John. Quite a few of us have decided to get together later this evening in the lounge bar of the Passage Inn. Let's go along there and have a drink."

"But Rosie, we always go up to Stacey Park after the carnival, to see the burning of the floats. We can't miss that."

"Oh," she said dismissively, "that's childish. And it seems so wasteful to see all that hard work go up in smoke. We can get together with the others instead, and have some fun."

"We've got to see the floats burned first. It's the tradition. We can have a drink later." Even to himself he sounded sullen and grudging, as though he was trying to avoid meeting the others.

Rosie was exasperated. "John, this is the first time the old mob have been together since the end of the summer hols'. Nearly everyone's back this weekend. We'll all be able to compare notes on courses. It'll be great to be together again."

John scowled. "Then I'll be out of place," he said. "I haven't got any notes to compare. I'm not at university any longer."

"Don't be stupid. Everyone understands what's happened and is sorry about it."

John wouldn't be appeased. "I bet Alan Hardacre will be there."

"Of course he'll be there. He's the one who's organised it. He and I have been ringing round all day, getting people to come along." She tried to persuade him. "Come on, John. Everyone else thought it was a super idea."

"He'll be crowing to everyone about the fact that I've not finished my degree. I notice nobody rang to invite me."

"You're not on the phone."

"No – nor likely to be." John continued to stoke his own resentment. "You'll be better off without having me in the way. I'm one of those dreary types who has to earn his living. I shall seem a complete boor compared with your cheerful lot."

She was furious now. "You certainly will, if you keep walking round with this enormous chip on your shoulder, feeling sorry for yourself."

"Right," he nodded. "Then you'd better go on your own. You won't want me mucking up your fun for you."

Rosemary faced squarely up to him. "John, what are you doing? It seems as though you're trying to cause trouble and upset me on purpose. You've hardly asked me anything about what I've been doing during the last seven weeks. All you've done is accuse me of going out with Alan."

"Well, haven't you?"

"So what if I have," she blazed. "If I know you, you won't have been staying in at nights doing nothing. Why do you expect me to behave like a nun?"

"Then you admit it."

She shook her head and turned away. "Oh, I can't be bothered to explain myself to a selfish, suspicious cuss like you. You must take me as I am or not at all." She looked at him. "Just tell me this - are you coming to the pub with me, or am I going on my own?"

John poked at her with his finger. "When I invited you out tonight, you didn't tell me you had already arranged to share it with a couple of dozen others."

"What do you expect? You didn't bother to come round to see me all day, until you picked me up at seven o'clock this evening. Do you expect *me* to run after *you* all the time?" Now there were furious tears in her eyes. "And don't poke me. It's rude."

"I'll do what I want," he retorted. "You don't seem to realise that I've been working all day to try and get a bit of extra money. I can't enjoy subsidised leisure any longer, not like you lot."

Rosemary stamped her foot. "There are more important things in life than money." She shook her head at him. "I'm not staying here with you in this mood. I'm going where I can see some friendly faces." She turned and almost ran down the road.

"I hope you all have a lovely time together," he yelled after her. But there was no reply.

John stood there with the trailing ends of the crowd eddying round him and cursed himself for his pride and his stupidity. Then he started to trudge alone towards Stacey Court.

17

"It seems a pity they're going to burn the dragon."

John paused briefly as he walked past the girl. "What?" In his present mood he didn't feel like idle conversation.

"I said - I don't want them to burn the dragon."

He turned to face the voice. There weren't any lights on at this side of the house and all he could see was a small white face surrounded by a dark hood. The girl sat on the stone balustrade and hugged her knees. She seemed so small that for a moment John thought she was a child, but her voice was more mature.

In the gloom he hadn't noticed her at first. Perhaps that was caused by the three lonely pints of beer that he'd drunk in the last half-hour. Her voice had startled him as he idly inspected the floats which were drawn up around the circular gravel drive in front of Stacey Court. Normally he wouldn't have lingered here on his own. He would have been where the action was. But it had suited his present mood of isolation to believe that he was alone.

The main activity was taking place round at the side of the house. As usual a part of the lawn had been lifted and a giant bonfire had been built on the bare soil. It was that which was consuming the fabric of the floats, one by one. Every few minutes a group of laughing men would come round the corner, strip off some more of the canvas and wood construction from one of the silently waiting trailers, and carry it off to be burnt.

The girl seemed unwilling to leave him to himself. "Don't you agree it's a splendid dragon?"

He nodded, but could only manage a grunt in reply. Couldn't she get it into her head that he didn't feel in the mood for casual conversation?

"I say - will you help me rescue it?" She sounded as though she was about to embark on some romantic adventure.

Despite his miserable mood of denial, John felt his interest stirring. "How could we make off with *that* great thing?"

"It's not very heavy. I can almost move it myself. You must be far stronger than me. I'm sure we could do it together." There was an infectious enthusiasm in her voice.

"We could only drag it," he said.

"Never mind. It's only a short way to the stable yard. We can hide it behind the tack room." She had jumped off the balustrade and was coming down the steps. Her face was still in shadow but he could see that her hair was tied up in a scarf. She was wearing a big sheepskin jacket with the collar turned up against the cold, and her slacks were tucked into short high-heeled boots. She picked up her feet in the delicate way of a high-bred filly. John began to feel the stirring of suspicion.

"Come on, let's give it a try." Her voice was full of suppressed excitement.

"Wait a minute," said John. "Someone's coming."

At that moment a pair of revellers came round the corner from the side of the house, picked up the wooden throne beside the dragon and returned with it to the bonfire.

"Quick," she whispered. "The dragon will be next." She hurried forward. "Let's pull it by the front legs."

Somewhat unwillingly, he followed her. The thing really was quite light. They set off dragging it backwards across the broad gravel area. As they neared the entrance to the stable-yard she suddenly dropped her side.

"Stop," she hissed. "Duck down round this side."

Another group of men came round the corner. They were joking and shouting. They seemed to have had plenty to drink. John and the girl crouched behind the dragon, almost bursting with suppressed laughter. As soon as the men departed with more fuel for the bonfire, they started pulling it again. Just a few more paces and they were sliding the tail across the cobbled entrance to the yard. Here they could drag it more easily. Just inside the gateway she stopped him again.

"Wait here a moment."

She returned to the drive. He began to follow her, but stopped. He saw she had lifted off the long tail from the dragon and was smoothing out the trail they had left in the gravel. He could see her profile clearly against the reflected light from the bonfire and now he knew for sure who she was. She turned and rushed back, laughing openly as some more men came round the corner. “OK. This is the last lap - across the yard and round the corner.”

Oddly enough, he still didn’t refuse to do as she instructed. They heaved and pulled in silence. She was surprisingly strong. As soon as she threw her weight beside him the contraption moved quite easily. It was all over in a few more minutes.

“That’s super.” She clapped him on the shoulder. “Thanks ever so much. Tonight we've accomplished a splendid feat of dragon preservation. I think you ought to feel proud of yourself.”

John affected an artificial mock-modesty. “It was nothing - really.”

“Oh, yes it was.” She was intoxicated with the fun of it all. “Here - I know what we’ll do. We’ll toast the dragon. I’ll get a bottle of sherry and some glasses. Just stay there for a minute.”

She disappeared across the yard and into a side door of the house. John stood and wondered what was going to happen next. Was this the opportunity he’d been waiting for?

She was back in a few minutes, glasses clinking in her hand. “Here you are. It’s daddy's best Amontillado. He’d be furious if he knew. But damn it - this is an occasion.”

He was handed a heavy cut glass wine goblet and she poured sherry into them both.

“Cheers. Bottoms up.”

She downed hers in one and refilled the glasses. “Good stuff, isn't it?”

John swallowed his more slowly, savouring the sensation. He agreed that it was very good.

“Let’s toast the dragon.” She raised her goblet. “I shall call her Esmeralda. To Esmeralda!”

“Esmeralda,” he echoed obediently.

“I say - what’s your name?”

“John,” he supplied

“Well John, thanks for your help. I couldn’t have done it without you. Here, have another glass.”

“That’s all right,” he said. “I haven’t finished this one.”

“Well I have.” She poured herself another. “By the way, I’m Alison. My father owns this place.” She swept her arm round in a casual circle.

"I know exactly who you are," said John. "I thought you'd gone back to finishing school in Geneva."

She still didn't seem to suspect anything. "Oh, I couldn't stand it. It's such a bore. We had this week off. Most of the Americans had flown home for Thanksgiving, so I decided to do the same. Daddy was furious. He said we can't afford that sort of thing. But I thought – 'sod that'. Being over-run by the plebs at home was better than being the only English-speaking person left with all those dreary nuns."

"I suppose you'd call me one of the plebs," said John slowly. The feeling of hostility was nearly choking him.

"Oh, no you're not - not tonight." The sherry was beginning to have an effect on her. "You've helped me rescue the dragon and I declare you to be a member of the ancient order of Esmeralda. Kneel, Sir John."

Feeling more than a bit foolish, John did as she bade him. He didn't understand himself. Why was he still playing along with her game? Alison picked up a stick from beside the stable door, stepped forward and tapped him on both shoulders. "Arise, Sir John, and have another drink."

"Can I claim my prize?" he asked, his eyes glittering.

For just a moment she looked at him a little suspiciously. Then the drink took over. "Name your prize, Sir Knight."

"It's this," said John. He stepped forward and took her in his arms.

Both her hands were occupied and she was too startled to protest. He kissed her full on her wide, ripe lips. He could smell the lightest scent of wood smoke on her cold, soft skin. For a fraction of a second she seemed to respond. Then suddenly she twisted her head away and John let go of her and stood back.

"That was my prize," he said, breathing heavily.

Her voice trembled as she answered him. "I think perhaps you have had a little too much sherry. Maybe now is time for you to go."

"I agree," said John. "It's time for you to return to your pastime of oppressing the peasants." His voice was full of mocking bitterness.

It was then that she recognised him. She pointed at him. "My God, I know who you are. You're Tucker's son. You're the lout who hit me last month."

"And you," said John, "are the bloody tart who lost her temper when I interrupted her while she was playing round with a married man."

"You - . You -." For a second words failed her and let him speak.

He pressed home his advantage of surprise. "And then you're the daughter of Sir Oswald bloody Stacey, who lives off the fat of other people's labours and doesn't pay them properly for it. I shan't forget *you* in a hurry."

She recovered remarkably quickly from his onslaught. "Get off my property immediately. If you haven't gone in two minutes I shall call the butler to throw you out."

"Still trying to threaten me with one of your non-existence hirelings? If you've still got one, the silly old sod will be half drunk at this time on carnival night. That threat is about as effective as your last one - to send the retired gamekeeper to rough me up. You seem to be living in some sort of old-fashioned fairy tale."

"Get out." She raised the bottle threateningly.

It was the threat of violence that made him go for her. He stepped forward and pushed down her arm. He was overwhelmed by a desire to do something to hurt her, to destroy her massive sense of superiority. He caught hold of both her biceps and dragged her towards him. Then he kissed her again, but this time it was cruelly and brutally with his mouth half open. He tasted blood as his teeth cut her bottom lip, but it didn't stop him. For a second she struggled then suddenly she went limp in his grasp. He heard the glass slip from her fingers and smash on the ground. The sound brought him to his senses.

He stepped back, panting heavily. He could see that tears were rolling down her face and that a small drop of blood was oozing onto her chin.

"You beast," she gasped.

John was shocked and horrified at the emergence of the animal in himself. He was on the point of humbly begging her forgiveness. But the next second she roused his fury again in the way she always could.

“Don’t you know that glass was lead crystal? It was probably worth more than thirty pounds.”

“Oh, bugger the bloody glass. Here’s my glass if that’s all that matters to you.” He tossed his glass to her but she made no attempt to catch it. It bounced off her shoulder and smashed musically on the cobbles, pieces tinkling into the far corners of the stable yard.

He expected her to fly at him in a rage, screaming at him and scratching his face. But there was no reaction. John turned his back on her and stamped out of the yard. He was bitterly humiliated and saddened by his own behaviour. He left the girl sobbing softly to herself, with her lip swelling under her tongue.

18

John went towards the bonfire at the far side of the house. He was aware that he had behaved like a crude oaf. It was the first time that he'd lost control of himself to anger since he was a child. He knew it was her superior manner which had infuriated him and caused him to lose his self-control. But that was no excuse. Now he was feeling deflated and miserable.

He certainly hadn't been a success with Alison Stacey. It would be wise of him to keep well away from her in future and hope that she would forget him and his behaviour. Yet at the same time he admitted the girl held a strange kind of fascination for him. It was like having something within reach but which couldn't be touched.

His feet crunched across the gravel turning area where the carnival lorries were standing. The remains of the floats at the front had been carried away to be burned. The area was dark and quiet. All the activity was round the corner. The noise and laughter drew him in that direction.

The grass from the area of lawn near the house which had been lifted was stacked in rolls on the empty flower beds. The massive bonfire was quite a picture, throwing flames fifty or sixty feet into the night sky. The great pillar of smoke climbed out of sight into the still, cold air. Straw had been strewn around for the hundreds of watchers to stand on. A large barrel of beer had been broached and there were glasses in nearly every hand.

John stood at the edge of the crowd, isolated and unnoticed. He was only half-watching the proceedings. His thoughts were still tied up with his shame.

"What? - all on your own on a night like this? I *am* surprised to see a good-looking fellow like you without a girl."

John glanced up, startled. He saw the speaker was Sarah Grant. He was still feeling a bit defensive. "Hello," he said cautiously, "I didn't notice you before."

She ignored his comment. "I thought your mother said that your girlfriend was coming home this weekend."

"We had an argument," he said shortly.

"It's the first time that you've seen each other for months, and you have a row?"

He felt the need to explain. "I wanted to come up here and see them burn the floats like we always do. She was more interested in going to the pub to talk to her friends. So we went our different ways."

She didn't try to preach to him as his mum would have done. She stood beside him and watched the activities around the bonfire. John looked at her covertly. She was dressed all in black. Her long woollen jacket was hanging open to reveal a tight, roll-neck sweater through which her breasts were prominent. Her trousers were black and she had on black socks and walking shoes with low heels. Only her hair was lighter and her face, which was without make-up, appeared a flickering white in the light of the bonfire. Watching the surreal scene, she seemed unaware that he was looking at her.

He felt the need to break the silence. "Are you on your own as well?"

"Oh, yes. Reggie's at some meeting of course."

"A meeting tonight?" John couldn't help being astonished.

"Oh - it's in Exeter - golf club or something."

"I should have thought it would be over by now."

A ghost of a smile touched her features. "You don't know Reggie. He'll stay on at the club for a few drinks and get home about half past eleven. That's Reggie's way of life."

She didn't sound bitter, just resigned. For John it was a new insight into his employer, who previously had just seemed to be rather remote and pompous.

"It's nice of Sir Oswald to let us have a bonfire in his front garden, isn't it?" she said.

He wondered whether she was being sarcastic and decided she wasn't. "No doubt he would stop it if he could," he said bitterly, "but it's become a tradition and he can't very well change that. I notice that none of the Staceys have come to join in. Back in the old days, Bertram wouldn't have missed it."

"I haven't been here long enough to know about these old village traditions." She half-smiled at him. "I suppose you don't like the Staceys very much after the way they treated your mother."

"They're not exactly my favourite people at the moment," he agreed.

"You mustn't let it poison your attitude to everybody, John. You must look at your present position as an opportunity for your life to take a new direction. That way, you'll make the most of it."

"I suppose so." John decided he'd better be careful how he replied. He didn't want to give offence to her by suggesting that working for Grant's was some kind of second best. On the other hand, he couldn't go around lying about being pleased he wasn't at Cambridge any longer.

As if reading his thoughts Sarah asked, "How are you getting on in the office?"

"All right, I think. It's quite interesting. Thanks again for recommending me."

"Reggie tells me that Bill Kingley's very pleased with you. I understand he's giving you more things to do. He wouldn't let most people learn to drive using the office car. It must mean he's thinking of letting you out on your own soon."

"That would be great. I'd certainly like a chance to do some site surveys." John felt a stirring of enthusiasm.

"If you ask me," said Sarah, "you're already better than that other dumb assistant of his."

"Oh, Jimmy's all right." But he couldn't suppress a smile of satisfaction at her words. "It's only that he hasn't got much ambition."

"I've told Reggie that I'm better at selecting his staff than he is, so he'd better leave it to me in future. Just you make sure you don't let me down." Somehow the look on Sarah's face suggested that she wasn't joking.

There was another period of silence between them. The bonfire was beginning to die down and people were starting to drift away.

Sarah suddenly turned to him. "So - if you're not currently tied up with other ladies, perhaps you would play the gentleman and escort me home."

"What?" John was startled at the invitation. "Oh, yes, of course. I'd be only too pleased."

"Come on then." She took hold of his elbow and firmly moved him in the direction of the main drive. After some initial confusion, he decided it was quite a satisfying feeling to have her walking beside him like this.

They said little as they went. He glanced down at her from time to time, seeing the fair hair bouncing beside him, and once she looked up and caught his eye and smiled in a way that made his stomach turn over. What, he wondered, did she have planned for him?

The Grants lived in a large house on the outskirts of town which overlooked Stacey Park at the back. They had to walk for half a mile under the trees beside the park before they reached her road. They were half-way along this stretch when they came across the louts.

A group of young village layabouts, rather the worse for drink, had decided to set up a human barricade across the road which everyone going that way had to get through. John knew quite a few of the young men. He had suffered the usual bullying as a schoolboy.

He paused. "Would you rather go round through the park?"

Sarah smiled up at him quizzically. "They're only clowning around. I'm a bit too old for them. Here you are - put your arm round me and pretend you're my boyfriend. I'll get you through."

John wasn't quite so sure about that. But Sarah's invitation was one he didn't want to refuse. He put his arm round her back and rested his hand lightly on her curving hip. He noticed the way her shoulder tucked neatly under his armpit as she turned slightly towards him. He could smell the smokiness of her hair. They walked towards the group of young men.

"Hello, my darlin'." Peter Parsons came towards them. He was one of the local bullies. John had felt his violent fists in various parts of his anatomy in his younger days. A group of lesser yobs trailed behind them.

"Come on, darlin'. Give us a kiss an' a feel, and we'll let you go."

One of the others peered at John. "'Ere, it's young Tucker. What you doin' with a married bird, Tucker?"

Parsons leered at him. "Tucker is it? I remember you,

Tucker. 'Ere you two, you look after him. I'll take the bird first."

John found he was struggling with a bloke hanging onto each arm. He felt hot with shame as he saw Parsons grab at Sarah. She turned away from him and he put a hand to her face to pull her round towards him. She ducked slightly and the next second Parsons let out a shriek and started to hop around. John was astonished to see the fellow's trousers round his knees and Sarah's hand was up between his legs.

"Christ, get her away from me," he howled.

But before anyone could move he had collapsed in a groaning heap on the road. Sarah straightened up and walked towards John. The others, like frozen automatons, stepped back as she took his arm and they resumed their walk.

"I rather think," she said conversationally, "that I took his breath away. I don't think he'll be troubling anyone else tonight."

John was open-mouthed with astonishment. "I've never seen anything like that before."

She smiled. "You pick up the strangest talents at acting school."

John looked down at her. She seemed so small. "That was fantastic. It makes me feel most inadequate," he said.

"Don't be silly. It was only the element of surprise that did it. That big fool just wasn't ready for me."

"But I was supposed to be escorting *you*."

"And so you were." She laughed and linked her arm through his again.

Within a few minutes they had reached her house. The gates were open and they started to walk up the gravel drive. They came to the open area in front of the house.

"Would you like to come in for a drink?" she asked.

John still couldn't get over the way she had dealt with Peter Parsons. "I'm sorry I wasn't much help to you," he said.

"You were a lot of help. I'm very grateful you were there." She reached up and stroked his cheek. "It might have been different if you hadn't been there to walk the rest of the way with me. Thank you very much for that."

John suddenly felt rather fond of her. Her face was very

close. He couldn't explain why he bent over and kissed her on her soft, half-open lips. For a second she started to respond, then she stopped and stepped back from him.

"Oh, John," she said, "I don't know what to think about you. I'm going to withdraw the invitation to come in for a drink. Perhaps we've both had enough of the opposite sex for one night." She smiled and turned away.

He watched her unlock the front door and disappear into the darkness of the hall. After a minute or so he saw that there was a light on downstairs. There was the sound of the front door shutting. He waited until another light came on upstairs, at the side of the house, and then he turned and slowly made his way back down the drive.

19

John and his mother moved into the little cottage in Orchard Street on the last Saturday in November. It was a rare, bright winter's day with a stiff breeze bowling the bundles of cloud across the sky. It was fortunate that the weather was friendly, because Sammie had only been able to borrow a small open lorry from Barker's for moving the furniture. But it took the three of them less than four hours to take what items would fit into the new place. More than half the stuff had to be left for collection by the second-hand furniture mart.

While Sammie accompanied the driver to return the lorry, John went back on his own to Riversmeet in order to check that nothing had been missed. He walked round the echoing, curtain-less rooms and surveyed the detritus that remained from his childhood memories. For one last time he climbed to the huge attic storeroom, where he had passed so many secret hours. He stood at the dormer window and looked out across the bare, winter mud-flats which had been left shining greasily by the receding tide. A single cormorant was perched on a buoy, patiently watching the expanse of mud for signs of edible life, its wings stretched out sideways to dry.

John felt a strange affinity with the erect, almost aloof creature. *He* also felt the need for his own space around him, just like the big bird. One of the things he liked most about Riversmeet was the way the house stood a hundred yards apart from the rest of the village, as if retaining its ancient private isolation. He felt as though the place was being stolen from him, although he knew he had no personal right to it. He had happily turned his back on it before when he went to Cambridge. But then he had known he could always come back again one day. His parents had lived there since soon after he had been born and he could remember no other home. Gazing fixedly at the Haldon hills, he swore to himself that he would get it back some time in the future. He didn't know when or how – but he was sure it would happen

After a few moments of dreaming, he shook his head. That

was enough of this foolishness. With a sudden, sharp intake of breath he swung round and strode noisily out of the room. He clumped down the uncarpeted stairs to the hall. Without a further backward glance, he went out through the front door, slamming it behind him, and down the grey-green steps. This was no time to be sentimental. If he were to come back here again one day it would be on his own terms.

Back at the cottage his mother was bustling about, tidying the kitchen. Sammie had returned and was being treated to a précis of her plans.

"I want a cupboard on the wall just above the table. That's so that I can get the saucepans out without having to bend under the sink. My back isn't up to that sort of thing any more."

Sammie was in her thrall. "That's a good idea, Mrs T. Cupboards can be made to look quite smart nowadays. There's a place on the Marsh Barton trading estate where they have the new white Formica doors. You can keep them clean by just wiping them with a cloth. They never need repainting."

"Are they expensive?" asked John.

"Ah. That I don't know," he admitted.

"I bet they cost a lot."

"Hmm. Well, in that case, they might have to be plywood to start with." His mother swung round. "And I'm going to get lace curtains for the window because I don't want everyone looking straight in here when they go past in the street."

"I'll put you up a wire with a couple of hooks," said John.

She put her head on one side. "What a pity the staircase was too small to get a wardrobe up. I suppose we'll have to make do with curtains across the alcoves. Could you make a top with a piece of picture rail to hang the curtain behind, Sammie?"

"I don't think it would be difficult to build wardrobes in those alcoves either side of the chimney breast in the bedrooms," he said. "Mind you, it would only be a shelf plugged and screwed to the wall with a hanging rail underneath and a couple of doors or a curtain if you can't afford the doors."

"Oh, Sammie, that would be lovely. But wouldn't it be a lot of work for you?"

He shook his head. “They would only take about an evening to make.”

“Mother,” interrupted John, “I'll do it. We can’t take up all Sammie’s time. He’s got plenty of his own jobs to do.”

“Yes, I’m sure he has, dear.” She smiled. “But you haven’t got any tools and Sammie was telling me he's got a whole workshop.”

“I’d be delighted to do it.” Sammie's honest, round face was beaming. “Is there anything else you want, while we’re talking about it?”

“These sliding doors under the sink.” His mother put her head on one side. “They're so thin that they won't push along. They just fall out of the grooves. Could we change those for something thicker, do you think?”

Sammie was bursting with enthusiasm. “I tell you what I’ve just thought of - Barkers have recently fitted out a kitchen for Mrs Smithson at the vicarage. It’s all in the new style, with everything matching. We’ve got her old stuff back in the joinery works and it’s in pretty good nick. I’ll ask Mr Barker if I can buy it. I reckon he’ll be pleased to get it out of the way. I think he’d let me have the lot for ten pounds. I’ve been thinking about having some of the shelves for my workshop. But there’s loads of stuff there. Far more than you’d need for this little kitchen. If you like, we could split the cost fifty/fifty.”

“That sounds lovely, Sammie,” she said. “But John is right. I can’t load too much work on to you. You’ve got your own work to do.”

“I tell you what - John can help me.” Sammie nodded to her. “I’ll provide the tools and he can provide the labour. I know he used to be top of the class in woodwork at school.”

John laughed at Sammie's enthusiasm. “It will still mean you’ll be putting a lot of time in yourself.”

“Oh, it’s no problem to me. I’ve got plenty of time.” He shrugged. “I usually spend the weekend doing things in my workshop anyway.”

“But you get paid for that,” protested John. “I think we ought to pay you something.”

Sammie pointed at him. “I tell you what - when I next want a hand with doing a job for someone, I’ll feel that I can call on you to help me. On some of my bigger jobs I really need help with carrying the work to the client's premises and fitting them in position. You can give me a hand when I need it. Of course, I know it would have to be at weekends. How about that for an arrangement?"

"Well - I suppose so . . ."

"Of course John would be only too happy to help you whenever you want him to," his mother chimed in. "And if you like, you can bring prospective customers here to look at the workmanship." She giggled. "Before you know where you are you'll have a business partnership going."

"Steady on, Mum. You can't muscle in on Sammie's enterprise. He's spent a lot of time building up his business. You can't expect him to share the benefits with us."

"Well, John, you say that," said Sammie seriously, "but loads of people are asking me to do work for them - and it's all coming by word of mouth. Everybody seems to want to have their houses modernised - new kitchens, new bathrooms, new wardrobes in the bedrooms. I could take on so much more if I had a partner. In fact, I think I could find enough work to keep me going full time, if I gave up my job with Barkers."

"There you are, John," said his mother triumphantly. "You're still thinking like an academic - not like a businessman."

Sammie agreed. "I've virtually got my workshop set up like a little factory. Two people could work there making all the units they needed. And then it would only take a day or two each week to take them and fit them into the clients' houses."

"Well, don't tell anyone about your workshop," warned John. "It's quite all right for your own use. But if you're running a business from the place, you'll probably find you're acting contrary to Town and Country Planning Rules. I've started to learn a bit about that in my job."

"John," said his mother, "sometimes I think you try to be deliberately awkward. You're not giving Sammie much encouragement."

"I am, Mother. I think he's got some damned good ideas. But I'm just saying that he's got to be careful to see he doesn't contravene the various regulations."

Sammie patted his shoulder. "I think that's a good point, John. I don't know anything about that sort of thing. It's with things like that where you could be a real help to me. Would you mind coming round to look at my place one night and give me some advice about what I ought to do? Perhaps that'll make you feel better about me helping you with your mum's kitchen."

"Of course I will." John felt a new warmth towards his friend. "We'll do it tonight if you like."

"All right," said Sammie. "How about seven-thirty?"

John nodded.

"Come to the shed door that leads onto the back lane. I'll be working there before you arrive."

"OK. I'll be there at half past seven."

Sammie turned to John's mother. "And I'll find out about those kitchen units on Monday, Mrs Tucker. We may be able to start doing them next weekend."

"Oh, that'd be lovely, Sammie. Thank you ever so much." She gave him an impetuous hug. John thought it was most unusual for her to do something like that.

Somewhat embarrassed, his friend extricated himself from her grasp. "It's my pleasure, Mrs T." He took a breath. "Well, I'll be off now. See you later, John."

John saw him to the front door then returned to help his mother sort out the furniture.

20

The station platform was cold, bare and windy. John sat with his coat wrapped tight around him. The train was late of course. Nobody quite knew why, but the porter suggested that it might have been something to do with the smog in London. Of course, John could have sat in the waiting room, but that was nearly as cold. Southern Railway didn't believe in lighting fires unnecessarily, even though it was the third week in December.

So he sat out in the open, surrounded by the stale smell compounded of steam and soot and dirt. But John didn't worry about the cold and the smell. He was warmed by the contents of the pink, scented envelope that nestled in his inside pocket. He reached in, pulled it out again and peered at it in the dismal light. By now he knew the contents by heart. He liked to just look at it, with its slightly curled edges, the small neat handwriting, the faint but fresh aroma of Rosemary.

> *My dearest John, I've been so upset since we had our stupid row and you stomped off into the night.* (Usual woman's exaggeration he thought to himself with a grin.) *Oh John, I've been feeling so miserable. Everyone keeps asking what's the matter with me. All the pleasure seems to have gone out of University life.*
>
> *John, how could you think that I was interested in Alan Hardacre? You've made me feel quite sick now, whenever I look at him. I hate his shiny hair and oily grin.* (John moistened his lips, and his eyes seemed to feel a bit damp.) *In another two weeks I'll be home for the Christmas holidays and I don't want this row to carry on.*
>
> *Of course you've probably got several other girlfriends by now. If you have, just let me know and I'll understand. Please write and tell me whether we can meet some time and at least make it up to the point where we can be good friends and you won't hate me*

any more.
Love forever, Rosemary.

He had waited a whole week before he'd replied:-

> *Write and tell me what time you're arriving, and I'll come to carry your bag. That is, unless you've already got somebody else to do it for you.* (Like Alan Hardacre, he'd thought. But at least he'd had the sense to resist saying as much.)

What he hadn't told her was that ten days ago he'd passed his driving test. Mr Grant had been mildly surprised. "I must hand it to you, young Tucker. When you go for something you really get stuck in and work for it. Well, best of luck to you." And he'd given him ten bob a week rise.

It had taken a lot of scheming to prepare for this evening. Luckily a young couple had come to the office wanting to view a country cottage. It was mid-afternoon and Mr Grant had already left. John had volunteered to take them to look round it. Bill Kingley had been quick enough to invent a reason why he couldn't do it himself. John had pointed out, that by the time he had run the couple back to the station, he would be unlikely to get back to the office much before seven. By then everything would be locked up. Nobody liked working late on a Friday night.

So, after much hesitation, Mr Cartwright had given John permission to take the pool car home that evening, as long as he returned it first thing the next morning. Now the Morris Ten stood outside in the station car park and John had paid five shillings to put two gallons of petrol in it for his own use. He hoped Rosemary would be impressed.

There was a whistle in the distance. His head jerked up out of its reverie. That must be her train. He looked at the platform clock. In fact it was only just over ten minutes late. He looked down again at the letter which still lay in his hand. Then he quickly tucked it away in his inside pocket. He got up and walked to the platform edge. The rails were humming with the noise of the approaching train.

When it came in to the station, there was the grinding sound of steel wearing away at steel as the brakes were applied. The mournful clanking of the connecting rods echoed across the platform as the great tamed monster rolled gently to a halt. The loudspeaker started to announce the arrival. A rush of warm air engulfed him as the engine pulled up, and there was a roar as clouds of billowing steam were released. The motion came almost imperceptibly to a halt and there were the thumps of doors opening.

John stood back and looked for her. There she was, her fair hair tied back in a pony tail. She climbed down, a heavy case hanging from each hand and a large bag hooked over her shoulder. Just behind her came a tall slim man. Had they been travelling together? A strange shyness came over John and he hung back for a moment, wondering if he had made a mistake in coming. But the next moment her searching eyes saw him. She dropped the cases and came rushing towards him.

She threw her arms around his neck. "Oh John, I was worried for a minute. I sent a letter to Daddy, telling him not to come, because you were picking me up. And it didn't occur to me, until I was about to get off the train, that you might not have been able to make it. It was such a relief to see that you were actually here."

"Rosie, you needn't have worried. Wild horses wouldn't have kept me away."

John felt slightly ashamed of the old cliché of his mother's. But Rosemary didn't seem to object. They went back to recover her tumbled cases. She hung on to his arm as he carried them up the stairs and out of the station.

"John," she smiled up at him, "even though the train's late, we'll still be able to catch the last bus, won't we?"

"I've got a little secret," confessed John as he led her into the station yard.

"What is it?" She turned to face him. "Oh, come on. Please tell me. John, don't keep me in suspense."

"See that Morris over there."

She spun round. "It's not yours, is it?" She seemed so excited.

"Well no," he admitted, feeling a little crestfallen. "It's the office pool car. I've only got it for this evening."

"But I didn't know you could even drive." She threw her arms round him again and gave him a big kiss. "Oh - how super."

He dropped the cases and grinned at her wickedly. "Of course we can still be home at the same time as the last bus."

"John!" She fluttered her eyelashes. "What *are* you suggesting?"

"I thought perhaps we could go up to Woodbury Castle."

"But that's miles away."

"Seven and a half miles, to be exact. It won't take much more than a quarter of an hour to get up there in the car. We can have half an hour alone together, and we'll still be home as quickly as if we walked back from the last bus."

Her eyes sparkled. "All right. It *is* a long time since we last had a proper talk."

"Well," he admitted, "I wasn't really thinking of doing much talking."

He wasn't quite sure if she'd heard him correctly, although she was silent as he put her cases on the back seat. Then he climbed in beside her. This was a modern version of the car with an electric starter. There was no need for the undignified business of getting out and starting it by swinging the handle. He let it into gear, pulled away, drove round the station yard and out on to the main road.

He'd carefully rehearsed the next speech. "I've got to thank you for writing that letter, Rosie. I wanted to say the same thing, but I didn't have enough sense to do it, even though I wanted to."

She looked at him and her eyes were dark. "Oh John, it seemed such a pity for our friendship to end like that, and over such a stupid misunderstanding."

"I know. It's all my fault. It wasn't even as though I really believed you'd been serious about Alan Hardacre."

"Oh, he's such a creep." She shivered.

"I don't know what got into me."

"Perhaps it was looking at Susan Plowright. Have you been out with her recently?"

"I haven't seen her since I last saw you." John was lying.

He'd plucked up the courage to invite her out the week after the carnival. But although he liked the girl's pneumatic figure he'd found her personality giggly and boring. The traffic lights ahead turned to red and he took his foot off the accelerator and coasted up to them. He pressed the clutch down to take the car out of gear and pulled up the handbrake.

"I would understand if you *had* been out with her," said Rosemary. "She's very pretty. She's got a very big bust and she doesn't mind showing it off."

John was startled to hear her talk so frankly. He couldn't look at her face, because at that moment the lights turned to green and he had to concentrate on getting into gear and pulling away. "I tell you, Rosie. I'm not in the least bit interested in Susan Plowright," and this time he *was* telling the truth.

"I'm sorry." She laid her hand on his arm.

"I know I've not been behaving very well recently," said John. "It's just that everything in my life seems to have got mixed up - what with having to leave university and find a job and move house. But I think I'm getting over it now."

Rosemary was all consideration. "Of course I understand. How do you like the new house, now that you've moved in?"

"Well, it's very small." John shrugged. "It's only got two bedrooms. But it's cosy - much warmer than Riversmeet. And it's got a small garden at the back surrounded by a brick wall. I must admit I've got quite used to the place by now."

"Riversmeet was so big. It always seemed sort of remote and cut off from the rest of the world." She gave a little shudder.

"I didn't mind the remoteness," said John. "But I see now that it was very out of date. Everything was pre-war. Sammie Joslin and I have started to modernise the cottage. We've fitted out the kitchen with worktops all round and spaces for the cooker and for a refrigerator and a washing machine, when we can afford them. Mum's tickled pink with it all."

Rosemary laughed. "I bet she is. Did you do the work yourself?"

They were out in the country now and John accelerated up to forty-five. He concentrated on the winding road, fighting to keep the wheel steady. “Well,” he admitted, “Sammie Joslin did most of it. He’s got all the tools, you see. He´s even got an electric drill. It cost quite a lot of money.”

“But you helped Sammie with the work?”

“I did some of it. In fact I did most of the design. Sammie’s very good with his hands but he doesn’t always think of the best way of setting things out. So I did some drawings to show him what I wanted. He agreed to do it like my sketches suggested. He said I seem to be better at that sort of thing than he is. Now he and I are starting to do work for other people as well, which has given me a bit of cash to spend on Christmas presents. Before that nearly all my earnings went on paying my mum and my travelling expenses.”

“Oh,” she said, “so it’s *that* money which has made the difference.”

John smiled. “I must say, I’ve decided I like designing.”

“That’s because you're a thinker.” She leaned her head against his shoulder as he drove. “I believe you’re starting to settle down now, John. You’re a lot more relaxed than you were at the carnival in November.”

He nodded. “I’m going to forget about Cambridge for the moment. I’ve decided this year is the one for making some money. I’m settling back into country life.”

“And your job at Grant´s? How are you getting on with that?”

They chatted cosily in the rattling, swaying enclosure of the car as they climbed onto the moor. At last they reached their destination and John pulled off the road.

“Now – we mustn’t stay long,” Rosemary warned him.

He checked his new watch. “The last bus leaves in five minutes. It’ll take twenty minutes to get there, then ten minutes to walk home and say goodnight. We’ll only take fifteen minutes to drive home from here, so that means we’ve got twenty minutes.”

“Quarter of an hour for safety.”

“All right then.” He grinned. “That means we haven’t got long for you to prove to me that you’ve forgiven me for the way I behaved at the carnival.”

“All right. Come here and let me show you.”

He bent forward to kiss her. Her cool, unscented skin smelled faintly of smoky railways. She kissed as she did everything - affectionately and cleanly and with an absence of sexual passion. Her lips were soft but firmly closed. When he opened his mouth a little there was no response.

He slid his hand inside her coat and cupped it beneath the swelling breast inside its protective linen blouse. He felt her stiffen a little but she didn't protest. He decided to see how she would react if he went further. His questing fingers located the top button of her blouse and undid it. He slid his hand inside and started to feel around the top of her bra.

It was then that she stopped him. "Please don't, John." She tried to make it sound like a joke. "I've heard about the kind of things that can happen when a man has a girl alone in his car on these lonely moors."

"And you don't fancy that?" He still kept his hand inside her blouse.

She looked at him. "What I fancy and what's allowed are two different things."

He made one more half-hearted attempt to reach inside her bra but she withdrew and turned half away from him.

"You know we mustn't, John."

"We're nearly twenty-two now, Rosie. Lots of couples are married and have children at this age."

She shook her head. "Well, we're not married. I'm sorry John, but I want to wait until I have a husband to let him do that sort of thing."

"I see." He let go of her and sat back in his seat. "Well, there's nothing more to be said then."

She turned back to face him, and he could see that her coat was already done up again. "I'm sorry, but I can't help the way I feel. I hope you understand."

"Of course I do." But did he – really?

"Please kiss me again, John."

He did as she asked but there was little enthusiasm in their kissing and soon they stopped. He started the car and began the drive back, to make sure that she was home by the time the last bus would have got her there.

21

John and his mother seemed to stand on the Grants' doorstep for an awfully long time after she had rung the bell. John stood in a glowering silence. He was in a bad mood. He hadn't wanted to come to the Grants for Christmas Evening dinner. But his mother had insisted on accepting the invitation. She said it was her first Christmas without her husband and she didn't want to stay in the cottage on her own.

As far as John was concerned, Christmas was turning out to be a pretty dreary affair. Despite his high expectations, he had seen very little of Rosemary. All he had been able to manage was a brief visit to her house in the late afternoon to exchange presents. They shared a few lingering kisses in the icy cold hallway and the promise to go out for a walk together as soon as the weather was a bit better.

Now he was standing outside the Grants' front door, freezing to death. At last, when even his mother was about to reach for the bell-push a second time, the door finally opened. It was Sarah herself who stood there.

“I'm sorry to have kept you waiting, Mary. I was in the kitchen, and of course everyone else left it to me to come and let you in.” She seemed a little off-hand, as though she had perhaps had an argument with her husband.

“That's quite all right, my dear,” his mother simpered, “I understand just how it is when you have to do everything yourself.” She edged into the hall in her apologetic way.

“Come in, John.” Sarah favoured him with something approaching a smile. “The cloakroom's over there.”

His attention was immediately caught by her bright red dress with its low-cut, frilly neckline which showed off quite a lot of her ample bosom. It was the first sign that perhaps this evening was not going to be all bad. Despite his earlier misgivings he found that some of his ill temper was beginning to evaporate. He obediently took the coats and hung them behind the cloakroom door.

“It's so nice of you to have us round, Sarah. It's not very

pleasant being on your own all day at a time like this. And John's not much help. He seems to be in a bad mood at the moment. I've noticed he's become more moody since his father died." Prattling away, she followed her hostess across the hall and into the large sitting room. John was left to trail behind them, admiring the expensive Christmas decorations as he went.

There were about half a dozen other guests in the brightly lit sitting room, none of whom John knew. As he looked round his heart sank once again. There was no-one else in the room under forty except Sarah. The Grants had no children and their friends all appeared to be middle-aged. The men were what his father would once have classified as stuffed shirts. The women were the type who liked torturing vowels at the top of their voices. He was going to have to try to make polite conversation with this lot for the next few hours and be on his best behaviour at the same time. Boy - was this going to be a Christmas to remember!

He was dragged round the room and introduced to them all as "Reggie's new assistant and the son of an old friend of the family". He supposed this was a pardonable exaggeration.

His mother immediately started chattering away to a couple of the other women, not at all worried that her twittering could hardly be heard among their raucous tones. The stuffed shirts were gobbling in a corner together like a group of wise old turkeys. John retired to one side of the room and watched. Sarah came by and pressed a glass of something sweet and fizzy and smelling of gin into his hand. John's dismay must have been showing on his face.

"Don't worry about these bods," she said. "I want *you* to give me a hand." And she treated him to an almost vulgar wink.

She passed on with his mother's drink but was back within a few minutes. "Dinner's nearly ready. Are you feeling hungry?"

"I always am," confessed John.

Sarah's high heels raised her forehead to the level of his nose. "I want you to help me carry the food to the table. Will you do that?"

"Of course I will," he said, not objecting to the pleasure of looking down her cleavage.

"Thank you." She gave his arm a squeeze. "I'll appreciate that very much."

There was a lot to carry. John decided that Sarah was a splendid cook. She had prepared so much food for the ten of them that he thought it likely that at least half of it would be left uneaten. The massive dishes kept him busy for some time.

"Will everybody come and sit down, please." She led the guests into the dining-room.

At the table John found he was seated between Sarah and a horsy-looking woman who was spent most of the time ignoring him. John tried to concentrate on the splendid fare, but he was aware of Sarah's scented bosom within a few inches of his nose as she leaned across the table, directing her guests in their choice of food. Finally she sat down and he could raise his eyes and survey the festive table. He took a mouthful of the fresh white wine from the frosted glass in front of him and found it just to his taste. He decided he was going to enjoy the meal, if nothing else.

Sarah leaned forward again and called down the table. "Have you settled into your new house, Mary?"

"I suppose so." His mother put her head on one side. "It's very small, but there still seems such a lot to do."

John was startled by suddenly feeling his foot being pressed twice underneath the table. Was that Sarah? Was she doing it on purpose? He felt himself start to perspire. He glanced quickly round the table and was pleased to see that nobody seemed to be paying him any attention at all.

"How do you squeeze everything in when you've moved from such a big place?" Sarah turned to her other guests. "Mary used to live at Riversmeet House," she explained.

"Well," said his mother, aware that all eyes were on her, "John and his friend Sammie have made me a wonderful fitted kitchen. And now they're starting to build wardrobes in the bedrooms. You see, the staircase is too narrow to get furniture upstairs."

"How lucky you are to have a son who can do things like that for you."

"Oh - Sammie is the trained carpenter. He has a lot of

special tools. But I must say John has come up with some clever ideas about the design and how to fit things in."

"I never knew John had so many hidden talents," said Sarah, giving his foot another firm press. She leaned forward to laugh at him, and John caught a tantalising glimpse of the top of a white lace bra.

"Oh yes," continued his mother. "You should see some of the drawings he has done to show me what things will look like when they're finished. Here, I do believe I have some with me."

To John's embarrassment she reached down, picked up her handbag and started rummaging around in it.

Mr Grant's voice boomed down the table. "Well Tucker, you're obviously a young man with hidden talents. I'm sure we'd all like to see these drawings."

There was a chorus of agreement.

"Reggie," interrupted Sarah, "You really ought to call him John, when he's a guest in your house. Keep "Tucker" for the office."

"Sorry, dear."

But he and all the others were gazing at Mary, as she started to circulate John's none-too-neat drawings. "This one is the kitchen from the back door. And this is the new sink unit. Oh - and this is what he has planned for the wardrobes in my bedroom."

The sketches were passed from hand to hand. One even landed in front of John.

"Let me have a look." Sarah leaned over. Her shoulder rubbed against his arm, her curls tickled his ear, her scent filled his lungs. Now he could hardly avoid gazing straight down the front of her dress, even if he had wished to.

"It really is very good, John," she murmured and her hand rested on his thigh under the table and squeezed firmly.

He felt an excited ache in the pit of his stomach. He couldn't even try to speak. His eyes seemed to mist over.

She took the sketch and moved to the person on her other side to discuss it. John didn't know whether he was pleased or sorry that she was no longer so close. He took a deep breath and tucked into his food, saying little to anyone, and remaining apparently unnoticed in the ebb and flow of conversation around the table.

From time to time during the meal, Sarah seemed to touch him in certain ways. When he helped her take out the dishes and bring in the puddings it seemed to him, that on several occasions, she pressed up against him. Her hand would rest on his arm or in the small of his back. She would face him when the others weren't looking and give him a secret little smile. John found himself enjoying the party even more, as time passed and the drink went down.

He sat back and looked round the table. His mother was deep in the middle of some meaningful conversation with the man beside her. He watched Sarah's hair waving as she agreed vehemently with whatever the stuffed shirt on her right was saying. At the other end of the table Reggie Grant seemed to be dozing quietly, occasionally opening his eyes to nod and to mumble "just so" to one or other of the women talking across him. Sarah turned back to him.

"Will you come and help me wash up?" she asked, giving him another enticing little smile.

John looked round in case her expression had been noticed, but everyone seemed to have consumed too much alcohol to be aware of anything. He got to his feet and started to gather some of the nearby plates. Sarah came and helped him to pile them on to the tray on the side table. She seemed a little flushed and unsteady herself. She fussed around him as he carried the massive tray outside.

"Put it on the draining board beside the sink. I think we'd better start with washing that lot up."

"Mother always tells me to do the glasses first."

"Good idea," she agreed. "John dear, before we start, can you go and get me my apron? I don't want to make a mess on my dress."

"Where is it?"

"Oh." She put her hand to her forehead. "I must have left it upstairs. It'll be behind the door in my dressing room."

"Never mind," he said. "I can still get it. Which room is the dressing room?"

"Of course, you wouldn't know. Follow me and I'll show

you." She led him across the hall and up the stairs. Her buttocks gyrated invitingly inside the tight silk skirt just in front of his nose. He found himself reaching out to stroke them. Sarah didn't seem to object.

He followed her down a short corridor on the left and took the first door. Inside the room she turned to face him. "There it is. Look - just there on the hook."

John pushed the door closed and put his arms around her. Her lips were soft and wet and moved against his to form a large inviting opening. He could feel the tautness of the muscles in her back. Otherwise her body was soft and voluptuous against his chest. He wanted to catch hold of those gorgeous inviting breasts. He pulled the strap of her dress off her shoulder and his hand burrowed inside the low, frilly neck. Her lips broke away from him.

"Ooh, you naughty boy," she teased, and her hand started to massage the lump growing in his trousers. He buried his mouth in her neck and pulled her dress down off the other shoulder. She let out a little shiver of a giggle.

Her strapless bra was stiffly boned and it needed both hands to pull it away and slide his hand under her breast and lift it up, then he bent down and fastened his lips upon the large, brown nipple.

"Oh John," she gasped and arched her back.

"Sarah! Where are you?" Reggie's voice came floating up the stairs.

John straightened up guiltily, letting go of her breast as if it were a hot coal.

"Don't worry, John. It's all right," she murmured.

"What if he comes up?"

"He won't. Don't worry - he's far too drunk to tackle the stairs on his own."

"Sarah?" It was Reggie again. "Are you there? The port's run out."

"No, it hasn't." She tucked herself back into her bra. "There's some more in the bottom of the sideboard."

"Well, I can't see any."

"All right, I'm just coming." She pulled the straps of her dress back up over her shoulders. "You'd better stay here,

John, until that big lump's gone down. There's a toilet through there if you want it."

The next second she was gone, carrying her apron and leaving John full of frustration. He stood near the window and looked out at the lights in the drive, taking deep breaths until he'd relaxed and recovered his composure. By the time he got down to the kitchen Sarah was well on with the washing up.

"I was hoping you were going to come back upstairs again," he said.

"I couldn't - not now. The horses are on the move."

"What?" said John, startled.

"The ladies with the teeth. I always think they look like two horses."

"Oh." John picked up a cloth and began to dry up. He started chuckling.

Sarah looked at him and smiled. "I was very impressed to hear about all the work you've done in your mother's cottage. I must ask her to invite me down to inspect it."

"Come any time you like," said John. "I'd enjoy showing you round myself."

"I'm thinking of having some work done here," continued Sarah. "Do you accept commissions from other people?"

"What me?" gasped John. "I don't know if I'd be able to."

"You could at least come and do a survey and give me a price," said Sarah. "I've checked my diary and Wednesday evening, the eighth of January, would be a suitable time. Reggie won't be here, because he has to go to London for two days. But he'll be quite happy to leave the decisions to me. I know exactly what I want."

The realisation of her real meaning almost took his breath away. This was a bit different from Rosemary and her forbidden zones.

"Will that be convenient for you, John?" she asked. "Or do you have other more important commitments that day?"

"No. Of course I haven't."

"So can you do that sort of thing?"

"Yes. I'd be pleased to." He felt his excitement growing again.

"Come straight round after work. You can tell your mother

that you're meeting a friend in town for the evening. Can you manage that?"

"Of course I can," said John, his mind working furiously. Christmas dinner had been a whole lot more interesting than he had ever expected.

22

John knocked at the workshop door. He had no doubt that Sammie would be there. He was always in the workshop before seven in the evening. There seemed to be nothing else he was interested in. He had never been a social person. John had occasionally dragged him to events but, although he took part, he clearly got little enjoyment from them. He just hung around on the edge of the crowd and only spoke to others when they talked to him.

There was the sound of bolts being withdrawn and next minute John was admitted to the storage part of the shed. This area helped to insulate the back lane from any noise in the workshop. John had to admit the arrangement worked very well. Sammie had told him that so far there had been no complaints from neighbours.

"Sorry I couldn't come yesterday," said John, "but it was Rosemary's last night. She went back this morning."

"Don't worry." Sammie was bubbling over with excitement. "I say, John, we've just been offered a big job. They're going to convert the auditorium at the Town Hall back into a cinema, again and they want the entrance all fitted out, with a box office and double doors and things like that. I said I'd get some drawings done and give them a price. Can you do that?"

"Well, I suppose I can . . ."

"It's all got to happen in a hurry of course. They want the job completed in time to open at Easter. They've only just decided to go ahead. There's no problem over money. The Town Clerk told me behind his hand, that they've voted a thousand pounds for the scheme. I reckon we can do it for much less than that."

John rubbed his chin. "Is it only the area at the front? No work in the hall?"

"No. The seats are already there. They've still got the old screen out at the back. We might be asked to fix it up for them. The Clerk said it used to be a picture house before the war and the projection room is still there, complete with projectors.

They've had an expert in and he says they can be put back into working order quite easily."

"Is that part of the thousand pounds?"

"Well." Sammie looked uncertain. "Yes it might be. But a thousand pounds is a huge amount. You could almost build a house for that. I reckon five hundred would be plenty for us."

"We'll have to say exactly what we're pricing for. How come you're being asked? Why haven't they spoken to some builders?"

"Actually that's how it came about. They spoke to my boss. Mr Barker's been the only local builder in the village since the war. But he wasn't very keen on it for himself. It´s nearly all carpentry. It's not much of a job as far as he's concerned, and it's wanted in a hurry. So he put them on to me. He's even said I can have some time off to carry out the work, and I'm allowed to use his equipment if I as well."

"Seems a bit strange." John frowned.

"Yes, it is," agreed Sammie.

"What do you think he's up to?"

"That's something I was going to talk to you about. He's made several comments recently about getting rid of the joinery shop. His foreman retires next May and that'll only leave him with one qualified joiner, plus me. I've got a feeling that he´s working up to the point where he might offer to hand that side of the business over to me. Then he would make me a sort of subcontractor instead of being responsible for everything himself."

"What about the workshop and all the equipment?"

Sammie pulled a face. "We'd have to talk to him about that. I reckon he'd give us free use of that stuff, provided we did all his work for him at reasonable prices."

"Er - what do you mean by we?"

"Well, I was sort of hoping you'd come in with me." He grinned disarmingly. "I'm all right when it comes to doing the carpentry. But I've realised these last few weeks that we need to offer a design service. That´s what you´re good at. You´re also better than me at estimating and organising things, so that we get everything ready at the right time. I've decided that I wouldn't be able to take it on without you."

John's mind was racing. "My problem, Sammie, is that I've only just started my Chartered Surveyor's exams. Those will take me the best part of two years. I can only take the exams if I'm working for someone who's already a qualified member of the Institute. Normally it takes up to five years to qualify, but they made a special exception for me when I got my professor to write to say I'd nearly finished my degree. So I wouldn't be able to work for you full time."

"I thought you didn't like the job at Grants," said Sammie.

"I don't much." John shrugged. "But it's a qualification. And I quite like going out and taking clients who want to look at houses. In the future I might be able to get a job as a land or building surveyor with a big company in London."

Sammie looked crestfallen. "Well, I wouldn't be willing to do it without you."

"Look, Sammie, I'd like to do it in a couple of years." John patted his shoulder. "Can't we continue on the present basis for a while, until I'm ready?"

"But what about this cinema job?"

"Oh, I'll certainly help you with that. And I'll keep on helping as long as it doesn't get me into problems at Grants. If that happens, perhaps we can take on a school leaver and I'll help you with training him on the paperwork side."

"All right. We'll carry on like that for the moment." Sammie grinned with relief. "I'll pay you a fair price for your work, John. We can add for your time in preparing the estimate and I'll pay you for that as well, and we'll share any profits fifty/fifty. That should help you build up some cash for the future."

"I still owe you for mum's work," John pointed out.

Sammie shook his head. "No, you don't. Look, John - you're a thinker. I need someone like that. You've paid me back several times over with the advice and the ideas you've given me." He paused. "I haven't told you this before, but I've already saved up more than eight hundred pounds from the jobs I've done for other people."

"Eight hundred! That means you've almost got enough to build your *own* small house if you want to."

"And that's all happened in two years. Think about it, John.

I reckon we could make a couple of hundred each, just out of this cinema job."

John grinned at him. "Sammie, you don't need me nearly as much as you think. It seems to me you've got a pretty shrewd business head on your shoulders."

"Oh, I'm not saying I'm a fool. But I haven't got the science and maths knowledge that you have. I understand that. There'll always be a place for you, John." He turned and led the way into the workshop. Some units were standing there half-built.

"What's this?" asked John.

"Some wardrobes for a Mrs Prince. She and her husband have just moved into the area. This is a good example, John. These people have moved into a new house. They haven't got any cupboards in the house. So they're willing to pay me sixty-five pounds to make these for them. The wood and the various bits and pieces cost just over twenty. It will take me about six nights to make them in the workshop and then I'll fit them over the weekend. That means I'll get about forty pounds for less than a week of my spare time labour, on top of my wages from Barker's. That's about three times as much as I'd earn from normal work, even allowing for some overtime."

"Wow!"

Sammie shook his head. "Mind you, there *is* a small problem. I agreed to accept twenty-five pounds down and ten pounds a month for the next four months because otherwise they said they couldn't afford it straight off. I've had to do that a lot. I'm owed more than a hundred pounds by people like that. Most pay up when they promised, but some are a problem. With one woman I had to go round and take the units out and refund part of her money in the end because she couldn't find enough to pay the balance she owed. It's obviously better if I can get jobs for people who can afford to pay up front."

"I might have picked up a job," said John. "My boss's wife, Sarah Grant, has asked me to go round on Wednesday to give her a price for some work. Old Grant will be able to pay. There'd be no trouble getting payment out of him."

"I'd heard you'd been seeing her."

The tone in Sammie's voice made John look up. "What do you mean?" he asked. "She's a friend of my mother's, and she's my boss's wife."

"I don't mean anything," said Sammie hastily. "I just heard that you'd been seen with her on carnival night."

John felt a bit wary. "Oh, I bumped into her at the bonfire at Stacey Court and she asked me to escort her home." He looked back at Sammie, who avoided his gaze.

"I expect it'll be her husband who decides on this," John lied. "He's no fool when it comes to spending money. So we may not get the work, but it's not worth doing it unless there's a good profit in it. I'll come round and tell you about it on Thursday. Now, what do you want me to do about the Town Hall quote?"

To John's relief the mention of Sarah was forgotten as they discussed the details of the survey for the cinema, the materials likely to be required, and the time involved in doing the work. John soon had several sheets of notes and rough sketches. They agreed to meet the next evening to go to go to the Town Hall and take measurements.

"Well, I'll go back and get some homework done tonight," said John. "That'll leave me free tomorrow night to work on this price."

He was a little surprised when Sammie shook him firmly by the hand. "What you're doing is much appreciated, John. I've already told you that I wouldn't be able to do it without you. I won't forget this when you need something in return. I want you to think of us as partners now."

John walked home with his mind churning over the possibilities of the next few days.

23

The driveway to Sarah's house was overgrown with big evergreen shrubs. The house was almost out of sight from the gate. It was a splendid house with a large bay window each side of the imposing entrance. John mounted the five steps to the front door, set in its projecting porch. He banged the great brass knocker which was at head level and retreated one step. His surveyor's clipboard and folding rule were tucked under his arm.

He could see there was a light on in the hall behind the inner door. The bay windows to either side were dark. He knew the one to the left was the dining room where they had enjoyed their Christmas evening meal less than two weeks ago, and where Sarah had squeezed his thigh under the table. He had a tight feeling in his stomach when he thought about it.

He looked up. The first floor windows above were also dark except that there was a glimmer of light reflected in the centre one. He gazed round the windswept winter garden. There were leaves blown into heaps in the corners by the foot of the steps. The driveway behind him opened out in front of the house. Then a side drive led round to the right to the garages at the rear. On the other side he could see the lawns sloping down to a pond, beyond which was a small wood. It was a large garden.

The light in the porch came on and the door swung quietly back. Sarah stood above him, outlined in the lights from the hall, the porch light glowing on her tousled fair hair. “John, I didn’t expect you so early. It’s lucky I heard the knocker. I was in the snug at the back. You should have used the bell.”

“Sorry. I thought you said I should call in on my way back from the office.” He sounded very formal to his own ears.

“Does your mother know you’re here?”

He shook his head. “I said I was staying in town this evening.”

“Well, come in.” She turned and led the way through the hall, leaving John to shut the door and then turn off the light behind them.

"We'll talk in the snug. It's warm in there. This house is such a great, draughty barn in the winter."

John followed her to the back of the house. Now he was full of doubt about why he was here. He had hoped that Sarah would be wearing the dress she had on at the party or something else more revealing. But she had on a big, loose, woollen jumper with a rolled collar. It fell almost to her knees over the top of some black trousers. Her breasts jutted through the thick fabric, putting shape into an otherwise shapeless outfit. Somehow it made her look quite small and defenceless.

"Are you all alone here?" he asked.

"Of course I am. Reggie's in London for a couple of days."

"Don't you ever worry about being all on your own in a big place like this?"

She laughed lightly. "Why should I? I'll lock the door after you go, and then I'll have an early night in bed with the wireless on and a book to read. Do you read?"

"I don't have much time at the moment."

"I love books." She turned to face him. "I like to read them. But I also love to just look at them and handle them. I don't think Reggie has read a book since he left university. Isn't that dreadful? I'd like to have someone like you to discuss books with."

John didn't know what to reply. He thought it safest to say, "I'd like that as well."

She smiled and at last he felt bit more welcome. "Would you like a drink?"

"Er - yes please." He noticed the room was oppressively warm. "Something cool and refreshing would be nice."

"I've only got gin-and-it here. But I've already introduced you to that, haven't I?"

John gulped and nodded. "OK. That'll do fine." He sat down on the small two-seater settee and waited for his drink.

"At the moment I'm just re-reading *Wuthering Heights* for about the fifth time." She bent over the little table in the corner to pour out the drinks and the loose jumper fell away from her, leaving her shapeless. "It seems to recharge my batteries. Do you like *Wuthering Heights*?"

"Er - I'm ashamed to say I've never read it," he admitted.

"I suppose you think it's a book for romantic women. But it isn't you know." She looked at him over her shoulder. "There's a huge amount of character construction and analysis in it. You should try it some time."

"All right," said John, wondering where this conversation was leading. "I will."

She brought his drink to him, then retreated to stand in front of the glowing coal fire. "Understanding the character of others is important in life. It helps you to get what you want from them. That's doubly important for a woman."

"I suppose it is."

"I'll lend it to you when I've finished it." She raised her glass and took a deep drink. Her eyes seemed to have an almost liquid sparkle. "What do *you* like to read?"

"Oh. Rather crude stuff like science fiction mostly." He shook his head apologetically. "I'm afraid I'm not very literary."

"Never mind. You can learn. I've decided I'm going to give myself the task of completing certain aspects of your education, which seem to have been overlooked." She said it almost to herself and left John wondering what to reply, or whether to reply at all. A silence settled in the hot little room. Sarah seemed happy with her own thoughts.

John anxiously cast around for something to say. "What was it you wanted me to look at?"

"Oh, we'll go upstairs and take a look at what I′ve got planned, when we've finished our drinks." She smiled at John's questioning glance. "I'm waiting for it to warm up. I switched on the gas fire up there just before you came. In fact I was on my way back downstairs when you knocked. I told you, this place is dreadfully cold in the winter. I keep going on at Reggie to put in central heating - he could easily afford it. But so far I haven't had any success." She winked at him. "Never mind. It's often an excuse to avoid a shag."

Her casual profanity left John speechless.

She laughed gleefully at the expression of his face. "Are you surprised to hear a woman talk like that about her husband? Well I'm not afraid to admit that Reggie's no good as a lover. For a start he weighs over eighteen stone. I can hardly breathe when he gets on top of me. And he's got no idea of how to get a woman roused. So I wear great thick woollen pyjamas if I go to bed with him in the winter, and that puts him off. Mind you, he doesn't seem to worry a lot. He prefers his golf and going to his club when he´s in London. I sometimes wonder if he's tumbling some little waitress up there. But she's welcome. She'll never get her hands on his money."

Was it the heat of the room or Sarah's chat that brought perspiration onto John's forehead? She crossed to him and rested her hand on his shoulder. "Don't worry, my dear. It won't be like that for you. That's why I put the gas fire on. It'll be nice and cosy in a quarter of an hour." She put her head on one side. "You're not shocked, are you?"

"No. Just a little bit - surprised." He took in a slow breath.

"You were quick enough to respond to me the other night. Don't tell me you're prudish when sex is discussed." She turned away again. "Most Englishmen are, you know."

"Give me a chance, Sarah," protested John. "I've never met anyone like you before. Most of the females I know are either young and scared of me, or else they're old women."

She stood back and looked at him. "And which am I?"

"Neither." He stood up. "That's what I was saying."

"Do you think of me as an old woman?" She put her on one side again.

"I most certainly do not."

She laughed. "Well, that's a relief anyway." She lifted her glass and downed the remainder of her drink. "Come on, let's go upstairs. Make sure you don't forget your surveyor's board."

When they reached the hall she said. "I'll just lock the front door. It pays to be careful. You go on up. It's left at the top of the stairs and straight ahead – but you know that already."

When he got there, John found he was in the little sitting-room where Sarah had taken him when he brought her the letter from his mother to tell of his father's death. He put down the clipboard and looked round.

He heard the door click, and turned as she walked towards him. He felt that he could see her body moving loosely underneath the sweater. He was almost certain that she wasn't wearing a bra. As she came close to him he reached out to cup her breast. The heavy feel of it excited him.

She laughed softly and held his arm. “My, you are keen. Let’s get the business over first, shall we?” She reached up and patted his cheek.

With difficulty John kept himself under control. “What do you want me to look at?”

“It’s in here.” Sarah led him through a side door into another smaller room. “I’ve got a little suite of three rooms up here. That one’s the sitting room. This is the dressing room and my bedroom’s through that door.”

“*Your* bedroom?”

“Reggie sleeps on his own most of the time. I insisted on that because he snores too much.” She made a dismissive shrug. “The only problem I have, is that the bathroom is down the corridor and I’ve decided that I want my own private shower room. I’ve thought quite a bit about it. I’d like you to build a partition round here. I want the middle part at an angle, with a door in it to make sufficient room inside for a toilet, a hand-basin and a shower.”

John felt a bit uncertain. “I’m afraid I don't know anything about plumbing.”

“Don't worry about that.” She shook her head. “I can easily find a plumber. You just build me the room.”

“What about the cornice?” He pointed to the ceiling.

She seemed to notice it for the first time. “Can you continue that round the outside of the new partition?”

“I expect so,” he agreed. “I’ll check with the plasterer. I think you’ll also need a fan to take away the steam because you won’t have a window in the new room.”

“All right,” she said. “Include for that as well. Do you think you could do the job?”

“Well, I think my friend Sammie could do it.” John went back to collect his clipboard from the other room. “When it comes to *doing* the work, I only help him.”

“Oh.” She wrinkled her nose. “I had the idea that you might do it yourself in your spare evenings.”

John suddenly understood what she was saying. He grinned and changed his mind. “Well, I reckon I could do most of it. I can tell Sammie that I want to prove to myself that I can do the work, by taking on one job on my own. He'll probably want to come and see it once or twice, to make sure I'm not making a mess of it. But I can do the rest."

"That's what I had in mind," she said with a nod. "If you need someone to hold things for you, I can always do that."

John considered the innuendo in her words, but didn't feel sure enough of himself to reply. He almost had the idea that she was laughing at him as she said, "Well, I expect you want to take measurements so that you can work out the materials that you'll need. I'll leave you to do that. I won't be a minute." She disappeared into the bedroom.

John opened his clipboard and started work. He drew a rough sketch of the corner of the room and the location of the proposed partitions and other fitments. Then he started measuring and writing down the dimensions. Later he would add the correct sizes for the shower and other fitments. He heard Sarah come back into the room and turned to ask another question.

"Which side do you want the door to -?"

Then he stopped. She was no longer in her loose sweater and trousers. Now she was wearing a long, gold-coloured, silk dressing gown. It only seemed to be held together by a belt at the waist. He saw that she had no shoes on her feet.

"I want the door hinges on the right side," she said.

"What? Oh." He made a note on his pad. "OK. I'll remember that."

"Have you finished now?" She came over and took the clipboard from him. "It's much warmer in the bedroom. Why don't you take your jacket off and come in there?"

John pulled off his coat and chucked it in the corner where Sarah dropped his clipboard. He watched her buttocks undulating under the silk, as he followed her into the bedroom. He caught up with her by the foot of the bed and put his arms round her from behind. His hands closed over her magnificent breasts. Now he was certain that she was wearing nothing under the dressing gown. He could feel the hardness of her nipples through the thin silk. His own erection was growing rapidly.

She looked up over her shoulder and he kissed her. Again

she had that soft, open-mouthed, inviting kiss that none of the girls he'd known seemed able to emulate. He tried to do the same, kissing with his mouth half open. But his teeth seemed to get in the way. His lips weren't as soft and ripe as Sarah's.

He reached a hand inside the deep V-neck of the dressing-gown and gently lifted a breast, softly caressing the nipple which became even harder under his thumb.

She shivered. "I think you like my breasts, John."

"They're the most beautiful I've ever seen."

"A woman's breasts get larger as she ages." She laughed softly. "Let me get on the bed and you can kiss them."

The covers were already pulled back, the pillows piled against the bed-head. She undid the belt of her dressing gown and lay back on them. Her body was half-uncovered. He could see the full length of her rounded thighs. He started forward.

"Hadn't you better undress?" she asked.

His mouth fell open. "What - everything?"

"Why not? Do you usually make love fully clothed?"

"I don't usually make love," he confessed, hurriedly stripping off his shirt and trousers and dropping them on the floor.

"Don't worry. You will soon get plenty of experience. You have a fine body. And with a great big cock like that you'll have no trouble with the girls."

John looked down. It was the first time he had thought about the size of his genitals. He climbed onto the bed and pulled her dressing-gown away from her breasts. Even in this position they still stood out beautifully, hanging heavily and turning up at the nipples. He bent forward and kissed one, cradling the other in his hand.

"You can take it right into your mouth," she said, "and suck the nipple gently."

He began to understand what she wanted. He kissed her breast softly, just taking the nipple into the ring of his lips. His tongue brushed softly round the circle of little bumps which surrounded it. He heard Sarah's appreciative intake of breath. He started to lick further, more wetly around the underside of her breast. Her hands were around the back of his head, running through his hair, pulling him against her. He transferred his attention to the other breast, feeling the cold wetness of her first nipple rubbing his shoulder. She groaned and he felt the urge to possess her. He suddenly sucked the whole of the end of her breast into his mouth, the nipple nudging against the back of his throat.

"Aah," she gasped and her body convulsed.

John let go. "Did I hurt you?"

"No. You just startled me. Here. Feel down here."

She took his hand and placed it deep between her legs. The flesh there was soft and warm and almost slimy. He could feel the dampness down the inside of her thighs.

"There," she said. "That is what kissing my breasts does to me."

John didn't quite know whether to be delighted or revolted. But the excitement was building up in him.

She wriggled down the bed until she was horizontal beneath him. He kissed her mouth again and her lips were wet and soft like the area between her legs. Then he knew what to do. He pushed his tongue into her mouth and she sucked it in. At the same moment his probing fingers found the entrance to her vagina.

He became aware of a bursting desire to enter her. He pushed his large excited penis into her, into the warmth and the wetness - a little at first, then deeper and deeper and deeper. The moist softness of her vagina wrapped completely about him, swallowed him in.

She let go his tongue and arched her head back. "Oh yes. That's nice, John."

Her enjoyment acted like a spur to him. He thrust into her again and again with increasing violence, and she gasped as he did it. The excitement mounted in him as the sweat broke out over his body. With a sudden bursting ecstasy, he reached a climax and ejaculated into her. There were a few more juddering thrusts and he collapsed across her voluptuous body, gasping for breath.

The sheets where he lay were wet with his perspiration. Her silk-clad arms were wrapped across his cold slippery back. She reached up and moved one of her breasts from under the pressure of his ribs.

"Did you enjoy that?" she asked.

"Oh, my darling." John struggled with the unused terms of endearment. "My sweetheart - I never knew it could be like that. It's the greatest thing I've ever felt in my life."

She snuggled up to him. "Well in that case," she whispered, "we'll have a little rest, and then we'll do it again. And this time I'll show you how you can make *me* enjoy it as well."

But she hugged him to show that, despite the way she was laughing at him, she still wanted him.

24

It was one of those bright, frosty January days - a good day to show people round a new house. Of course, the garden was just a patch of bare earth. But at least Mr Forrester had ploughed the area at the front. There were new fence posts between the plots and a concrete path to the front door. Prospective purchasers didn't have to wade through deep mud or clamber over piles of rubble, as they often had to on other estates. John decided old Forrester knew a thing or two about selling houses.

Mr and Mrs Partridge were due in five minutes. Bill Kingley said that Old Man Grant had always been strict in his instructions that negotiators had to arrive with or before the prospective purchasers. John didn't mind that. He had unlocked the house, taken a quick look round to check everything was reasonably clean, and was leaning against the porch in the welcome sun.

Last night he'd worked late on the price for Sarah's shower room. Sammie hadn't been any help. He wasn't interested in Sarah's job. He said it wasn't really the sort of job they wanted.

"It's a lot of hard work fitting something like that into an old house and making it look nice. It'll cost a lot. And you see - when it comes to it, she won't want to pay the proper price." He shrugged. "But you can do it if you feel we have to."

"I'll do most of the work myself," said John, and hurried on. "I'd like to help her, since she's the boss's wife."

Sammie looked at him suspiciously. "That sort of person doesn't need help. Given half a chance, they suck people like us dry. Of course," he added, "I suppose it might put you in your employer's good books."

John was surprised at him - not so much at the bitterness in his voice, as the perception he showed. John had never thought of Sammie as a social reformer.

"Well," he said, "I've sort of promised."

"OK," said Sammie. "You do your part cheap, if you like. You've got to learn by your mistakes. But you'd better write in ten pounds for my help from time to time, and also something for the electrician."

"Of course I will."

In the end John felt he had erred on the safe side. He kept telling himself that Sarah would just have to pay a fair price for the work. He wasn't going to let last Wednesday night influence his business decisions.

He smiled at the recollection of their love-making. He had never experienced anything like it before. His previous loving relationships had all been with single girls about his own age - primarily Rosemary. In those affairs he had been the leading person. With Sarah it was different. She was the teacher and he was the apprentice. It was the first time he had made love to anyone so completely. Sarah knew exactly what she wanted and was prepared to tell him precisely what he should do to provide it. But she had shown him that the sexual act could be a stupendous experience. And when they reached a climax together, she reacted with refreshing freedom. There was no modest turning of her face to the pillow or beseeching him to hold back.

By the time she had finally had enough from him on Wednesday evening, it was already after eleven and he felt completely drained. When he got home, he told his mother that he had missed the last bus and had walked all the way back. That had explained to her why he was so late and so tired.

John was aroused from his reverie by the sound of a car drawing up outside. He straightened up and walked down the path the meet the visitors as they alighted. "Mr and Mrs Partridge?"

"That's right." Partridge was a short, bustling Londoner in his forties. Mrs Partridge was younger and slightly taller with fair shoulder-length hair. She was rather thin to John's eyes. She was overdressed for the country in a light blue suit, flowery blouse and a straw hat. She said nothing, but gave him a welcoming smile from startling blue eyes.

Partridge rubbed his hands together. "Well then, young man, what have you got to show us? You'd better understand that I want my money's worth. Mind you, there'll be no problem with cash, because my company's paying. They're moving me down here, so they've got to pay for my services." He led the way towards the house. "All right then, you can tell us all about this place."

"Well, Mr Partridge," began John. "This is a brand new, modern-style house. Best quality materials have been used throughout. Everything . . ."

"Don't bother me with all that rubbish, young fellow," Partridge interrupted. "Let's look around. I want to make sure there's enough room for everything to fit in."

John led the way towards the front door.

"Is there a garage?"

"No," said John, "but there's plenty of room to build one."

Partridge came to a sudden halt. "I've got to have a garage. I'm being given a brand new car. I said to them - a Regional Sales Manager's got to have a new car. Now then, I can't leave a new car out on the road, can I?"

"Well," John felt the day was beginning to turn dull, "I can ask the builder . . ."

"Don't just ask him, laddie." Partridge's head darted forward like an angry turkey. "You tell him it's *essential*."

"A garage would cost more but I'm sure the price would be reasonable."

The man was affronted. "Now, look here, I can't afford to pay *extra* for it. If a garage isn't in the price of the house, you can forget it."

"Houses with garages cost much more that this one, Mr Partridge."

"Well, perhaps we should look at some of those then," he said aggressively.

Mrs Partridge chimed in. "Now that we're here, Lionel, I think we should at least look at this one. It's seems such a nice house from outside."

"Of course we will, Susie. Of course we'll look at it. Why do you think we're here?" He turned back to John. "Lead on, my son."

John did as he was instructed. "This house follows the modern concept of a straight through sitting/dining room . . ."

"Huh. I don't think much of that idea," said Partridge. "I prefer somewhere separate to eat my Sunday dinner."

"But it's so light and roomy." Mrs Partridge looked around,

her face glowing. It made her look pretty. She wasn't John's type of woman of course. He noticed how small her breasts were - much smaller than Sarah's.

"There's a serving hatch from the kitchen at the dining end," offered John.

"All right," said Partridge. "Let's see the kitchen, then."

"Just through here and turn right."

Mrs Partridge was bowled over by the kitchen. "It's so big," she enthused. "And it's lovely to have views over the fields at the back. Our flat in London looks out on a brick wall."

"But where are the shelves?" Partridge was obviously in a complaining mood. "We've got all those shelves at home. This kitchen has only got a sink."

"Oh, yes. We'd need to have some shelves," she agreed.

John had a sudden bright idea. "I know a company who can put in a fully fitted kitchen for less than a hundred pounds."

"A hundred smackers?" gasped Partridge. "Good god. That sounds a hell of a lot to me."

"Oh no, Lionel." Mrs Partridge turned her blue eyes on her husband. "Ellie and Joe's new kitchen was nearly *two* hundred."

John looked at her gratefully. He noticed that the skin of her cheeks was so smooth and clear in the morning sunlight as to be almost luminous.

"But we can't afford to spend that sort of money," her husband remonstrated.

"Yes we can," she pointed out. "We'll have the money which is left over from selling the flat. We could spend it on a smart new kitchen."

"Don't argue in front of the salesman, Susie. There won't be enough money for a fitted kitchen. Anyway, I want a new set of golf clubs." He turned his back on her. "Let's go upstairs and look round."

Mrs Partridge and John trailed up the stairs behind him. Partridge went first into the main front bedroom and looked around. "There's nothing to see in here," he complained. "No cupboards, no shelves, nothing."

"There's space to put wardrobes in the alcoves each side of the chimney," John pointed out.

"But we haven't got any wardrobes. Our flat's all fitted out. There are cupboards everywhere." He turned to face John. "We've got to have cupboards, haven't we Susie?"

His wife was gazing at the view, which was across open fields to the woods near the stream. In the distance were the grey peaks of the moor. She was as still and as perfect as a statue. "It's so beautiful," she breathed. "Everything's so sunny and bright."

"It's a sunny day." Partridge stumped over to look out of the window. "It won't look so good when it's pouring with rain and blowing a gale. In any case, you can't hang suits on a beautiful view."

She turned to face her husband and John could see the longing in her face. "The flat's so dull and dark even on a sunny day."

"But it's no good having a place without cupboards, Susie. We'd have nowhere to put all our stuff."

She looked up at him with her eyes bright. "We can easily buy cupboards - or you could make them."

"Here - you know I'm no good at that sort of thing." He backed away defensively. "It's no good expecting me to make things if the house hasn't got them to start with."

"Perhaps," John intervened, "I could talk to the builder about all these things - the garage, the kitchen and some fitted wardrobes. Obviously he'd have to put the price up, but you could probably increase the mortgage to cover it. I expect your payments would be a bit more per month but -."

"What do you say to that, Lionel?" She was breathless with excitement. John thought she had a very pretty face when she smiled like that, with those beautifully curved lips and those bright blue eyes. It was a pity about the small breasts. "You've said that we'll be saving money by moving from London, and with your rise for the new job. . ."

He placed his hands on her slim shoulders. "Now Susan - I've told you I don't want us to discuss this in front of the agent."

"No," she agreed, "but he could at least see if he can arrange something like that and tell us how much extra it would cost. And then we could make a decision."

Partridge softened. He turned to John. "Can you do that, young man?"

"Certainly," said John.

"There's no commitment, mind you." He put his head on one side. "I might decide the new price was too much and want to go somewhere else."

John nodded. "I understand that. Of course, if you decided to go ahead, the builder would want a deposit before he started the extra work. That would be in case you had to back out for some reason."

"What!" For a second Partridge looked as though he was going to explode, and John wondered if he'd made a mistake in mentioning it at this stage. Then the man regained control of himself. "Well - I suppose so." He fiddled around in his top pocket. "Here's my business card. My home address and phone number are written on the back."

"Very well, Mr Partridge," said John, pocketing the card. "I'll talk to the builder and tell him that you'd like the house if he'll do these extras at a reasonable price. We'll get some drawings done to show you what they'll look like. I'll also arrange for a new quotation. And when I've got it all together, I'll ring you to give you the details. I should have the information ready by the end of the week."

Susie Partridge turned her glowing eyes on him. "That'll be lovely, won't it Lionel? Thank you ever so much." It gave John a great feeling to believe that he'd made her happy.

As he stood at the door, wishing them goodbye, John noticed how trim her ankles were and how slim her waist was beneath the belted jacket. He thought he would almost be able to touch his fingertips, if he stretched his hands round it.

He remembered Sarah's comment that it was the wife who really made the decisions about buying a house. John had the feeling that he was going to make a sale here. He must remember to ask old Grant if he could have the normal commission.

As the car pulled away Susie gave him a bright little wave. John waved back. He decided that he would choose the middle of the day to telephone the price to them. That was when he was most likely to catch her on her own.

He turned to see old Forrester making his way across the garden from the next house. “Well,” the builder demanded, “what did they think of it?”

“Er - they liked the setting very much. Mrs Partridge really liked the views.”

“But what about the house?”

John scratched his head. “They liked it. But the trouble is they want a garage and a fitted kitchen and fitted wardrobes in the bedrooms.”

“Don’t be daft,” Forrester burst out. “If I did that it would cost me more than my profit on the place.”

“Oh,” said John, “I think they’d be prepared to pay extra as long as it could be added to the mortgage.”

“A garage would need Planning Approval.”

“Not if it was beside the house and behind the building line,” John pointed out.

Forrester shook his head. “I’d have to put in a double gate and a driveway as well.”

“Yes, you *would* have to do that.”

The old man paused and weighed the idea in his mind. “I don't really want to mess around with fitted kitchens and things like that.”

“The problem is,” said John, “they’re moving out of a flat in London where everything’s fitted. They haven’t got removable wardrobes and kitchen dressers and things like that.”

“Then they’ll have to buy them.”

John shook his head. “That’ll cost them a lot of money. Their alternative is to buy a house with these things already fitted. It’ll cost them more, but the mortgage payments will only go up a little bit and they won’t notice it so much.”

“It´ll be difficult to find a house round here that´s all fitted out like they want.”

“Well, that´s what they´re looking for.”

“And I haven’t got a joiner who can do work like that.” Forrester waved his arms around. “Dammit. I’m a builder. I don’t mess around with fitted furniture and things like that.”

“Well,” said John. “I know a young joiner who can do that sort of thing. Shall I ask him to come along and prepare some sketches and a price for you? I think the Partridges would be interested in something like that."

Forrester shook his head. "I haven't got time to play around with things like that."

"All you'd need to do is add the quote to your price. I'm sure my friend will include an extra five percent for you if you want him to."

John found that Mr Forrester was suddenly interested.

"I hope he realises," said the old man, "that he wouldn't get paid for all his trouble if the Partridges didn't go ahead."

John nodded. "He'd understand that. I've told the Partridges that they'd have to pay a deposit before the extra work was started."

Forrester looked at him cannily. "You seem to have thought of everything, don't you? All right. I'll look at this offer from your friend," he pointed a finger at John, "but without commitment, mind. And I don't want to be involved with doing any of the work."

"What about the garage and the drive?"

"Would he do that as well?" Forrester looked interested.

"I could ask him to include for it."

"All right." Forrester clapped him on the shoulder. "He might as well quote me for the lot. It'll save me a lot of trouble."

"OK. That's no problem."

"And remind him he's to include the five percent for me on all of it."

John smiled. "I'll make sure he does that."

"Come back to me as soon as you can. I'll leave you to lock up." Forrester turned and stumped away. John went out to the car and collected his tape and clipboard to measure up the rooms for the fitted units.

25

Worn out by three hours furious shopping Camilla Forbes Prendergast collapsed into a chair near the window. Her voluptuous body slumped with exhaustion. Her plump, cupid lips and dark eyes were damp with perspiration. Her spikey red hair had flopped on to her forehead

"Oh, my god," she complained, "I don't know why they sent me to St bloody Teresa's. The shops in Geneva are frightful. I haven't been able to find a thing that fits. If only Daddy hadn't banned me from going to Paris." She shook her head. "I don't know what I shall look like when I go home at Easter. *And* I'm desperate for a coffee." She gesticulated furiously at the waiter across the restaurant.

"You haven't done too badly." Alison surveyed the pile of bags surrounding her friend. "Just look at *me*, Millie."

Camilla was aghast. "My dear - one solitary bag. I'm sure you're not feeling well, Alison. You haven't been the same since you came back from England. What happened to you at Christmas?"

"Nothing." Alison sat opposite her friend and looked out across the *Rade de Geneva*, past the spectacular water jet, and up into the snow-covered mountains. But she saw none of it. "That's just it. Nothing happened at Christmas."

"Darling - surely something must have happened to you. I had a furious time. I must have lost my virginity five or six times." She ordered coffees and *pains au chocolat* from the waiter who had just arrived. "Didn't you go to any parties or anything?"

"Oh - yes." Alison continued to stare at the view. "Yes, I went to some parties."

"Didn't you meet anyone there?"

"No. No-one special - just the usual boring bunch of infantile schoolboys pretending to be grown-ups, talking in loud voices about their conquests, and groping in corners."

"You should have come to London. We had some wild parties in London. Why didn't you come to London?"

Alison turned her eyes on Millie. “I couldn’t. Daddy’s so bloody tight at the moment that he wouldn’t give me the money. Besides I didn’t feel much like parties, even in London.”

“Not feel like parties?” For a few seconds Millie was deprived of words. “Alison - last year you used to be the original raver. If you don’t feel like parties, you must be ill.”

Alison shook her head. “I’m perfectly all right.”

“Or in love. That’s it - you’re in love. Wait till I tell the other girls.”

“Millie, I am *not* in love.”

“Yes, you are.” Camilla pointed at her. “You can’t hide it from me. I know who it is. I saw Ambrose just before we came back. He let on that you were having an affair with some married local farmer. I bet you spent the hols rolling around in the straw. Well, I must say it’s the best way to keep warm at this time of year.”

Alison sighed. “Millie, you are crude at times. There’s no affair. It was all over before it ever got started. Some local yob blundered into us in the middle of a clinch and scared the shit out of Ralph. He’s kept clear of me ever since.”

“Really - how decadent,” gasped Millie. “Tell me more. Where did this happen?”

Damn Ambrose for letting the cat out of the bag. Alison knew she’d never be able to keep it quiet now. “Oh - in the woods near home.”

“Yes, but when?” asked Millie. “Was it over Christmas?”

She shrugged. “No. I was out riding early one morning last autumn. You know - the time I went back to try and get more money out of Daddy.”

The waiter brought the coffee, but Millie paid him no attention. “You’d known this Ralph fellow for some time?”

“We’d met a few times in the summer at parties and barbecues and things like that. He’s a member of the local sailing club where Ambrose is a leading light.”

“I didn’t know Ambrose sailed.”

“Oh, he’s good at it,” said Alison bitterly. “Brilliant at everything is our Ambrose, as long as he doesn’t have to work his brain too hard.”

But Camilla wasn't interested in that. "So the romance blossomed out on the water."

"Nothing much happened then - just a few words, a few touches." Alison smiled in reminiscence. "But when I came here in September, Ralph started writing to me. We arranged to meet secretly when I went home. It seemed as though it was going to go on from there. But it didn't, because of John bloody Tucker."

"John Tucker?"

Alison sighed. "He's the yob who broke it up."

"So you know him? You let some damned yokel ruin the start of a good affair?" Camilla was incensed. "I hope you told him where to get off."

Alison looked down at the table. "I did more than that. I hit him with my riding crop and ordered him to get off our land."

"Well done. I should think so too."

"Also," she said quietly, "I got him and his mother thrown out of their estate house. Because of me he has had to leave university and get a job to support his mother."

"My god, Alison. He really *did* get under your skin. And the fellow was clever as well. You've probably wrecked his career."

"I realise that now," Alison admitted. "I don't feel very good about it."

"He might cause trouble, you know." Camilla drew a pattern with her index finger in a puddle of coffee on the shiny surface of the table. "These clever plebs can turn nasty when they think they've got a grievance. Have you heard anything from him?"

"I met him when I went home for the weekend in November. I told you - it was the local carnival."

"So?" Camilla couldn't wait. "What happened then?"

"Well, we sort of bumped into each other in the dark. In fact, he kissed me."

"Go on! Go on!"

"I think he'd been drinking." Alison paused as she remembered. "We didn't recognise each other at first. Then, when he knew who I was, he kissed me really roughly - like you imagine a working-class kiss would be. He actually cut my lip. Then he told me just what he thought of me and threw the glass he was holding at me and stormed off."

Camilla concentrated hard on the shape of the coffee puddle she had drawn. "How very interesting."

"The strange thing was - I felt as though I wanted him to do it again - to hurt me some more." Alison looked up at her friend. "I nearly ran after him and said I was sorry and would he forgive me - all that sort of stuff. I've never felt like that before in my *life*."

"Oh dear," said her friend. "That sounds a bit like love to me, little girl."

"That's rubbish, Millie. How can it possibly be love? I've only met him the twice – er - three times. And I don't even *like* him. In fact, I think he's pretty revolting. I just think he must have appealed to some base side of my personality. Perhaps I have some strange compulsion to experience things that are grubby and dirty."

Millie's face was alight. "But did you go grubbing around with him over Christmas? Did you meet up for some sort of furtive self-flagellation or anything?"

That finally made Alison laugh. "No, there was nothing like that. In fact nothing worth talking about happened at all. I didn't see him or Ralph or anyone else of note. It was almost a relief to come back to the excitements of Geneva."

"Oh, my God." Camilla raised her hand to her forehead. "You really are a lost cause, Alison. It's about time you got drunk. Let's have a *pernod* to set us on our way." She waved furiously again in the direction of the waiter.

26

It had been a bad week for John. Monday lunchtime he'd rung Sarah to give her the price for the shower room. She'd seemed surprised that it had been so much. "One hundred and forty pounds? Are you sure? Does that include the plumbing?"

"No," said John. "You said you knew someone who could do that. I'm sorry, Sarah, but it's a rather fiddly job. It'll take a couple of weeks in the evenings and the plasterer will want three days."

There was a brief silence from Sarah. Then she said, "Oh, well. I'll have to think about it."

"Would you like me to come round and go through it with you?" asked John hopefully. "We could check if you want to change anything."

"Not at the moment. I'll come back to you."

He made one more try. "I don't know when you wanted the work done - only we're going to be very busy up to and around Easter."

"That's no problem. I'm not in a hurry."

She had been distinctly offhand. It was almost as though she was annoyed with him about something. It seemed such a big change from her mood when he was with her the other night. John shrugged to himself. He supposed women were like that at times.

Then on Wednesday a bombshell had burst on John and Sammie. They had thought it would be a good idea to get a trailer to carry the longer and larger units which they were building. So they decided to fit a tow-bar to the second-hand van they had recently bought from Barkers. John had taken the van and the new trailer to pick up a load of timber. But on the way back from the sawmill the clutch had burnt out going up a hill.

This had caused them a real problem. They'd had to get Mr Blake at the local garage to make two trips to tow back the trailer and the van and that alone had cost them nine pounds ten. Then old Blake had given them an estimate of thirty-five pounds for replacing the clutch. John and Sammie had come close to having a row about it.

"I reckon we ought to try to do it ourselves next weekend," said Sammie. "If we asked him nicely, old Blakey would let us use his ramp. I reckon the bits would cost us less than twenty quid."

"But that's daft Sammie. Even if you're right, that would only save us fifteen pounds. Between us we usually earn thirty or forty pounds over a weekend just making fitted units. More important than that - it will also put us back a week on our programme for the cinema reception area."

"Then we'll just have to put some more hours in. I am not going to work all weekend just to pay old Blakey for repairing the van." Sammie had a tendency to get obstinate when things didn't go right.

John sighed. "But we're already working all the hours God made. You've got to face the fact that unexpected problems will occur from time to time when you're in business. We've just got to pay up and get on with the work. Besides," he admitted, "there's a film I want to see at the Gaumont next week."

"Why can't you wait until it comes down to the Palace?"

In the end John had to tell Sammie that he'd be working on the van on his own, before he'd agree to give the work to Blake's. His partner grumbled about it for weeks afterwards. He was only slightly mollified when John spoke to Mr Barker and the builder offered to make a contribution of ten pounds towards the cost, because he admitted that the clutch must have been on the way out when they bought the van from him.

It was nearly one o'clock on the Thursday morning by the time John got home. As a result, he was feeling a bit fractious when he was called to the phone by Janice soon after he got in to the office next morning.

"John. It's a Mrs Partridge for you."

"Partridge?" For a second he was puzzled. "Oh - Mrs Partridge." John bounded across to the phone and picked it up breathlessly. "Hello."

"John. It's Susie."

John was surprised at the informality. She'd hardly said a

word to him a couple of weeks ago.

"My husband's travelling away this week so I decided I'd come down and have another look at the house. How is the builder getting on with his designs for the kitchen and the other stuff?"

"Er, well. He wants *me* to do the drawings," said John, almost truthfully.

"Oh. How are you getting on?"

He took a breath. "I've sort of started."

"I was hoping I could see something. Perhaps you could meet me and explain to me what it's going to look like."

"Meet you? Of course," said John. "When?"

"Later today?" she suggested.

"Today?" John was startled but hastily corrected himself. "Er - OK. I'll see if I can borrow a car for this afternoon."

He put the phone down and went in search of Bill Kingley. "I've got a Mrs Partridge on the phone. She's the lady I took to look at Forrester's new house at Clyst St Andrew a couple of weeks ago. She wants to go and have another look this afternoon. Is the pool car available?"

"Don't worry," said Bill. "I'm free this afternoon. I'll take her. Tell her to get round here at two o'clock."

John thought quickly. "Er - I've done a few sketches for her of fitted kitchens and bedroom units which they want. If I explain them to you, can you tell her how they'd look?"

"Why, John?" demanded Bill. "What the hell did you do that for? That's not part of your job."

John wrinkled his brow. "They won't buy the place unless it's fitted out. I asked old Forrester about it, and he wasn't interested in doing anything. So I volunteered to do it myself."

"That's a bit beyond the call of duty isn't it?"

"I don't mind," said John. "I want to get a sale."

"Hoping to get your one per cent commission, are you." Bill laughed. "All right, young John. You can have the car. Make sure it's back here by five o'clock though. I don't want to be late tonight."

"Thanks, Bill." John almost ran back to the phone. "Hello Mrs Partridge. I've been able to arrange a car. When shall I meet you? After lunch?"

"Do you know the Cranford Lodge?"

"The hotel on the by-pass?"

"I'm staying there. Come round at one and I'll treat you to lunch."

"All right," said John. "Thank you very much."

How different she was today, John thought to himself as he put down the phone. She had seemed such a quiet little thing when she'd been with her husband the other day. Now she was treating him to lunch in a posh place like the Cranford. But there was no time to think about that. He had to work on his sketches for an hour, so as to have something to show her.

He went to get the keys to the car at twelve forty-five.

"Using the car to go home for lunch?" asked Bill, with a slightly malicious smile on his face.

"Actually," said John smugly, "I've been invited to have it with Mrs Partridge."

Bill laughed. "I think you ought to reword that slightly, young John. Sounds as though you've made a hit there." And he tossed the keys across the desk.

The Cranford Lodge Hotel was linked to the country club and golf course. It had always seemed incredibly posh to John. He hadn't previously formed the opinion that the Partridges were rolling in money, and he wondered how Susie Partridge was able to be so extravagant.

She met him in reception. "Hello, John. Can I call you John?"

"Of course you can."

"Call me Susie. It's silly to be formal, isn't it."

John agreed. He thought she looked absolutely stunning. She was wearing a blue woollen dress with long sleeves that moulded itself to the shape of her slim body. Her bright blue eyes seemed to reflect the colour of the dress. Her fair hair was tied up on top of her head in a curling ponytail and she looked younger than she had on the previous occasion he met her, and somehow she was also much more vivacious. Even her breasts seemed larger than he remembered them. It was as though she changed personality when she was no longer repressed by her husband.

"Come and sit down," she said. "What will you have to drink?"

"Let *me* get the drinks if you're treating me to a meal."

She had a trick of looking straight into his eyes which was almost disconcerting. "OK, then. I'll have a dry martini."

He handed her his clipboard. "All I've done so far are some foolscap sketches. You might like to look at them while I'm getting the drinks."

When he came back to the table that she had decided to occupy, he found his sketches spread out all over it. She was poring over them.

"Did *you* do these?" she asked

He nodded.

"They're really very good, John. You've got quite an artistic talent."

"Thank you."

"No I mean that." She looked up at him again in that direct way. "I did a year at art school, before I left to get work. I assume you haven't had any training."

"I'm doing draughtsmanship in my evening classes at the moment," he admitted.

She leaned back in her chair. "Yes. But these drawings show imagination - not just draughtsmanship. They give me just the sort of picture I want to see. Although there *are* a few alterations I'd like to make if you don't mind."

"Of course not."

John went out to the car and collected his sketch pad so that he could incorporate her amendments. Then they sat down and started to go through the proposals in detail. He was very aware of her lithe, vibrant personality beside him and the light scent which wafted in his direction from time to time.

After a while a waiter came, and she ordered lunch. They ate while they talked and John sketched. A very pleasant hour passed quickly. After lunch he drove her to look at the house again. They were able to stand in front of the appropriate walls and hold up the sketches so that they could get an indication of what each would look like. He was surprised to find that she knew precisely what she wanted. Presumably it was her art school training which made it easier for her to decide which colours to choose. He had brochures showing Formica and paint colours, but she also knew what she wanted in natural wood tones. By now he was convinced that she was going to persuade her husband to go ahead and buy the place with the proposed additions.

He found himself happy and relaxed in her company, although he was still aware of her sexuality. She *also* seemed to be enjoying herself. John complimented himself that she liked being with him.

As he drove her back to the hotel she said, "Thank you very much, John, for all you've done. It's been most helpful. When do you think I can expect to get the prices?"

"I'll check with the joiner, but I don't see why you shouldn't get something early next week."

"That'll be super. Well, thank you for a lovely afternoon. Cheerio." And she went into the hotel reception, leaving John feeling a little crestfallen.

He put the car into gear and started to leave. Then he suddenly remembered he had forgotten to give her two of the sales brochures that she'd requested. He reversed the car back into the parking space and returned to the hotel with the brochures in his hand. As he entered the reception area, he immediately saw her bright blue dress across the foyer near the lift doors. He started towards her, but just at that moment the lift doors opened and a man came out. He walked towards her. They embraced and he kissed her full on the mouth. Then they turned and, with his arm about her, they went back into the lift.

John froze. The man that Susie Partridge had just kissed so enthusiastically was certainly not her husband.

27

The Convent de St Thérèse was open to visitors on Thursday afternoons in term-time from four until six. The reception took place in the entrance hall, which was a great barn of a room. The young ladies sat around in small groups on upright chairs while tea was served to them and their visitors by the nuns. And no-one would dream of missing it, because it was the only chance most of them had of seeing casual visitors from home.

Millie had ensured that she and Alison were occupying a prominent position just inside the front door where the draught was excruciating but the opportunity for seeing the new arrivals was the greatest. Even at this moment they were watching a couple of young men removing their coats and scarves in the porch.

"It's Henri again," said Millie. "Did I tell you that Henri Maeterlink is Awstrian but his mother is first daughter of the Countess of Aylesbury and they've got oodles of lollie."

"Sounds just your sort, Millie."

Camilla looked at her sideways. "Don't joke about it, dear. He may be half a foreigner, but he went to Harrow and Oxford and stayed on in England during the war. One could do a lot worse."

"I'm sure one could," said Alison primly.

"Oh, my God!" Millie clapped her hand to her forehead. "He's got that fool, George Carter-Smythe with him. George is third son of the Marquis of Shrewsbury - Eton, Grenadier Guards and a ghastly bore." She smiled. "But at least *Henri's* rather sweet."

"He must be at least thirty-five," said Alison cheekily. "And he's almost bald. Wouldn't you hold that against him?"

"My dear, he's the permanent bachelor. That's what I hold against him." Millie waved to him as he came through the door and he made for them. "Alison - meet Henri Maeterlink. I think he's something big in banking."

"Hello." He bent over her hand with exaggerated gallantry.

Alison laughed at his performance. She decided she liked

him, with his round smiling face and his short, slightly hunched figure. He was like a middle-aged, fully-dressed cherub.

"Camilla," he said, "you know George Carter-Smythe, don't you? Have you met him, Alison?"

"No." She was thinking how perfect Henri's English was for an Austrian. Of course, he had spent most of his life in England.

"George. This is Alison Stacey," introduced Millie. "Please sit down."

"Not one of the Norfolk Staceys?" George perched his six foot nothing ramrod back on the edge of one of the chairs.

She looked up at him. "No. We live in Devon."

"Alison's father is Sir Oswald Stacey," said Millie. "They live at Stacey Court, near Exeter."

"Oh, really?" George's speech was all tortured vowels. "What does he do?"

Alison wasn't quite sure. "Do? Well, just runs the estate, I suppose."

"A country squire. How jolly interesting." But Carter-Smythe looked far from interested.

"What brings *you* to Geneva, George?" asked Millie.

"I'm here for the winter sports. You know - skiing and bobsleigh and things like that." He inexpertly mimed the action as he turned to Alison. "Do you ski?"

"We have lessons on Mondays," said Alison.

"But we're not allowed out on the slopes," said Millie.

"George doesn't ski either," said Henri. "Not yet, anyway. He still has to learn to relax. At the moment he skis like a Grenadier Guardsman - most of it on his bottom."

Alison felt like bursting into laughter but managed to contain herself.

"One has to learn." George didn't appear to be the least embarrassed as he switched topic. "Shall you be in London for the season?"

"No," said Alison. "I live too far away."

Millie didn't agree with that. "You most certainly will be for some of it," she said. "My birthday occurs during Henley week, so Daddy's hiring one of the marquees. You'll certainly be at *that* ball."

“I don’t have anything suitable to wear for that sort of thing.” Alison felt like a gauche little girl.

“I don’t know. How about shirt and jodhpurs - what?” George snorted at his own joke, but nobody else laughed.

“You can hire a gown,” said Millie. “Everybody does it nowadays.”

But Alison felt humiliated.

“I think I would like to visit Devon in the summer.” Henri appeared to be good at changing the subject. “I haven’t been there since I was a boy. Might I call on you when I’m down in your area?”

She smiled at him. “Of course we’d be delighted to see you.”

“Are you sure about that, old boy?” said George. “Nowadays Devon fills up with plebs in the summer. It’s a dreadful place. *I’ll* be in Cannes myself.”

“I’m sure,” said Henri facetiously, “that Alison will know some lovely places which are well off the beaten track and where there isn’t a pleb in sight.”

“Oh!” Carter-Smythe looked genuinely surprised. “Is that so?”

Alison smiled sweetly. “I’ll try to think of somewhere during the next few months.”

She decided Camilla’s views on the two men were very accurate. It would be nice to see Henri again. He certainly was rather sweet. But while the conversation turned back to the expectations of the next summer season, *her* thoughts were much closer to home.

28

John was concentrating on writing the description of a new property he and Bill had surveyed the previous day. It was the first time the chief clerk had asked him to do it and he realised it would be carefully checked, so it was important he got it right. Miss Brain came out of the boss´s office where she had been taking down some shorthand and stood by his desk.

"Mr Grant would like to see you in his office, Mr Tucker."

"What - now?"

"That´s right. Please don´t keep him waiting." She gave him a prim smile and turned away.

John hastened to obey the summons.

"Well, young Tucker, how do you think you're doing so far?" Grant stretched his considerable bulk in the leather-upholstered chair until it creaked alarmingly. He had allowed himself the luxury of taking off his jacket and John was fascinated by the way his braces stretched across his large torso.

"Well, I hope I'm doing OK, Mr Grant. All I *can* say is that I'm doing my best."

"Yes." Grant nodded. "Bill Kingley said that you're putting a lot of effort in."

John smiled. "That's kind of him."

"He tells me that you're doing all sorts of extra things to try and get this Partridge sale. Is that right?" There was a deceptive lightness to his tone.

"Well," said John, "I suppose I *am* trying extra hard, because it's the first sale which I've really handled all by myself."

"Apparently you're doing drawings of what the house would look like with the furniture in it. Then I hear that you take the office car and spend the whole afternoon explaining these drawings of yours to Mrs Partridge, if you don't misunderstand me." Grant eyed him suspiciously. "Are you sure all that is necessary?"

"Well," said John, "yes, I am. I think they've appreciated

the effort I made on their behalf."

"I hear you've even arranged for some mate of yours to build their garage and fit out their kitchen and do various other things for them. Do you think that's the role of an estates surveyor?"

"All I can say, Mr Grant, is that they've signed to buy the place and I believe they wouldn't have bought it without the extra work that´s been done. I don't think Mr Partridge originally intended to buy it. I think they were really looking for a place which was all fitted out."

"And didn't we have anywhere like that on our books?"

John felt his heart sinking. "Er - I can't think of any."

"Did you check *all* the files?" Grant was still leaning back in his chair, but he suddenly seemed more alert.

"Well, I suppose I didn't check everything," confessed John miserably.

"What I want to know is whether you checked anything at all?" asked the boss.

John took a breath. "I discussed it with Bill."

"So - Bill Kingley's the expert on all the properties we've got on the books, is he?" Grant was enjoying himself now.

"Yes, I thought so. But not only that." John tried desperately to think of excuses. "Obviously Miss Brain had been through their requirements in detail before she sent them the particulars. Of the stuff she'd sent them, they'd only shown interest in this one property."

Mr Grant showed his ponderous irony. "So - as well as the chief clerk, you relied on the secretary, did you? Do you know exactly how many brochures she sent them?"

John shook his head. "I'm sorry. I'm afraid I don't."

"Of course you didn't think to ask for any advice or guidance from Mr Cartwright or myself?"

"Well, you were busy . . ."

"Now look, Tucker," said Grant severely. "There's a right and a wrong way to go about these things. This is a professional office. I understand you want to become a professional surveyor. So don't go around behaving like a brush salesman."

"I thought I was encouraging a sale," said John weakly.

"As a surveyor, you don't encourage a sale in that way. Ask for help from me or Mr Cartwright. You must remember to be professional above all else. Don´t forget that you are representing both the seller and the buyer. The estate surveyor has responsibilities to both parties."

"I thought that's what I *had* been doing," said John. "I *was* trying my best to discharge my responsibilities to both parties."

"Have you thought what might happen if these plans of yours go wrong? Suppose, for instance, that this friend of yours doesn't do a good job."

John shook his head. "I'm sure he will do a good job. I've seen his work."

"Suppose these - er - Partridges don't like the finished units. What then, eh?" Grant sat upright as he thought about it. "You'd be in a pretty pickle then, with all that money spent and with them refusing to buy the place."

"That was my reason for doing the sketches," John explained. "When they had the sketches, they couldn't complain that they didn't know what the finished job was going to look like. They've also agreed that they'll put down a deposit and sign the contract before the additional work can start. I agreed all that with Mr Forrester."

"Oh." Grant tried heavy sarcasm. "So at least our client knows about it."

"Of course he does. I discussed it with him before I started anything, and then again yesterday when Mrs Partridge confirmed they would be going ahead. Forrester said he would tell his lawyer, so that everything's included in the contract of sale." John didn't say that the builder had also promised to send an order to Sammie Joslin.

Grant stuck his thumbs under his braces and ran them up and down. "And what if these sketches of yours are wrong? Have you thought what would happen then?"

"But they're not wrong," protested John.

"We don't know about that, do we?" Reggie Grant shook his head. "You young fellows always seem so sure of yourselves after only a few months training. You don't seem to learn any humility. I've got it from all sides. Firstly, there's Bill Kingley on one side saying what a lot of bright new ideas you've got, and then Sarah keeps on telling me what a clever young chap you are." Grant wagged a finger at him. "Well, young Tucker, just you make sure that you're not *too* damn clever. That's all I've got to say."

John tried to look contrite.

"I wonder whether I've been giving you too much of free a hand up till now. Perhaps I'd better keep a closer eye on you myself in future."

"Why? Has anyone complained?"

Grant pulled a face. "Not complained, no. In fact, I met Jack Forrester yesterday evening and he was singing your praises. He seemed to think you were a real Mr Fixit. He was the one who was carrying on about these damn sketch things of yours."

"But he didn't think I'd behaved incorrectly?" John asked anxiously.

"No. He was just surprised. He said that I was making you work damned hard for your commission." Grant chuckled. "Is that what you want, young Tucker - a nice big commission cheque?"

"Well, I did hope . . ."

His boss switched tack. "My wife tells me you're going to get this same joiner fellow to build her a shower-room."

John nodded. "I've given her a -. I've told her how much it would cost. She said she'd think about it."

"She told me all about it," said Grant. "Sounded bloody expensive to me."

"The joiner tells me it's an expensive sort of job." John tried to look earnest. "There's a lot of work involved. She wants the existing cornice continued round the partition. That'll make it look much nicer of course - but it all adds to the cost. And then I had to point out to her that she'd need a power ventilator to prevent condensation because there won't be any windows in the new shower room. That power ventilator costs twelve pounds, just to buy it."

Grant held up a hand. "Hmm. Well, yes. But the price still seems a bit steep to me. What I was going to say was that if you did her a good cheap job, I'd see it was reflected in your commission."

"What about the materials and the labour of the joiner and

the plasterer?"

"I'd pay for that, of course. I wouldn't want to see you out of pocket on the job. But any profit would be included in your commission payment. Does that seem a fair deal?"

"Well -." John hesitated, then decided it would be politic to accept. "Yes, I suppose so. Does that mean I'm to go ahead and get the materials?"

Grant shook his head. "Not yet. Do her a revised quote taking off your twenty-five pounds commission for the Partridge sale. Then she'll give you her instructions."

John's brain was doing feverish calculations. He'd need to talk to Sammie about this, because there was another twenty pounds in the original price for his own time, but he thought he could persuade him to accept Grant's proposal.

"Well, that's all." Grant rubbed his hands together. "You'd better get on then. Can't keep the customers waiting, can we?"

John got to his feet. "Thank you."

"That's all right," said his boss. "Remember my door's always open, if you want advice or help in deciding what course of action you should be taking - that's providing I don't have clients or visitors with me, of course."

"Thank you. I'll remember that."

John went back into the outer office, taking a deep breath of fresh, unhypocritical air as he did so. He decided he'd ring Sarah up with the revised price during lunch-time. She might suggest he went round and discussed it.

29

At six o'clock it was light, but the sun was not yet up. The sky was a deep indigo overhead, which said that it was going to be a beautiful Saturday - not that John expected to see much of it. This morning he and Sammie were starting work on fitting out the cinema reception area. He had promised to be there by eight o'clock.

Last night they'd worked until eleven, stripping out the existing furnishings and fitments, rolling up carpets, taking down lights, removing doors. Then they'd loaded out the timber and tools to build the new partitions and the supports for the new units. These were prefabricated and waiting in Sammie's workshop for delivery when the preparations were ready. Today the serious work started on site.

It was going to take three weeks to do the complete job. Sammie had been given the time off by Jim Barker - part holiday, part unpaid. His boss was doing everything he could to help them with this job. But they still weren't quite sure about the old man's intentions.

In any case John couldn't ask for time off during the day. So he felt honour-bound to work evenings and weekends to give his partner as much help as he could. Sammie could do a lot of the work on his own. But he needed a second pair of hands for some of the tasks. Already they were wondering about taking on a young lad to be a trainee.

It was vital that this contract was finished on time, in order to achieve the Easter opening required by the council. After that they had to start straightaway on making the fitted furniture for the Partridges′ house, because the couple had said they were going to accept John's proposals and they wanted to move in before the end of April. It seemed that this part-time business of theirs was starting to become a full-time job for at least two men.

At the same time there were several new enquiries coming in. Sammie passed all these to John. That resulted in him doing the designs and the estimating in his bedroom in the odd hours, early and late. Nowadays he only saw his mother at mealtimes in their cramped little cottage. She didn't seem to mind that he was so busy. However, he found it was a relief to be able to get out for the occasional early morning walk in the fresh, cold air.

The grass in the rides was starting to grow again. He could feel the wetness of it through his boots. The damp, dark forest either side was silent, faintly exuding the scent of pine needles. At this moment he felt as though he was the only person awake in the world, as he trudged towards the rising sun.

Gradually he became aware of a new sound - a hollow, socketing rumble, which slowly grew from behind him. By the time he was fully conscious of it, the noise had already grown and resolved into the sound of a horse cantering up the ride towards him. He turned to look back, just as it came over a rise a quarter of a mile away. John moved to one side and waited for the rider to pass. On he came, lazily swaying to the movement of the horse, a flat cap on his head and his coat tails flying.

Suddenly the man saw John. He reined back the horse and came to a halt just a few yards away. The horse was blowing hard. Flecks of spittle were spattered along the sides of its jaw and neck.

"Good God. It's young Tucker."

"Hello, Ambrose. I'd have thought it was a bit early for you to be up and about."

The handsome young fellow pulled off his cap and grinned. "Well, I've accepted an invitation to hunt this morning. So I decided I'd better get a bit of practice in, as I haven't ridden since the autumn."

"Just back for the weekend?"

"That's right. The old man summoned me. He wants to get all serious about me doing a job and earning some dough when I leave Trinity." He laughed mockingly. "It comes to all of us sooner or later."

John found that now he could smile back without rancour. "I know what you mean. How are things in Cambridge?"

"Bloody awful. Everybody's rushing around, panicking about the finals. Looks like I'm going to have to join them."

"Surely Ambrose," said John, "a fellow with your

connections can find out what the questions are in advance?"

Ambrose raised his eyes to heaven. "I probably can. But I haven't got anyone to work out the answers for me, now that you've gone. The new bloke I'm sharing rooms with is a right pratt. He keeps on complaining about me getting in late and waking him up."

That raised a laugh from John. "As if you would."

"I'm serious. The fellow had the beadles up twice last week." Ambrose effortlessly controlled his horse's sudden desire to set off up the ride again.

"And how's Old Coggy?" asked John.

"Oh, the old bugger's more of a misery than ever." He sighed. "The man keeps rabbiting on about losing his star pupil. The way he talks, you were the brightest thing in living memory."

John grinned. "He made sure he never let me know it."

"Well he wouldn't, would he? That's not like him." Ambrose leaned forward and patted the horse's neck. "I tell you, it's a relief to get away from the place for a few days. And now my old man's starting on at me. He says I've got to earn some money - reckons he's found me some boring bloody job with a merchant bank in the city - arranged interviews and all that crap." He shook his head. "I think I deserve a few weeks to get rat-assed and relax a bit after three years of the academic grind."

"You poor chap." John couldn't help being amused by his ex-colleague's suggestion that he'd been studiously working for the last three years.

Ambrose wagged a finger at him. "It's all right for you to grin. I was hoping to tap pater up for an increase in my allowance, but the silly old codger tells me he's stopping it altogether from the end of September. What the hell am I going to do then?"

"I know what you mean." John shook his head. "Life's tough at the job-face."

"It bloody well is," said Ambrose. "I mean - I don't mind going to London. After all, that's where all the action is these days. And Guy Bagworth's offered me a share in a flat in Chelsea. But I understand that I'll be expected to put in an appearance at the bank before ten each morning and that the buggers will complain to the old man if they think I'm slacking. He claims he's some sort of shareholder or other."

"My heart bleeds for you."

"Don't be so bloody cheeky." Ambrose jerked the horse's head up and it backed away, eyes glaring. "Do you know, I'm even going to have to lay the car up and go back by train on Monday. I got a puncture on the way down and the garage says I need four new tyres. I mean - where am I going to get twenty quid at this stage of the term?"

John suddenly had a bright idea. "When are you down next?"

"It'll be in two weeks - for Easter. Why?"

"I'll offer to do a deal with you," John suggested. "If you lend me your car till Easter, I'll put on a new set of tyres for you."

"Why do you want to do that?" Ambrose demanded. "I didn't even know you could drive."

"I passed my test before Christmas."

"And what does somebody like you want a car for?"

John just managed to keep smiling at the fellow's cheek. "Among other things," he said, "I want to go up to Sheffield and collect my girlfriend from university for Easter."

"I see," said Ambrose. "Want to show off a bit, do you? Want to have her knickers off on the back seat. Why do you expect me to help you to score with your girlfriend, Tucker?"

Despite his understanding of the man´s attitude, John felt his anger rising. "Do you want a free set of new tyres, Ambrose, or not?"

The other man shrugged. "I suppose I might as well. It's no skin off my nose, since I can't use the bloody thing anyway." He pointed a finger at John. "You'd better not crash it though."

"It's insured, isn't it?"

"Of course it is."

"Well," said John, "I'll pay any costs which come up while I'm borrowing it. And you know that you can trust me to take good care of it for you."

Ambrose leaned forward in the saddle. "You're talking as though you're flush with cash. Where do you get your money from all of a sudden?"

"You wouldn't want to know about it." John smiled. "It's an old-fashioned concept called work."

"Don't give me that," said Ambrose cynically. "I heard you were training with Grants - trying to sell houses or something. But even I know that Reggie Grant's a mean old bugger. You're not trying to tell me that he pays you enough to be able to flash around five-pound notes. You've got to have some sort of side-line going."

John gave him a nod. "Well - opportunities come up when you're meeting people. Let's say I'm in the business of property improvement. But I tell you what - it means bloody hard work and very long hours."

"I bet it does." Ambrose laughed. "But never mind. The best of luck to you, young Tucker. I reckon you'll go a long way. You and I must have a talk together some time. We may be able to help each other."

"Have we got a deal about the car?" demanded John impatiently.

"Yes - why not? Come round early this evening and I'll let you have the keys." He grinned at the look on John's face. "Don't worry, Alison's still in Switzerland."

John looked at him suspiciously. "What do you know about that?"

"More than you think." Ambrose laughed. "She told me you'd kissed her and cut her lip. She tried to get me to come round and thump you. I said it probably served her bloody well right, and she shouldn't be so stuck up. They get ideas above themselves at these expensive finishing schools. It's about time she came down to earth."

"She's got quite a temper," said John reflectively.

"Don't worry about it. I'll get her to toe the line. I'll tell her to make sure she leaves you alone in future." He sat upright. "After all, we never know when you might be useful to us."

John snorted. "I can't imagine what use I could be to someone like Alison."

"Oh, she's not too bad," said Ambrose. "She's not one of your brainless little birds. She can talk some sense if she tries. Do you know - I reckon she's got more brains than I have."

“Well, there’s a confession.” John shook his head in surprise.

Ambrose laughed as he gathered in the reins. “Bloody hell - five minutes talking to you and I’m getting maudlin. Go on - bugger off on your walk and I’ll see you this evening.” He raised a hand. “Cheerio then, young Tucker.”

He swung round and kicked his horse straight into a gallop as he headed back down the ride towards his hunting arrangement.

30

Not for the first time, John was telling himself that he didn't really fancy the profession of estate agency. He would much rather do something active, like being on building sites, especially on a beautiful early spring day like today. But Sarah's arrival in the office made him forget all that. It was then that he realised that he hadn't seen her for nearly three months.

She was wearing a simple light green dress with a scoop neck, if anything could be called simple once Sarah was inside it. John couldn't help noticing the tan on her cheeks and the darker, almost coppery sheen to her hair. It reminded him that the Grants had recently returned from a holiday in southern Spain.

"Phew, I'm whacked," she announced to the office. "Can someone take my bags."

John beat the rest of the office to her side by a good ten feet. He relieved her of the two heavy carrier bags for which he received a twinkling smile which made his stomach turn up at the edges.

"Darling." She strolled into her husband's office. "I'm in such a pickle. The garage wants to keep my bloody car. Apparently there's something funny with the steering."

John could hear Grant waffle on about something. "A man like that doesn't deserve her," he thought to himself as the office door swung shut behind her undulating hips. He placed the baskets beside his desk and resumed his bored checking of house descriptions. Once again, he decided that estate agents ought to have more interesting things to do in the quiet periods.

He'd hardly checked out the dining-room dimensions when the door creaked open.

"Tucker, can you come in a moment?"

John followed Mr Grant into his office and stood awkwardly just inside the door. He noticed Sarah was sitting back elegantly in the most luxurious of the clients' chairs and her skirt had ridden up to expose most of her shapely thighs.

"Tucker, Mrs Grant's car is u/s. I want you to take her home in the Armstrong. Take care now and don't rush it, but don't hang about either. I'll expect you back about one to one-thirty."

"Darling," said Sarah, "I've got a few errands I must do. Could John help me with those as well?"

"What!" Grant frowned. "Yes, all right. I suppose so."

"They may take two to three hours. Can you spare him that long?"

Her husband sighed. "All right. You can have him all afternoon, if you want. Just as long as he's back here with the car by five o'clock."

Sarah leaned forward and rose languidly from her seat without apparent effort. John caught a momentary glimpse of white brassiere as her neckline fell open. But the next second she had straightened up and the tantalising vision had disappeared.

"Do you want a drink before you go, Sarah?"

She patted her husband's shoulder. "I don't want to keep you from your work, darling. Do you have the keys?"

Grant fished in his pocket and dangled them out to her. John backed out of the office in front of her and went to retrieve her bags. They seemed to weigh a lot.

"Come on then," she said to him. "Reggie says the car's parked in Barnfield Road."

Obediently he followed her as she swept out of the office. He was well aware of the envious glances of the other staff as he staggered, half a pace behind her, across the well-mowed lawns of the Close. He was grateful for the thin shade of the plane trees which were just bursting into leaf.

"Isn't the weather gorgeous?" said Sarah.

Breathlessly, John agreed that it was.

"It must be so boring to have to work on a beautiful day like this. I thought how nice it would be for you, if I came to your rescue. I hope you're going to be grateful."

John grinned and assured her that he would be very grateful indeed.

"And my car *isn't* behaving very well these days. Besides, nothing much seems to be happening in the office at the moment, does it?"

"It *is* quite quiet," John agreed.

"I expect you're bored out of your mind. I know I would be. I know that *I'd* be very pleased to have an opportunity to get out of the place for the rest of the day." Sarah giggled. "You're really very lucky to have me as a friend, you know, John."

When they reached the car, she unlocked the passenger door and reached inside to release the others. "Open all the windows and let the car cool down a bit. These black cars get so hot. It's quite overpowering in there at the moment."

She stood back while he did as instructed. Then she handed him the keys. "Here you are. Put the bags in the boot."

John did as he was told. After a minute she climbed into the front passenger seat and he went round and shut the door behind her. Then he sat on the warm leather of the driver's seat and turned on the ignition.

"It'll be cooler once we're moving," he said.

"Poor John. You *are* looking hot. Come here a minute and I'll take your tie off."

Obediently John leaned forward. Her strong, capable fingers removed his tie and undid the first three buttons of his shirt.

"There! That'll make you feel better." She gave his chest a little pat. "I hadn't noticed before that you've got quite a hairy chest for a young man. I rather like hairy chests."

John didn't quite dare to say at the moment that he liked Sarah's very smooth chest. Instead he started the car up and drove gently out along Southgate. For a long time, as they were driving out of town, she said nothing. Her head was slightly on one side to let the breeze from the open window ruffle her hair. Her arms were relaxed on her lap.

At last she looked at him. "You're quiet, John. What are you thinking about?"

"I was brought up to speak when I was spoken to," he said truculently.

"Don't be prissy with me, John Tucker." She regarded him languidly. "Shall I try and guess what you're thinking?"

"If you like."

"OK, then." She looked at him through half-closed eyes. "You're thinking - why has she avoided me like the plague for the last three months since she seduced me, and now suddenly she turns up and gets me to run her home. I wonder what she has planned for me? Am I right?"

"You're not far out," admitted John.

"Well - to answer you, there are reasons why I haven't spoken to you for a while. Some of them I can't tell you. But one of them was that you were trying to be too greedy."

He looked sharply at her and then back at the road. "I don't understand what you mean?"

"I think your price for the shower-room was too high." She leaned back in her seat and looked out of the window. "I decided, at that price, that I'd better get the job done by someone else. Now Reggie has stepped in and accepted for me. But don't get ideas above your station, John Tucker. I don't need to pay to get a lover."

The comment took John's breath away. "I never for a moment thought that you did," he protested.

"It didn't occur to you, I suppose," said Sarah, "that you might have offered to do the job for me for nothing. Of course, I would have paid for the materials and other costs."

"I don't think Sammie would have agreed with me doing that," he pointed out. "Also, I needed the money. Things are a bit tight just now."

"What did you need the money for?"

He shrugged a shoulder. "Among other things I'm saving up to get a car."

"Well, that's perfectly all right. You should have talked to me about that. I could arrange things like that for you." She turned to face him. "Don't you think, John, that you should decide who are your friends and which ones are merely your customers?"

He was silent for a long time. "I'm sorry," he said at last, "I hadn't really thought about it before."

"Well," she leaned across and rested her hand on his knee, "it's about time that you *did* start to think about it. I've got plans for you, John Tucker. It would be a pity to spoil all those plans at this early stage."

He concentrated on his driving and felt confused and uncomfortable. It was only another mile or so to her house. The journey was completed in silence.

As they turned in at the drive, Sarah said, “Take the car round to the garage at the back. It’s shady there.”

As soon as he’d pulled up, he went round to help her out. But she ignored his proffered hand. Feeling foolish and rejected he followed her, carrying the heavy bags, to the back door and into the kitchen.

“Put them over there.” She indicated a worktop. “Would you like a drink? I don’t mean alcohol - something long and cool.”

“Yes, please.”

“I’ve got some real home-made lemonade. It´s great with ice. How would that suit you?”

“Sounds fabulous.”

He stood awkwardly while she mixed the drinks, got some ice from the fridge, and topped it up with water. He thought how competent and efficient she was at doing things like this. She was much more adept with her hands than his mother, who tended to fuss and fiddle in a way that got on his nerves. She brought the drinks over and set them down on the work top beside him. Then she crossed the kitchen and bent down to get a tray from between the cupboards. As she straightened up, John saw that the zip on the back of her dress was partly undone. She came back with the tray.

“You’re coming undone,” said John.

“What?”

“Your zip is coming undone.”

“Oh yes, it’s a silly one on this dress. Do it up for me - there’s a dear.” She turned her back towards him.

John stepped towards her and caught hold of the tab on the zip. Then he slid it slowly right down her back to her waist and over her bottom. The dress peeled away like the skin on a banana, revealing an expanse of sun-tanned back and a white bra-strap.

“John,” she said, “I thought I told you to do it up.”

“I wanted to look at your suntan.”

“Will you do me up, please?” She leaned forward, resting her hands on the work-top.

“Not yet. Did you have a nice holiday?”

“Yes, thank you. It was very restful.”

"Did you ever think of me?" he asked.

"From time to time." She dropped her head and her hair cascaded over her face. "Have you seen all you want to?"

"No, I haven't." He put his two hands on the strap of her bra and unhooked it. "You've got a beautiful back." He bent forward and kissed her in the nape of her neck and she gave a little shudder. "Did you have anyone on holiday who told you that?"

"What do you think?"

"I would have liked to be with you on holiday." He slid the dress and bra off her shoulders and it shimmied down her arms to her wrists. He moved up close behind her with his hips pressing against her bottom. He pushed her against the table. Then he reached round her and cradled her wonderful breasts in his hands.

"Did anyone do this to you on holiday?"

She turned her face towards him. "No, they bloody didn't." Then they were kissing and he knew he'd been forgiven.

He pulled her away from the table and turned her towards him. He started to push her dress down over her hips. It was then that she stopped him.

"I'm afraid I've got bad news for you, John."

"What do you mean?"

"I've just started a period."

"What?" For a second he couldn't take it in. "But why did you bring me back here?"

"Because I wanted to talk to you. And also because I wanted you to take me in your arms and comfort me. Just because I can't have sex for a few days, it doesn't mean I don't want to be cuddled. That's something else you've got to learn." She pulled away from him. "Here, bring the tray and the glasses and we'll go upstairs."

She held her dress in her hand as she walked half-undressed out of the room. He picked up the tray and trailed behind her up the stairs. In the bedroom, at her prompting, he undressed and they lay side by side with nothing on and drank their iced drinks and discussed the near future.

"Reggie's away over Easter on some golfing trip. I've told him I'll get you in to do the shower-room during that time. I'll make it up to you many times over at Easter for what you can't do today. You can even stay overnight if you think you can find a decent excuse to give to your mother."

"I've got a bit of a problem at Easter. Rosemary will be coming home for the holidays and she'll want to see me. We've not seen much of each other during the last six months."

"I see. Does she make love better than me?"

He shook his head slowly. "You know that she and I have never made love in the way that *you* and I have."

"Well then, you'll have to say that it's the only time you can do the work." There was irritation in her laugh. "Goodness gracious, it'll only be for five days. She'll be able to see you during the rest of her holiday."

John thought quickly. "I suppose she'd accept something like that, if I put it the right way. I was hoping to get time off to go up and collect her from University in Sheffield. I've come to an arrangement with Ambrose Stacey to borrow his car. She would have to accept it, if I did that for her."

"You're starting to learn, young John." She smiled her secret smile. "I think you're proving to be quite a good pupil. I do believe you and I are going to go a long way together."

"I hope so, Sarah." He paused. "It seems a long time since we last made love together."

"All right then," she murmured. "Just because I can't enjoy it, it doesn't mean that you have to go without."

She slid down the bed. One hand cupped his testicles and squeezed them gently, the other clasped his erect penis and pressed it into her cleavage. Then she lowered her head and began to take him into her mouth. John groaned and abandoned himself to a new love-making experience.

31

Bill Kingley allowed John to have the Friday afternoon off, because he'd been putting in some extra hours earlier in the week. Just after one-thirty he was pulling onto the A38, heading for the North, with six hours driving ahead of him. Ambrose's little sports car had a new set of tyres and a full tank of petrol.

He had spoken to Rosemary two nights ago. "I'm sorry, Rosie. I can't get away any earlier. So I'm afraid I shan't be there till about seven o'clock."

"Don't worry," she said. "I've got lectures anyway on Friday morning. We can put you up on the settee in our flat overnight and then we'll come back the next day."

"You understand that we'll have to leave as early as possible on Saturday morning," John reminded her, "because Sammie and I are putting the finishing touches to the Palace for the Easter opening."

"What is the Palace?"

John laughed. "The new cinema they're installing at the town hall - they're going to call it the Palace."

"What a funny name," she said. "It sounds more like a castle than a cinema."

"I don't know about that. It's certainly got a smart reception area. We've had lots of compliments about it, and at least one councillor has asked us to do some work at his offices." John had to admit that he felt proud of the job they had done.

"Oh, that sounds good," she said loyally.

"I'll give you a private showing one morning."

There was a pause while they both thought about that.

"Well," he said, "I've got to do the quote for this councillor tonight, so I'd better ring off. I'll see you on Friday evening."

She lowered her voice. "I'm looking forward to it ever so much, John. If you're here in time, I'll be able to take you round and show you a few of the places in Sheffield. You've got the directions on how to find us, haven't you?"

"Of course I have. I'll try to be there by seven. 'Bye." He rang off, feeling guilty about his plans for Easter.

In fact it was nearly a quarter to eight by the time he pulled in to the Sheffield street of rather grand Victorian houses, many of which had been converted into student flats because they were near the university. Rosemary shared a floor with two of her friends. There seemed to be a party going on as he made his way up the stairs to the second floor. He stood at the open door to the flat and looked around. At least a score of youngsters (he presumed they were students) were sitting or standing round in groups, shouting at each other over the noise of the music. He approached the nearest group.

"Do you know where Rosemary Williams is?"

He got two blank stares and one shake of the head. But one girl was a bit more alert.

"Do you mean Rosie? I think she's through there in the kitchen." She pointed the direction he should take.

In the kitchen the cacophony of music was a bit lower, but the noise of debate was if anything higher. He saw Rosemary at once by the sink, dressed in tight trousers and an old loose, orange jersey. Not without difficulty he made his way over to her and joined the group. For a few minutes she was so busily engaged in the argument, that she didn't notice his arrival. Then suddenly she saw him.

"Hello. I wondered when you'd get here. Nobody seems to be in a hurry to go home for Easter so, as you can see, we're having a bit of a party. Isn't it fabulous?"

John thought that she didn't seem very pleased to see him. She didn't kiss him or touch him. She hardly bothered to introduce him. Nobody took much notice of him anyway.

One young chap, sporting an attempt at a beard, deigned to speak to him briefly. "Where do *you* stand on Marx?"

"Probably with my foot across his mouth." John was aware that he sounded surly and uncommunicative.

Rosemary leaned across to interrupt. "Don't listen to him, Jasper. Since he left Cambridge last autumn he's turned into a right old capitalist."

"What a strange man." Jasper turned away to talk to someone more sympathetic.

John was stung into a retort. "I suppose you might say I'm a bit strange if I enjoy having enough money in my pocket to take a girl out for the evening." But he realised no one was listening. They'd all gone back to their much more interesting conversation about Marxism.

He stood for a while and watched them, feeling out of place in his dark blazer and grey flannels. He was struck by how young and idealistic they all sounded. Even Rosemary, whose behaviour was more mature than most, seemed to be years younger than he felt now, although their actual age difference was less than three months.

He suddenly realised that not once since Christmas had he thought seriously about Cambridge or the academic career which he'd missed. It was as though his life there had existed in a different time. Admittedly he had never taken part in the various debating societies and other clubs, even when he was at university. However, he presumed that six months ago he would have looked and talked like everyone else in this group. Now he felt as though he belonged to a different world, several years older.

After a while he found himself a glass, rinsed it out under the tap, and filled it with some fizzy drink from a half-empty bottle. No-one seemed to notice as he drifted back into the noise to explore the rest of the flat. The place was in a dreadful state. It didn't look as though it had been cleaned or tidied for months. He was surprised that someone like Rosemary, who he had previously thought of as being so meticulous, was prepared to live in this state.

John massaged his forehead. He was feeling tired after the long drive. He went down a short corridor from the main room and pushed open a door on one side. It led into a bedroom. There were muffled grunts coming from the bed and he could see a pair of bare buttocks rising and falling furiously. It seemed as though there *were* still some students who had more important priorities than disputing the possible benefits of Marxism.

The man's head turned for a second. "Bugger off. Can't you see we've reserved this one?"

Then John knew who it was. "Oh. Sorry, Alan."

He withdrew and returned to the living-room, aware that

he'd probably ruined the fellow's climax, but not feeling in the least regretful about it. He'd always suspected Alan Hardacre of having dishonourable intentions towards women. But he had no right to feel superior. He supposed the chap was just like himself. At least he was grateful that it wasn't Rosemary's knees which were sticking up either side of those white, bouncing buttocks.

His head was throbbing painfully now. He just couldn't stand this noise any longer. His body felt exhausted after several days of long hours and short nights. There was only one haven left to him. He decided to go back to the car. He could be fairly comfortable there and sit in peace.

He went outside and climbed into the passenger seat, hoping that Rosemary would hurry up and get bored with political disputes. Within a few minutes asleep.

He awoke in the cold light of dawn. He checked his watch. It was five-thirty. He climbed out of the car, feeling stiff, and shivering in the keen wind. He walked up and down for a few minutes, stretching his body and looking up at the flat. All was quiet. The music and the discussion seemed to have come to an end. He reached inside the car for his windcheater and put it on. Then he entered the house and mounted the stairs to the first floor.

Luckily the door to the flat was unlocked. He went in and wandered round. There were a few bodies slumbering on settees and on rugs in corners, but nobody was awake. The kitchen was deserted. He found a glass, rinsed it and filled it with tap-water to assuage his thirst. Then he went in search of the bathroom. From there he decided to take a peep to see if Alan Hardacre was still in the bedroom. Instead, he found Rosemary stretched out on the bed where the fellow had been performing earlier. She was still in her orange sweater and black trousers but at least she was on her own. He shook her shoulder gently.

She was instantly awake. "Where have you been, John? I was worried about you."

He sniffed. "Not sufficiently worried to come outside and look in the car."

"Of course." She clapped her hand to her forehead. "I didn't think of that."

"No matter," he said. "I'm sorry I didn't hang around, but I was tired after the long drive and needed some sleep."

"You could have had my room."

John kept his reply short. "It was occupied."

"I'm sorry, John." She reached out and patted his arm. "I should have prepared something for you."

"Don't worry," he said. "I'm rested now. But I would like us to get off as soon as we can. I suggest we find a transport cafe on the way back and stop for some breakfast."

Rosemary stood up. "But I can't go without helping with the cleaning up."

"Rosie - I told you I wanted ~~to~~ us to get away early. You should have cleaned up last night."

"They'll all moan at me," she protested.

"They'll moan at you a hell of a lot more if you start cleaning now. Most of this lot won't wake up till lunchtime. I suggest you leave a note to say I've dragged you away, and you'll do your share next time."

Somewhat uncertainly, she agreed to this. She packed her things and left a note on the kitchen table after she had cleared a space. One or two of the other students surfaced briefly as they departed, waved a hand in their direction and fell asleep again. John loaded Rosemary's somnolent body into the passenger seat and her bags into the boot. Then he started off, leaving Sheffield to the early morning electric milk-floats and delivery lorries.

Rosemary was soon asleep again. She slept through Chesterfield, Derby, Burton and Lichfield. South of Birmingham, John found the transport cafe he was looking for. As he pulled in to the parking area she woke.

"What's the time?" she mumbled sleepily.

"Just after half past seven. Fancy some breakfast?"

That brought her fully awake. "Ooh. Yes, please."

"I'm absolutely starving," said John. "I haven't eaten anything since yesterday lunch-time."

"Neither have I, except for a few nibbles."

He decided a little moan was in order. "I couldn't find

anything to satisfy the hollow feeling in my stomach when I looked round last night."

He got out, locked the car and they went into the cafe.

"Oh, I'm sorry, John." Rosemary caught up with him and grabbed his hand. "I suppose I should have looked after you better, but we were having such a good discussion - the best of the term. If you'd come and shaken my arm, I'd have got you something. Are you cross with me?"

John grinned reluctantly. "I must admit it would have been nice to have had a bit of a welcome. But I didn't want to impose myself on you. I didn't think I'd be very popular if I broke up the argument."

"So instead you went all grumpy and took yourself off and hid in the car," she accused.

"I did *not* go all grumpy," he protested. "I was just tired. I went to look for a bedroom but all I did was interrupt Alan Hardacre in the middle of shagging some bird."

To his surprise she wasn't shocked by his language. "Oh, yes. Alan and Melanie have discovered what sex is all about. They're at it all the time now."

"Do you want a full breakfast?"

She nodded and he went up to the counter to order the food. He came back with two steaming mugs of sweet tea.

"If Alan's into sex," said John. "I hope he's taking precautions."

"Of course he is. He's a mature adult."

"If he is, he's the only one that I saw last night," he said acidly.

"Don't be so superior, John Tucker, just because you've got money in your pocket and a posh car to drive around in." She shook her curls at him and looked smug. "It doesn't impress we intellectuals."

"It impresses you enough to accept a lift home in it."

"That's only because *you're* driving it, sweetie." She smiled. "I haven't asked you yet - how did you manage to get something so smart?"

"It's Ambrose Stacey's. It was off the road because it needed new tyres and he couldn't afford any. So I paid for the tyres in return for borrowing it until Easter."

"Wow," she said. "That must have cost you a lot."

"Not really. Only twenty pounds."

"*Only* twenty pounds?" Her mouth opened wide. "That would cover me for nearly half a term's expenses. I thought you were complaining that you were only earning five pounds a week."

"Ah, things have changed a bit since I started helping Sammie. We can earn twenty or thirty pounds each in a weekend now. My share from the cinema reception will be more than a hundred pounds. I've got twenty-five pounds' commission to come from selling a house to a couple from London and I'm working on Sarah Grant's shower-room over the Easter weekend." Too late he stopped himself.

But Rosemary had caught on. "What's this about Sarah Grant?"

"Sarah's my boss's wife."

"I know *who* she is. What has she got you to do?"

"We're building a shower-room in the corner of one of the bedrooms."

"We?" She looked at him sharply.

"Sammie and I, of course."

Rosemary sniffed. "You mean Sammie's getting you to help him."

"Not all of it." He prodded her. "On this one *I'm* going to do a lot of it. Sammie will give me a hand from time to time. It'll be good experience for me."

"And Sarah Grant's going to pay you for it?"

John nodded. "Of course she is. Not a lot admittedly. I've agreed special terms with her husband, because I'm getting the full commission on this house sale."

Rosemary pointed her teaspoon at him. "I think you ought to be careful about what you do for Sarah Grant. People might get the wrong idea."

"I can't see why," said John. "After all, she's my boss's wife."

"She's also a scheming woman. You could be letting yourself in for all sorts of problems. Remember - just be careful."

John was saved further embarrassment by the man behind

the counter shouting out that their breakfasts were ready. After that they were quiet while they tucked in to the food. Later he was able to steer the conversation along more suitable paths.

32

"Are you Sammie Joslin?"

"Yes." Sammie looked up from sanding the varnished moulding along the front of the reception counter.

"I'm Sarah Grant."

His gaze took in the fairly short lady with the large bosom who was dressed as though she was going to a summer garden party at just after nine o'clock on a Saturday morning. "Yes, I know," he said and returned to his sanding.

"I understand that you and John Tucker are business partners."

"Well, I wouldn't put it as strongly as that." Sammie decided he'd better be a bit careful when he talked to the wife of John's boss. "We do some jobs together in our spare time."

Sarah looked round the reception area. "Have you done the whole of this?"

"Yes," he admitted.

"I would hardly describe this," she indicated the area with a sweep of her hand, "as an odd job."

"No." Sammie was discomfited. "This is the biggest thing we've ever done. I've taken some time off, with the agreement of my boss, so as to get it done on time."

"I take it that *John's* boss knows nothing about his part in this."

"Er - well, I don't know really," he stammered. "You'll have to ask him."

Sarah smiled triumphantly. "Don't worry, Sammie. Your secret's safe with me. John has told me all about what you're doing."

"Has he?" said Sammie slowly. "I don't know whether he should have done that."

"I said 'don't worry'." She leaned close to him and her expensive perfume mixed with the fresh smell of the sawdust in his nostrils. "I have no reason to spoil your enterprise by telling my husband. In fact I applaud it. I might want to take advantage of it myself some time in the near future."

"Oh, yes," said Sammie suspiciously, "I heard about that."

"What do you mean?"

"There's a shower-room that you want him to build."

She nodded. "Yes. There is. In fact that's why I called in to see John and have a chat with him. Do I take it that he's not here?"

Sammie shook his head. "Not yet. He's on his way back from collecting his girl-friend in Sheffield. He should be here after lunch."

"Never mind," she said. "Since you're partners, I expect you can help me just as well as John. This shower room will be quite an interesting little project for you, don't you think?"

"Well," Sammie scratched the back of his neck. "To be quite honest, I'm more interested in joinery and fitted furniture. There are all sorts of jobbing builders around who do bathrooms and things like that."

"Really?" Sarah's good humour seemed to fade a little. "Well - I'm sorry, but John has agreed to do it now. I hope he's not going to let me down." She puffed out her very large chest. "In fact that's why I'm here. I came to check whether everything will be ready to start on Good Friday morning."

"I don't know really." Sammie stood up and wiped the back of his hand across his forehead. "I shan't be doing much on that job. I'm busy on other work and John will probably do most of it himself."

"But surely you must know whether the materials have all been ordered - that sort of thing. You *are* his business partner, after all."

He shook his head. "I'm afraid I don't, Mrs Grant. John's handled it all himself up to now. All he told me, was that it's being done over Easter. He didn't say anything about Good Friday."

"Dear, oh dear." Sarah planted her hands on her hips and regarded him angrily. "That's not very good organisation, is it? Can I take it, that at least you'll have finished this job by then?"

"Don't worry." Sammie grinned infuriatingly. "This won't cause any delays to *your* work. You can see that everything here has been virtually completed already. The last bits and pieces will be tidied up by tomorrow night. We hand over the keys to the council at nine o'clock on Monday morning. They intend to be open for business on Thursday."

"Well, that's one thing at least. I'm afraid I have little interest in activities at the local flea-pit." Sarah turned away dismissively. "However I must emphasise that it *is* important that I get confirmation about the start on my place. I have to make all sorts of preparations before the work can begin. Can you make sure, Sammie, that you ask John to contact me, as a matter of urgency, the moment he returns."

"He'll be in touch with you just as soon as we've had a chat about it," said Sammie, a trifle ominously.

"Thank you so much." Sarah noted the inflection in his voice but decided not to comment as she walked away from him with a rather exaggerated sway of the hips.

33

The day before Good Friday was the first day the weather was good enough for John and Rosemary to go on the day-long walk they had planned. Suddenly the dull, damp westerlies of the last week were pushed back and a day dawned fresh and bright. The good weather had been forecast on the wireless, although there was a warning that it might turn to rain later. John had called round the night before to tell her he was taking a day’s holiday and to make arrangements.

He picked her up soon after nine o'clock. Rosemary was dressed in a tight woollen jumper and grey corduroy trousers with flat lace-up shoes which meant that she scarcely reached to his shoulder. She looked like a young girl again, clean-smelling and fresh and bursting with goodness. It made his heart lift to see the sun sparkling on her shoulder-length golden hair. He saw the last of the puppy fat bulging over the belt which was pulled a little too tightly at the waist. He looked at the swelling of her breasts, the tendons in her neck as she held her head high. She flushed as he studied her.

"John - you shouldn't stare like that."

He tore his gaze away with an effort. "Don't you like me to look at you?"

"Of course I do, but you mustn't let my dad see you. He would never let me go out with you if he saw that look on your face."

"Why on earth not? Did he raise objections to us having the day out together?"

Rosemary chuckled. "Not really. He was suspicious as usual, but mum was on my side. She always says that she thinks you're nice. I don't know why."

She stepped back with her eyes full of mischief and held the front door wide for him to enter.

Her mother was in the kitchen putting the finishing touches to the picnic lunch. She was a plump, homely woman with a hint of Devon burr in her voice when she spoke to him. “Hello, young John.”

"Hello, Mrs Williams. Lovely day."

"Remember to keep an eye on the sky. I've a feeling it might turn wet later. Make sure you take a waterproof, Rosie." She looked at her daughter. "Now - I've put four apples in. Do you want me to put in another couple?"

"Goodness gracious, Mum. There's enough to keep a regiment on the march. I don't know how we'll carry it all."

"Oh, you've got a strong young man to do that."

"We'll share it" said Rosemary.

"No, you won't. You let him do it. You start off as you mean to go on." And Mrs Williams gave him an affectionate pat on the forearm.

John laughed. He enjoyed her pulling his leg. "You wait," he said. "We'll get round the first corner and I'll dump everything on to Rosemary, turn her into a beast of burden and wear her out."

"And don't you hurry to get there," said her mother. "Rosemary's not used to long walks like you. She's got lazy up at university. She prefers to be transported everywhere."

"Mum, it's only twelve miles."

"Still, that's enough for you to overdo it."

"If you keep talking like this we'll be late leaving," said Rosemary. "Then we'll miss the bus back and you won't know what time we're going to turn up."

"That's another thing," said Mrs Williams. "Her father wants her to make sure she's back before dark."

John stood to attention and made his boy scout's salute. "I solemnly vow -" he began and ducked as Mrs Williams went to clip him round the ear.

"Go on with you. You'd better get off while you can. I might decide to join you myself next, and then where would you be?"

John packed all the stuff into the haversack he had brought and they departed. Once they had left the town, their route followed a footpath which led into the woods beyond the Stacey plantations. They walked side by side a yard apart, he with the backpack hanging from one shoulder, she with her fair hair ruffling in the light breeze. The early spring sun was warm and the sky was blue, although betraying a steely glint which didn't augur well for later in the day.

The dew beaded their shoes and the shadows under the trees were dark and cool. The woods carried on for a mile and then they began the climb towards the moor. Here the path ran into a plantation of large conifer trees put down in the First World War and now approaching maturity. Their route followed a broad green ride. Rosemary fell quiet under the slightly oppressive influence of the surrounding woods and now they only talked occasionally in low tones.

When they came out onto the open moor their mood lifted. The brown bracken had been beaten down by the winter rains and was now less than knee-high. The path over the sandy soil was covered with twigs and fronds and seemed to bounce under their feet.

"It's ages since I was up here," said Rosemary.

John looked at her and smiled. Her face was pink and freshly scrubbed. Her eyes were sparkling. She laughed at him.

"When did you last come up here, John?"

"I went for a long walk the weekend after the carnival." He remembered the loneliness, the misery he had felt as he walked.

"Who did you come with?"

"Nobody. I wasn't very good company at the time."

She was silent. But the memories came flooding back to John. The feeling of being alone after the recent death of his father. His university dreams were in ashes. They were moving from the house of his childhood to a tiny, poky cottage. His youthful love affair seemed to have come to an end. He was starting a boring job in a provincial office. He remembered the vow he had made that day - to fight until he had won back everything he had just lost. Was he keeping to his resolution?

These thoughts made him feel morose. The sun seemed to have gone out of the day. John’s mind turned over the autumn memories as he walked. Affected by his mood, Rosemary lapsed into silence and trudged along at his side, just casting the occasional glance in his direction.

After a couple of hours they had crossed the moor and began the descent towards the sea, glinting silver in the distance. Unnoticed, a veil of cloud had crept up from the west. Suddenly they found the sun was blanked out and a cool breeze had sprung up sprung up. They were out in the open countryside of the foothills below the moor. Here the farming was mainly arable and mixed crops with a certain amount of stock and dairying. The hedges were lower and the trees fewer.

They stopped, took their sweaters from the rucksack, and put them on. The footpath had led into a narrow country road. It was quiet and there was no traffic. After a while it started to rain - not heavily, but gradually increasing towards a steady drizzle.

"We'd better shelter somewhere" said John. "Let's try that barn."

It stood back twenty yards from the road. The doors were open, and it was three-quarters filled with square bales of straw from last summer's harvest. They ran into the barn and dragged off their damp sweaters. The place was warm. It had that slightly overpowering, sickly scent of fermentation which pervaded the dry, dusty straw.

"Are you hungry?"

She nodded. "It's early but we might as well have lunch while we wait to see if the rain will clear."

"We'll climb up to that sort of platform." He helped Rosemary up the steps made by the bales.

They settled down on the edge of a large shelf of straw twenty feet above the ground and John took out the picnic stuff and handed it to Rosemary. He could tell that her mum had gone to great trouble. Rosie spread a check tablecloth between them and took out the various foods, each wrapped in greaseproof paper, and opened them. John watched as she did it. She seemed perfectly happy sitting there, with her damp tousled hair and her pink jumper pulled tight around her waist. He could imagine she would make a good housewife, intelligent and humorous, yet practical and competent at the same time. He wasn't quite sure whether to be pleased or disappointed.

After the meal John lay on his stomach and watched the rain steadily falling outside. The morose mood brought on by his memories had returned. Rosemary tried to start a conversation on several occasions but without success. Finally she gave up, packed the picnic away and climbed the remaining six feet or so to the top of the stack. Up there she was only a few feet below the metal roof and the drumming rain. There was a long, pregnant silence. John continued to look out at the worsening weather and think dark thoughts.

He scratched at his head. It must have been a fly which took off as soon as he scratched. A few minutes later it was there again. He scratched it again - still nothing. A third time the tickling started. He reached up suddenly and touched a piece of straw. He felt around for it, but it had gone again.

There was a snigger from above. He looked up to see Rosemary sitting on the edge of a pile of straw bales. Three long pieces of straw had been tied together to make something to tickle him with. She roared with laughter as he leaped to his feet. She lifted her legs back over the edge of the straw bales as he reached out for her. The next minute she shrieked as the pile collapsed with her on top and everything landed in a heap at his feet. Rosemary was all pink and gasping with laughter. She looked absolutely delightful.

John leaned forward and grabbed her straw fabrication then he climbed up over the heap of jumbled bales to the top of the stack and stood with his head only a few inches below the roof. Rosemary jumped to her feet and chased after him. He held it behind him as she tried to reach it, turning each way to frustrate her efforts. Finally she got fed up and pushed him over on to his back.

"Give me my straw thing." She jumped astride him.

As he reached up she caught hold of his hands and used all her strength to try and pin them back on the straw.

"What straw thing?" he gasped, laughing.

"You know very well, John Tucker."

Her face was flushed. Her eyes were bright and excited. Her breasts were rising and falling with the effort of holding him down. He could feel the exciting sensation of her buttocks pressing against his pelvis.

"I don't know what you're talking about," he taunted.

"Oh yes, you do." She redoubled her efforts.

Suddenly he let his right arm go and pushed up with his left. Caught off balance, she fell. In a second he had rolled over on top of her and was lying between her parted legs. He could feel her breasts thrusting up beneath his shirt. Now she had gone quiet and her face was serious. Her eyes seemed dark and soft.

He kissed her, gently at first, trying to soften his lips in the way Sarah had shown him. Their wide-open eyes were staring deep into each other. Her lips were warm and yielding. They kissed with more urgency, more excitement. Their mouths were half open, their tongues entwined, drinking each other in. She released his hands and put her arms around him. He began to stroke up her side to cradle her breast in his right hand. Still she kissed without reservation. He half rolled over and began to push up her jumper. It came out of the waistband of her trousers. He reached up inside it and pulled at her bra. The shoulder-strap came away and her left breast was in his hand. The excitement began to mount in him.

Then she was dragging at his arm. "No, John. Please don't."

"Why not? I won't hurt you. I wouldn't do anything that might hurt you."

"I know, but you may not know when to stop."

"Rosie." He could just reach her nipple with one finger. But she was pulling hard at his arm. He felt an animal urge to have her. He let her pull his arm away but instead moved it straight it back to her waist. He pulled roughly at the zip on her trousers and it burst apart. His hand began to probe between her legs through the silky material of her underpants.

"No, John. Oh please, John. I don't want you to."

Still he tried to force his hand in. He was possessed by an intense, murderous desire for her body. Then suddenly she slapped him across the face. The stinging shock of it woke him to what he was doing.

"John, leave me alone. Take your hands off me. I've never known you behave like this before."

He gazed at her. He felt dazed.

"Look, John. You know I can't let you do that. Just think what my mother would say."

He knew she was right. The excitement went out of him and he felt weak and deflated. "I'm sorry, Rosie. Please forgive me. I shouldn't have touched you."

"It's all right John. I know how you feel. I want it just as much as you, only I have to think about the consequences."

Suddenly she was soft and compliant and loving again. She pulled his head down against her shoulder and murmured sweet words into his hair. She pulled her sweater across her chest but he could still see the nipple through the fabric. He placed his hand gently about her waist and hugged her. They cuddled together and she murmured endearments into his ear. But he felt unable to respond. It was as though she wasn't enough for him any more.

After a while they became aware that the rain had stopped. They stood up and straightened their clothes. John hoisted the haversack onto one shoulder. Then they walked to the main road where they could catch the bus. They travelled home in companionable silence. But he was feeling guilty because he couldn't help thinking about tomorrow when he would be getting so much more with Sarah.

34

After Easter John was feeling rather defensive when he faced Sammie. He was aware that his partner didn't think much of him taking on Sarah's job. Nor had he been pleased by the way she'd buttonholed him at the Palace to try and find out what John had organised about ordering the materials. Finally, John had made a couple of mistakes while he was doing the work and had to call Sammie in to solve them for him.

"Thank you for sorting out those problems with Sarah Grant's shower-room."

"That's all right. The electrics are done and the plasterer goes in tomorrow. You said he knows how to run that cornice?"

John nodded. "He told me he does. I showed it to him at the weekend and he said it was all right."

In fact the chap had nearly caught him in bed with Sarah, because he'd arrived half an hour early for the appointment. John barely had time to pull on his working clothes as he went down to let him in. He had wondered what the bloke was going to think when he saw Sarah drifting around in her silky negligee. However she had completely disappeared by the time they'd got up to the bedroom. The windows were wide open and the heavy-scented smell of lovemaking had been largely blown away.

Sammie was watching John with a concerned expression on his face. "She said she's going to do the paintwork herself?"

"That's right."

"Well, it should all be over by next weekend." Sammie paused and John waited for the censure. "I did tell you it was a mistake to take that job on. We've got enough work to be selective now."

"I know you did," said John. "I promise to listen to you in future."

Sammie continued, "Of course, I understand it was for your boss's wife and everything."

"Don't worry." John shook his head. "There won't be

anything else like that."

"It's delayed me a couple of days with the Partridges' work," Sammie pointed out. "They haven't complained, but I don't think you ought to take on any more of these jobs by yourself in future."

John turned to him. "What do you mean?"

"Well -." Sammie looked awkward. "You're great when you're helping me with something. But you didn't go about building Mrs Grant's shower-room the right way. The setting out was all right, but you should have got the service carcassing through before you started boarding the partition."

"I wanted to break the back of it over the Easter weekend. I couldn't ask the electrician to start in the middle of his Easter holiday."

"Why not?" demanded Sammie. "I would have done. He could only say 'no'."

"Yes. Well, I just didn't think I could." John couldn't admit to Sammie that he didn't want anyone else at Sarah's house over Easter.

He had never before had a weekend like that one with Sarah. She'd given him a key so he could wake her up and made love to her every morning before he started work. Then he'd spent most of the rest of the day working on the shower-room. She had helped when he needed her and that had twice led to further sex in their work-clothes. At times he thought that she was insatiable. They had also spent the evenings in bed and he even contrived to pass the whole night with her on one occasion. By the end of the four days he was absolutely exhausted. And he knew that he hadn't put the work in on the shower-room which he should have done.

Sammie seemed to echo his thoughts. "It took you much longer than I thought it should have done, John. Thank goodness we're not paying you by the hour. I think in future you ought to concentrate on the surveys and the estimating, and leave me to do the actual work."

"You can't do it all on your own, Sammie. You've still got your daytime job to do."

"Oh, you can help me when I need you. But I think you should spend your main time on the thinking work. That's what you're best at. We've had three new enquiries over Easter. The latest is from the chairman of the council. He rang me earlier this evening. Our name's starting to get known in the locality. It's amazing how many people want their houses updated in some way or another. So surveys and estimating have got to be your priority in future."

"That's understood," said John. "Of course I'll always put the surveys first."

Sammie took a breath. "There is another thing that I've been thinking of putting to you. There's a young chap at Barker's called Jamie Smith. He's not an apprentice. Old man Barker was a bit crafty and took him on as a trainee. His parents didn't buy his indentures, so that means the old man can get rid of him whenever he wants." He paused. "Well - now that Barker has started to cut back a bit, he's getting very choosy about the sort of work he takes on. Personally, I think he's planning to retire soon." He took another breath and ended in a rush. "Anyway, he's told me he′s thinking of getting rid of young Jamie. So I think we ought to offer him a job."

"What – full time?" John wrestled with the idea of becoming an employer. "Where would he work?"

"In my shed, of course. That'd be no problem. He's a real good lad, and only expects to earn two pounds ten a week." Sammie had obviously been spending some time thinking about this. "My idea is, that if you prepare cutting lists of the materials we need for each new job, then I can give him targets for preparing and part-assembling the stuff. If he does better than the targets, well - we'll give him a bonus. That way I'll be able to concentrate on assembly and get much more done in the time that I'm working on the job."

"Aren't you worried about him being left all on his own in your shed?" asked John.

His partner shrugged. "I don't see why. He'll only be using hand-tools and I'm sure he can be relied on to use those properly. I'll check him twice a day to make sure he's turning out good quality work. I'll have to do that because I′ll be assembling the stuff." Sammie plunged on when John nodded. "It'd be a pity to miss him really. Who knows what he'll do if he leaves Barkers?"

John didn't know why he was feeling a bit suspicious about the idea. He realised he ought to be all in favour of it. It was unusual for Sammie to consider taking risks of this sort. He wondered if there was another reason for this new idea of his, such as trying to make sure that John didn't do jobs on his own for people like Sarah Grant in future. But he knew he mustn't let suspicions like that affect his judgement on the proposal. He had no personal objection to taking on a new lad. He was all for expanding the business, now that it was proving to be so profitable.

"Well, I don't mind," said John. "There *is* the point, of course, that we'll have to start keeping accounts if we have an employee. We'll need to deduct tax and things like that."

"Oh god, will we?" Sammie looked uncomfortable. "Can't he do that for himself?"

John grinned. "I shouldn't think so. But I don't really know. I'll look into it."

Sammie shook his head. "I don't want to have anything to do with that sort of thing. That'll have to be your job, John."

"I don't know much about accounts either. But it would be a pity to make that stop us from developing the business. I'll talk to an accountant to get advice about what we ought to do." He tapped Sammie on the chest. "That reminds me - now that we've started the Partridge job, we should have had the deposit from them. I'll have to ring Susie Partridge to see if they've sent off the cheque."

"That's important," said Sammie. "I want to start fitting the kitchen units next weekend."

"You haven't forgotten," John reminded him, "that I'm taking Rosemary back to Sheffield on Sunday."

"That's another reason why I was thinking of young Jamie. I could try him out next weekend. I thought I might offer him fifteen bob a day to help me on Saturday and Sunday. It'll give me a chance to see what he's like out on site."

John grinned at Sammie's cunning. "Good idea. We could probably also do with a third pair of hands when Partridges' wood panel garage turns up. I've ordered that for delivery on Friday week, so that we can put it up over the following weekend." He turned to more practical matters. "Now then, do you want me to give you a hand with assembling those drawers?"

So talk was forgotten and they got down to some serious work.

35

It was the night of the local hunt ball. It was one of the top events of the year and it took place at the Grand Hotel outside Exeter. The sound of the band playing a slow foxtrot came echoing from the ballroom into the reception area.

John watched Rosemary walk towards him from the cloakroom. He always forgot how pretty she was when he was away from her. Tonight her hair was piled up on top of her head where it sprouted in a mass of curls. It showed off the smoothness of her neck, the high bloom of her cheeks and the rich colour of her lips. Quite a few heads turned to watch her as she walked towards him, her back upright, her breasts prominent beneath the crossover top of her dark blue ball-gown.

"Wow! Where did you get that dress?" he asked. "I couldn't see it properly I picked you up."

She smiled at his reaction. "Oh - just in a shop in Sheffield. Do you like it?"

"I think it's fantastic." He took her elbow and steered her towards the hall. "I notice that everyone else thinks so too. Have you worn it to any events at university?"

She bridled slightly at his questions. "No, I *haven't*. I got it specially for tonight."

"How can you afford to buy something like that on a student's grant?"

"You are nosey, John Tucker," she accused him. "If you must know, it was in the sales. And also mum helped me a bit."

He stopped her at the edge of the dance-floor. "What did your mum think of it when she saw you in it?"

"She liked it." She giggled. "But she said you've got to make sure to take me straight home after the ball."

"You mean she doesn't trust me with you?" He feel really incensed. "That's a laugh. She doesn't know what you get up to every night in Sheffield."

Rosemary had a knowing smile on her face. "She's not worried about the people I meet up there. They're just students.

She says you're a dangerous man of the world now."

"That's not fair," he protested mildly. "I'm still the same person who was at university six months ago."

"No, you're not." She was suddenly serious. "I know what she means about that. You've become a man. You're not a boy any longer. And she knows that men have to be watched much more carefully."

They paused to look round the room, already half full of dancing couples. They caught sight of a crowd of their friends and moved towards them.

"I can't help it," said John, "if I've had to mature more quickly than some others."

She smiled up at him. "No - you can't. And I like you for it. But it seems to mum as though you've suddenly grown up and left us behind. The rest of us are still youngsters compared to you."

"I don't know about that," he said. "*You* look pretty grown up in that dress."

"I think it's that which worries my mum. I look as though I'm a woman, but I'm not nearly as mature as you."

John laughed. "It all sounds a bit complicated for me."

"Perhaps you're right. Well, let's not be serious this evening." She turned away from him to talk to a couple of the other girls.

John went to get some drinks. When he came back he got drawn into job-talk with some of his friends. The university students, several of whom were at tonight's ball, were all starting to think about the future after they graduated. Very few would settle in Devon at the end of the summer holidays. Most were looking for graduate jobs in London, the Midlands or the North. Some were staying on for post-graduate work at university. Listening to them, John was surprised to find that he didn´t feel the faintest twinge of envy at missing out on their excited plans for the future.

The latest dance came to an end and the dancers drifted back to their seats. He looked across to where Rosemary was deep in conversation with her friends. What were her plans when she left university? She hadn't discussed anything with him yet. He listened with half an ear to the discussion beside him as he glanced at the group.

"You always seem to be on the edge of things, watching the others."

John swung round at the sound of her voice. But he knew from the extended vowels, before he saw her, that it was Alison Stacey. He hadn't seen her arrive. In fact he hadn't thought about the possibility that she might be there at all. She was wearing a grey sheath dress with a high neck but no sleeves. Her dark hair was wrapped into a pleat at the back and she wore a pearl choker necklace. She looked very glamorous, very mature. That must be the effect the finishing school was having on her.

"Hello." He felt slightly nervous as he stood in front of her. Was she going to make a fuss? He knew that she had every right to be furious with him after the way he'd treated her last November.

"Have you come here alone?" she asked. "Whenever I see you, you always seem to be alone."

John shook his head and pointed to Rosemary. "There's my girlfriend. What about you?"

She gave Rosemary only the most perfunctory of glances. "I've only just got away from my escort. I said I wanted to go to the loo. He's such an awful bore."

Her comment made John smile. He could imagine that she would bore easily.

"I like you better when you smile." She put her head on one side. "You always seem to be gloomy."

"I do?" John was astonished. Then he admitted, "Perhaps you haven't caught me at my best."

"No. Perhaps I haven't." She paused and it was clear that her thoughts had also gone back to the events after the carnival. "Do you know the dragon is still in the stables? Daddy was most intrigued when he found it. I told him I was preserving it for posterity."

"What did he say about his glasses?"

"He was furious. He would have had your guts for garters if he'd known the truth. I had to tell him that I'd dropped them. He said he was going to stop twenty pounds out of my allowance - but of course he forgot."

Her tone was mild. Was that a sign that she had forgiven him? Was she trying to make peace with him? His suspicious mind asked him why.

She moved close to him. “Take a look at my face,” she said. “You cut my bottom lip with your teeth. Do you see the scar?”

John searched the beautiful mouth. “No,” he answered truthfully.

“Well,” she shrugged, “it's there. It must be covered by my make-up. I think I’ll always have it. You have left your permanent mark on me.”

He refused to feel guilty. He tried to look at the lovely face objectively, but he felt his lungs fill with her expensive perfume and his stomach began to contract. The band started to play again. “I like that scent,” he said. “What is it?”

“It’s something special my aunt gets from Paris. You can’t get it in the shops here.”

There it was again - that superior manner that seemed to treat him like a lackey. He felt his hackles rise once again. But she seemed unaware of the way she annoyed him.

“Do you dance?”

“All right.” He smiled at her surprised look as he took her by the hand and led her into the middle of the floor. The music they were playing was a waltz. At least that was easy.

He put an arm round her waist, and she moved against him. After the first few steps he knew she was a good dancer. She leaned back from the waist and her hips were flat against his stomach. Her legs effortlessly followed his own. John felt as though they were floating across the floor.

“My,” she said, “you really *can* dance. Most men can't, you know.”

He wasn’t going to tell her that it was easy with her. “I don't want to talk,” he said. It seemed that they only argued when they talked. He smiled again at the nonsense of the thought. But there was pleasure in holding her, in swivelling and swooping and surfing on the flood of romantic music.

Inevitably it stopped after a few minutes. They came to a halt, but still his arm was round her waist and her hand rested on his shoulder, as though they were waiting for the next dance to start. She was looking straight up at him and her lips were close. Suddenly the light caught them and he saw the scar, almost exactly in the centre of the lower lip.

"I can see it now." He still wasn't going to apologise.

"You behaved very badly." But she didn't say it as though she was annoyed.

Why did he have this urge to kiss her, to gently caress her lips and beg her forgiveness for his behaviour? But he only had to remind himself that she was a Stacey, to destroy that feeling. He would never allow himself to apologise to *her*. And by just the slightest movement she seemed to hold herself aloof from him, as though she knew how he felt.

"I behaved badly too." Her voice was very quiet. "I'm sorry about it now. But, at the time, I thought it had to be done."

He stared at her. "What do you mean?"

"I wanted to make it clear to you that I'm not a good person to cross. Why do you think you were thrown out of Riversmeet? My father would never have had the guts to do it. It was I who arranged for you to be given the notice to quit."

John went cold. "What did you say?"

"It was far too big for you anyway. And someone from a better family than you wanted it, and was prepared to pay good money for it. So I don't think it was the wrong thing to do. I'm sure you and your mother are much happier in your cosy little cottage in the village."

She tailed off, aware that his hands had fallen to his sides and had bunched into fists.

"I said - I'm sorry about it now."

"You bitch! You reckon you've got some divine entitlement to play God, do you?"

She stepped back a pace. She seemed genuinely surprised by his reaction. "What are you going to do?" she asked, a slightly worried look crossing her face.

"I don't know yet." John struggled to keep himself under control. "Just be warned that I won't forget this. I'm going to find a way to make you regret the things you've done to us."

"Are you going to resort to violence again?"

He shook his head, a twisted kind of smile on his face. Before he could reply there was an interruption.

"John - what are you doing?" It was Rosemary.

"Er - nothing." He shook his head. "I've been dancing."

She was at his elbow. "But the music's stopped."

"Who is this?" asked Alison.

"I'm Rosemary Williams. I'm John's girlfriend."

"Oh. Hello." Alison turned and looked her up and down.

John forced his hands to relax and drop to his sides. The next minute they were surrounded by dozens of people. Everybody seemed to be talking at once. John watched Alison. Now she was the centre of attention. Everyone wanted to catch her glance, to talk to her, to obtain her approval. He felt like shouting aloud to tell everyone just what she was like. But he kept his mouth shut.

Rosemary was beside him. "John, what were you doing, dancing with Alison Stacey?"

"Doing?" He thought about it. "Well - actually she asked *me*."

"I don't believe you."

"It's true. Don´t forget her brother and I shared rooms at Trinity."

She held her head up. "All right. Now it's my turn. You haven't even asked me yet."

He put his arm round her waist and pulled her towards him. This was the way to forget Alison Stacey. They started to dance comfortably and happily. Rosemary didn't have the fluency of Alison, but he mustn't think about that. They should find something different to talk about.

"The reason I didn't invite you to dance was because you were all too busy discussing the future for me to get a word in," said John.

"No, we weren't," she responded. "We were talking about clothes."

"Rosemary - what have you decided to do when you finish at Sheffield?"

She realised, by the way he used her full name, that he expected a serious reply. She took a breath. "I haven't finally decided yet, but I think I may try to become a librarian. I like books and my English degree will help me get a job in that sort of thing."

"Will you come back to this area to work?"

“I don’t know.” She thought about it. “I think that partly depends on you.”

That surprised him. “On me? Why?”

“Once upon a time, John Tucker, I felt sure of you.” Rosemary stopped in mid-dance and regarded him seriously. “But in the last few months I don’t seem to know you any longer. I don’t know what you’re going to do next. It’s a bit like being close to an active volcano, emotionally speaking.”

“That’s ridiculous,” he said. “Don’t forget that I’ve had to concentrate hard on earning money over the last few months. I haven’t had time for esoteric discussions. Now I’m just starting to get on top of things, but I’ve still got a long way to go before I can see a settled future ahead of me. It’s work that has been taking up all my time.”

She put her head on one side. “I understand that, of course. Among other things, your weekly letters have become shorter and shorter.”

“Well, as I said, we’ve got so much to do. Sammie and I are getting a lot of jobs and we’ve got to do it all at weekends and in the evenings.” Why couldn’t he seem to make her understand?

“I’m not sure about Sammie’s influence on you,” she admitted. “Knowing him, I suppose *he’s* even working this evening.”

“He works all the time. He’s an absolute nutter for work. And I don’t feel I can let him down. It’s thanks to him that I had the transport to bring you tonight.”

She laughed. “A second-hand Dormobile van?”

“Don't sneer at it, Rosie. It would have been a taxi otherwise.”

“A taxi might have been better.” She shook her head. “We were the only people to turn up in a massive great van.”

“I’m sorry, but we can’t run to a car yet. We need the van for delivering our units. We bought it cheap off Barkers, the builders. Sammie’s boss let us have it for seventy-five pounds.”

She stepped close and gave him a hug. “I’m not complaining. I don’t mind what I travel in. I think you’re doing marvellously and I’m very proud of you. But don’t you see -

that's what I mean about you. You've moved on to other things. I feel as though I'm only a sideline to you now - we write once a week and meet briefly about twice a term. I'm only a tiny part of your life. You've got so many other things which are more important."

"You can't blame it all on me. After all, it's *you* who's got to go back to Sheffield on Sunday. At least I'm taking the trouble to run you back."

"Oh, I know it's me as well," she admitted. "But you did say you were going to come up and visit me one weekend last term, and you didn't make it. What are the chances that I'll see you during the summer term?"

The music started again and they moved into a slow dreamy fox-trot.

"I'm sorry about last term." He took a breath. "As you know we were working on this cinema refit every weekend so that they could open at Easter. Lots of people are giving work to us now and we can't afford to let them down."

"I'm not asking you to let people down, John. I just want you to allocate a bit of time to us - to *our* relationship."

"All this work is also worth money," John still argued. "I reckon I'll soon have enough to buy a car of my own. Then I'll be able to come up and see you later in the summer."

She shook her head. "It'll be finals then and I'll be working all the hours that God made. There always seems to be something keeping us apart. I haven't seen much of you over Easter because you´ve been doing that job for Sarah Grant."

"But be fair, Rosemary. You'd already told me that you wouldn't be able to spare much time because you had to do a lot of swotting."

"Yes," she agreed, "they've given us loads of homework and it's all got to be done some time."

"Well, we'll have to wait until the finals are over." He searched for alternatives. "Perhaps we'll be able to make up for it in July and August. Perhaps we can have a holiday together."

"But that's nearly four months away," she wailed. "I don't know what will have happened to you by then." They came to a halt in the middle of the floor.

He spread his arms wide. "But what else can we do? You've

already said that you’re going to be too busy on your exams to have much time to spare.”

There were tears in her eyes as she said, “Oh, I don’t know. I don’t want to talk about it any more.” She turned away. “I’ve lost interest in dancing. Let´s go and talk to our friends.”

“Why don’t we leave and go up to Woodbury castle on our own?” he suggested. “We can be alone together up there. It may be our last chance for months.”

“John, you know we can’t do that,” she said. “Everyone would talk.”

“Let them talk. It doesn’t worry me.”

She shook her head dismissively. “No. We’ve got to stay here. It’d only get back to my parents. And I can’t have that happening at the moment.”

She turned and walked back to their table with John trailing behind her, thinking that this was how all their meetings seemed to end these days. She was such a lovely girl, but he couldn’t seem to get close to her. It was just as though they were leading different lives.

36

Ambrose had surprised John by his willingness to lend him his car again for a couple of days to run Rosemary back to university.

"Of course you can," he said when John broached the subject. "We chaps have got to help each other out. By the way, you couldn't lend me a tenner, could you? I'm a bit tight at the moment."

With a grin, John handed over the money. "Treat it as a donation to cover wear and tear. Thanks, Ambrose. Of course I'll also leave the tank filled up when I return the car."

They shook hands and parted. John guessed they would never become real friends but he could see that they might be useful to each other in the future.

The traffic was light on the return journey and Rosemary was chatting happily all the way back. The time seemed to pass quickly.

When they arrived at the flat in Sheffield no-one was there. She unlocked the door and they went in. The place looked almost tidy – far different from the state it had been in three weeks ago when they left.

"Someone seems to have made a bit of an effort to clean up," said John. "But where is everyone now?"

She smiled. "I expect they'll start turning up over the next couple of days. Don't forget we came back early so that you can get home tomorrow in time for work first thing on Monday morning. No-one will have lectures here till Tuesday."

"It's a tough life being a student."

"Rubbish." Rosemary was easily irritated these days. "Most of our work has to be done on our own. I'll start studying as soon as you've gone tomorrow morning."

"I was only joking," he said. "I know you've done a lot over Easter."

"It's a jolly good job I had *something* to do. I've hardly seen anything of you. You seem to have been working all your leisure hours on that job for Sarah Grant." Rosie seemed insistent on telling him off about it. "On the few times I've seen you, you've been tired out and keen to get off to bed."

John grinned. "The trouble is that you'd never agree to come with me."

"Well," she bridled, "perhaps you've got your opportunity now."

He was suddenly alert. Did she mean it or had he misunderstood her? "Opportunity for what?" he asked.

She tossed her head. "Oh, don't be silly, John." She looked like a mettlesome filly, with her head back and a flush on her cheeks.

He noticed the way her long, golden hair cascaded down her back. It seemed to have grown during the holiday. Her breasts, now fuller than he remembered them before, seemed to jut out. Even though her blouse was buttoned up to the neck, there was the tight little belted waist and the skirt flaring out over her soft hips. She looked very inviting to him at the moment. Although he was tired after the long drive, he felt the ache for her building in the pit of his stomach.

She was watching him carefully. John wondered if she could guess at the lascivious ideas which were growing in his imagination. For a second the thought crossed his mind that she might be subtly manipulating him, but if she was, he didn't mind. He smiled at her. "Come on. Let's go out and have a meal and a bottle of wine to celebrate."

"Celebrate what?"

He put his head on one side. "How about being alone together for almost the first time in our lives?"

"Oh, I don't know about that," she chided. "The last time we were alone together was in that barn on the other side of the moor, and look what happened then."

"In the end - nothing. Are you complaining?" He took her hand. "Let's find somewhere nice to eat."

They got back two hours later. They'd had a lovely evening. They had talked as they used to in the old days - quietly, heads together, discussing plans and memories. It was one of the happiest evenings John had experienced recently. As the food was eaten and the level in the wine bottle went down, Rosemary seemed to become softer and more affectionate. They walked back to her flat with their arms around each other.

There was disappointment when they got back. They were no longer on their own. Another couple had arrived and were sitting on the settee drinking coffee.

"Hi, Jill," said Rosemary, "what time did you get back?"

"Oh, only half an hour ago." Jill was dark and skinny, with worldly-wise eyes. "We're both shattered. We left Inverness at ten o'clock this morning. This is Alastair, by the way."

"Hello, Alastair. This is John."

Alastair looked as though he hadn't washed for a week. John hesitantly shook his sticky hand.

"We're going straight to bed," said Jill. "See you later Rosie."

They picked up their mugs of coffee and disappeared into one of the bedrooms.

"Do they sleep together?" asked John.

"I suppose so." Rosemary grinned. "I mean - afterwards." John thought the comment seemed a bit risqué for her.

"Have they known each other a long time?"

She shook her head. "I don't know. I've never seen him before."

"And yet they're going to bed together," he persisted. "Does everyone do that sort of thing at this university?"

"No, they don't," she protested. "Jill's just more of a free-thinker than some. Don't tell me, John Tucker, that you're sitting in judgement on her. Do you know - I think that you're a prude underneath your sexy exterior."

That made him stop and regard her. "Sexy? Do you think I'm sexy?"

"You are when you look at me like you did earlier this evening - through those half-closed, hooded eyes - just like you're starting to do now." She moved close to him. "It's enough to make a girl go weak at the knees."

It was then that he kissed her. The sensation was extraordinary. It was as though an electric current had passed between them. He knew from her gasp that Rosemary had felt it too. It had never been quite like this before. It was so different from the practised kisses of Sarah. Those were soft, sensual and exciting, but there was nothing like the explosion which occurred inside him when he kissed Rosemary this time.

He gathered her in his arms and kissed her again. It seemed to him as if she opened up to him and invited him in when he did it. He had never felt such a sensation of togetherness with another person. And this was only from a kiss. His hands began to fumble with the buttons on her blouse. Their lips were hardly separating for breath before they kissed again. It was as though they couldn't bear to lose contact with each other. This was different from the other day in the barn. He knew now that Rosemary desired him. Her blouse was already open to the waist.

"Let's go to my room."

It was only a little room with a single bed. John noticed, as an aside, that somebody had made the bed where Alan Hardacre had performed before Easter. He was watching Rosemary. She undid the zip and slid her skirt and petticoat to the floor. She bent down and took off her shoes. Then she was kissing him again. John reached behind her to try to find the hook on her bra.

Still they kissed as she started to undo his shirt. She seemed better at undressing her partner than he was, and it came undone quite quickly. He unbuttoned the cuffs and dragged it off. He pulled down his trousers and let them fall to the floor while she held his face between her hands and kissed him wetly.

They let go of each other. John reached down and awkwardly got his shoes and socks off so that he could remove his trousers. Rosemary turned from him and took off her blouse and bra. Then she pulled back the bed covers. When she turned back to him she seemed suddenly shy. She still had her pants and her suspenders and stockings on. But her lovely breasts were uncovered, and the pink nipples were hard with desire.

He took her in his arms, and they were kissing again. He could feel the mounds of her breasts pressing into his chest. The excitement made his penis swell instantly rigid inside his underpants. And still they couldn't stop kissing each other.

When they got into bed and pulled the covers over them, the

sheets felt sticky and cold until their own warmth pervaded them. As they kissed again, he cupped his hand under her breast and stroked the nipple. Then her hand was inside his pants, releasing his great stiff penis. He was astonished. Was this the same Rosemary who had pushed him away when they were in the barn only a couple of weeks ago?

"Oh Rosie, I want you," he groaned.

"And I do. Have you got a protective?"

"A what?"

"You know - a Durex. A french letter."

"Oh." He was taken aback. "No."

"I haven't got anything either."

"Sod it. Isn't that stupid of me?"

"Never mind," she said. "Let's take the risk. I only had the curse last week. I'm probably still all right."

He pulled back. "No. We mustn't risk it."

"Go on, John, please. I want you so much."

"So do I." But he couldn't do that to her.

"Please! It may be our last chance for months."

"If you got pregnant it would wreck everything, Rosie. You know it would."

She looked into his face, her eyes glowing. "What would it matter if I did get pregnant? You're doing well now. We could be married and you could look after me. I wouldn't mind forgetting my career."

"But what would your parents say?"

She shrugged. "Oh, I suppose they'd be upset at first. But they'd soon come round. Mum likes you ever such a lot." Then suddenly she pulled back from him, her face full of suspicion. "You don't *want* to marry me, do you?"

"I - I don't know." Then, when she turned her head away, he went on, "Oh, don't be so daft, Rosie. We've never even talked about it before. We haven't had a chance to really get to know each other that well. We've only met up for a few days every now and again in the holidays. For God's sake, this is a decision that would affect the whole of the rest of our lives. We can't just rush into it on some sexual urge."

She turned back to him. "I can't believe I'm hearing this. Always before it was you who was trying to persuade me to let *you* go further. Now, when I agree, you suddenly start inventing excuses. You'd better admit it, John Tucker - the fact is that you're not willing to commit yourself to a serious long-term relationship."

"Well," he demanded, "who is at our age?"

"Millions of people. You said yourself that thousands of couples get married when they're younger than us." She sounded so betrayed.

He had to convince her. "But at least I would expect that they've talked about it and realise what such a decision means. Why are you suddenly ready to throw away all your studies and your hopes for the future? We're just on the brink of making real lives for ourselves. In two or three years time we'll be ready for marriage. We just aren't ready at the moment."

"You mean *you* aren't ready. All *you* want is the sex without commitment," she flung at him. "And I thought you had matured. It just shows how wrong I was about you."

"That's rubbish, Rosie," he accused. "In the morning you'll know it is. Good God, here are you begging me to shag you one minute and the next minute you accuse me of only wanting sex, even though I've just refused to do it."

"Oh, and won't *that* be something for you to crow about to all the other lads. Rosie Williams offered herself on a plate and I turned her down." She burst into tears.

John reached forward to comfort her. "Rosie, you know I wouldn't -."

"Leave me alone and get out," she shouted. And when he still tried to reach out and touch her, "Go on! Get out, before I call Jill and her friend in here to chuck you out."

Not quite sure of what had hit him, John got out of bed and dressed. Then he went back into the living room. He sat down for a while and waited, but Rosemary didn't appear. He checked his watch. It was just after half past eleven. He stretched out on the settee and tried to get some sleep, but the flat was cold and damp. After a quarter of an hour he gave up. He went into the kitchen and managed to find some coffee. There was no milk or sugar. He brewed himself a cup of black coffee and sat with it cradled between his hands, thawing them out. Should he go back into her bedroom to try to make it up?

But somehow he knew that wouldn't work. Their evening together had been wrecked and he didn't really know why.

In the end he decided there was no point in staying here. It would be more comfortable in the car with the heater going. He didn't feel tired now anyway. So he decided to start the drive home. He finished his cup of coffee and set off.

37

John arrived at the Partridges' new house just before lunchtime. He checked the front door. It was locked. He still had the agent′s, key so he unlocked the door and opened it wide to let fresh air into the house. However he decided he should wait outside for a couple of minutes before going in. He backed the pool car up the smart new concrete drive and parked in front of the stained cedar-wood garage which they'd put up last weekend. Then he sat and surveyed the rough patch of earth which was going to be the front garden. Lionel Partridge was going to be busy this summer trying to lick the place into shape.

It was a beautiful spring day. John wound down the window and listened to the birds singing in the trees across the road. It was on days like this that you felt as though summer was just around the corner. He got out of the car and took off his jacket and threw it on the front seat. He rolled up his sleeves and felt the warmth of the sun on his forearms. Memories flooded over him of the excitement he had felt as a youngster, at simply being alive at this time of year. It was different now.

It was ten days since he had taken Rosemary back and they had experienced the extraordinary scene in her bedroom. He hadn't heard a word from her since. But then, he didn't expect to. What was there to say? Even if he wrote to her and apologised and said it was all his fault and that of course they ought to get married, he somehow doubted if it would change her attitude. He felt as though she'd tried to force him into making a decision without giving either of them a chance to discuss their plans.

Maybe she was right. Perhaps he wasn't ready to commit himself. He certainly wasn't yet ready for something as final as marriage. He was approaching twenty-three. He accepted that there were thousands of people of their age who were already married, and that a lot of them had children as well. It was all very well for them, but he wasn't ready for all that yet. Nor did he really think Rosemary was, if only she'd admit it to herself.

He was prevented from further dark thoughts by the arrival of a taxi. Susie Partridge got out and bent to pay the driver. Then she turned and walked up the path towards him. She was looking fresh and bright in a white linen costume with colourful flower patterns all over it. Her belt was pulled in to accentuate her tiny waist. Once again John found it hard to understand how she had brought herself to marry a middle-aged slob like Lionel Partridge.

"Hello." She seemed to be bubbling over with suppressed excitement. "Isn't it a lovely day?"

"It certainly is," he agreed. "Well, you'll see that we've nearly finished all the work. Are you looking forward to moving in?"

"Oh - yes. It all happens next Monday and Tuesday." She took his arm and shepherded him through the open door into the house. "John, I'm bursting to tell someone. I've got a new job. It's a very exciting one. I've just had the interview and I've been told that I've been accepted. I start work on Monday week."

He laughed at her enthusiasm. "Is it down here?"

"Of course it is. I gave up my work in London several weeks ago."

"What are you going to do?"

She turned to face him. "I'm to be personal secretary to Sir Oswald Stacey - a real baronet. I'll have an office in the big house - Stacey Court. Do you know it?"

"I live within a mile of the place." John couldn't help smiling. "I often walk around the home park and through the woods."

"Well, I never," she marvelled. "Is the public allowed to walk through the place? Isn't that nice of Sir Oswald?"

Her innocence made John laugh. "It's got nothing to do with Sir Oswald. People have had the right to walk on various public footpaths all around Stacey Court for generations. He'd probably stop it if he could."

She pulled a face. "It sounds to me as though you don't like him very much."

"I don't," admitted John. "I think he's a miserable old skinflint. He'll take every penny he can out of the local population to pay for his holidays in the South of France and for his daughter to go to finishing school in Switzerland, while he does little for anyone in the village. He's not a fraction of the person his father was."

"Oh, dear." She sounded disappointed. "He seemed ever so charming to me."

He looked at her pretty face. "Well, he would be to you. I should think everybody is charming when they talk to you."

"You're very sweet, John," she smiled. "But I take it that you don't approve of my new boss."

"Oh, you have to get work where you can." He shrugged. "Just be warned that he's not likely to be a generous employer."

"I'll remember."

"So," John mused, "Sir Oswald's having a new private secretary, is he? He's obviously decided to pension off the old battle-axe who was there before."

"Do you know Mrs Bailey, as well?"

"Know her? She also used to be in charge of the local Catholic church." He grinned at the recollection. "I remember her trying to chase us out of the aisles when we went in there to shelter from the rain."

"Is that why you call her an old battle-axe?"

"Mind you," admitted John, "I suppose we used to make quite a lot of noise. The other thing she didn't like, was that we used to stick our fingers in the holy water in the stoup just inside the door and dab it on our foreheads. I remember her coming in and catching us drinking it once. We obviously thought it would cleanse our souls the direct way, but she didn't share the belief."

Susie laughed delightedly. "You and your friends sound as if you were a right bunch of rogues."

"I suppose we were in a way." John thrust the memories behind him. "Anyway, I'm glad you've got a job near your new home. And it'll be nice for you to work in the old house. What sort of job did you have in London?"

She smiled. "I was a secretary, but quite an important secretary. I worked for the general manager of a big company in Enfield. So I had quite a lot to do with the preparation of accounts as well. I think that's one of the things that Sir Oswald liked. It means I can do his book-keeping for him."

"Of course he does. It'll save him from employing two people. That sounds just like him. You'd better be careful not to get caught up in any fiddles that he's involved in."

"John, you do sound bitter," said Susie. "That's not like you at all. I always think of you as being so cheerful and positive about things."

He snorted. "Not where the Staceys are concerned. I have no reason to like them. They seem to think that they've got rights above the law and everybody else." John shook his head. "But let's forget *my* prejudices. Did you know that Grant's collect the Stacey Estate rents? So we may meet up on business from time to time."

"Oh, that'll be nice."

"Yes." He found himself thinking it might be *very* nice. "Well, do you want to have a look around the house? Come and see your new kitchen first. It was finished on Sunday." He led the way towards the back.

"Oh, John, this is lovely," she said as soon as she saw it. "I've never had such a lovely kitchen. The colours are so bright and sunny. I didn't know it would be so shiny. You were going to let me have a brochure to show what the colours were like, but you forgot to leave it with me."

"Yes. Well, I remembered the brochures when I got back to the car. I picked them up and took them into the reception to see if I could catch you. But when I got there, I could see you were with someone else. So I thought it prudent to forget it at that stage."

"Oh!" Susie was staring at him. The colour seemed to drain gradually from her face, leaving her small and pale and childlike.

John cursed himself for opening his big mouth and letting out his knowledge of her secret meeting. "Don't worry about me, Susie. I'm not interested in whoever you might have been meeting – or why. I know it's got nothing to do with me."

"It's not what it seems, John," she said. "Honestly it isn't."

"Well, I haven't told anyone, and I don't intend to tell anyone. So don't worry about it."

But she still fixed him with her withered gaze. "What do you want me to do?"

"What are you talking about, Susie?" He shook his head. "I don't want you to do anything."

She didn't seem to hear him. When she spoke it was as though he wasn't there. "It's all starting again. I thought, by coming down here, that I could get away from it. But I suppose I'll never get away." She looked into his eyes. "Please don't make me start it all again."

"Start what again?" asked John, confused.

She shook her head. "I'm sorry. I can't tell you. Just tell me what you want to do with me."

"I've told you, Susie." He raised his voice. "I don't want to do anything with you."

"Men always want . . ."

"Well, *I* don't." He gripped her arms and she shrank away from him. "Look Susie. I *like* you. Through you I've had my first chance to sell a house on my own and earn myself some commission and get some work for my friend. I'm grateful to you. I don't expect anything else from you. Your private life is nothing to do with me. I've never asked anyone to tell me anything which they didn't want to. You have nothing to fear from me. Do you understand?"

She nodded but still kept away from him.

"I promise any secrets you may have are safe with me." He let go of her arms. "Now, let's forget it. Come upstairs and see what we've done in the bedrooms. We'll be finished over the weekend."

She trailed up the stairs behind him and said she was pleased with what they were doing. She allowed him to show her the inside of the garage although she didn't appear to actually look at anything properly. She accepted his offer of a lift back to the station and let him buy a platform ticket and take her down to the platform where he bought her a coffee while they waited. But the sparkle had gone out of her because of his one stupid comment.

The only thing which cheered him up was, that after the train had arrived and he had found her a seat and put her case on the rack, she came back to the door with him and hung out of the window and kissed him on the cheek and said, "Perhaps you really *are* the first nice man I've ever met."

And she stayed hanging out of the window and waving and getting smuts on her lovely costume until the train curved out of sight at the end of the platform.

38

Tuesday was college day for John each week. That was the day he had off from the office to learn about building construction and building administration and surveying techniques. It was a relief to be away from the dreary office routine, but he found it difficult to get excited about some of the more obscure subjects like law and quantity surveying.

The class broke for lunch at twelve and everyone made for the canteen where it was possible to have a two-course meal for a shilling. As he walked down the steps to the car park with some friends, he saw Sarah sitting on a seat. She looked fabulous. She was wearing an olive-green sheath dress with a high neck but without sleeves. The dress seemed to mould itself to her figure and the colour deepened the suntan on her arms.

"Wow! Look at that," said one of the other lads under his breath.

As they walked towards her, Sarah uncrossed her legs and rose to her feet, smoothing down the stretch material of her skirt as she did so.

"Hello, John," she said. "Can I take you to lunch?"

"You can take us all," offered another of the lads.

She smiled radiantly at them. "I'm afraid this is business," she said to them, as she took John's arm and directed him towards her car. "I've got something I want to show you."

Their departure was followed by a series of cat-calls and whistles, and John knew he was going to have problems later when he tried to convince them that Sarah was just a friend of his mother's.

"Well, we managed to pull that off without anyone noticing," he quipped as he climbed into the driving seat. Sarah liked to be chauffeured.

She smiled at him without humour. "I hadn't realised you were likely to be surrounded by a crowd of friends. It's difficult to be inconspicuous in a situation like that."

John thought that Sarah wouldn't know how to be

inconspicuous if her life depended on it. He started the car and drove out of the college.

"Take the Woodbury road," she instructed.

"Where are we going?"

"Don't ask questions." She had a smug smile on her face. "I'll show you when we get there."

John sighed loudly. "All right. Your wish is my command - as always."

"I find it difficult to get an opportunity to speak to you these days, John," said Sarah. "I can't just barge into the office and sit down beside you, can I? But now that my plans are starting to mature, I need to see you more often. I thought of us having a regular fortnightly meeting. You could come to my place on Wednesday evenings when Reggie's always at the golf club. What do you think about that?"

He took a deep breath as he steered round a bend. "Well, that sounds all right to me."

"It wouldn't necessarily be just so you could shag me." She leaned back against her door and regarded him with hooded eyes. "I′ve got lots of plans of things I want to do. Sometimes we'd just talk about those."

John grinned. "OK. So some meetings would be better than others."

"And it would probably be wise for you to ring up to check the coast was clear before you came round - just in case something had come up. We wouldn't want Reggie getting any wrong ideas, would we?"

"No," he agreed strongly. "We certainly wouldn't. How about if I ring you next Wednesday at seven? I'll tell Sammie I want to have one night a week to myself."

"That sounds an excellent idea."

They drove in companionable silence. After a while she said, "What time do you have to be back for lectures?"

"Quarter to two."

"Oh, that should be all right. We haven't far to go." She pointed ahead. "Turn right just along here."

John noticed for the first time that they were approaching the village on the road which led from the moor.

Just before they reached the first houses she told him to

stop. "If you open that gate on the right, we can drive into the field."

"Won't Farmer Fisher object?" asked John.

"No. He doesn't own it any longer."

"What do you mean?"

She looked at him with a benign smile on her face. "It´s mine now."

"You own this field?" His brain was reacting slowly. "You mean you've bought it from him?"

She nodded.

"But, Sarah - how did you get the money?"

"Well - if it's anything to do with you," she smiled, "I've actually got quite a lot of money which my father left me when he died. I told you that he had died, didn't I?"

"Yes." John nodded. "You said that you missed him a lot."

Sarah shrugged. "I suppose it was bound to happen sooner or later. We have to accept that death comes to all of us. If nothing else, it has given me the opportunity to buy this field."

"What do you want to buy a field for?" He was mystified. "Are you going to keep horses or something?"

"No." She had a smug smile on her face. "It's my investment in the future. And you're involved. I want you and me to build houses on it. I told you I've got plans for you. This is the start of them."

John seemed to have difficulty in grasping her intentions. "Houses? How many houses?"

"I don't know," she said. "How many do you think we can get on it?"

"What about planning permission? You *do* know that, under the Town and Country Planning Act, you need to get permission now before you can build anywhere?"

"Yes, I did know *that* much, John. That is one of the few advantages of being married to an estate surveyor." Sarah abandoned the sarcasm and explained. "I spoke to the Planning Officer of the Rural District Council before I made my offer. We'll have his full support on this one. The council want the village to expand as a dormitory area for Exeter." She nodded at him. "Come on now. Don't hang about. Open the gate and drive in. I want to show you what we've got."

John did as he was told. He drove just inside the gate, switched off the engine and put on the handbrake. Then he opened the door for Sarah and they started to stroll down the field through the knee-high grass.

"There's a small stream down at the bottom," she said, "so I thought we could leave a strip of ground alongside it for a play area and for dog-walking and things like that. The other side of the stream is the start of Stacey Park, so that's likely to remain open country. But the western end of the field already has houses along the other side of the hedge. That means this is a logical extension of the village."

He was impressed. "How big an area is the field?"

"Just over eight acres."

"Well," he said, "at the moment old Forrester is doing two developments of about ten houses to the acre. If you were willing to build in short terraces, I think you would get over twelve to the acre - say a hundred altogether on a field of this size."

Sarah linked her arm through his. "And what would they sell for?"

"Let me think." John halted as he worked it out. "I suppose they'd fetch between two thousand and two thousand five hundred each. There's a big demand for small economical houses at the moment to replace the ones which were destroyed in the war. By undercutting people like Forrester you'd probably find them quite easy to sell."

Sarah put her hand to her throat. "One hundred houses at two thousand pounds each - that's two hundred thousand pounds. Is that right?"

He nodded. "How much did the field cost you?"

"Fifteen hundred pounds." She took a breath. "How much will it cost to build the houses?"

"Well, I'd need to work it out, but they say it's roughly the equivalent of two years pay for a building worker - maybe a bit less for terraced houses. Let's say a carpenter gets fifteen pounds a week, to be on the safe side. Based on those figures, the houses ought to cost less than fifteen hundred pounds each to build." His jaw dropped. "That means you could make a profit of about fifty or sixty thousand pounds in something less than two years." He shook his head. "You'll be rich."

She hugged him excitedly. "You too, darling. We're going to be equal partners in this. I have the capital - you supply the know-how."

"What?" John tried to digest this sudden, huge change to his fortunes. "I - I don't know whether I've got enough know-how to take it on."

Sarah stepped back and looked at him. "You're not going to duck out on me, are you John? I'm relying on you. I don't want to be left with an eight-acre field that's no good for anything but grazing cows."

"But -" he stammered. "But you haven't thought of the problems."

"What problems?"

"For a start," he pointed out, "what does Reggie think about the idea?"

She shook her head. "He doesn't know, and I don't intend that he should know for quite a long time, until the development is well under way. This is *my* money which I've inherited and which I want to invest in the way I choose. If he knew about it, *he'd* want to take over my money and use it for some purpose of his own. And I don't intend that should happen. So this project is to be a secret which you are to keep to yourself, John. Do you understand me?"

John was silent for a while, digesting the full meaning of her words and starting to think about all that was involved.

"Sarah," he said, "this is a big project. It's going to need a full building organisation. Have you thought how it would be set up?"

"Actually I have, darling." She smiled in a superior way. "I've been to see an accountant and he is forming a limited company for me. I will be a forty-nine percent shareholder with the shares held by him as a nominee to protect my confidentiality. You'll be the same and the balancing two percent will be held by my solicitor, James Robertson. You will be the director and we need to appoint someone to be company secretary. I believe it's only a nominal position. I thought you might have some ideas about who could do that."

He considered the question. "I don't think Sammie would be

interested in a role of that sort."

"I don't want Sammie to have anything to do with this company," said Sarah positively. "We can employ him to do the work if you wish. But I'm afraid I don't want to have both of you as partners. I would feel outnumbered." She raised her chin and looked at him defiantly. "Besides I don't think he's got anything useful to offer this business."

John was bewildered. "What have you got against Sammie? He's a damned good worker."

"OK." She shrugged. "I've already said we'll employ him to help build the houses if you want to. But I don't want him to be one of the bosses. I want to separate the development company from the work that you and he do. *Our* company will be the employer. The company that you and Sammie have, can be the contractor. Do you understand me?"

"OK. So you want to separate the building work from the selling." John was surprised that she was so vehement about it. "Well, that's fair enough, if that's the way you want it. I don't expect Sammie would want to be involved with the sales side anyway."

Sarah smiled with satisfaction. "I just wanted us to be clear on that before we started."

He didn't really notice her comment at that moment. He would remember it later.

"I think," he said, "that I may have come across someone who would make a good company secretary. We've been doing some work fitting out a new house for a couple called Partridge who are moving down from London. The wife has just got a job as private secretary to Sir Oswald Stacey and she tells me she used to be secretary to the general manager of a large company in London. I think she might be interested."

"The important thing is - will she be able to keep confidence?"

"Oh yes," said John smugly, "I think I can ensure she does that."

Sarah looked at him. "You wouldn't be taking sexual advantage of her, by any chance?"

"No, I'm not." He was almost shocked by her question.

"Good." She nodded. "I don't expect you to be exclusively

mine, John. But I don't want to find that I'm competing with someone else in my own company."

John digested that piece of information. Sarah smiled as she watched him. "Will we need anyone else, do you think?"

"Er - well - I'll need some help with doing the survey and preparing the planning application." He thought rapidly. "The ideal person to help with that is Bill Kingley. He knows a hell of a lot more about this sort of thing than I do." He thought carefully. "How could I get him on our side?"

"He mustn't know anything about me being involved," said Sarah.

John scratched his head. "What if I just tell him that I've been offered the job of doing the survey and the application by a developer who wants to remain anonymous? I can say I've been offered two hundred pounds for doing it and I'll split the money with Bill if he'll help me. I should think he'd be grateful to pick up an extra hundred, wouldn't you?"

"There's something else we need to discuss." She took his arm again. "If you're going to be travelling around doing all these extra jobs, you're going to need a car of your own. You can hardly keep borrowing Reggie's pool car."

John looked crestfallen. "I haven't saved up enough yet to buy a car."

"Ah, but I have an idea," said Sarah. "I could do with a new car. I think I'll let you have my old one. You can buy it off me for ten pounds a month. You could afford that, couldn't you? How about if I charge you two hundred and fifty pounds? You can pay me ten pounds down and ten pounds a month for the next two years."

He was impressed by her splendid offer. "What? But your car's too flashy for me. I was only going to buy a Ford Eight or something cheap like that."

"You must think of the future, John." She started walking again, directing him towards the top end of the field. "You've got to start bettering yourself. You are going to be a person of substance." She threw her head back. "I've decided I'm going to have a Sunbeam Talbot. I think they're good-looking cars."

John was surprised to hear a woman talking so knowledgeably about cars.

Sarah looked up at him. “Of course, you’ll have to get your own insurance. I’ll put you in touch with my broker and he can give you a cover-note. You can collect the car next Wednesday evening when you come to see me. By the way, I don’t want Reggie to be told about this, just in case it starts him thinking. So you won’t be able to brag about it in the office.”

“Of course I won’t,” said John, upset by her tone. “Although I presume it’s all right if I’m buying it from you at a fair price.”

Sarah smiled indulgently. “I think you’ll find a *fair* price would be nearer five hundred pounds.”

“Really, but -”

“Don’t worry, John,” she said gently, “you’ll pay me back in plenty of other ways.”

They had been gradually walking up the field beside the stream. Now they had nearly reached the top corner, a shadowy glade out of the bright sunlight.

“Well,” said Sarah, “it seems as though we have the bones of a nice profitable arrangement in place. Do you agree?”

John nodded. “Yes, I do. Thank you for thinking of me.”

“My darling,” she said, “I’ve told you that I have all sorts of plans for you. I think this is a good place to seal our new contract, don’t you?” She moved close to him and put her arms around his neck.

He felt his excitement begin to rise. “Won’t it make a mess of your dress?”

“Never mind,” she murmured as she undid the front of his shirt. “It’s the right colour and it’ll wash. Besides - I’ve never been shagged fully clothed in the middle of my own field before.”

“Sarah, you are crude sometimes.”

The stretch material gave way enough to let him pull her skirt up over her bottom. She subsided onto the long grass. As he lay on top of her he thought that he was going to be late back for the afternoon lecture. But he didn’t let that distract him.

39

It was about ten days later when Bill Kingley came into the shop from the back carrying his jacket and wellingtons. It was just after nine. “Come on, young Tucker. No more hanging around chatting up the staff. We’ve got to go and survey a place up on the edge of Dartmoor. It’s going to take us most of the day, so we need to get moving.”

“We never seem to see you nowadays, John.” Janice stopped arching her back and flaunting her bosom and started concentrating again on her typewriter. “You’re too posh now to mix with the ordinary staff.”

“Sorry to drag him away from you, my dear, but some of us have work to do,” said Bill. “You may not have noticed it, but we’re busier in this office than we’ve ever been. All the world and his wife seem to want to buy houses at the moment. Do you know where the quick-set level is, John?”

“It’s already in the boot of the pool car.”

Bill pulled his jacket on. “Right, then - we’re off.” He spoke generally to the office. “Don’t sell too many while we’re gone.”

There were various reactions from happy farewells to groans as they walked out. John looked sideways at Bill and decided he looked hugely cheerful. Now might be a good time to talk to him about the field survey. But Bill seemed to have his own agenda. “You’re not interested in that Janice bird, are you?”

John shrugged. “Not really. I just like to be polite.”

“Polite, my foot. She’s got nothing to offer but a big pair of tits. I can tell she’s interested in you, from the way that she sticks them up under your nose. But I thought you had a bit more discernment.”

“You are crude, Bill,” said John thinking of the last person he’d accused of that sort of language. “No, I’m not interested in Janice. I haven’t got time to be interested in anyone at the moment.”

“Come off it. I don’t miss these things, even if Reggie Grant does.”

"I don't know what you mean."

They reached the car and started checking the equipment.

"You know damn well what I mean. Why has Sarah Grant bought a smart new Sunbeam Talbot? Why are you driving round in a car that looks remarkably like Sarah's old car? And why do you carefully park it two streets away so that no-one knows that you've got a new vehicle, when I'd expect a young lad like you to flaunt it under the noses of the big-titted brigade?" Bill slammed the boot and climbed into the passenger seat. "You can drive as usual."

John got in and started the engine. "You don't miss much, do you? Has anyone else said anything?"

"Not to me, they haven't. But then I wouldn't expect them to. I've been wondering about you and Sarah Grant for a while. I've heard before that she has a taste for the lads. I reckon you're playing a bit of a dangerous game, young John. So you'd better be careful and watch your back."

"My god," John said as he drove out of the car park, "I hope that sort of story isn't going the rounds."

Bill smiled. "I don't think it is. Certainly no-one's spoken to me about it. And I've said nothing to anyone. Your secret's safe with me. What is the dastardly secret anyway?"

John had a quick think and decided to do a hasty rearrangement of the truth. "Well, Bill, the situation is this. Sarah Grant came to me and said she'd been left a lot of money by her father when he died last year. She already had a pretty good idea of what she wanted to do with it, but she needed someone to help her with the practicalities. So what she's done, is buy a field on the edge of our village where she says she's confident of getting planning permission to build about a hundred houses. From what you've been saying, they ought to sell like hot cakes."

"They certainly will in that location," Bill agreed. "It's a pretty village and quite close to Exeter where there's plenty of work with those new companies moving their offices down here. There's bound to be a big demand as long as the prices are reasonable."

"That's where you come in, Bill. I've been waiting for an opportunity to talk to you since she told me about this last week. You see, Sarah doesn't really understand all the technical problems involved. And I've got to admit that I'm a bit of a greenhorn at the moment. So I said to her that she'd need to employ someone like you to do a survey and work up an outline scheme. Would you be willing to do that in your spare time, if I gave you a hand? I suggested she should pay you a hundred pounds to prepare the planning application. What do you think about that?"

Bill pursed his lips. "Hmm. I don't see why not. How much work is involved?"

"Well - you obviously know that better than me. I thought we could probably do the survey and some sketch layouts in a weekend. Then I'll go into college in the evenings for a couple of weeks and draw it up in their drawing office. They've got all the gear there - the skins and the printing facilities which I can use free of charge because I'm a student. You could go over it with me a couple of times so as to get it right, and I'll update it. While I was doing that, I thought you might fill in the forms."

"Why don't you use an architect?" asked Bill. "That would be the obvious way."

"Firstly because he'll take three to six months to work up a scheme and Sarah wants things to start moving faster than that. Secondly, I think it's the cost and the fact that an architect wouldn't do it just as she wants. And thirdly - because she would find it difficult to keep it confidential if an architect was involved. Apparently she's doing all this without her husband's knowledge. He doesn't know about the windfall from her dad. If he did, she's afraid he'd probably want to have the money and stick it into the business or some scheme of his own, and she doesn't want that to happen. She's one of these ladies who values her independence."

"So why does she turn to you then?"

John was ready for the expected question. "I suppose it's circumstances really. You see, she's known my mum for some time and has watched me grow up. She was instrumental in getting me the position at Grant's when it was important that I got a job fairly quickly. I think she feels I owe her something for that. Then she got me to do some work in her house at Easter."

"I heard something about that."

"What did you hear?" John looked at him suspiciously.

"Only that the job was done over the weekend while our Reginald was away." Bill grinned. "I think that you're a bit of a dark horse, young Tucker. But you tell me what really happened."

John turned his full attention back to the road. "Sarah's shower-room? Well, I brought in a friend of mine to help and she was very impressed with the result. I think she sees us as a team for the future." He decided to expand on the idea. "The point is, that *you've* got the know-how and could be a part of the team as well, if you're interested."

"And why should I be interested?"

"If you don't mind my saying so, Bill, I think you're grossly under-valued at Grant's." John briefly glanced sideways at him to gauge his reaction. "I reckon you're the bloke who holds the whole business together. Without you, I think Grant's would be nothing more than a little surveying practice which never got any work worth talking about." He took a breath and plunged on. "And yet I gather you'll never stand a chance of becoming a partner and making the money out of the business that you deserve - just because you're not qualified. I don't think you owe Grant's anything." He paused, and when Bill still didn't say anything, he said, "Sorry if you think I've overstepped the mark."

The older man was quiet for a long time. Finally he said, "You're very straight, young John. So, it's *that* obvious, is it?"

"No, it isn't," said John miserably. "It's just the way *I* think, that's all. And I admit I know nothing about it really."

"I don't know about that. 'Out of the mouths of babes and sucklings' and all that sort of thing. You may have put your finger on something that I've not been willing to face up to." He shrugged. "But what can I *do* about it anyway."

"Well," said John, "if you accept the offer I've just made you, who knows where it might lead? After all, you've got nothing to lose and you're not doing anything wrong. It's no crime to accept some weekend work to augment your income in these tight times, is it? Will you at least think about it?"

"I don't need to think about it, John. I'll accept. As you say -

why shouldn't I? I know where I can borrow a theodolite, so let's get started this weekend, shall we?"

"Thanks a lot, Bill." John heaved a sigh of relief. "I must admit I was worried about trying to do it myself without your experience and practical knowledge. Of course, you won't say anything that might get back to Mr Grant."

"You can rely on me," Bill smiled. "Now take this next turning left. The property we're to survey is just down the end of the lane."

From then on he was strictly professional.

40

As summer advanced the riverside came to life again. People from all around the area came to the village, either to venture out on to the water or to watch others making a mess of it. In the evenings the pubs were crowded with drinkers who overflowed onto the Strand and the nearby quays. Once again it became the place to meet people and to while away the time.

It was nearly ten o'clock when John decided to give up estimating work for the evening. He had also been working on drawings for the new development planning application, which would be submitted in the next couple of weeks. If the application was successful, work on the new housing estate should be able to start in July. The diggers would go in straightaway and the main drains, roads and foundations should be well on the way before the winter rains came. The first houses might be on sale before Christmas, even though it would probably be next spring before the real sales would start. Sarah said she had no worries about funding the work until then. Her bank manager was very supportive about the whole project. John was aware that she had her own special way of dealing with her business contacts.

He felt that he needed some fresh air before he went to bed. He was physically tired, but the weather today had been warm and pleasant, and he felt a short walk was called for. The last of the sunset glow still lit up the sky and the scent of a bonfire lingered in the air. He decided to take a stroll beside the river before going to bed.

He went to the end of the Strand but resolutely turned his back on Riversmeet and strolled along the riverside through the village. When he got to the Passage Inn he decided he felt like a drink. So he went in and ordered a pint. He turned away from the bar with the beer in his hand and the intention of going to sit beside the river to drink it.

Then Ambrose Stacey loomed in front of him. "Blow me, if it isn't young Tucker. This *is* a surprise."

"Not such a surprise really," John pointed out, "since I also happen to live here. How are you, Ambrose?"

"Depressed." He detached himself from the group he'd been talking to and latched on to John.

"What on earth have you got to be depressed about?" asked John. "You're not worried about the finals, are you?"

Ambrose raised a hand. "God, no. They're bound to give me some sort of degree - just for lasting the course. That's all that I will need to get a job in the city."

John grinned. "That'll be what you're depressed about - the idea of having to start work."

"You've got me all wrong, Tucker," protested Stacey.

"What - you're looking forward to *working*?"

Ambrose nodded. "I tell you - work can't come quickly enough. I want to get to London as soon as possible. That's where it's all happening." He shrugged. "Besides, I desperately need the money."

"Still tight for cash, are you?" John shook his head. "I don't understand you. Your father must give you handouts worth three times as much as I earn, yet you're always broke."

Ambrose tapped him on the chest - evidence that he'd had a little more beer tonight than he should have done. "What you don't realise, young John, is that I have a position to keep up. Everybody expects Ambrose Stacey to be where the action is. Oh yes!" He silenced John's unspoken protest. "I tell you - it's a big responsibility. In fact, I don't mind admitting it's starting to get me down."

"Poor old Ambrose," laughed John. "I never realised how you suffered."

"It's all right for you to laugh. I hear you've got a very nice little sideline going in addition to the daytime job for old skinflint Grant." He patted John on the shoulder. "A little bird told me you're raking it in."

"Really?" asked John. "And who would that little bird be?"

Ambrose rubbed the side of his nose. "Never you mind. But I understand it's a nice little earner. I hear you're making a fortune out of fitting out houses for the *nouveaux riches*. Is that correct?"

"I suppose it's a close enough approximation to the truth to suit you."

"I thought so." The other chap nodded. "I don't often get these things wrong, you know. Of course, you realise you're firing wide of the mark with this new business venture, don't you?"

"What do you mean?" John took a long draught of his beer and waited.

Ambrose tapped him on the chest again. "What I mean, is that you could be making an even bigger fortune if you were in there dealing with the seriously *riches* instead of just the *nouveaux* ones." He leaned forward in conspiratorial fashion. "You see, the upper classes are looking to upgrade their houses as well, now that the money's starting to flow again. But the silly fools think they've got to go to Chelsea or Mayfair to get companies to do it for them, and those fellows charge the earth. There's a pot of gold out there just waiting to be tapped."

"And you think you're ready to tap it, do you, Ambrose? Your financial crisis should soon be at an end in that case."

He shook his head. "Not me, Johnny boy. You're the one poised to make the fortune. All you have to do is get the right introductions. And of course it's more than possible they could come from me." Ambrose warmed to his theme. "Now listen, John. Here's what we do. I go in first. You know - invited for dinner, or something like that. I start waxing lyrical about how beautiful their house could be made, using this new fitted furniture stuff. Then, when they're all enthusiastic, I tell them about this great chum of mine who'd do them a super job for a fraction of the price charged by the Chelsea boys. All I have to do then is make an appointment for you to go to see them and, "hey presto", you're in."

"And what would you get out of this?" John felt naturally suspicious.

"A ten percent commission, of course," said Ambrose, "to be paid when you get the order."

"Oh, no!" John was a bit sharper than that. "The commission would be five percent. After all, you're only getting us an introduction. And it would be paid when we're paid. How would I know you weren't setting me up?"

"Really, John," said Ambrose huffily, "is there no honour in this world? How can you doubt me and my friends?"

"Well, the alternative is that you tell them I always insist on a twenty-five percent deposit. Then I'd pay you two and a half percent on receipt of the deposit and the other two and a half when the bill was settled. Is that honourable enough for you?"

"Ambrose shrugged. "I suppose it'll have to do. When do you want me to start?"

"Start tomorrow." John grinned. "The sooner you get us some clients, the sooner you'll start getting the cash."

Ambrose nodded. "OK. I'll be on the blower first thing. Anything else you want me to sell for you while I'm about it?"

"Well, there may be some houses later. But they'll only be little boxes. They're not the sort of things your rich friends would want to buy."

"Nevertheless - I'll consider it." Ambrose eyed him thoughtfully. "Now - here's something else for you to think about. Did you know my little sister is coming home next week?"

"Alison?" John looked at him. "Why are you telling me about it? She and I are hardly bosom friends at the moment. I expect she'll want to keep out of my way."

"I'm not so sure about that." Ambrose nodded thoughtfully. "You may be wrong about her, you know."

John shook his head. "I don't think so."

"Really," he urged. "I think she feels badly about the way she treated you. You ought to give her a chance to apologise. Alison's not such a bad lot when she's away from the influence of her London friends."

"Why are you so interested in mending fences, Ambrose? I wouldn't have thought you'd have given a hang about how I get along with your sister."

"Well - you know me." He leaned back with a cherubic smile on his face. "All I want is for the world to be a great big happy place."

John couldn't think of anything to say in reply to that.

"I tell you what," said Ambrose. "How would you like to come sailing on Saturday week? I could do with a crew. My regular's away. Perhaps Alison will be there and you'll be able to meet on neutral ground, so to speak, after the race."

"All right." John eyed him cautiously. "I wouldn't mind

that."

"We'll call it a date then. The race starts at two, so you ought to be there about one-fifteen to help me get the boat on the water."

"OK - I'll see you on Saturday week." John downed the last of his pint and put the glass on the bar. When he turned back to continue the conversation, Ambrose had already buttonholed some long-haired woman who was smoking her cigarette through a holder. He shrugged. It seemed as though the chap had as quickly forgotten about him.

In any case he decided there was still time for him to get another hour's work in, before he went to bed. There was a busy weekend ahead of him with three different kitchens to be fitted. John mainly did the delivery bit while Sammie and the lad did the fixing. All the same, Ambrose's comments about Alison were interesting.

41

Sarah was shown into Harold James' office after being kept waiting for no more than two minutes.

"Hello Harry," she said. "Thank you for agreeing to see me at such short notice."

The chief planning officer stood up and came round the desk to greet her with his hand outstretched. "Not at all. It's a real pleasure, Sarah."

She knew that it *would* be - for him. She had put on the light grey costume with the plunging neckline which she kept for such occasions, and she hadn't bothered to put on a blouse underneath. She had also sloshed perfume down her cleavage just before she got out of the car. Now, as she lowered the bundle of drawings which she had been carrying like a shield in front of her, she was aware that she had Harold's very close attention.

"It's very kind of you, Harry, to give me personal help with this application. Of course I'm not actually making the application myself. But I have a lot of interest in the outcome, if you understand me."

"Certainly I do."

She was aware that he hadn't heard a word she was saying. His eyes were glued to her cleavage and his head was swimming in a cloud of Chanel No 5. It was obvious from their last meeting that Harold was a man with a liking for large breasts.

"Do you remember the Rotary Ball at the end of January, Harry," she reminded him.

"I most certainly do. We had three dances together. You weren't so sun-tanned then."

"You're a very good dancer. We had an enjoyable time together." In fact she had found it almost impossible to unhook his nose from inside the neckline of her dress. "It's difficult to get good partners. Reggie doesn't dance. He spends most of his time propping up the bar. When I come across a man who can actually dance, it's a real bonus."

"Well," enthused Harry, his head bending towards her midriff, "let me know any time you want another dancing lesson."

"I'll remember that. However - to business first." She turned sharply away, her boobs almost banging him in the face. "Can I spread the papers out here?"

"What? Oh, yes." Harold scurried around, clearing the desk and helping her spread out the drawings and forms.

"I realise that these planning applications can take a long time to process. But it's important for us that we get the roads and drains and foundations in before winter is upon us. Do you think you can hurry things up a little?" Sarah leaned over the drawings and her costume jacket fell half-open.

"Oh, yes, I'm sure I can." Harry was performing contortions to try and get into a position to peer down her front.

"When is the next Planning Committee meeting?"

"What - er - oh, I think it's on Tuesday fortnight."

"Would you be able to put us on the agenda for that one?" Sarah smiled and half-turned towards him, giving him a brief view of her left nipple before she straightened up. She guessed that the vision would stay with him for the next two and a half weeks.

"Of course I can," he gasped, his eyes fastened on what he could see of her brassiere.

"Oh, thank you, Harry. I knew I could rely on you." To his intense regret she turned back to the drawings. "Now let me explain our plans. We have just over eight acres on the outskirts of the village. You've already told me it is Council policy to expand into this area. We're proposing a hundred and four semi-detached and terraced houses in short rows set at different angles to each other to improve the aspect. We've allocated nearly an acre alongside the stream as an amenity area for the benefit of the whole village. You can see the proposed layout." She leaned back, providing him with a full frontal. "Do you think you would be able to support these proposals?"

"Er - yes," he agreed, "I should think it will fit in very well with our overall plan. The road access is adequate, and you can link in to the main sewer which more or less follows the line of the stream." Harry was regretting that he wasn't tall enough to see down her cleavage at this stage.

"We've filled in five copies of the form and there are five sets of drawings for your distribution. That's correct isn't it?"

He clasped his hands together. "Perfect."

"Will you support our application with a strong recommendation, Harry?" She smiled invitingly at him.

"Sarah," he cooed at her, "you can be assured I will."

"Do you think the committee are likely to approve it in those circumstances?"

He nodded enthusiastically. "I can virtually guarantee it."

"Oh, thank you, Harry." She leaned forward, generously giving him a view down her front almost to her waist. "You don't know what this means to me." She planted a kiss on his forehead as it bent forward. "What time is the meeting?"

"Pardon," he mumbled, lost in contemplation of the magnificent view.

"Harry - the time of the Planning Committee meeting on Tuesday fortnight - is it in the morning?"

"Oh, yes. Yes." He tore his eyes from contemplation of her breasts and raised them reluctantly to hers. "It's ten-thirty. Do you want to come?"

"I don't think that's necessary," said Sarah in her most seductive voice, "but you could call on me after lunch to bring me the committee decision. I should really be ever so grateful if you were able to tell me that we'd received approval."

Harold James could hardly believe his ears. He suddenly found it difficult to breathe. He managed to mutter. "Oh, yes, I'd be only too pleased -."

"There's one other thing, Harry. I'd be ever so grateful if nobody but you knows about my involvement in the project." She smiled her most alluring smile. "I'd like this to be another little secret between the two of us."

"Of course. Of course," he assured her, moving as close to her as he dared. "My lips will be sealed."

"You're such a nice person to deal with. I'm sure we're going to get on very well together." She giggled as she wriggled out from under his gaze. "You can bring your dancing shoes if you like."

"Pardon?" Then he smiled as he saw the joke. "Oh – I'll make sure I do."

"Can I take this brochure with me?" Sarah picked it up and read it. "It's a copy of the annual report and accounts for last year."

"Yes, of course. There are plenty around." He shook his head in surprise. "Why do you want to read the annual report? We're already well into the new year."

She turned and favoured him with a withering smile. "I don't want to read it, darling. I'm just particular about who I have peering down my cleavage on the way back to the car."

The next minute she was gone, with the annual report and accounts clutched to her chest and leaving the chief planning officer to his fantasies.

42

John drove his friend to meet old Forrester in the smart new Hillman Minx that he′d acquired from Sarah. He was aware that Sammie was worried about the meeting. He had dressed in a dark suit and had put on a tie.

"What do you think he wants to talk to us about?" asked Sammie.

"I don't know. He just rang up and asked if we could meet him in his office at nine on Saturday morning. Hopefully he'll be handing over his cheque for the rest of Partridges' work."

"Do you think they've complained about the standard of the work?"

"Of course not. I went to meet Susie Partridge a few days before they moved in. She was delighted with what we'd done."

"Well, it's got to be something important to drag us away from work on a Saturday morning." Sammie still wore a worried frown. "Does he know how much work we've got on?"

"We had to meet him some time," John pointed out. "I can't get away during the week. It was lucky I wasn't on duty this Saturday, otherwise I'd have had to suggest tomorrow, and a Sunday wouldn't have looked very professional."

His partner sighed. "That would have been just as bad anyway. We've got so much to do that I'm working Jamie seven days a week as it is, not that he′s complaining. He likes the extra money."

"Is he doing well?"

"Yes," nodded Sammie, "but he and I can't cope on our own, even with a bit of help from you. We're going to have to do something about it."

John had been waiting to discuss this with him. "Sammie, it's time that we seriously considered how we're going to develop the business from now on. I was just as surprised as you when that big job turned up so quickly from Ambrose Stacey's contact. It was only just over a fortnight ago that we had our chat in the pub. To be honest, I hadn't expected to hear any more from that source. It just shows how wrong one can be."

"Oh, I'm not complaining," said Sammie. "It's a really good job. You say there's over a thousand pounds' worth of work?"

He nodded. "And the profit margin is good. I reckon we should make between three and four hundred pounds on top of your labour and the material costs. And there's another much bigger project I want to talk to you about. I know you haven't been keen to go into general building, but I reckon there's a lot of money to be made from constructing new houses. *And* I can guarantee the return on this one, because it'll be on a cost-plus basis."

"What's all this about?" Sammie looked baffled.

"It's a big housing job right on our doorstep." John broke off. "Well, here we are at Forrester's. I'll tell you about it on the way back."

He turned into the yard and parked beside Forrester's big Wolseley. As they got out of the car, the old man came out of the office door. "Good morning, Mr Forrester," said John. "I don't know if you've met Sammie Joslin. He's the chap who made the units for the Partridges' house."

"Call me Jack." Forrester shook hands firmly. "Come on in. I've got a proposal to make to you two lads."

The old man led the way through a short corridor into his office, affecting the exaggerated limp that John had noticed he used before when he was meeting people. He winked at Sammie as they followed him.

"Take a seat. Make yourself at home." Jack lifted a pile of papers off one chair and staggered round to the back of his desk. "Do you want a cup of tea?"

"It's a bit too early for me, thanks," said John and Sammie also shook his head.

"Well, I expect you're wondering why I asked you round here," began Forrester without further ado. "The fact is that I've been very impressed by the work you've done at Plot 15, Meadowlands."

"That's the Partridge's house," translated John.

"That's right. You see those layouts on the wall." They

turned to look at the area he indicated. "The one on the right is Meadowlands. It's been running for just over a year. I've sold seventeen houses there at the rate of one or two a month and I've got plans for another forty-two to be built in the next two years. The layout on the left is Vicarage Lane. That's bigger. There are seventy-two plots altogether of which only eight have been sold so far in the last eighteen months." He turned back to them. "Now then, since you've done that work at No 15, I've been taking potential buyers in there to show them how the houses can be fitted out, if they're interested. The result is that I've had four firm offers at Meadowlands and two at Vicarage Lane. Every one of them wants a fitted kitchen and three of them are prepared to pay the extra for fitted wardrobes as well. What do you think of that?"

John heard Sammie's sharp intake of breath, but he answered. "And you want us to do the work?"

Forrester nodded. "That's right. *And* they all need doing in the next six weeks. Can you achieve that?"

"Six kitchens and three lots of wardrobes in six weeks?" gasped John.

To his surprise, in view of his partner's earlier comments, Sammie answered for him. "Yes, Mr Forrester, I think that can be done with a bit of reorganisation on our part."

John gulped and looked at his partner. Sammie grinned reassuringly at him.

He turned back to the older man as a new thought struck him. "Will you be paying us on the same basis of twenty-five percent deposit and the balance as soon as they move in?"

Forrester smiled. "Don't worry, I haven't forgotten." He opened his right hand desk drawer and drew out an envelope. "Here's your cheque for the work you did at Partridge's."

"Thank you, Jack." John pocketed the letter. "OK. I don't see why we shouldn't continue to work on the same basis."

Sammie nodded, not concerned with the financial arrangements.

"There are a couple of extra conditions to this new order," said Forrester with the ghost of a smile on his face.

"What do you mean?"

The old man put his elbows on the desk and leaned forward.

"Well, since you're able to do all six in one go I thought you could give me a further five percent discount. That's ten percent altogether." He raised a finger. "Also I want you to do show-houses on each estate, so that I can show them to potential purchasers without having to ask the permission of the people who've already moved in." He leaned back in his chair. "Does that sound reasonable?"

John was a bit cautious. "How would we be paid for the show-houses?"

"In the same way as the others." Forrester shrugged. "Twenty-five percent with the order and the rest when they're sold."

"But they might not be sold for years."

Forrester shook his head. "I don't know about that. I haven't done this sort of thing before. But your Bill Kingley told me that, in his experience, it's often the show-houses that sell first. You'd have to take your chance on that, just like I do."

"I tell you what," said John, "you know we're only a small business just starting up. Cash-flow is important to us. Can I make a suggestion?"

"Go ahead."

"What if we fit out all eight kitchens and five sets of wardrobes and you pay us in full less twelve and a half per cent as soon as we've finished each one? That gives you more profit, but it helps us as well, by our getting paid before we've got to stump up for the materials."

Forrester thought about it for a minute. Then he nodded. "All right. I'll give you the order on that basis. The first ones will be wanted in about four weeks' time. Can you do that?"

John looked at Sammie, who nodded. "Yes - that shouldn't be a problem."

"Good. I look forward to this becoming a regular business arrangement." Forrester stood up and saw them to the door. "By the way, I'll be starting a third site quite close to the city in the autumn. We'll discuss a similar arrangement on that one when the time comes."

As they drove away, John said, "There you are. Nothing to worry about, was there? That's a good order, by the look of it, and there'll be more to come. Were you happy with that?"

Sammie shook his head doubtfully. "I didn't understand your mathematics. Can we afford that arrangement?"

"Well," John explained, "it'll be an order for about eighteen hundred pounds all together after Forrester's discount. You know how much the kitchens and the wardrobes cost to build for the Partridge's house. You multiply the kitchen figure by eight and the wardrobe price by five. What does that add up to?"

Sammie was quiet while he worked it out. "A bit less than twelve hundred pounds."

"In that case there's a profit of over six hundred in it for us even if we don't improve our efficiency when we're doing eight off in one go."

"You're right," agreed Sammie, a trifle reluctantly, "and I reckon we can save at least another hundred by proper planning of production."

"We may get a discount on materials if we're bulk-buying."

Sammie grinned. "O.K, partner. It looks like you did a good job there."

"The only problem," said John, "is whether you can cope with the workload after what you said earlier."

"Yes." His partner was quiet for a while. At last he said, "Well, now is the time for my news. I think we're going to need it."

"Go on then." John suddenly sensed that this was something important.

"Jim Barker called me in to his office yesterday afternoon. You know I told you that he seems to be running the business down recently? Well, he's now admitted to me that he wants to retire. Apparently he's put a few feelers out to see if there's anybody around who's willing to buy him out, but he hasn't had any response. So he's offered to hand the whole company over to me. What do you think?"

John was struck dumb by the way it was all happening. "Wow!" was all that he could manage.

"Of course, I said I'd want you in as a part-time partner and he says that's up to me." Sammie turned to him. "I'd need your backing, John," he said seriously. "I couldn't do it on my own."

"You mean," asked John, "that we'd take the whole thing over - the yard, the workshop, the blokes, the vehicles, everything?" He swallowed. "What's the catch?"

"Well, I suppose you'd say there are two. Firstly he'll keep the ownership of the premises and lease them to us initially for three years at five hundred pounds a year. The other thing is that we have to pay him a pension which starts off at a thousand a year and rises by two per cent each year."

John was trying to work the figures out in his head. "We ought to be able to afford that all right. We could more or less pay that much now from the money we're making on the fitted furniture. What about the blokes who are working for him?"

"I told you his foreman retires in May. Now that Jamie's left, there's only me and old Daniel in the yard. The old guy's about five years off retirement and I don't see any problems with him. There are six other blokes out on the sites - two youngish brickies who also do a bit of plastering, a chippie and his labourer that I could use to help with the extra fitted furniture work, and two decorators. And then there's Angus, the foreman. He's the one we're most likely to have problems with. He may think that he should have been offered the business instead of us."

"Is he any good?"

Sammie nodded. "Yes. He's the only one at Barkers who's not a youngster or an old man. He trained with Jim Barker before the war. Then he was called up and served in the Royal Engineers and returned to Barker's when he was demobbed. He's got a very practical head on his shoulders, but he's not so good with the money side of things. I think that's why Jim Barker came to me."

"Leave him to me," said John. "It sounds as though I might have just the job for him."

"What do you mean?"

"I was telling you, when we arrived at Forrester's, that I've got a new project." He swallowed. "Well, I've been approached by a developer who wants to build a hundred and four houses on a field just outside the village. Your Angus sounds like the chap we need to run that site."

Sammie looked startled. "A hundred and four houses - how

big is that?"

"It will give us a turnover of about a hundred and fifty thousand pounds," said John. "We'll be paid on a cost plus ten per cent basis. That's a profit of fifteen thousand pounds spread over two years. We'll need a labour force of about fifty men altogether. That means we'll need a good site foreman. Your man Angus should be just the ticket."

"But John, we'd never cope with all that work." Sammie was aghast. "That's about five times Barker's present turnover. Where would we find all the men?"

John spared him a sideways glance. "Advertise. Go to Bristol if we need to. I've been reading that there are lots of building tradesmen looking for work up there. I also want us to use the latest modern equipment. These new tractor/diggers are worth looking at. They can be fitted with forks at the front for unloading and moving materials around the site."

"But all this costs a lot of money."

"You don't need to worry about that," John assured him. "This new developer has plenty of money and is willing to help us with funds. In any case we'd get a monthly cheque on account to pay us for the work we've done to date. And we've already got nearly three thousand pounds put away ourselves, which will be there if we need it."

"Who is this developer?"

"Er - I've promised not to say." This was the question he'd been expecting and didn't quite know how to answer. "You could say they're quite well-known locally."

"They?" Sammie grinned, not at all put out by John's reticence. "That sounds like the Staceys. Oh, maybe it's Ambrose. You've been seeing a bit of him recently. Have they come into money or something?"

"I'm sorry, Sammie. I asked if I could tell my partner, but they said it wasn't to go any further at the moment. All I can tell you is that the money's there if we do the work. I want us to go ahead and accept it. It could give us a real chance of getting on our feet."

His partner took a deep breath. "Well, I've always known you were ambitious. I suppose I might have guessed that something like this was likely to happen sooner or later. I hadn't expected it quite so soon though."

"I think we'd be mad to turn down an offer like this, Sammie."

His friend was quiet for a long time, thinking it over. At last he said, "I don't want to be involved in building, John. I don't think I know enough about it. We've got so much fitted furniture work that I don't see how we can take on something as big as this."

"Sammie, new housing is the future. Millions of houses were destroyed during the war and the local councils are too slow in building replacements. Grants are being besieged by people desperately looking for new houses. Every new one which comes on the market immediately has half a dozen people booking up to look at it. And particularly they want new, cheap houses. This is what we're going to give them."

"It's what *you*'re going to give them, John. I don't want anything to do with that side of the business." He shook his head. "Oh, you can still run the business from Barkers yard and use whatever stuff you need, but it's going to be your show. Let me concentrate on the furniture."

John looked at him. "Are you suggesting we split up and just share the premises?"

"No. I still need you as a partner on the furniture side. I don't want to get involved in all that administrative stuff – accounts and payroll and invoicing and things. I want you to carry on doing that for my side. So we'll be equal partners in the furniture company." He took a breath. "But the building side is separate. That's your own business. I don't want to be involved in it." Sammie looked at him. "But one thing's for sure, John. It means you'll have to leave Grant's and join us."

"In my mind I've accepted that will have to happen when the building starts."

"When *does* this job start?"

"Probably later in the summer. They've still got to get final planning approval although I'm told it's been promised." John tried to be reassuring. "When we know the start date, I'll make the necessary decision."

"Right," said Sammie, "so that's it then. I'm to tell Jim Barker that we accept his offer."

John looked at him seriously. "I'll work all the figures out on paper this evening and show them to you tomorrow morning. As long as they work out as we expect at the moment, I think we'll have to, Sammie. We'd never be able to face each other again if we pulled back now, just when it's all about to happen."

"You'd better come and meet Mr Barker and we'll talk about the details. How about this afternoon?"

"I'm afraid I can't," said John. "I'm sorry, but I've agreed to go sailing with Ambrose Stacey. Besides I think we ought to make sure nothing comes up that we hadn't foreseen when we talk over the figures."

Sammie grinned. "I see. Well that's enough said. I can see the way things are going. Shall I ask the old man if he'll meet us later tomorrow morning? I think he'd probably prefer to do it over the weekend with none of the blokes about."

"That'll suit me fine."

"I'll say provisionally eleven o'clock," said Sammie. "If there's any change to that, I'll put a note through your door."

John felt a rush of warmth towards his partner. "Thanks a lot, Sammie. Where do you want me to drop you - by your shed door?"

"Yes. Jamie will be there. He can let me in."

"I can give you a hand for a couple of hours if I can be of any use," John offered. "I'm sorry about not being around this afternoon."

"Don't worry," said Sammie. "What you're doing is just as valuable for our future."

John thought to himself, as he parked the car, that he couldn't have found a better friend to go into partnership with than Sammie.

43

John arrived at the sailing club at least ten minutes before he needed to. A few of the early starters were already at work on their dinghies, stripping off canvas covers, topping up buoyancy bags, tensioning forestays, bending on sails. The first couple of contestants were running their boats down the launching ramp, wires slappiting against masts in the brisk breeze.

"Have you seen Ambrose Stacey?" John asked.

"Oh, he won't be here for half an hour. He always leaves it to the last minute."

Feeling a bit out of it, John sat on a low wall near the launching ramp and watched the activities going on busily around the boat yard. The warm sun soaked into his back and he took off his sweater.

The majority of the boats were on the water and the junior class had already started racing before Ambrose's sports car turned in through the entrance gates. John walked over to meet him and stopped when he saw that Alison was his passenger.

She half smiled at him. "Hello."

"Great!" Ambrose looked straight past John. "Adam's back."

Alison jumped out. "He's *my* crew today."

"Rubbish. Adam's always my crew."

"Not today, he isn't," said Alison. "You've already asked John."

"Well, John understands that I'm bound to take the best man available." Ambrose didn't deign to look at his sister. "*You* can have John. I can see that Adam's already got your boat ready. You can go straight out and give the fellow some practice to get him into shape."

He slung his bag over his shoulder and strode towards the clubhouse. He appeared to have completely forgotten them.

"Sod him." Alison stamped her foot in frustration. "He always does this. He always has. He only does it because he's a man and a couple of years older than me. And Adam's so wet that he lets Ambrose walk all over him. So that means I'm left with the bloody rookie again."

John couldn't help grinning. "Well, it's nice to have the two of you fight over me like this."

She rounded on him. "Now, listen to me. I want to beat that bugger and teach him he's not so bloody clever as he thinks he is. You're going to have to learn fast. You'll have to do what I say. And remember - on a boat, the skipper's always right."

As Alison turned away, John caught her arm. "Now, *you* listen too. I'll do my best. But if you start losing your temper and shouting, as you've been known to do in the past, then I'll stop being your crew and turn into a passenger. Is *that* clear?"

For a second they faced each other, eyeball to eyeball. John wondered if she was going to strike him. Then suddenly she relaxed and smiled. "All right. That's a fair arrangement. We'd better get started. I suppose you haven't got any waterproofs."

"Nothing but what I'm wearing."

"I hope you don't mind them getting wet," she advised. "I know it looks nice now, but things can change. You'll probably go home soaked."

John inclined his head. "That's all right. It won't be the first time."

"OK. You just wait by the boat while I change." She grabbed her holdall from the back seat and made for the clubhouse. But she was out again in a few minutes, dressed only in a sweater and shorts with plimsolls on her feet. Her long dark hair was tied up behind her head. John noticed the admiring glances that followed her as she crossed the dinghy-park towards him.

"Not bothering with the waterproofs?" he asked innocently.

To his surprise she blushed. It made her look quite pretty. "No time. Race starts in quarter of an hour. Help me push her to the slipway. Then I'll hang on while you bring the trolley back. We'll need to hurry."

When John returned from parking the trolley, she told him to hold the bow while she climbed into the dinghy to ship the rudder and centre-plate and to raise the sails. He stood thigh-deep in the water. Down here the breeze was more noticeable. It made him shiver. He thought perhaps she was right and the two of them would be frozen by the end of the race.

"OK. Push the bows out and pull the side of the boat towards you," she instructed. "Now - you can get in behind the shrouds - just there. That's right - sit here beside me. Grab that sheet and pull it in gently. That's enough."

They were off. Already they seemed to be moving remarkably quickly. Alison manoeuvred the tiller as they worked away from the slipway, swooping over the short wavelets. As if to celebrate, an explosion cracked out above their heads.

"Ten-minute gun," explained Alison. "There's one at five, and the minute guns start at three. You will have to work the stopwatch. Here it is. Hang it round your neck on the lanyard. The reset button's on the top. Press once to start and again to stop. Twice to reset. Is that clear?" She looked about her at the other boats. "I think we'll get upriver out of the crowd, because I've got to teach you how to go about. We do that whenever I shout "Lee-oh"."

In the next few minutes John was introduced to the first few rudiments of sailing. Alison seemed surprisingly patient, explaining where to sit and what ropes to hold. But when the five-minute gun came, they had to start working their way down to the starting buoy.

"Water. Water. Out of the bloody way." Ambrose and Adam went creaming past, leaning out as they swept by. "Pull your finger out, Alison, and watch where you're going."

John turned to see Alison's eyes blazing with fury.

"Why's he moving so much faster than us?" he asked.

"What?" She shook her head. "Oh, he's on a reach, while we're tacking. It's a faster point of sailing in this wind. But he's also got one of the new moulded hulls. Only weighs half as much as this one and slips through the water better. Nothing but the best for brother Ambrose."

John wondered at the bitterness in her voice. Perhaps this pampered, favoured girl didn't always have everything the way she wanted it. For the first time he felt an unexpected sympathy for her. He was quiet, thinking about it, as they tacked across the river.

She explained the course. "First we go downriver to Turf.

That should be a straightforward reach in this wind. Then we run across to Riversmeet Buoy in the mouth of the Clyst with the wind behind us. You can't quite see it from here. Then we've got to work back to the start. That'll be the problem today, especially on the second lap when the tide will be ebbing fast and the mud-banks will be starting to show. That's where Adam's so good. He knows the river like the back of his hand. He can tell you whether you'll get through some of the channels before the tide runs off. There have been times when I've been sailing with him, with the plate right up and less than three inches of water under the keel. The boat following thirty yards behind us was left high and dry when the water suddenly rushed off the top of the mud-banks. Do you understand what I'm talking about?"

"Of course I do." John's voice was a bit sharper than he had intended.

A boom downriver gave them a sense of urgency.

"Start the stopwatch," instructed Alison. "That's the three-minute gun. They come at one minute intervals now. The tide's still making a bit so we'd better get as close as we can to the starting buoy. But we must stay behind the start line, that's an imaginary line from the flag on the starter's balcony to the buoy where all the boats are. If you're not this side of the line, you have to turn back and cross it again before you can start racing."

John looked at the press of boats jostling round the buoy. "Wouldn't it be better to keep a bit clear of the others? Then we could approach the line at speed with no-one in the way."

"If there was any sense in that," she said witheringly, "everyone would be doing it."

"But if you keep going like this, you'll cross the line too early."

Alison stared at him. "How can you tell that?"

"I don't know." He shrugged. "Just by eye, I suppose."

She suddenly made a decision. "All right then. We'll see if you're right. Let's go about. Come on," she shouted. "Lee-oh."

John ducked under the boom as it swung across and hauled in on the other jib sheet as she'd told him. The dinghy crept across the river towards the mud-banks on the other side. Its sails quivered as it appeared to head straight into the wind. John watched the burgee at the mast-head which gave the lie to this sensation.

The two-minute gun boomed.

"The stopwatch is right," said John

"We'll have to go about again before we run aground." Alison was fidgeting. "Nobody else is so far from the line. Ambrose will think I haven't got the guts to race."

"Look at them," he indicated. "They're all flapping about, getting in each other's way."

At that moment there was a scrape below them.

"Up plate," she screamed. "Forget the jib sheet. Pull on that rope before the wind has us over."

The dinghy stuttered to a halt, sails flapping wildly as John hauled up the heavy cast iron drop-keel. The boat fell away before the wind with its bow pointing upriver.

"Oh, Christ," cursed Alison. "We'll be the laughing-stock of the clubhouse. Why the hell did I listen to you?"

"Can't we get moving again?" said John.

"We haven't got room to go about. We're going to have to gibe. That could be dodgy in this wind." She was on her feet. "You sit down in the middle of the boat."

The minute gun echoed across the river.

"We're going to be miles behind." Alison was almost weeping with frustration. "Forget the jib. Grab hold of the boom and, when I say so, pull it across to the other side. Are you ready? Now! Pull like hell."

John struggled to pull the boom over his head as she hauled in on the main sheet. Then he stood up to beat the wind out of the bellying sail when she told him, and the boat rocked violently.

"Quick," she screamed. "Sit up on the gunwale or we'll capsize. Now - drop the plate half-way and pull in on the jib."

For a few seconds it was all frantic activity.

Then -

"Oh, you little beauty," she breathed.

Suddenly the dinghy was transformed from a mess of sails and ropes into a smooth, racing thoroughbred. It accelerated towards the line like a greyhound released from its leash.

"How long have we got?" she asked.

John checked the stopwatch. "Forty-five seconds."

"Are we going to make it? Will we make it?" She seemed to be talking to herself.

"Pull a bit closer to the wind," he suggested, and checked the stopwatch again. "Thirty seconds."

Now they appeared to be heading directly for the buoy. But he knew the tide would carry them off it.

"Fifteen seconds."

Alison was laughing like a demon as they came hurtling down on the mass of flapping boats. "Water. Water," she screamed. "Out of my bloody way. Get off the fucking river, Ambrose."

Miraculously they seemed to miss everyone. The starting gun boomed and the next second they creamed round the buoy and headed down towards Turf. Looking back, John could see that the other boats had suddenly all straightened up and were purposefully pursuing them downriver. A couple were on the other tack, clawing back towards the buoy. One of them was her brother.

"Ambrose cocked it up," she exulted. "He collided with one of the others and they've both got to restart. It'll take him an age to catch us."

But in fact the moulded-hull boats were soon closing on them. Alison and John were still in the lead when they rounded Turf buoy. Running before the wind across the river, they just managed to hold their position. But close-hauled on the third leg, they were overtaken by several of the lighter boats, and they rounded the start buoy to begin the second lap in fifth position. Even more galling for Alison was that Ambrose was now only just behind them. On the first reach of the second circuit he drew level.

"Get that old tub out of my way," he mocked. "I don't know why you waste your time with it, Allie. It's only fit for going fishing."

"You're taking my bloody wind, Ambrose," she yelled.

"Come and get it, then."

John watched her breathlessly as she screamed at her brother, "If you get too close, I'll ram you. I promise I will."

"Not a chance. Bye, old thing." His mocking laugh came across the water as he altered course a point and presented his stern to them.

Alison fumed with frustration. She accused John of not keeping the jib tight enough. Then he'd got too much plate down. He was trailing a sheet in the water. But no matter what they did, her brother drew inexorably away from them.

On the run to the Riversmeet buoy the wind began to die away and blow in fitful, irregular puffs. The boats trailed each other, rocking gently on the smoothing water. They had to set their sails goose-winged to catch whatever breeze they could. But the lightweight hulls moved even further ahead. The leading boats rounded the mark ten minutes ahead of them and started to cross the mud-flats towards the main channel.

When they reached the turning-point the ebbtide was already bubbling round the buoy. They began to creep back across the river.

"I don't know whether we'll make it across the flats in this wind," said Alison anxiously.

John tore his eyes away from contemplation of Riversmeet House. "Why don't we follow this side-channel," he suggested. "We'll be helped by the tide for the first part. And then we'll be on a reach back to the finish."

"It's half as far again," she wailed. "Ambrose will leave us miles behind."

"He will anyway. We're seventh at the moment, and we're not going to catch that lot up. Our only chance of beating them is if they run aground."

Alison looked at him oddly. "All right. Why not? Maybe you're bringing me beginner's luck. You were right about the start. Perhaps you'll be right about this."

Five minutes later she was cursing him again as the wind almost died away altogether. They found themselves drifting along with the sails hanging limply most of the time.

"But look at the others," John pointed out. "They're just as bad."

The lead boats, separated from each other by no more than fifty yards, lay motionless above their broken reflections. Astern, the rest of the fleet was scattered, some following John and Alison, some risking the short cut across the mud-flats and some still creeping towards the Riversmeet buoy.

As John watched, the water a few yards from them made a sudden swirl and a gurgle. It was as though a great, gleaming monster moved just below the surface. Then it heaved itself gently upwards and the water rushed off its shiny, cratered back. He let out his breath with a sigh. The tide had dropped to expose the mudflats.

"God, look at that."

He looked to where she was pointing. The six leading boats were suddenly all awry, their masts at strange angles, their sails loose and flapping. Already the crews were out of the boats and walking round them, ankle-deep in water and soft mud. They were pulling down sails, trying to right the boats. They'd all been left high and dry.

Alison clapped him on the shoulder. "Isn't that bloody marvellous," she exulted. "You really *do* seem to bring me luck. Now all we need is some wind to get us back to the finish before the committee decide to abandon the race."

As if she'd been heard, there came the sigh of a breeze and the sails flapped a little and filled. Gentle and fitful at first, but steadying and increasing all the time, the new breeze out of the South West blew them home to a resounding victory.

It was more than two hours later when the rest of the fleet managed to drag themselves off the mud-banks and limp home. John and Alison had cleaned the boat and stowed it away long before the others arrived. Then they were treated to drinks at the bar. Alison was the centre of attention, complimented by everyone on her victory. She revelled in the success, particularly in beating brother Ambrose, who had returned mud-covered and weary. Then John became aware that a group of younger sailors had gathered round them, and here came Ambrose.

"Come down to the jetty," said her brother to the two of them. "We want to make a little presentation."

Despite his suspicions, John went with them down the steps and along the floating pontoon to the end where the last of the ebb tide swirled around the muddy uprights.

"We always have a little ceremony when a new rookie has

his first taste of success." Ambrose had a broad grin on his face. "Are you ready lads?"

John was grabbed from behind. His feet were lifted from under him. He found himself suspended by his legs and arms in the middle of a laughing mob. He noticed Alison was one of them.

"Why me?" he protested. "I was only the crew. Why don't you do it to the skipper?"

"Come now, John." Ambrose quizzed him. "Where's your gallantry? You wouldn't expect us to throw a lady in."

"I don't see why not," said John. "Women float just as well as men."

He was being swung backwards and forwards. The momentum was building up. He looked up at the circle of grinning faces. Alison and Ambrose were together on his right arm, their earlier vicious rivalry forgotten.

"OK, lads. One - two - three."

As John swung upwards and outwards, he made a despairing grab at Alison's loose sweater. With a scream she followed him in. They landed together with an explosion of spray in the mixture of deep mud and dirty water.

John struggled to his feet, waist-deep in the disgusting mixture. He looked round, waiting for Alison's spluttering fury to emerge. She came to the surface with her hair plastered over her face and her clothes filthy.

"I don't know why I haven't learned about you," she shouted at him. "You always get me into some sort of a mess. You're nothing but bloody trouble, John Tucker." But, to his astonishment, she was laughing.

He helped her across to the end of the jetty and she let him put his arm round her as she stumbled up the steps. Mud and water were pouring from their clothes as they made their way back to the clubhouse and the hot showers.

"I reckon you owe me a drink when I've showered and changed," she said.

He suddenly felt full of cheek. "I haven't got a change of clothing. I'd better go home and have a bath. So – instead of a drink, how about if I take you out for dinner this evening?"

She paused for only a second. "All right," she agreed. "Pick me up at half past seven."

So John squelched home, well pleased with himself.

44

Alison took a lot of care with her appearance as she prepared for dinner that evening. She wasn't quite sure why. She'd had enough education in social matters by now to be able to judge both John, and her attitude to him. He wasn't the sort of person she particularly admired or was likely to be interested in. His social graces were decidedly stunted. Although he spoke well, he had an unfortunate habit of being very direct in his personal comments, which would get him kicked out of any decent house in London as soon as he started airing his opinions.

It was true that he was tall and slim and good-looking in a slightly Nordic way, but he wore his mousy brown hair cut too short, and he tended to hunch his shoulders and jut his head in a way that looked almost aggressive. As far as she was aware, he didn't ride or shoot or even play golf. And he was far too bloody clever for his own good. His unfortunate wife, when he acquired one, would struggle to keep two steps ahead of his thinking. She could imagine he would be jealous, demanding and a thorough bore to live with - not at all the person for someone similarly self-centred - like her.

Then why, she asked herself as she backcombed her hair with the dryer, should she be taking so much trouble? She thought about it and decided it was the element of competition, that she felt when she was with him, which led her to make the effort. She had the uncomfortable and wholly unusual feeling that, while they were talking, he was watching her and judging her actions. Most men she went out with were only interested in discussing themselves, the people they knew or the latest places they'd visited. They didn't actually take any interest in her as a person. They only seemed to exist because of their contacts with others.

John Tucker, for all his humble origins, was the first person she had met who seemed to exist in his own right. She had the oddest feeling that, even if the rest of civilisation were to be swept away, he would still be able to stand up on his own. He was intensely individual. In fact, he was quite a frightening person to know. That was why she had to be ready for him.

She put on her simple pearl necklace and the matching single-drop earrings. As she did so she heard the doorbell ring, but she didn't hurry to go downstairs. Annie, the cook, would go and let him in. She didn't think her father would want to be introduced to him, so he could be left to wait in the hall or in the morning-room. He ought to find that a little daunting. It should put her one up on him for the start of the evening. She wondered what he would be doing when she got down there.

Here came cook now, puffing up the stairs, to tell her of his arrival. What would she make of him? There came a tap at the door and the old dear poked her nose round the door.

"John Tucker's 'ere, my lovely." She paused and clasped her hands together. "My - you do look nice."

There was something funny about her expression.

"What's the matter, Annie?"

The cook took a cautious breath. "Is 'e takin' you out tonight, my lovely?"

"Why? Shouldn't he?" Alison demanded. "He hasn't got the plague, has he?"

"Oh, no." The old dear scratched her head. "But that's a *lovely* outfit you've got there, my dear."

Alison sighed. "It's only a bloody cocktail dress, Annie. I'm not expecting to be presented at court or anything like that."

Cook ducked her head to one side in embarrassment. "But 'e's only wearing a blazer and an open-necked shirt, my lovely."

"He's *what*! I thought -." Alison leapt to her feet and grabbed her stole and evening bag. She went out through the door, along the corridor and down the stairs two at a time before cook could utter another word.

At the foot of the stairs she froze. She saw that the glass doors to the central bookcase were wide open for the first time that she could remember in her life. John Tucker was standing there, leafing through one of the ancient, morocco-bound books.

"What *are* you doing?" Astonishment robbed her question of any sting.

He smiled up at her innocently. "Pardon."

"What are you doing with that book?"

"I was looking at it. I decided to while away the time until you were ready." He smiled at her disarmingly. "It's really quite interesting."

She heard cook gasp behind her.

"But nobody ever takes those out of the bookcase," said Alison. "They're probably worth thousands."

John looked up at her. "Well, I can tell you that they won't be worth thousands for much longer. They're in a dreadful state of preservation. Look at the mildew on these pages and the way the leather's turned green around the bottom of the spine. They'll be unreadable in another few years."

"Nobody has *ever* read them." She was horrified. "Nobody has even had them out of the bookcase. Please put that one back straight away."

He shrugged. "OK, but you ought to suggest to your father that he gets some advice from an expert on the preservation of those books before they become worthless." He returned it to its place on the middle shelf and turned the key in the door. "This whole place is obviously dreadfully damp."

Alison ignored his advice. "I thought," she said heavily, "that you'd offered to take me out to dinner."

"That's right. Are you ready?" He smiled infuriatingly. "You don't need to hurry. I know you ladies like to take your time."

She drew herself up to her full five foot eight. "The question is, are *you* ready?"

"What do you mean?"

"They won't let you into the Royal Clarence dressed like that." She nodded at him. "You can't even get into the Cranford in the evenings without a tie."

His hand strayed towards his throat. "Ah, that. Don't worry, we're not going there. I don't need a tie where I'm taking you."

"I am *not* going to some bloody pub for a snack dressed like this."

"You look absolutely devastating," he said seriously, "and you'd slaughter everybody wherever you went. I promise you'll go down a wow where I'm taking you. Oh - and it's not a pub."

"I'm not sure that I want to slaughter everybody, as you put it." But Alison found it difficult to remain serious with him. "Where *are* we going then?"

He grinned. "Do you know The Harbourside."

"Where's that?" she demanded.

"It's a very pleasant little restaurant at Teignmouth which specialises in shell-fish. They will only have been landed just this afternoon. They're always delicious."

She pouted. "But I shan't know anyone there."

"Is that important?" John couldn't resist a shrug.

"It means," she said viciously, "that I won't be able to talk to anyone but you all evening."

To her fury he actually grinned. "All right, you can bring a book. But please hurry up. I'm ravenous. Mud-swimming is obviously good for the appetite."

Alison decided she couldn't still be angry with him. "Come on, let's get going." Then she had a sudden thought. "You're not planning to take me on the pillion of a motor-bike or anything like that, are you?"

"How *could* you think such a thing?" He feigned shock. "Mind you, my car's not very special. You'll be used to much smarter vehicles with your other escorts."

But when they got outside, she saw it was a nice little Hillman. The seats were quite comfortable, and he even turned the heater on low to combat the cool evening air. They had a pleasant drive across the Haldon Hills with the sun setting far to their right over the high tors of Dartmoor. The conversation was gentle, relaxing.

They arrived at the restaurant just after eight. Alison waited for him to get out of the car, but for some reason he was fishing around in his blazer pocket. The next moment he'd pulled out a striped tie. "I'd better look my best if I'm escorting such an elegant young lady."

"You sod, John Tucker," she exclaimed. "You were working me up all the time."

He grinned as he did up the tie in the mirror. "Alison, you must try not to be so predictable. Ouch," he exclaimed as she punched him in the bicep. "Is that the way you always resolve your arguments with men?"

"No, it isn't." His comment made her think. "In fact, you're the only man I can remember who has annoyed me enough to make me feel like hitting him."

"If I try hard enough, I might turn that into a strange sort of compliment." He got out of the car and slammed the door.

As he opened her door, she replied. "You're the only person who would have enough conceit to see a compliment in it." But he didn't seem to want to argue any more.

It was the start of a good evening. The little restaurant was a delightful place, almost the equivalent of a French bistro. The seafood was delicious - as good as any she'd tasted in London or Geneva. Even the wine was passable.

She entertained him with tales of her experiences at finishing school, the strange standards of the nuns and her forays with friends into surrounding France and Switzerland. He told her a little of his work at Grant's and the developing fitted furniture and building business which was starting to bring him in more money than he would ever earn as a surveyor. Three hours passed quickly, and it was well after eleven when they set out for home.

They pulled up on the gravel drive outside Stacey Court at a quarter to twelve. There was still a light on in the hall, but the rest of the house seemed dark. Cook would have gone to bed and Ambrose wouldn't be home for at least a couple of hours. Her father would still be in his study at the side of the house, but he would be well down his bottle of gin by now. She would just poke her nose round the door to say goodnight and he would mumble something. Suddenly it seemed a bare, empty place to live.

She turned to look at John. He was leaning back, watching her.

"What are you thinking?" she asked.

"I was wondering," he said, "whether you'd let me kiss you goodnight."

She leaned her head back. "Of course. That's only fair, isn't it, after you've spent all that money on me."

"I'll be a little more gentle than I was when I kissed you last."

She said nothing but turned her face as he moved towards

her. He kissed her *very* gently. In fact, his mouth seemed surprisingly soft and inviting. His lips were slightly parted, and the cold straight line of his teeth came through them. But that made the kiss even more exciting. She wanted him to kiss her some more. She opened her mouth in invitation and he responded by kissing her all around her lips. They seemed to massage their faces together, parting only for a gasping breath before they did it again.

Only then did she become aware that his large, warm hands were stroking her body through the silk of her dress, raising ripples of excitement around her ribs and in the pit of her stomach. Maybe it was the wine she'd drunk, but she didn't want him to stop. His lips slid off her face and he buried his head in the hollow of her neck. She took in a great, gasping lungful of fresh air and pulled him against her, feeling the muscles of his back under her fingers. He worked his mouth down her chest and she knew he was going to pull her dress down and kiss her breasts and she wanted him to do it. Then suddenly he stopped. He let go of her and sat up.

She became aware there was a knocking on the window. It was Annie, the cook. They sat up and adjusted their clothes and Alison wound down her window.

"Oh, I'm so glad you're 'ere, my lovely. It's your dad. 'E's flat out on the floor an' I can't move 'im no matter 'ow 'ard I try."

"What's the matter -?" began Alison.

But John was out of the car. "Where is he?"

"In 'is study. Through the library an' on the right at the back."

John ran across the gravel, up the steps and disappeared into the house. Cook hurried behind him. Alison straightened her clothes rather more slowly. She got out of the car and followed them. By the time she reached the study, John and cook had lifted the old man onto the *chaise longue* and loosened his tie. But his face still looked deathly white.

"Have you rung the doctor?" asked John.

"Yes, just afore I saw you was back. 'E should be 'ere any minute."

Alison was looking round the room. She went over and

picked up a little bottle from near his desk. She read the label.

"Oh my god! This bottle had aspirins in it. But there are none here now. Do you think he's swallowed them all?"

"Get a bowl," ordered John and Annie scuttled out. "Here, help roll him over." He stuck his fingers into Sir Oswald's throat, thinking how he'd have liked to have done it if the fellow had been conscious.

Stacey didn't respond at first. Then he coughed. John poked again and he spluttered and retched. A little fluid came up. John repeated the treatment and he retched more violently once and then a second time and the whole lot came up. The cook arrived with the bowl just in time to catch most of the evil smelling liquid. There was little in the way of solids in it.

"I think it's mainly gin," said John. "How much will he have drunk tonight?"

Alison retrieved a bottle from the wastepaper basket. It was empty.

"I din' do 'e no supper tonight. 'E said 'e'd get 'isself somethin'" said Annie.

"I don't think he got that far," said John. "I presume those little white balls are the aspirin tablets. There must be at least twenty of them." He pushed Stacey onto his back where he lay and snored with his mouth open. "You'd better keep that bowl to show the doctor. But I should think you can clear up the mess on the floor."

Cook busied herself with mopping up and Alison went to get another bowl in case her father was sick again. She returned bringing the newly arrived doctor with her. John explained what they had done.

"Well, that seems all right," said Doctor Morton. "You can throw away that stuff. Will you all wait outside while I take a look at him? You can stay, Alison, if you wish."

So John found he was left on his own while cook disappeared into the kitchen with the bowls. He went outside and closed the car windows and collected the ignition key. Then he came back and sat at the foot of the stairs.

He didn't have long to wait. The study door opened, and Doctor Morton came out followed by Alison.

"It's not too serious," he said. "Sir Oswald has come round

now. He said he had a bad headache. It appears he must have taken an accidental overdose. On top of the alcohol, it would have been enough to kill him. Fortunately, you made him sick before he could absorb too much aspirin and he should be fine in the morning." He turned to Alison. "I think it would be as well if he slept in the study tonight to avoid overworking his heart by taking him upstairs. I'll call round and check up on him in the morning. But I don't expect there will be any serious repercussions." He nodded. "Good night, then."

"I'd better leave you," said John. "It's late and you'll be wanting your beauty sleep."

"Thank you for helping – for being here."

He smiled crookedly. "That's all right."

"I enjoyed tonight." She came over and kissed him, but pulled back quickly, aware that cook had returned and was watching.

"Cheerio." John walked down the steps, got into his car, started up, and drove away from the disaster that was Stacey Court.

45

John was waiting in his car outside her home when Susie was dropped by taxi at just after half past five. She paid the driver and went indoors, apparently without noticing him. He gave her five minutes to take off her coat before he went and knocked at the door. She opened it almost immediately.

"Hello, Susie. Can I have a short chat with you?"

He saw the fear leap into her eyes. "Why?"

"Look, it's nothing to worry about." He shook his head. "I just want to ask you if you're willing to do something for us. You'd get paid for it."

"Us? What is it, John?" She was obviously deeply suspicious of his intentions.

"Can I come in just for a minute to tell you about it," he urged. "If you're not interested, I'll go as soon as you ask me to."

"All right." She stood reluctantly aside to let him in, and indicated the living room door. John walked in. "Can I sit down?"

She nodded silently.

He sat in one of the big comfortable armchairs. He noticed that Susie remained standing.

"Susie, can I first of all explain something about myself that I hope will set your fears at rest." He had been thinking about this carefully. "Less than a year ago I had to give up my degree course at Cambridge and I was fairly fed up about it. However, since then I have got myself a job at Grants. I have also started up a business with my friend Sammie Joslin, which is going very well, and I am about to start another business project which is what I want to talk to you about." He paused and took a breath. "I have a girlfriend at Sheffield university. I've recently started to get friendly with Ambrose and Alison Stacey, and I have another very good lady-friend, who I'm going to talk to you about now. I have no interest in any secrets - er - arrangements you may make with anybody, unless they connect in some way with my affairs, which I'm sure they don't." He looked at her very directly. "So you have no need to fear me. In fact, I would like you to regard me as a business friend - nothing more. Do you understand what I'm saying?"

She shook her head hesitantly. "Not really."

"I've probably not put it very well." He sighed. "I'll approach it from the other side. I'd like you to keep what I'm going to ask you to yourself, even if you refuse to help me with it." He stretched out his hand placatively. "It's nothing illegal or wrong in any way, but we don't want certain people to hear about it yet. Will you agree not to talk about it to anyone else - in the same way that I'll keep quiet about anything that you tell me? That obviously means that, if I let you down, I know that I'll suffer as well."

There was a pause while she digested this. "All right. That seems a fair deal."

"Thank you." He took a breath. "Well, what I want to ask is not very difficult. The situation is this - Sarah Grant, my boss's wife, has recently inherited some money from her father. For her own personal reasons, she doesn't want her husband to get his hands on it. Instead she wants to invest the money in property development. Is that clear so far?"

She nodded.

"So you can see already why I want you to keep it to yourself. She has started a limited company to run this development business and has asked me to be a director of it. Don't ask why she has chosen me. She seems to think I have the potential to be a success at this sort of thing, and I guess it's got something to do with the fact that I'm a young chap, who's less likely to go off in whatever direction I choose for myself and therefore I'm more likely to do what she wants me to do." John grinned and was rewarded with an answering smile.

"Well - as I say, she's been to an accountant in Plymouth who arranged the limited company for her. She doesn't want to appear on the list of company officials in the new company in case her husband decides to check up on this new development company. Therefore she's asked me to be the company director. But we also need a company secretary. The long and the short of it, is that she asked me if I knew anyone who might be suitable. You had already told me that you'd done this kind of thing in London. So I thought you would be the right person to ask, and I also thought your other experiences would make you realise it was important to keep the business confidential."

She put her hand to her mouth. "But what about the job I've just started at Stacey Court?"

"Oh, it wouldn't affect that job in any way. This position wouldn't involve you in much work (at least, not to start with) so it's something you can do in your spare time. You'd just be a name on the company register and would be asked to sign a few documents from time to time. We'd pay you a pound an hour for your time plus any expenses."

"I suppose that sounds all right." But she was still a little hesitant.

"If the job were to become more demanding," he said, "you could choose whether to come and work for us on a full-time basis. Otherwise you would resign, and we'd have to find someone else." He half shrugged. "By then the whole thing would probably be out in the open and Sarah would have made peace with her husband. The question is, would you be willing to help us?"

Susie smiled and nodded. "Of course I would."

"That's great."

John jumped up and gave her a hug. She seemed to like it and smiled radiantly up at him. The next moment they were kissing with surprising passion. Suddenly realising he shouldn´t be doing this to a married woman, he broke off and stepped back.

"I´m sorry, Susie."

"That´s all right. I liked it." She gave another little smile. "I don't think I've ever met a man before who was quite like you, John."

"Really?" He blinked. "The fact is that I'm pretty naive in my dealings with other people. I expect you've been used to much more sophisticated men."

"Maybe I have. But It´s a lot nicer dealing with you." She seemed to be relaxing now. "Do you want a cup of tea?"

"Have you got any coffee? I quite like instant."

She nodded. "Of course I have. Do you like milk and sugar?"

"Just milk." He followed her into the kitchen. "How do you find the fitted cupboards? Are they as good as you hoped?"

"They're super. I'm really pleased with them." He found her enthusiasm stimulating. "They're so easy to keep clean, and all the worktops are great. What a difference from the ancient stuff they've got at Stacey Court."

"I bet." John leaned against the sink and regarded her. He realised he had come close to putting his arms round her again and he forced himself to think of other things. "How's your new job going?"

"Well - I like it." She hesitated. "But it's quite a strange place to work. I haven't got an office of my own. I've just been given a desk in the corner of Sir Oswald's study."

"I was there last Saturday night. Did you hear about the overdose he took?"

"No!" exclaimed Susie. "What on earth happened?"

So he told her about finding Stacey unconscious on the floor and the subsequent events.

"That would explain why he was in bed for a couple of days at the start of the week," she said. "The funny thing was, that I had to go up to his bedroom and go through his post with him and take some dictation. But he never said anything to me about the overdose. He just said the doctor had confined him to bed for a few days."

He shook his head. "Working for Stacey is not like a normal job, is it?"

"I haven't really got enough to do at the moment," she admitted. "I was told that I was also going to do work for the estate manager. However Mr Cavanagh (he was doing that job) gave in his notice before I started." She handed him his coffee.

"He didn't last very long."

"Everything's in utter chaos at the moment. I don't know what's going to happen. Sir Oswald's going to have to make a decision about it." Susie picked up her cup of tea and went back into the living room. He followed her and they sat down facing each other. Now that she had started, the talk seemed to flow out of her. "People keep ringing me up and asking what's going to happen about the leaks they've got in their roofs and all sorts of other repairs. Some of them get quite nasty, and threaten to withhold their rent and that sort of thing. I just don't know how to handle them."

"It sounds as though old Stacey needs an urgent replacement for Cavanagh." He smiled at her. "Did you know that my dad used to be the estate manager until he died last year? When I was a kid, I often used to go round with him to look at the various properties."

"You wouldn't like to take it on now, would you?" Susie enquired hopefully. "Whenever I pass on these complaints to Sir Oswald, he just says, 'They'll have to wait till the new estate manager comes'." She shook her head. "But he's done nothing about advertising for a replacement and it's going to be months before someone starts. Meanwhile the complaints are starting to build up and I think he's going to have some serious problems on his hands before too long."

"I couldn't take it on," said John. "I've got too much else on my plate in my spare time. I don't see why Grants couldn't do it though - at least as a temporary measure while he's finding a new estate manager. Of course, they'd expect to charge him for the privilege, but it would only be on a time-basis for the actual hours they put in. By the sound of it, he needs to sort out something fairly quickly, before he starts to have problems with getting the rents."

"That's a good idea. I'll suggest it to Sir Oswald. Then, whenever I have a complaint, I can ring you up and ask you to deal with it, and you can send me a report when you've solved it."

John grinned. "I don't think it would be me you'd speak to. Probably Mr Grant or his partner would want to deal with something as important as that. Anyway, if old Stacey is interested, you can tell him to ring Mr Grant."

"I'm definitely going to do that." Susie stood up. Now she was all sharp and efficient. "Sir Oswald has got to take this matter seriously."

"Otherwise," he said, changing the subject, "you've settled into your new life happily enough, have you?"

"I love it down here," she confided. "You've no idea how dreary it was in London. I love the countryside and the less complicated life. Lionel doesn't seem to be impressed with

Devon. He still spends a lot of time in London. He's a Londoner at heart. So I only see him at weekends. For the rest of the week, he's away up there or travelling round the country."

"What a strange chap he must be." John shook his head, mystified. "He's got a well-furnished new house and he's married to such a pretty wife, and yet he ignores them most of the time. I must say I don't understand him."

Susie smiled. "You claim to be innocent, young John, but it seems to me that you're very good at flattery."

John had the feeling that an opportunity was there to make more of their relationship if he chose to, but he decided he ought to leave things as they were at the moment. Susie was something of a mystery to him. So he steered the conversation onto more general topics and left her after he'd finished his coffee.

46

"I've got a problem," announced Rosemary.

Jill snorted. "Haven't we all. They're called men."

"How did you guess?"

"I wasn't thinking of you, lassie. My problem is that shit, Alastair."

"I thought he'd gone back to Aberdeen and good riddance, you said."

"He did," she wailed, "but now I miss the bugger."

Rosemary sighed. "It looks like we've got the same problem. The question is, what do we do about a solution?"

"You mean – 'Come back, lover. Everything's forgiven.' Not very subtle, is it. And I'm not sure it would work with Alastair."

"I'm sure it *wouldn't* work with John."

"John? You mean that gorgeous guy I saw you with at the start of term?"

"He's been my boyfriend since the fifth form. Everybody assumed we were going to spend the rest of our lives together, but that doesn't seem very likely now."

"What went wrong?"

"Well," Rosemary shrugged. "I think it all started to fall apart when his dad died last autumn. His mum decided she couldn't afford to keep him at Cambridge to finish his degree, so he had to leave and find a job. A few other things went wrong at the same time and he sort of felt the world was against him."

Jill shook her head. "Sounds like he's got a right chip on his shoulder. But that's none of your fault."

"He didn't exactly blame me for it. But he kept on making comments about the fact that I was still studying, and he had to go out and earn money."

"Huh. He should complain. At least he doesn't have to try and exist on a student's grant."

"Oh, he knows that," said Rosie. "He's a clever bloke and he's doing very well. He's got himself a car and two jobs and he's got quite a bit of money saved now. In fact, money and success seem to be all he's interested in now. That – and other women."

"What do you mean?"

"You know how it is." Rosemary shrugged her shoulders. "Boys are always trying it on – hoping you'll be drunk or so keen on them that you let them do what they want. Of course, John's been like that as well and, like the others, he never used to argue when I said 'No'. However recently he's got a lot better at it. He makes it much more difficult to hold him off."

"And you're complaining?"

"Well, I keep wondering where he learns it all. There are several local girls who I think he might be interested in, and who probably wouldn't refuse to let him have his way with them. And then at Easter I found he was spending quite a lot of time at a married woman's house." She tossed her head. "Oh, there was a good excuse. He was fitting out a shower-room for her or something like that. But I made a few enquiries and found out that her husband was away while he was doing all this."

"Wow. Did you accuse him of having an affair with her?"

"No. I didn't accuse him of anything. I just told him to be careful."

"What did he say to that?"

"Oh, he made light of it, of course. And I didn't have any actual evidence - only a few suspicions. But it meant we had a fairly fraught time over Easter."

Jill frowned. "It seemed to be all right between you when he brought you back after the Easter hols."

"It was," said Rosie. "He's a different person when I get him away from Devon and the influence of that woman. In fact, we were getting on so well that I thought – well – I thought, why not let him go all the way. I thought that if he was having it with other women, then perhaps I'd better let him do it with me. The way we felt when we kissed – it was like an explosion – I thought he ought to find it better with me."

"Bloody hell, girl. That sounds a bit dangerous. Were you drunk or something?"

Rosemary smiled bleakly. "I *was* a bit squiffy, I suppose.

But I really wanted it. Anyway, it turned out that he wasn't prepared. He didn't have a durex."

"So that was that."

"No. Not exactly. I'd just finished a period, so I said I was willing to take the risk. In any case, if things went wrong and I got pregnant – well, then we could get married." She took a deep breath. "And, do you know, he turned me down. I felt so humiliated. I lost my temper and said, that if he wasn't willing to commit himself, then he'd better get out. And," she concluded quietly, "he went."

There was a long silence. Finally Jill said, "And now you wish he'd come storming back."

Rosie gave a little nod. "There's never been anyone else for me like John. And that's not just childish idealism. I like everything about him, even though I feel he's sort of moved on and left me behind. But I want to catch him up again if I can."

"So how are we going to get him back again?"

"I don't know."

"I take it that it's no good just writing and apologising."

She shook her head. "I did that once before when we had another row."

"Did it work?"

"Not really. Oh – we made it up and things were all right for a while. But we soon started moving apart again. In any case, I don't think I want to try that again. I think I've got to do something in my own right – to show him that I'm meeting him on equal terms. Do you know what I mean?"

"I think so." Jill pulled a face. "But it's bit difficult for you to do much until you've finished your degree. Perhaps *then* you can become your own person."

Rosemary nodded slowly. "I think you're right. I've been thinking about it a lot. I was all ready to go back to Exeter and get a job in the county library when I finished my degree so I would be near him again. But I'm not sure he would be pleased about that. Now I wonder whether to take the job I′ve been offered in London. It would be my statement that I'm choosing to go in my own direction. The only thing is how to get it through to him."

"Just tell him you're going to London. That should make

him think. If I was in his shoes, and I was really keen on you, I wouldn't like that at all. After all, London's nearly as far away from South Devon as Sheffield is."

"I know," agreed Rosie, "and that's my problem. Before, I would have taken the Exeter job without hesitation. I'm not that worried about carving out a brilliant career for myself, although my tutor would be horrified to hear me admit it." She smiled weakly. "If John would tell me how he really feels, I would be able to decide. But I don't know how I can get him to talk about it."

"That's easy. Invite him to the graduation. You can work on him then and at the ball afterwards. Make yourself really desirable, the way I know you can. You'll be a sure-fire success. By the end of the night he'll be begging you to give it all up and marry him."

That made Rosemary laugh. "I love your optimism, Jill. But I do think you're right in one respect. The graduation would be a good way to get the message across to him. I'll make sure I send an invitation to him. Oh," she giggled, "and I'll use the excuse of asking him to drive my parents up to the event so that he thinks I'm only using him. He can hardly refuse to come then, can he?"

Amid many giggles they proceeded to plan the detailed entrapment of John Tucker.

47

Sir Oswald Stacey was having a sandwich and his first gin of the day when Alison walked into the library. "We're back, daddy. How are you feeling today?"

"As well as can be expected." He put on his sad, bloodhound expression.

"It would help if you kept off the gin," she suggested. She didn't feel like being sympathetic at the moment.

"I don't know about you youngsters these days." Her father sniffed with self-pity. "Don't they teach you any respect at these finishing schools?"

She ignored him. "We had a lovely time at Caroline's ball. Even Ambrose said he enjoyed it."

"You'll have to make the most of this season, Alison." Stacey shook his head. "I shan't be able to continue your allowance for much longer. You're going to have to find someone else to pay your bills."

"What are you saying?" she demanded. "Are you telling me I've got to get married or something? Don't forget I'm only just twenty-one."

"Your mother was barely twenty-two when we were married. It's a perfectly good age for marriage. It's only after you're married that you can begin to carve yourself out a place in society."

"Daddy," complained Alison, "that might have been all right before the war. But things have changed now. Not many people get married straight after the season nowadays. I'd certainly like a few years to look around before I decide."

Her father pulled another long face. "Well, who am I to advise you. I wish your mother was here to tell you the right way to go about it." He shook his head again. "But I have to tell you that I cannot pay for you to gallivant around for several years while you're making your mind up."

"What do I *do* then?" She spread her questioning arms wide.

"I would have thought it was obvious," said Sir Oswald. "You find somebody else to pay for you or you provide the funds yourself."

"But daddy - what happened to all the money that mummy left for me?"

The old man shook his head mournfully. "It's all gone. That damned finishing school of yours cost me an arm and a leg. Of course," he suggested, "you could always get a job."

"A job?" demanded Alison furiously. "What sort of a job?"

"I don't know." His bloodshot eyes gazed at her. "What have you learned at Saint Theresa's?"

"Oh, god knows - how to talk to people, how to be a hostess, how to dress properly - that sort of thing." She shook her head. "Nothing that would help me to get a job."

Stacey wagged his finger at her. "I don't know so much. Nowadays there are all sorts of openings for a good-looking, presentable girl. I'm told there are positions for receptionists and private secretaries and things called personal assistants. What you need to do is bend the ears of some of these swains who escort you about and dance with you at these balls and things." He dismissed them with a wave of his hand. "You've got to sell yourself, instead of spending all your efforts on having a good time and doing various mad things that you won't remember the next morning."

"That reminds me." Alison laughed. "Ambrose and some of his friends threw George Ponsonby-Smythe in the river."

"Hmm," he snorted. "That sounds like the kind of puerile behaviour I'd expect from your brother. Where *is* Ambrose by the way?"

"Just putting the car away. He'll be here in a minute." She returned to her memories of the party. "George deserved it. He was drunk and was being pompous. Do you know, he actually said in front of me, that he mightn't mind marrying some daughter of the - "rustic squirearchy" - he called it. Those were his actual words." She straightened up. "Of course, I realised he was referring to me. Well, I told Ambrose and he told George to withdraw and when he wouldn't, Ambrose threw him in the river."

"Goodness gracious!"

"There were plenty of people to help him do it, I can tell you. It made Ambrose quite popular for the rest of the evening."

Stacey snorted. "I can't understand such foolish behaviour." He drained his glass and poured himself another double. "It won't help him when he's looking for a job. The Ponsonby-Smythes are an important family. They know a lot of the right people in London."

"Everyone laughed when it happened," said Alison.

"I don't need the help of the Ponsonby-Smythes." Ambrose came into the room. "I've got an interview of my own next week with Henri Maeterlinck."

"Who?" His father peered at him distastefully.

"Henri Maeterlinck. He's a partner in Schubert's, the merchant bankers."

"Sounds like a hun to me," said Stacey.

Alison turned her eyes to heaven. "Don't be such a bloody snob, daddy. He's Austrian."

"Same thing." Sir Oswald shook his head dismally. "They were on the same side in the war."

"Well, Henri wasn't," she countered. "He was educated at Harrow and spent the war over here. His mother's an English countess. He seems more British than you or Ambrose."

"Oh," said her father triumphantly, "then he's a damned Jew, I expect. That's why he's in Schubert's."

"Well, you'd better get used to it, father." Ambrose slumped down in the chair across the desk from the old man. "I met him last night at Caroline's and I've got a formal interview with him on Thursday. He as good as told me he'd offer me something. Apparently they want a presentable type on the sales front."

"And," said Alison, "he's coming to call on us in three weeks. He's planning a touring holiday in the West Country."

"Calling on *us*?" Sir Oswald was startled. "Why does he want to come here?"

Ambrose snorted. "Why do you think he wants to come here? He's interested in our little girl, of course." He turned to her. "Have you slept with him yet?"

"No, of course I haven't. Henri's too much of a gentleman to suggest that sort of thing right away. That's the sort of behaviour I'd expect from some of the reprobates that *you* hang around with."

"I don't want a Jew interested in Alison." Sir Oswald stood up, his head shaking uncertainly, his gin temporarily forgotten. "It would make your grandfather turn in his grave."

"Why shouldn't he be interested in Alison?" demanded Ambrose. "If I'm prepared to go and work for the bugger, why shouldn't Alison climb into bed with him?" He shook his head. "We don't even know he *is* a Jew anyway. And if he is, so what? They're the ones with the money these days. I would have thought *that* would interest you."

Stacey looked from one to the other, his determination wavering. "You say he's a banker?"

"Not just a banker," said Ambrose. "He's a partner."

"How old is he?"

He shrugged. "I don't know - late thirties, forty?"

"He's just over thirty-five," said Alison firmly.

"Is he good looking?"

"No." Ambrose chuckled.

"Well," said Alison diplomatically, "he's quite nice really. He's a bit like a cuddly teddy bear."

"He's short, bald and has an idiot grin," said Ambrose. "But who cares? He is *seriously* rich."

Sir Oswald came close to smiling. "Very well," he said. "You may present him to me when he calls. I suppose we've got to learn to live with all types. Now leave me to finish my lunch."

He resumed his seat, reached for the gin bottle and topped up his glass.

48

When John called in to Sarah's for their regular Wednesday evening meeting, she had the news all ready for him.

"We've got our approval. I had the chief planning officer round here yesterday afternoon and he confirmed the committee passed it in the morning."

"Whoopee, we're in business." John gathered her up and swung her round in the hall.

Sarah couldn't help thinking how much nicer it was to feel his strong, young arms round her than the furtive, clammy grip of Harold James which she'd had to endure for an hour and forty minutes the previous day.

"Let's go upstairs and celebrate. You say Reggie's away tonight." He grabbed her hand and rushed her up the staircase, two steps at a time. In the bedroom he pulled her into his arms again. "You're looking all pink and pretty. It suits you to be an entrepreneur."

"Is that what you call me?" She let her head fall back as he began to kiss her neck and transfer his lips towards her cleavage. "I feel more like a female Machiavelli, with all my manipulating and organising."

"I'll tell you what you feel like. You feel softer than silk and as juicy as a ripe peach." He had her blouse undone to the waist and was sliding the strap of her bra off her shoulder.

"Well," she squealed, "don't take a bite out of me in your excitement. I might find that hard to explain to my husband."

"Don't worry. Your delicate skin is safe with me. All I want is your virtue." And he tossed her onto the bed and pushed her skirt up around her waist. "Hey - you haven't got any knickers on."

She parted her legs joyously. "I might have known that's all you're interested in. And it's too late for me to scream now. You'd better have your wicked way with me while I close my eyes and think of England."

"That's not all I want," he threatened. "I also want a half your wealth. I'm not just a ravening sexual beast. I'm also possessed by demonic greed."

"Oh, that's all right then." She giggled. "You had me worried for a minute."

"But," he said, "we have to get our priorities right."

Sarah gasped as he entered her. "Oh, John. I think a lot of your priority."

"Your body comes top of my list at the moment, my darling. You could say you're at the top of my in-tray."

Maybe it was the way she was lying, arched over the edge of the bed, but she reached one of the quickest orgasms she had ever achieved. John's climax came at just the same moment and it continued for what seemed a long time.

"Oh," he moaned, "that was almost painful. Was I too quick for you again, Sarah."

"No, you certainly weren't, my darling. I was right there with you. I think I'm learning to be faster at the same time that you're controlling yourself better," she gasped. "But can you please move? You're breaking my back."

Without uncoupling they wriggled their bodies onto the bed and he collapsed on top of her with one leg hanging over the side.

"Oh, Sarah," he murmured in her ear. "It's so good being with you."

She said nothing, but she hugged him to her. At that moment she felt really happy. They lay there quietly for a time as the excitement drained out of their half-clothed bodies.

"So, when will we receive the notification and the forms?" he asked at last.

"I don't know exactly. But my friend Harry said he'd try and hurry it through for us."

He supported himself on one elbow and looked down on her. "Well, I can start getting set up for the diggers to move in. I've got some quite competitive quotes, as long as they can get the work done before the winter rains start. We'd better see about putting some signs up. Shall we use Barkers as the front company? They can organise the selling and everything if you like."

"That´s a good idea," she agreed. "That would avoid some of the risk on this first project. What does Sammie Joslin say about it all?"

"I think he's happy to leave it to me." John absent-mindedly stroked the fine hair behind her ear. "He thinks we've bitten off more than we can chew. But I've promised him that all the financing will come from this mystery developer. And your offer of five thousand up front has helped. I've taken on Barker's foreman, Angus McIntyre, to run the site and he's really excited about getting his teeth into a proper project at last. Over the last few years, he's only being doing little refurbishment jobs. I think the man's going to be quite good."

"That's nice," purred Sarah. "You also said on the phone

that your little friend, Susie, is willing to be company secretary. Does she know about me?"

He nodded. "But I explained why you wanted your position kept confidential, and she understood. I think there's some sort of complication in the relationship between Susie and her husband, but I haven't had the cheek to ask her about it yet."

"It all sounds most mysterious." Sarah smiled, half to herself.

"I'll tell you about it when I know the facts," said John. "Meanwhile I was going to suggest we could all meet at the accountant's on Saturday morning to sign the necessary papers. Would that suit you? I'm not working this Saturday and Susie says she can pretend to Lionel that she's going shopping."

Sarah agreed. "That won't be a problem for me. I'll set it up for ten-thirty."

"And then we're all ready to start." He let out a large breath.

"We ought to have a celebration drink," she giggled.

"All right then."

He rolled off her and got to his feet. He washed himself in the smart new shower-room and tidied his clothing. Then he went into the boudoir to pour out the drinks. He didn't need to ask her what she wanted any more. As he finished pouring she walked in, wearing her silk dressing-gown. He watched her as she drew the curtains. He could tell she had nothing on under the thin silk and already he felt the urge rising in him again. It boded well for the rest of the evening.

Sarah was looking down into the drive. "Good god," she burst out, "here comes Reggie."

"Bloody hell! What do I do now? I'd better get out fast."

"Don't be silly." Sarah seemed calm again. "He's seen your car. I'll have to explain that to him." She walked took a breath. "Here's what you have to do. Tidy your clothes, go downstairs and wait in the sitting room. Turn the light on. He'll take the car round to the back to park it. He always spends several minutes wiping it down. He thinks more of it than he does of me." She gave him a little push. "Go on. I'll be down in a minute, and I'll bring some stuff that we can say your mother sent you round to collect for the Women´s Institute jumble sale. Is that clear?"

"OK."

John scuttled downstairs with his drink. He went into the sitting-room, turned the light on and sat down with his heart beating. He tried to look as though he'd been casually waiting for the last ten minutes. After a little while he heard a door bang at the back of the house. A light came on and a few seconds later Grant appeared.

He looked in at the door. "Good heavens. It's young Tucker. What on earth are you doing here?"

"Oh, hello," said John with a nervous gulp. "I'm -. I'm collecting some stuff for my mother. Sarah - er - Mrs Grant is upstairs getting it at the moment."

"Stuff? What stuff?" Was it John's imagination or was the man´s tone rather aggressive?

"Um - I don't know exactly." John's hands flapped guiltily. "I gave the note to Mrs Grant."

"Oh -." Grant nodded. "I see you've got a drink."

"Yes. Your wife offered me one while I was waiting."

His boss threw himself in a chair. "I could do with one of those."

"Oh," said John. "Right."

"Can you do me one?"

"Yes - er-. Where is it?" He gulped. "I mean -"

"Over there, of course." Grant gestured impatiently in the direction of the huge sideboard which stood at one side of the room.

John rose to his feet and started towards the drinks. At that moment Sarah swept in carrying two huge brown paper bags. She was dressed in trousers and an old shapeless sweater. John could see, from the sag of her breasts, that she wasn't wearing any underclothes.

"Hello, dear," she said casually. "Now then, John. That's all the jumble I can put my hands on at the moment. Tell your mother I'll see if I can come up with some more in the next few days."

"Oh. Oh, thanks."

She turned to her husband. "I wasn't expecting you back tonight, Reggie."

"No," he said. "I had to change my plans. In fact, you're

involved in it, young Tucker."

John gulped again. "I am?"

"Yes. I was called over to see Sir Oswald Stacey and his secretary this afternoon. Pretty little thing she is. What's happened to that drink?"

"I'll get it for you." Sarah made for the sideboard.

"Anyway, Staceys want Grants to take over the day to day running of the property on the estate. Apparently the estate manager's gone missing. The secretary bird asked for you personally. Says she knows you, or something. Obviously you impressed her somehow or other. I shan't ask how. Ho, ho - what."

"Don't be crude, Reggie," said Sarah, bringing his drink. "We're not in your club now."

"Oh. Sorry, my dear. Well, apparently it's very urgent. So I promised we'd get on with it straight away." He turned back to John. "You'd better come in and see me first thing in the morning, young fellow."

"OK, I'll do that." John drained his glass and got to his feet, anxious to get away. "Thank you for the jumble, Mrs Grant. Give us a ring if you've got any more, and I'll come over and collect it from you."

He made for the door and Sarah accompanied him. As she opened the front door she said to him, "I want those clothes back again, John. Keep them in your car boot and let me have them back at our next meeting."

She let him kiss her briefly on the mouth and then he was crunching across the gravel to his car with a large carrier bag in each hand.

49

Summer had come to Sheffield a few days before the graduation ceremony took place, so the crowds of families and friends were able to turn up with the men in their smart suits and the ladies wearing pretty dresses and colourful hats. Sammie had to admit it was a splendid sight as he drove in to the university campus.

Rosemary was waiting for them at the bottom of the grand steps to the senate building. She was resplendent in her long black gown with the green and white striped trim and was carrying her mitre-board. She came rushing over to greet them and then froze when she saw Sammie. This was the moment he had been dreading. He took a deep breath and opened the car door.

But Mr and Mrs Williams were ahead of him. They leaped out and rushed to hug their daughter.

“Oh, Rosemary, don’t you look smart.”

“Isn’t it exciting? This is the proudest moment of my life.”

Sammie walked gingerly round the car. “Hello, Rosemary.”

“What’s happened?” she asked, a look of horror on her face. “Is John all right?”

“Oh, it’s such a pity for him,” said her mother. “He was so disappointed. And it was so kind of dear Sammie to step into the breach the moment John had to pull out.”

“I was pleased to have the chance,” said Sammie.

Rosemary’s face was still frozen. “But what’s happened to him?”

“There’s nothing to worry about, my dear.” Mr Williams pulled himself up to his full height. “John had a very important meeting which came up at the last minute and which he couldn’t get out of. Apparently his company has just been given all the work for the Stacey Estates and the meeting was set up by his boss with Sir Oswald for this morning. They’d asked for him personally and John said he didn’t feel he could let them down.”

“I see. It was easier for him to let *me* down.” She nodded.

"John always gets his priorities right."

"Oh, don't be like that, my love," her mother cooed. "He knew how disappointed you'd be. He was disappointed as well. But he said that the most important thing was for *us* to be here for this afternoon's ceremony. So Sammie, bless him, moved heaven and earth to make arrangements to step into John's place. He's driven us all the way here with only one stop."

"That's kind of you, Sammie. John's lucky to have you as a friend." Rosemary gave a bitter little laugh. "You're the sort of person he doesn't deserve."

"Now be fair, Rosemary," said Mr Williams sternly. "John's got a lot on his plate at the moment. You can't expect him to spoil his business opportunities just to come to your graduation ceremony."

"Actually I was pleased to do it," interrupted Sammie. "We've got the company set up now so that I can spare the odd day off. And it was rather nice to have a break. I've never been to something like this before. Also I've enjoyed driving his car." He turned to the others. "It's very comfortable, isn't it?"

"Oh, it is," agreed Mrs Williams enthusiastically. "John didn't hesitate about that. He filled it up with petrol and arranged to get himself about by taxi. I'm sure he did everything he could so as not to spoil your big day."

Rosemary turned away dismissively. "Of course he did. It doesn't matter to me, anyway." She straightened her back. "Now - come with me. I've got nice seats for you near the front of the balcony. I'll show you where they are, and then we can go and have a buffet lunch before the ceremony starts."

"Buffet lunch? Isn't it exciting, Harry." Mrs Williams bustled along behind her daughter.

"I'd better just go and park the car," said Sammie.

"OK. You'll see the parking areas sign-posted over there." Rosemary pointed. "We'll meet you in the marquee on the side lawn. Mum and Dad will show you where the seats are later."

Sammie got to the marquee before the Williamses. He hung around near the entrance until they turned up, and then they queued for their lunch. Rosemary arranged for him to be in front of her in the queue.

"I really do appreciate you putting yourself out like this, Sammie," she said. "I don't want you to think that I'm annoyed with you for being put in the firing-line by John. He's the one with the excuses to make."

"Rosemary, I promise you John was really disappointed about letting you down." Sammie smiled a little too readily. "He only heard yesterday morning about this meeting and the fact that it had to be him attending personally. Stacey Estates must think very highly of him."

Rosemary shrugged. "He's got to decide what his priorities are. I suspect that John will always be having those sorts of things happening to him. The question is," she looked at him quizzically, "are you here to substitute for him in all ways."

"I don't understand what you mean?" Sammie felt himself going pink.

"First of all I'd better explain about your accommodation." She giggled. "Don't look like that, mother. I've booked you and daddy into a private hotel just round the corner from our lodgings. But I haven't got you tickets for the graduation ball. I assumed that you wouldn't want to be the only adults among a thousand youngsters."

"You can say that again," said her father.

"I'm afraid that means I won't see you this evening." She tucked her hand through her father's arm. "I assumed you'd like to go to the pictures or something like that tonight. There are loads of lovely cinemas in Sheffield with all the latest pictures on. Is that all right?"

"Of course it is, my dear," said Mrs Williams. "Have you booked a room for Sammie as well?"

"Well - no. That's just it." Rosemary smiled unconvincingly. "The ball will go on until dawn and afterwards we'll probably all go down into the city centre for an early breakfast in the market. It's ever such good fun. But we won't be doing a lot of sleeping so I thought there was no point in booking a room that wasn't going to be used." She turned back to Sammie. "Of course, I thought it was going to be John."

"Is that going to be all right with you, Sammie?" asked her mother anxiously.

Sammie hoped his grin looked confident. "Of course it is.

I've had plenty of nights without sleep before."

"You can have a rest in my room this evening before we go to the ball," said Rosemary. "It doesn't start until nine. And then you can have another sleep after breakfast tomorrow, before we set off back, while I'm showing Mummy and Daddy round the city-centre. Will that be enough, or do you want me to see if I can find you a room?"

"That's no problem." Sammie shook his head. There was a worried look on his face. "But John didn't warn me about any ball and I've only got this one suit. Will it be all right to wear that?"

"Of course it is. Perhaps I'll see if I can borrow you a more colourful tie." She patted his arm. "But don't worry. The men will be dressed in all sorts of things. The ball is mainly a chance for all the girls to show off their ball-gowns."

Sammie's mouth dropped open. "Have you got a ball-gown?"

"I'll be wearing the same thing that I wore to the hunt ball at Easter." She smiled. "It's quite lucky in a way, because you weren't there and so you haven't seen me in it. All my friends will want to know who my new escort is."

They had reached the head of the queue. "Here, Sammie," she said, "take one of these plates and serve yourself to anything you want."

Sammie did as he was told. But he only had half his mind on the excellent food in front of him. He was also trying to cope with the idea of being the official escort of a very pretty girl in a beautiful dress for the first time in his life. There would be a whole evening of dancing and heaven knew what else. He was in a reflective mood as they filled their plates and found a half-empty table and the others chatted their way through the splendid fare.

50

John took the pool car when he went to inspect the North gatehouse to the Stacey Estates. He parked the car under a tree just inside the gate and walked back to look at the house. It had once been a rather fine single storey building of cut limestone with a slate roof. But the beautiful pediments were now badly spalled by the frosts and there were signs of wet rot in the window frames.

He walked over and knocked on the door. After a couple of minutes a middle-aged woman opened it. She had a cigarette dangling from the corner of her mouth.

"Mrs Harris?" asked John.

"That's right."

"Hello, I'm from Grants, the estate agents. I had a call from Sir Oswald Stacey's secretary this morning. She asked me to inspect your property. I understand you've been having some problems."

The woman removed her cigarette. "'Bout bloody time someone came to look at it. We bin complainin' for more'n a year now, since they did the alterations to the roof, an' you're the first person we seen."

"What alterations did they do?"

"I dunno." She shrugged. "Took off the lead an' put on some new modern stuff what they said was better. All I know is - it 'a'n't bin any better. 'Ere," she beckoned, "come an' look at this."

Obediently John followed her into the hallway and from there into what he presumed was the living room. The place was very untidy. He immediately saw that there were large black stains on the outside walls which hung down from the ceiling like great festoons of spider's webs. The wallpaper below the picture rail was bubbling and peeling away from the wall.

"I tried to wipe that black off," she assured him, "but it just come back again after a few more days. Look in the corner 'ere."

He looked to where she pointed. He could see that the ceiling was badly discoloured and it sagged under the weight of water which had seeped into it. In one area a small piece of plaster had broken away from the supporting laths.

"May I?" He took a chair to the corner and stood on it to inspect the ceiling more closely. He poked his pen into the plaster. It was soft and had clearly been subjected to a lot of moisture.

"Thanks." He returned the chair to its former position.

"It's the same in every room." She took the cigarette from her mouth and wiped her hand across her upper lip. "Come an' look."

John followed her from room to room, noting the same problems, nearly always on the outside walls and the ceilings near the eaves.

"This were a lovely 'ouse when we come 'ere nearly eight year ago," said Mrs Harris. "Me and my Charlie really loved it. We was as snug as two bugs 'ere. Fact is, that's the only reason that Mr Tucker what's dead now got Charlie to move from 'is old job." She shook her head. "We wouldn't never 'ave come if the 'ouse wasn't so nice. *Now* look where it's got us."

He was interested. "You knew Mr Tucker, did you?"

"Yes." She nodded. "'E were a nice gen'leman. We was all right when 'e were 'ere. But nobody seems to bother no more."

"Well," said John, "I'm his son. I've only just been asked to look into the problems by Sir Oswald. But I promise you *I'll* bother."

"Oh." She turned to regard him, removing the cigarette from her mouth again, the better to look at him. "What you goin' to do about it then?"

"I want to find out the cause of the problem first," he said earnestly. "To do that, I think I need to go on the roof. Have you got a ladder I can borrow?"

Mrs Harris put the cigarette back in her mouth and thought for a moment. "Yeah, I think Charlie's got one in the shed out back. I'll show you where."

She led John through the kitchen to the back door. From there she indicated the shed. "It's not locked. Just lift the latch."

John went to look in the shed. It was large - virtually a garage. When his eyes got used to the gloom he made out a timber ladder in a somewhat doubtful condition located between the roof trusses. With some difficulty he got it down, carried it outside and leaned it against the rear wall. Then, taking his life in his hands, he mounted it with his clipboard between his teeth. The ladder was too short to get quite to the top so he had to reach up and put the clipboard on the parapet, and then he had an uncomfortable moment while he felt over the parapet for a hand-hold to pull himself onto the roof.

As soon as he was there, the cause of the problem became obvious, even to someone as inexperienced as he was. Where the hips and gutters and copings to the top of the walls would once have been covered with lead, they now had a kind of pitch material spread over them. The pitch had expanded and contracted with changes in the temperature. It now had many cracks in it. In some places it had peeled away from the stonework and the roof slates. This was obviously allowing water to seep in when it rained. He could see places where complete pieces of the material had broken away and there was nothing to prevent the water from soaking into the roof timbers. John began to feel quite unsafe walking around on joists and rafters which might already be half-rotted through.

Gingerly he made his way back to the top of the ladder. Mrs Harris was standing near the bottom. She had started a fresh cigarette.

He called down to her. “Who exactly told you that this new material was better than the lead which was already here?”

“I dunno.” She shrugged, shaking the ash off her cigarette. “The man what done it, I s′pose.”

“Do you know who *he* was?”

She shook her head vacantly, gazing up at him.

“Why did you let him go ahead and do it, Mrs Harris?” he asked, a shade brusquely.

She stiffened at his tone. “Nothin’ to do with me. ’E said ’e’d bin sent by Sir Oswald Stacey. Warn’t no right of ours to stop him comin’ in, were it?”

John sighed. “I suppose not.” Very carefully he eased himself back over the parapet on to the top of the ladder, remembering at the last minute to pick up his clipboard.

Then he had the business of putting the ladder away. He returned to the back door to find her still standing there with the cigarette in the corner of her mouth, a wisp of smoke drifting into her yellowing hair.

"Well, Mrs Harris," said John, "I think I know exactly why you've got these problems. I must say I'm not *at all* happy about the work that's been done on your roof. I'm going to go back to my boss and report what I've found. Then I'm pretty sure some action will be taken to rectify your problems. In any case, I'll come back in a few days and tell you what's happening. Is that all right?"

She nodded rather vaguely. "I suppose it'll 'ave to be."

John reached out and shook her hand. "Well, I'll see you again soon."

He left her gazing after him with the butt of her cigarette shrinking towards her hairy top lip, and drove back to have a chat with Bill Kingley. He was full of misgivings. He had a nasty feeling that, in taking this job on, he'd bitten off a bit more than he could comfortably chew.

51

When Rosemary came out of the bedroom dressed in her ball-gown she took Sammie's breath away. He thought he'd never seen anyone who looked so beautiful. He half rose to his feet then sat down again, unaware that his mouth was wide open.

"What's the matter?" She grinned at him. "You look as though you've seen a ghost."

"What? Oh - sorry." He wanted to tell her that he felt more as though he'd seen a vision than a ghost, but he didn't quite dare say that to John's girlfriend. "You look absolutely fantastic, Rosemary."

She coloured and arched her back. "Well, it's nice to be appreciated by *someone*. Here, I've got a brighter tie for you to put on."

Her comment brought Sammie back to earth. "I'm sorry. I'm going to look an awful mess beside you. John's been on at me to get some smarter clothes, but I've never bothered before." He gulped. "I see what he means now."

"Rubbish." She patted his arm. "You're not going to look a mess at all. Just pop into the bathroom and brush your hair and put this tie on. Then remember to stand up straight. You're very good-looking, Sammie. All you need is a little bit of self-confidence."

"Really? Do you mean it?" He scuttled off into the bathroom to do as she said.

When he came out again Rosemary had put her coat on and had hidden the beautiful dress, except where it burst out from the restraints of the coat around her ankles. But her lovely golden hair was still there, gathered up in a mass of curls behind her head.

"Come on then." She took hold of his arm. "It's not far to go. And the weather's nice. Don't forget what I said about standing up straight."

Sammie felt prouder than he could ever remember as they walked down the street, round the corner into the main road, and the further quarter of a mile to the main entrance to the university. There were dozens of people going the same way, some of whom Rosemary greeted. But none of them, to his mind, looked a fraction as beautiful as she did. He fancied that other people were looking at him. He didn't doubt that they were wondering to themselves how he had managed to get the position of escort to someone as lovely as Rosemary.

They mounted the steps and went into the Senate Building. In the entrance hall she left him to put her coat in the cloakroom. He stood in a corner, trying to be as unobtrusive as possible. When she reappeared his heart sank, for she was with a group of several girls. Even as he watched, they were already being surrounded by a number of smart young students. He knew he didn't stand a chance of matching up to them.

Then Rosemary saw him. She beckoned him over and came to meet him. Suddenly he was in the middle of everything, being introduced to everybody as her boyfriend's business partner, having a dozen immediately forgotten names thrust at him. But he was surprised to find that everybody was interested in him. He was being asked questions about what sort of business he was in, how many people he employed, was the business expanding. He began to realise that he was knowledgeable about a subject outside the experience of these clever students. The realisation did wonders for his self-confidence.

As a group they drifted into the main hall where the graduation ceremony had taken place. It was now cleared of the rows of chairs which had filled it this afternoon, so as to make room for the dancing. Around the edge were dozens of large tables, each surrounded by chairs. Rosie's group occupied one of these. Nobody seemed to object when he took the seat beside Rosemary, and he continued to busily field questions as best he could, until the band started playing, and conversation became more stilted. Sammie sat back to watch the others.

Rosemary turned to him. "Would you like to dance?"

He shook his head. "I can't."

"Of course you can," she urged. "Everyone can dance. All you have to do is shuffle around in time to the music."

"Well, I'll have a go, but I don't think I'll be much good."

She giggled. "Don't worry. I don't mind a few damaged

toes."

She got to her feet and Sammie followed her onto the dancefloor.

"How do you feel, now you're here?" she asked.

"Actually I quite like it. Your friends weren't as intimidating as I'd expected."

"Intimidating?" She seemed astonished at the suggestion. "Of course they're not. There's nothing to fear from this lot."

He tried to make amends. "I agree - now that I've met them. They seem a very nice group of people. Are these the ones who've been taking the same degree course as you?"

"Yes, mostly," she said. "They're a good lot. We've had plenty of fun together. It's disappointing that we're going to have to break up now that we´ve graduated. But everybody's promised to keep in touch. We'll try to meet up somewhere in a few months' time to compare notes on our forays into the big, bad world."

"Oh. What are *you* planning to do in this 'big, bad world'?"

Rosemary sighed and shook her head. "That's the problem. I can't make up my mind. I was thinking of going into library work and I've been offered a job in the central library in Exeter. But I've also recently been offered a research post in the V & A in London and that is quite exciting. It would be a really good career move, as well as paying more money. My tutor says I'd be mad to turn it down."

"Blimey," said Sammie. "I shouldn't think John would be very pleased about you going to London. I know I wouldn't like it if I was in his shoes."

She nodded. "I know, and that's the problem. Before, I would have taken the Exeter job without hesitation. I'm not that worried about carving out a brilliant career for myself." She smiled. "And it *would* be nice to be living at home again."

"Oh." Sammie sighed with relief on behalf of John. "There's not a problem then."

"Well, I'm not sure." She pulled a face. "You see, John was saying at Easter that it was important that we both developed our own careers. He said we couldn't possibly think about anything like marriage until we were both properly established." She added hurriedly, "Not that we've ever talked about any firm arrangements anyway. But I think that John might want to encourage me to take the London job for a couple of years." She tailed off. "He's sort of got used to me not being around all the time."

"Well, if I was John, I wouldn't think like that at all. I'd want a person as pretty as you to be somewhere close to me where I could keep an eye on you," said Sammie forthrightly.

Rosemary couldn't help laughing at him. "Sammie Joslin, you're so old-fashioned you're almost feudal."

"I'm sorry." Sammie blinked with embarrassment. "But that's how I feel."

She gave him a heart-stopping hug. "I don't mind. I think it's rather sweet." She shook her head. "But John is much more modern in his approach. I suppose I'm just going to have to discuss it with him, and sort out how he feels about the whole thing, before I give my reply to the museum." She sighed. "I was going to discuss it with him tonight if he had come. I must definitely sort it out next week."

They lapsed into silence as they danced, both thinking their own private thoughts. Sammie had to admit that he didn't understand John sometimes. If he had a beautiful girlfriend who seemed to be waiting for him to make up his mind about their future together, he wouldn't have a problem in coming to a decision. He'd snap her up straightaway before somebody else became interested in her.

But Rosemary's thoughts still seemed to be with the doubts she had about John. At last she said, "There is one thing I'm bothered about. What do you think about this Sarah Grant woman?"

"Sarah Grant?" Sammie was startled. "Do you mean John's boss's wife?"

"That's right. What do you think of her?"

He decided that he had better be careful. "Well," he said, "I don't really know her. I've only met her a couple of times."

"Didn't you do that job for her at Easter?"

"Yes, we did," he admitted, "but I didn't have much to do with that. John did most of the work himself. I only went round there for a few hours to help him finish it off. And I only saw her briefly then."

"Just a minute, Sammie." Rosemary had halted in the middle of the floor, her eyes glittering. "Do you mean John did most of the work himself, without you helping him?"

Sammie was puzzled. "Well, yes, but that was all right. It didn't the need two of us most of the time. And John could call me up if ever he needed me. He made a couple of little mistakes and he took quite a lot longer to do it than I thought he would - but otherwise it went OK. I thought it was good experience for him."

"I *bet* it was," Rosemary burst out.

"What do you mean?" He felt extremely nervous. Was she about to blow up at him?

"Oh, don't *you* worry," she said hurriedly, sensing his embarrassment. "It's just that I don't trust women like that. They don't seem to follow any of the normal rules. Have you seen anything of her recently?"

"What - Mrs Grant?" Sammie shook his head. "I think she keeps well clear of me. I wasn't very pleased when she turned up on the cinema job and started throwing her weight around. I told John about it and I think he must have said something to her. I noticed, when I went to her house, that she looked at me a bit carefully."

"Indeed!"

He thought that Rosemary managed to imbue that one word with a wealth of meaning. He had a nasty feeling that she wasn't happy about something he'd said. In fact the evening, which had seemed to him to be developing rather well, became gradually duller. Rosemary seemed to retreat into herself. A couple of her friends even joked to her about it, without getting any real response from her.

Rosemary decided she wanted to leave the ball far earlier than any of the others and later Sammie found himself trying to sleep on the settee in the sitting-room at her flat. There were people forever coming and going, wanting to stop and chat or drink cups of coffee. He felt thoroughly miserable. It was as though Rosemary had thrown him onto the scrapheap. He wondered what on earth he'd done wrong.

52

John was full of misgivings when he pulled up in front of Stacey Court. He'd discussed the problem of the roof to the North gatehouse at some length with Bill Kingley, and they'd agreed there was nothing they could do other than to put the facts in front of Sir Oswald Stacey. The Grants were on holiday for the week. Bill had had nothing to do with this side of the business and Mr Cartwright refused to get involved. The responsibility rested on John's shoulders. But he didn't relish the prospect of coming face to face with the man he hated above all others.

He got out of the car, mounted the flight of steps to the front door and rang the bell. While he waited for someone to come, he looked round. Although Stacey Court still looked splendid from a distance, it was less elegant when seen from close up. A lot of the projecting stonework on the main face of the building had spalled and worn away. The once splendid portico above the front door was crumbling at the edges and, as far as he could see from the detritus surrounding the house, the main cornice at roof level must be in the same condition. The window frames showed signs of rot, inadequately covered by a fairly recent coat of paint. The gravel drive was well-raked, and the borders weeded and the grass trimmed. But the hoop-iron fencing alongside the drive was rusted and bent, and wouldn't withstand the onslaught of many more winters. To the competent eye the whole place was showing signs of neglect.

John's reverie was interrupted by the door opening behind him. He turned to find himself face to face with Susie. As usual her bright appearance and cheerful smile lifted his mood.

"Hello," she said. "We got your message that you'd be calling. Sir Oswald will see you in the library. That's the room I now use as my office."

"How are you settling in?" he asked as he followed her into the hall.

"I love it." She smiled and shepherded him through the main reception room. "I never thought I'd have the chance of working for a real baronet in such a lovely place as this."

She led him across another reception area and into the smaller library on the corner of the house. Through the tall french windows he could see there was a wide terrace and then the land fell away, providing great vistas of parkland interspersed with occasional large trees and grazed by cattle. John had to admit that it was still a splendid sight.

"Will you have a coffee? Sir Oswald will be down in a minute."

"Yes please."

Susie poured him a cup from a silver jug on a tray which had obviously been prepared for them.

"I must say, Susie," said John, "that you seem to have taken to this life like a duck to water. You even talk with a slightly reverential quietness." He took a sip of his coffee which was already only lukewarm.

Susie's laugh was infectious. "Do I really? I suppose the atmosphere of the place gets to you after a while."

"And is the organisation of the Stacey Estate now running like clockwork?"

She raised her eyes to heaven. "There wasn't much organisation when I came. I think my predecessor was a genteel woman who had been taken on by Lady Stacey to keep track of her engagements and gradually she had been handed more and more of the estate duties. As far as I can tell, she never had any secretarial training." Susie shook her head. "There was no sort of filing system at all - just a diary - and a lot of letters were thrown away when they seemed to be out of date. It's going to be a long job getting things into order."

"Do you do the accounts as well?"

"Not yet, she doesn't." Sir Oswald stood in the doorway. "We have to be sure of her trustworthiness before she can take on that part of the job. Well, young man, Mrs Partridge tells me you want to report to me about your inspection of the North Lodge."

John noticed Susie blush and wondered how long Stacey had been standing there listening to their conversation. He guessed not long.

He said, "Yes. I thought it was sufficiently important to

bring to your attention straight away."

"All right." The old man inclined his head. "Go on then."

John handed over the three pages of typed foolscap. "This is the detailed report for you to read at your leisure. But briefly, all the outside walls of the building are running with damp and the living conditions inside are below what one would normally consider the minimum for healthy occupation."

Sir Oswald's only reaction was to raise his eyebrows. "Really?"

"The reason for this deterioration is that somebody stripped all the lead out of the gutters around the perimeter of the roof, and off the valleys and hips, and replaced it with an inferior pitch material which has cracked and lost adhesion in a lot of places. There are now dozens of leaks all round the building."

"Oh - ." There was no sense of regret in the old man's voice. It seemed as though he was merely disappointed that John had managed to discover the cause of the problems.

"In addition," said John, "the lead has been stripped off the copings and cornices. This has allowed moisture to soak into the stone. Frost action has caused the stonework to start to crumble. Within five years the building will be damaged beyond repair, unless urgent and expensive remedial action is taken."

Sir Oswald said nothing. The silence seemed to stretch into an eternity.

John ventured a further comment. "I have discussed this with my superior. It seems to us that somebody has stripped all this lead off in order to sell it. The price of lead has become extremely high since the war. The cheap material which has been used to replace it is useless. Somebody has effectively committed theft against the estate."

John paused, breathing slightly heavily. He was aware he had just made a serious accusation against somebody unknown. He was expecting Stacey to be either furious or suspicious of his conclusions, but he didn´t react at all.

"In our opinion you should take action as soon as possible against whoever did this damage." John paused. Then he went on hesitantly. "Er - we think you could recover the cost of replacing the lead on the building. There is also the cost of repairs to the stonework and redecoration to the interior. You would have a substantial claim against the perpetrators of this - this crime." He paused again, but there was still no reply. "Remedial action should be taken before the winter sets in. Would you like us to talk to your solicitors?"

The old man still said nothing. John wondered if he had understood what he was telling him.

"I really think it's urgent that -."

Sir Oswald shook his head. "*I* will speak to them."

"Pardon," said John, a shade insolently.

Stacey raised his eyebrows. "Thank you for your report, young man. I will read it thoroughly and talk to my solicitors, and Grants will receive my instructions in due course." He raised his hand as he saw John was about to speak again. "Please leave it to me. I will now deal with it."

John subsided into silence.

"Goodbye." Stacey inclined his head slightly and left them without another word or a backward glance.

After a minute John turned to Susie. "I think he knows more about this than he's saying. Do you think he's protecting someone?"

"What do you mean?"

"This lead wasn't just taken by some casual thief. Whoever has done it, has replaced the lead with another material, although it is cheap and inadequate. Somebody on the estate must have known about it. Whoever that person was is as guilty as the thief."

"I see," said Susie slowly. "Perhaps that's why he won't let you talk to his solicitor. Perhaps he wants to speak to somebody himself before he takes action."

John had a sudden idea. "That estate manager must have known something about it. What was his name?"

"Do you mean Mr Cavanagh?"

"Maybe. From what you said he must have left about two or three months ago."

"I've got his letter of resignation here." Susie went to the pristine new filing cabinet in the corner. "This is one of my innovations. I managed to get him to buy it, although he didn't want to. He hates spending money on things like this." She searched through the files and emerged triumphantly with a letter in her hand. “Here you are. I don’t see why you shouldn’t read it, since you’ve taken over the job.”

The letter was very brief, comprising only three short sentences giving notice of Cavanagh’s intention to leave at the end of March. No reason was given for his decision and there was no information about where he was going. John made a note of the man’s address on his clipboard.

He handed the letter back. “Thanks, Susie.”

“That’s all right. Do you want another coffee?”

John shook his head. “No. I’d better be going. We’ve got a lot on at the moment. I’ll be in touch soon. Sarah wants us to have an initial meeting of the development company. It’ll probably be one Wednesday evening. Would that be all right with you?”

“Yes, of course.” She saw him to the door and said goodbye.

John drove away from Stacey Court, troubled by Sir Oswald’s lack of response to his report.

53

"Come in, Ambrose, and take a seat." Henri Maeterlink ushered him into his plush third floor office. The place was very grand with large windows giving sweeping views south across the Thames. There was obviously a lot of money on display here.

Ambrose considered carefully what he should say as an opening comment. He didn't want to appear cringing, but he felt he ought to flatter Maeterlink's vanity a little. So he said, "Thank you for giving me an opportunity to tell you about what I can do, Henri."

"Oh, we know what you can do, Ambrose." Henri held up his hand. "I was impressed by what you told me at the ball the other day about this fellow Tucker, and the way he is paying you to get him introductions. I've talked to the board. That's the sort of thing we´re interested in."

"What?" Ambrose was taken aback.

Henri made a throwaway gesture. "I don't imagine you'd make a good banker or accountant or that you would even want to. It's not your line at all, is it? But socially you're a real asset."

"I am?"

"Absolutely, old chap. You know hundreds of the right people. You are presentable and you can hold your liquor. But above all, you seem to be acceptable to most people in society. That's what this bank wants."

Ambrose gaped at him. "I don't understand."

Henri sat down opposite him, rested his elbows on the desk and interlinked his fingers. "You must remember, Ambrose, that Schubert's is a merchant bank. We don't have branches all over the place holding balances for thousands of little people. Our smallest investor will have over a hundred thousand pounds vested in the bank. Quite a few of them have more than a million." He leaned back in his chair and wagged a finger at Ambrose. "No, our main task is to find the right opportunities to invest in. This country and the whole of Europe is waking up from an investment drought covering most of the last thirty years. There are people everywhere who are sitting on huge assets which are grossly undervalued and underused. *We* want to find the enterprising individuals who will help those wealthy people put their assets into profitable use. Do you follow me?"

Ambrose wasn't quite sure that he *did*. "Can you give me an example - show me the sort of thing you have in mind?"

"Certainly I can," said Henri. "A very good example is this chap Tucker, who you were telling me about. I suppose you didn't stop to think about what he was doing with your introductions." He hurried on before Ambrose could interrupt. "Well, I'll tell you. He's making a lot of money out of them. What happens is this. You give him a customer. You tell me that he's not in competition with anyone, except with some big London company who would charge a fortune - and that's not competition at all. As a result, he's got a very profitable outlet for the service he's providing. I would be surprised if he isn't charging your contact at least twice what it costs him to do the work. That's fifty percent profit on turnover, which is a very nice return. There aren't many businesses which are making that level of profit at present."

"The bounder," Ambrose burst out, "and he's paying me a miserable five per cent. Right - he can forget the idea of getting any more work through my contacts."

Henri shook his head. "That is entirely the wrong approach, my friend. If he's making so much money out of it, we want him to expand as much as he can - a hundred-fold if possible. And we want to be a part of it. He needs to set up an organisation to run a much larger business. He needs the funds to open depots all around London, in Brighton and Bournemouth and wherever else there are suitable market opportunities - Paris and Nice immediately spring to mind."

"Ah." The light began to dawn on Ambrose. "You provide him with the funds to do this - at a good rate of interest, of course."

"We do much more than that, Ambrose. We take a stake in his company. In return for a forty per cent slice of the business we provide all the capital he needs to expand wherever he wants." Henri paused. "Subject to our approving his plans at each stage, of course, and subject to satisfactory returns being maintained. But we do even more than that. In addition we will also provide finance to his customers to enable them to have their houses completely upgraded - not just the kitchen or a bathroom. We may well decide to fund the purchase and complete the fitting out of a number of suitable houses to have something we can show off to the public to get them thinking along the right lines." Henri tapped the side of his nose. "In a few years, Ambrose, a lot of people are going to be a great deal wealthier than they are now, and they'll soon be falling over themselves to have smart new homes to show off to their friends. We want to be in the vanguard of this new world order."

Ambrose smiled with self-satisfaction. "So you want me to deliver this chap Tucker to you?"

"Well, you could put it like that. But it won't only be Tucker. It'll also be all his contacts and his suppliers. And then we'll want you to be on the lookout for others like him. Chaps like Tucker are going to be the engines which drive our expansion programme. You are going to be the man out there looking for them."

Ambrose wasn't fooled that easily. If Schubert's were going to make a fortune out of John Tucker, he wanted to see that a slice of it came to him. "Sounds like a very important job," he said. "Presumably the rewards are commensurate with the importance."

Henri smiled benignly. He looked even more like an overgrown gnome with that smile on his face. "Ah, now. You're right in thinking that this is a post we value most highly. Therefore, like all the best jobs, we're going to pay by results."

"What exactly does that mean?" asked Ambrose suspiciously.

"You'll get a minimum basic salary of twelve hundred a year."

Ambrose gaped. "But I can't live on a hundred a month in London. That's less than pater's allowance at Cambridge."

"Listen to me." Henri held his hand up. He was smiling even more broadly. "You must understand, Ambrose, that this job is not a sinecure. I have said we want to see results and we will pay highly for those results. On top of your salary you will get a generous expense allowance. You will put in a weekly report of your meetings. Any reasonable expenses - meals, hotels, entertainment, whatever you consider you need to spend to pull in your target - will be paid in full on a receipted invoice basis. Do you understand me?"

"Yes, but -."

"Wait a minute. In addition, you will meet me twice a month and you will be given specific targets. We will give you bonus payments when these targets are met. For example, we will pay you one thousand pounds the day that John Tucker sits down with us to discuss our funding of the expansion of his business. Does that seem reasonable?"

Ambrose was stunned. "One thousand pounds? Well - yes, I suppose it does."

"You can continue to get your five percent from him for the introductions you make to him - at least for the present. We may want to change that later. I think that's quite generous, don't you?"

He looked up to see Henri smiling across at him. "Oh, yes - yes I do. When do you want me to start?"

"Well - as soon as possible. Shall we say the first of August?"

"First of August?" Ambrose asked, startled.

"Why not?" The round face beamed at him. "It's hardly going to interrupt your lifestyle, is it? Were you planning a holiday?"

Ambrose shook his head. "I may go to some friends in Shropshire for a few days. But, as you say, they could well be customers." He decided to be a bit crafty. "Of course, I shall need some funds to get myself a flat or something."

"That's a reasonable suggestion," said Henri. "I'll send you a cheque for two hundred and fifty – an advance on your Tucker bonus with your letter of appointment. Will that do?"

"It would be a help." He was thinking that he needn't let the old man know about the start of his new job for a couple of months, so he should be able to keep receiving his allowance at least until September.

"I think this could be the start of a very good arrangement for both of us." Maeterlink stood up.

Ambrose nodded. He experienced a warm glow of satisfaction. When he thought about it, the interview had worked out even better than he had hoped. There was going to be none of this business of getting into work before ten in the morning and sitting at some dreary desk all day, pushing a pen. "Yes. I agree. Thank you very much." He stood up, took the proffered hand and shook it firmly, as he had been taught at prep school.

"Very well," said Henri. "I'd like you to be in this office at eleven o'clock on the first Monday in August to discuss precisely how we will set about netting this chap Tucker. I don't want you to say anything to him about our plans before then. But of course there's no reason why you shouldn't get on as well as you can with him, and continue to give him sales contacts as before. Are you happy with that arrangement?"

"I certainly am."

"By the way," said Henri. "I shall be on holiday for the next two weeks. I was thinking of calling on you and your lovely sister some time next week. Is that likely to be all right, do you think?"

"I'm sure Alison will be delighted to see you," replied Ambrose smoothly, making a private note that he must warn her to be ready.

"Then I'll see *you* on Monday in three weeks time. Goodbye. Your letter of appointment and the cheque will be in the post." Maeterlink ushered him to the door.

The whole thing seemed to be an excellent arrangement, thought Ambrose, as he made his way out into the rich July brightness of the City.

54

Rosemary had been home for a week before she got in touch with John. She had been hoping he'd come round and see *her* first. After all, she thought, he knew Sammie had brought her back from university, but there had been no approach from him. However it was important for her to make a decision about her future. So, early one evening, she went round to see him in the little cottage in Orchard Street. She tapped on the knocker and John's mum came to the door.

"Why - hello, Rosemary," she said. "Come in, my dear."

"I suppose John's not home yet?" She followed the dumpy little lady into the front room. She noticed how dingy it was in here behind the net curtains, despite the bright sunlight outside.

"No," said Mary. "I don't know what time he'll be back. I hardly seem to see him these days, he's so busy. He just pops in for his meal and then rushes straight out again."

"You *are* expecting him this evening, then?" Rosemary had begun to wonder whether she'd even be able to catch up with him at his home. "I didn't know whether he expected me to ring and make an appointment or something."

Mrs Tucker seemed unaware of the sarcasm as she picked up a pile of ironing to make a chair free for Rosemary to sit down. "Oh, yes, he always rings if he's not going to be able to make it." She proudly indicated the new telephone on a small table by the front door. "He's put a phone in at home now. He says it's important to be in touch with people all the time. He's also put one in at the new site office, so that he can telephone the foreman whenever he needs to. And there's one at Barker's, of course."

"Goodness," said Rosemary, "it's becoming quite a business empire."

"It is indeed. John finds it all so exciting. But I *do* wish he'd take a bit more time off. All work and no play – you know the saying." She turned to smile at the girl. "Well - perhaps he will relax a bit, now that you're home. You must talk to him, Rosemary, and try to get him to take a break for a few days.

Why don't you suggest to him that the two of you do something like you did last summer? You all went cycling then, didn't you?"

"I've been home a week already, Mrs Tucker, and I still haven't even heard from him." She felt almost outraged.

"Goodness." His mum shook her head absently. "Did you tell him when you were coming back? He hasn't said anything to me about it. He'd have been sure to have said something if he knew."

"Well," said the girl, "he knew Sammie was bringing me back from Sheffield last Sunday. After all, the graduation was the week before last, and there wasn't any real reason to stay on after that." She added bitterly, "or didn't he even tell you about my graduation since he didn't bother to come."

Mrs Tucker turned to face her. "Oh, you mustn't say things like that, Rosemary. He was most disappointed that he had another meeting which he had to go to. It was some new work which Grants had got for Stacey Court. He was given the work personally, you see, so he couldn't ask anyone else to go to the meeting in his place. It was so kind of Sammie to step into the breach. He's a real gem, that Sammie."

"Yes he is," agreed Rosemary with feeling. It seemed to her that there was a conspiracy among their parents' generation to avoid telling John the truth. She had no doubt that the subject would now be changed.

"Have you seen the lovely kitchen he and Sammie made for me? Do come and look." Mrs Tucker led her into the back room.

Rosemary noticed the kitchen was much brighter and more cheerful than the sitting-room. The window looked out on to the back garden. There were no net curtains obscuring the light and the garden was still speckled with evening sunlight.

"Look at these lovely units," said his mum. "See - I've got a built-in sink and a place where the oven fits in and John has just bought me a new refrigerator. This is luxury compared to the old kitchen at Riversmeet."

"You didn't mind leaving Riversmeet House then?" asked Rosemary. "I thought John resented having to get out and move to a smaller place."

Mrs Tucker patted her on the arm. “As far as I’m concerned, it’s the best thing we ever did. That old barn of a place was so cold and damp. This is much more cosy. The shops are just round the corner and there are plenty of people to talk to. At Riversmeet we were a quarter of a mile from the nearest neighbours, and they were a couple of old dears who never had anything much to say. And there’s so little housework to do here. I can buzz round with the dustpan and brush in half an hour.” She shook her head. “No, I don’t regret moving one bit.”

“Don’t you mind not having the views?”

“She never looked at them, did you, mum?” John’s sudden arrival made them both jump.

“My, you startled me,” said his mother. “It’s that new Yale lock you’ve put on the front door. It’s so quiet that I don’t even hear the key turn.”

“You had it on the latch. Anyone could have walked in. I just pushed it open.” He turned to Rosemary. “Hello, Rosie. You look lovely.”

He bent forward and pecked her on the cheek. It was rather less than she thought he owed her after all this time apart.

“Hello, John.” Now she was face to face with him she suddenly felt shy. He seemed so smart and self-assured in his dark grey work suit and striped tie. There was nothing about him any longer of the casually dressed student, which she remembered from last year. For the first time since she had known him, she was made aware of her appearance. She had only pulled on a cardigan over her blouse and skirt to come across and see him. She wished she’d taken more trouble.

Mrs Tucker seemed to appreciate her embarrassment. “Why don’t you two go and sit down in the other room. I’ll make a pot of tea.”

“I’ve got a better idea,” said John. “Let’s go down to the Passage Inn for a drink. Then I’ll take you out for a meal.”

“Are you sure you can spare the time?” Rosemary was aware that her comment sounded bitter and sarcastic.

John raised an eyebrow but didn’t react. “I’ll ring Sammie and tell him I can’t go into the office this evening. He’ll understand. After all, it’s not every evening that you get back from university. And for the final time too. Are you coming, mum?"

She shook her head. "No. You can count me out. I've got a meeting at the Women's Institute this evening. We're making kneelers for the church," she explained to Rosemary. "We want them to be ready for Christmas."

"I can't go either," said Rosemary. "Besides I'm not dressed to go out."

"Rubbish. You look super just as you are. Doesn't she mum?"

"Of course she does," said Mrs Tucker loyally.

"I am *not* going out dressed like this."

"All right, I'll take you home to change and I can chat to your mum and dad while I wait for you." John disappeared to make his phone call before Rosemary could protest. She raised her eyes to heaven.

"I *know*," said Mrs Tucker, shaking her head. "It's rush, rush, rush all the time. He tires me out sometimes, just watching him. I quite liked the idea of having a telephone in the house at first. And I must admit I find it very convenient at times. But it means that John's never out of contact with people. Someone always seems to be ringing him up."

"He hasn't even told me your number," protested Rosemary.

John reappeared. "I'm sorry. Sammie's just reminded me that I've got to go into the office for half an hour to sign some papers and other things. I'll drop you at home, Rosie. Then I can clear up my work at the yard while you're changing. After that the evening's ours."

"No it isn't," said Rosemary with a firmness which she hadn't intended. "I've been trying to tell you, but you wouldn't let me get a word in - I'm already going out this evening. I only popped round for half an hour to let you know that I'm home, since you hadn't called in to check."

There was a moment's silence. "Ah," said John. There was a glint in his eye as he looked at her. "Well, am I allowed to join the queue for a future appointment?"

Despite herself, Rosemary grinned. "I think I could spare you Friday evening."

"OK. I'll book us a table somewhere." John's answering

smile seemed a little forced. "I'll pick you up at seven, is that all right?"

Rosemary nodded her agreement. She still felt a little nettled at the way he had so easily accepted her comment that she couldn't see him tonight. He hadn't seemed particularly upset about the fact that she wasn't available.

"Does that mean," asked Mrs Tucker, "that you'll be eating here this evening after all?"

"Yes I will, mum. I'll just walk Rosie home and I'll be back inside half an hour. Is that all right?" He crossed to the front door.

"Of course it is. Your meal will be ready for you when you get back."

As soon as they were outside and he had closed the door, John said, "I'm sorry I couldn't get up to see your graduation, Rosie. I hope Sammie explained that this new job had just come up at Grants and I couldn't refuse -."

"Yes, Sammie explained it all, just the way you told him to." Rosemary started off at a fast walk, her head in the air.

John rushed after her. "It could have affected my career if I'd turned it down."

"So everybody keeps telling me," she said between clenched teeth. "It didn't matter anyway. We had a lovely day and your absence didn't spoil anything. Sammie was a smashing escort at the ball, even though you hadn't warned him about what he was letting himself in for."

"How could I?" gasped John, struggling to keep up with her. "I didn't know much myself. In any case, it all had to be arranged on the phone, because the other meeting came up at the last moment. I warned him to wear a suit." He took a breath. "Well, I think it was very good of Sammie to do it. It's not his cup of tea at all."

"I've already told you that Sammie was absolutely brilliant. God knows what situation my parents would have been left in, if Sammie hadn't come to their rescue. And I'd have looked a pretty big fool going to the ball in my beautiful new gown without an escort, wouldn't I." She was quite proud of the snap in her voice.

"For god's sake, Rosie, why are we in such a hurry?"

She paused for him to catch up. Then she rushed on again. "I can't hang around. I've got to be ready to go out at half past seven. If I'm going too fast for you, then forget it and go back home. I hadn't realised how unfit you'd become, now that you're doing a sedentary job all day."

"Look," said John, trying to smooth things over. "I've said I'm sorry and I really am. But I've told you this other meeting was important to my career. I'm afraid that has to come first until I´m established. I can't allow clients to think that I'm not fully committed to their projects. I've got to think of the future."

His remark made Rosemary even more furious. "Sod your future, John Tucker. We've done nothing else in our last few meetings but talk about *your* future. The rest of us also have futures, you know. Or don't we matter?"

"That's totally unreasonable, Rosie," he complained. "All *you've* talked about recently is exams and graduations and getting married. You don't seem interested in planning a future for either of us."

"That just shows how little notice you have taken of what I've said," she spat at him over her shoulder. "Well, as it happens, I've already sorted out what I'm doing - not that you'll be interested."

He was getting nearly as angry as she was. "Of course I'm interested. It's part of *our* future, together isn't it? What have you decided - since you obviously weren't prepared to discuss it with me before you made up your mind?"

"I've decided," she said, "to accept the job they´ve offered me at the V & A. It's a very interesting post in document research." She paused for a second. "As usual with these special opportunities, the salary isn't very good (only about five hundred a year) but the high profile will be good for my future prospects."

To her fury he smiled. "I think that's brilliant, Rosie. You'll really enjoy that sort of work. You can rent a nice flat nearby in Chelsea or somewhere like that and I'll be able to come and visit you."

"Do you have any idea of the cost of flats in Chelsea?" she demanded. "There's no way I could afford to rent a flat on that salary."

"Well," he said, "I might be able to help with that. I'm meeting the bank next week about expanding our activities into the London area. I could probably do with a base somewhere like that."

Rosemary swung round and faced him. Her face was white with anger. "You just don't understand, do you, John? I want to do this on my own. I don't want to be patronised by you, just to show how much cleverer you are than me. If you want to get a pad in London, get your own. I do *not* want you descending on me any time you feel like it – making use of me when it suits you. I want to live my own life. Is that clear?"

John was shocked into temporary silence by her attack. Rosemary resumed her charge for home. He trailed along behind her, aware of the strange looks they were getting from passers-by.

"I'm sorry you think of me in that way, Rosie." He tried to sound reasonable. "I thought we were both aiming for the same thing in the end. I wanted to help both of us. I didn't mean to insult you."

"Well you *did* insult me," she threw at him over her shoulder.

"Then I'm sorry."

"So where are *you* going to get the money from to get a place in London?" Rosemary asked venomously. "You're not earning that much from Grant's and, from the way Sammie was talking, it sounds as though you're over-stretching things at Barkers, with all the extra work you're taking on. So who's providing this sort of money? Is it your friend Sarah?"

"That's what I'm going to see the bank about." John seemed even more breathless than before. "And what's the point of the jibe about Sarah?"

"Is it your reward for services rendered over Easter?" Rosemary paused with her hand on her front gate and faced him.

John shook his head. "I don't understand what you're talking about."

"Come off it, John." She was shocked at the vitriol in her own voice. "Sammie didn't tell me this of his own volition. I tricked it out of him. But he made it clear that he hardly did any work at all on Sarah Grant's shower room. According to you the two of you were working on it all over Easter. He also said he was surprised it took you so long. I didn't have to be very clever to work out why." She compressed her lips. "What had happened to Mr Grant while all this was going on?"

She couldn't tell whether it was breathlessness or embarrassment which had turned his face scarlet. He shook his head twice as though he'd just been hit and was trying to think straight. Then he recovered his fighting spirit. "So your jealous, vindictive little brain has been festering away about this for weeks, I suppose, constructing some great big sordid affair out of it all between me and a woman fifteen years older than me."

"Well, isn't it true?" she accused. "If it isn't, you have only to tell me just what did happen. Then we can forget about it and start all over again."

"Why the hell should I have to explain myself to you? We don't own each other - as you've already made perfectly clear. You have no idea what business Sarah and I are engaged in, and I don't intend breaking confidence to tell you." He took a breath. "If you want us to remain friends, you'll just have to forget about Sarah - at least at the moment."

"Who said I want to remain friends with you?" she screamed at him. "Why should I want to have anything to do with someone who shows me so little consideration?"

She burst into tears, wrenched the gate open, rushed up the garden path, pushed open the front door and slammed it violently behind her.

John continued to stare after her, aghast at the sudden collapse of their relationship. "Bloody hell, John. You do seem to have a talent for upsetting young women," he said to himself.

Slowly he turned and made his way home. His appetite for his mother's cooking had disappeared.

55

Sammie drove to the Pound Lane housing site in the new company van. He was delivering the kitchen units and the fitted wardrobes for the show house. This had become a priority now that John was already getting lots of enquiries about houses on the new estate. It seemed there was a desperate need for new housing, from the interest that was being shown by the public.

It was the first time he'd been to the place for a couple of weeks. John was directly supervising Angus McIntyre, dropping in every evening to go through the day's progress with him. He had told Sammie how he was full of praise for the way Angus was running the site and had told his partner how much more quickly the houses were being built than they had anticipated. But Sammie was curious to see for himself how things were going.

He noticed there was a smart new Sunbeam Talbot parked outside the site office. Sammie thought it was rather a posh car for a potential buyer of one of these small, cheap houses. And when he went inside, he found Sarah Grant was sitting across the desk facing Angus.

"Hello," said Sammie. "What are you doing here?"

Sarah looked at him in that superior way which so annoyed him. She appeared to be weighing in her mind whether she would bother to talk to him at all. "I often pop my nose in," she said after a minute's hesitation. "I'm interested to see what's going on."

"You know that building sites can be dangerous." Sammie felt nettled by her casual attitude. "There are unmarked holes that you can fall into and low scaffolding that you can bang your head on."

"Oh, I don't let 'er go anywhere on 'er own, Mr Joslin," said Angus hastily.

"It also happens to be private property," continued Sammie. "We wouldn't accept any responsibility for any accidents which might happen when somebody is on site without the authority of a director. For example, I wouldn't like one of the diggers to bump into that smart car outside."

"Don't worry." She smiled at him infuriatingly. "I have authority to be on site."

"Do you mean John's given you permission?" Sammie made a mental note to take this up with him.

Her smile was even wider. "If you like."

"I'll have to have a word with him." Sammie shook his head. "If he authorises you to wander round, then he ought to accompany you to see that you don't go anywhere that you shouldn't."

"Sammie," she said. "If you ask John, I'm sure you'll find he has delegated the authority for looking after me to Angus."

"Is that correct, Angus?"

Angus looked shamefaced as Sarah answered for him. "Of course it is, and a very good job he is making of it too."

Sammie thought she seemed to be challenging him to make an issue of the matter. He had a nasty feeling that was because she was confident she would win, if it came to a conflict. He decided he must talk to John about Sarah's position in the order of things. He changed tack.

"Well, if you can tear yourself away from chatting to ladies, in order to do some work for a few minutes, Angus, perhaps you'd like to help me unload the kitchen units for the show house."

"Don't let me get in the way of your work." Sarah unwound herself from her chair. "I'll be off now. Thank you very much, Angus, for being so sweet, and for explaining to me how everything is progressing. I'll see you again soon."

She smiled at Sammie as she left but he noticed there was a hard glint in her eye.

He turned to Angus. "What exactly *is* she doing here, Angus? The way she talks, it's as though she's often in here."

"Well - she of'en is, Mr Joslin - at least once or twice a week. I got the idea from 'er that she was somethin' to do with it all. She asks quite a lot of very straight questions - about 'ow many bases we got laid an' when the show 'ouse is likely to be finished an' that sort of thing. I mean, she doesn't take a lot o' my time, like. She only stays for about ’alf an hour each time she comes. An’ she’s always very polite.”

Sammie began to suspect that Sarah *did* have more interest in the site than his partner had let on. “Has John - er, Mr Tucker -? Has Mr Tucker ever been with her when she came on one of her visits?”

“Yes,” nodded Angus, “she was ’ere once when ’e turned up. ’E di’n’t seem to mind ’er bein’ ’ere at all. ‘E took ’er off an’ showed ’er everythin’ what was goin’ on an’ explained it all to ’er. I thought it was all right after that. Did I do wrong?”

“No. Don’t worry, Angus. I’ll talk to Mr Tucker about it.” Sammie decided that John owed him some explanations, about some of the things that were happening. “Now then, let’s get these kitchen units unloaded. Have you got someone to fix them? I believe John wants to start advertising the houses in a couple of weeks.”

56

Henri Maeterlink came to visit Alison on a beautiful July evening when Stacey Court looked at its best. He had had the good sense to telephone her in advance and invite her out for dinner so that she was wearing a black cocktail dress and was ready to go out when she came down the stairs to greet him. She couldn’t help smiling at him as stood in the hall. He gazed owlishly up at her with a broad beaming grin on his face.

“You look delightful,” he murmured gallantly as he hastened to greet her and press her hand to his lips.

“Oh, Henri.” Alison laughed. “You managed to say that as though it was the first time you have ever uttered those words.”

“I promise you that I have never been more sincere.” He grinned broadly at her. “Can you suggest somewhere for us to go for a meal?”

“I certainly can. In fact I’ve already booked a table at the Royal Clarence in Cathedral Close for eight o’clock.” She smiled. “Was that presumptuous of me?”

"Not at all. It's what I would expect of a talented hostess, which is what I'm sure you will soon become." His compliment seemed a little clumsy, even to his own ear.

She ignored it and took his arm. "It gives us time to have a quick chat with Daddy and a glass of sherry on the terrace before we drive into town. Shall we get the duty bit over before we start to enjoy the evening?"

"Come now," he protested, "I've been looking forward to meeting your father."

"And he you," lied Alison, leading him towards the library.

She had instructed her father to keep the gin bottle out of sight. Only ten minutes ago she'd been down to check that he was still behaving himself. But she saw, as they went in, that his glass was freshly charged. Henri appeared not to notice. Sir Oswald rose to his feet, a trifle hesitantly.

"Daddy," she said, "this is Henri Maeterlink. I've told you about him."

"Good evening, sir." Henri strode across the little room and shook him firmly by the hand.

Her father seemed to be taken aback. "Oh - good evening."

"May I compliment you, sir," said Henri, "on having a such beautiful and charming daughter."

"Oh." Alison could tell that the old man was deeply suspicious. "Oh, thank you."

She thought she should change the subject. "Henri and I are going to have a sherry on the terrace, father. You're welcome to join us."

To her surprise he accepted. They trooped back through the reception hall and out of the side door. At Alison's instruction, Annie had put a tray on the cane table by one of the pillars with the sherry decanter and two glasses. Now she had to go and find another glass while Henri brought an extra chair from the hall. But her father seemed not in the least put out. He seated himself with his back half to the park. The golden evening sun was streaming across his shoulders.

"The sherry's a fino," said Alison, pouring it out. "I hope that's to your taste." She offered a glass to Henri.

"Are you allowed to drink alcohol on a Friday?" Stacey leaned forward and peered at him.

"Father!"

To her chagrin, Henri burst out laughing. "Actually I'm a Catholic, Sir Oswald. The only thing I'm supposed to do on a Friday is eat fish."

"Oh," said the old man, backing down a little, "don't you insist on the children being brought up as Catholics, or something like that?"

"When they get married, devout Catholics give an undertaking that they will make every effort to ensure the children follow the true faith." Henri was still smiling. "I regret to tell you that I am not a devout Catholic, despite the fact that my family can trace its Catholic origins back to the Holy Roman Empire."

Her father digested this while he sipped his sherry. He raised his bloodshot eyes to his daughter. "Thin, acid stuff - this, Alison," he opined. "I prefer something with more body to it."

She ignored him. The evening was not starting the way she would have wished.

Fortunately Henri was sensitive to her feelings. "This is a beautiful part of the country where you live, sir. You are very lucky to own such a splendid estate in this area."

She could tell the old man was pleased by the comment. He made a throwaway gesture. "My family have been here for over two hundred years." He shook his head mournfully. "Of course this is all a poor imitation of the splendour we used to know. Death duties and all these other taxes have done for us all now."

"Are you receiving professional advice on how to minimise your tax losses," asked Henri diplomatically. "There have been some new advances in this field in the last two years."

Stacey shook his head again. "It's all too late for us, I'm afraid."

"It doesn't have to be," Henri said. "You still have this great asset of the estate which you need to protect."

"This is such a dismal topic for so beautiful an evening," said Alison hurriedly, anxious to stop her father sinking back into his normal depths of self-pity. "Tell us where you've been on your tour round the West Country, Henri, and maybe we can suggest some other places you should visit."

He responded immediately to her suggestion. He was clearly an enthusiastic traveller. The evening began to brighten up. They soon felt the call of hunger and left her father to finish off the sherry he'd complained about, before he went back to his gin. By the time Henri had returned her to Stacey Court at half past eleven, they were well on their way to becoming friends, and had made an appointment to meet in London when his touring holiday had ended.

57

John looked at the peeling signboard. “Carter and Smith, general builders,” it said. He walked through the open gateway into the yard and looked round. His now-practised eye told him the place was in chaos, with untidy heaps of surplus materials dumped wherever there was a square yard or two of space. When he looked at this sort of place, it made him very glad that Sammie was so well-ordered at Barkers, with everything kept in its correct position. His arrival at this builder’s yard in South London was the conclusion of several days’ investigation. The previous day he had run Peter Cavanagh to earth. At first the man hadn’t been willing to talk to him.

John had even surprised himself with the way he threatened the man, in order to get the information he wanted. “Mr Cavanagh, we’ve been called in by Stacey Estates to investigate the theft of this lead. Either you tell me what you know about this business or I report the theft to the police, with the comment that you had refused to volunteer any information to me. No doubt they’ll start asking questions all over the place, and that’s not likely to do your reputation a lot of good.”

“I know nothing about it,” Cavanagh insisted. “It had all been carried out and finished by the time I started. Stacey must have arranged it himself. Frankly I don’t understand it. He would never let me spend any money on maintenance or improvements even though they were desperately needed. That was one of the main reasons why I decided there was no point in continuing to work for him.”

“Do you know who did the work?”

“I think it was some London firm. I seem to remember seeing an invoice from a set-up called Smith and Partners lying around somewhere.”

So John had gone back to Susie. She had hunted around in the records which she was trying to get into some sort of order. After an hour of searching, she had rung him back with the name of a company called Carter and Smith who had a yard in the Croydon area.

Just inside the yard gate on the left-hand side, was a shed which had seen better days. John rapped on the door of the shed and pushed it open. A fairly scruffy, burly, middle-aged man was sitting behind the desk smoking a cigarette.

"'Ello. What can I do for you then?" John noticed the marked London accent.

"Are you Mr Smith?"

"'Oo wants to know?" the man demanded.

"Er - my name's Tucker." John handed over his card and sat in the worn leather chair facing the man. "We've been retained to look after the estates of Sir Oswald Stacey in South Devon."

"Oh, yeah." He leaned back in his chair and looked out of the window. "That's right. I remember 'im."

"*Are* you Mr Smith?" John persisted.

He shook his head. "No, mate. Mr Smiff's bin dead these last ten years, God bless 'is cotton socks. I'm 'is former partner - Mr Carter." he sat forward again in his chair. "Wot can I do for you, then?"

"We've been told," said John, "that Sir Oswald Stacey employed you to strip the lead off the roof of the North Gatehouse on his estate and replace it with pitch, is that right?"

Carter nodded insolently. "That's right. If I remember rightly, 'e did."

At last John felt he was getting somewhere. "What did you do with the lead?"

"Do wiv it?" Carter regarded him with astonishment. "Sold it of course, like what 'e told me to. Wurf a lot of money these days - is lead."

"What did you do with the money you got for it?"

Carter sat upright and poked a finger at him. "Now look 'ere, sonny. I did what I was instructed to do. I sold the lead and took off my price wot I quoted 'im and I sent the balance back to 'im. It was all done straight and above board wiv proper receipts. I kept copies for myself." He shook his head. "'E's got nuffin' to complain at me for."

"And you received a written order from him to do the work?" John was feeling confused.

"Too right I did," said Carter. "I knows enough, to realise 'e might come back later on for more. I made sure I was covered."

"Can you let me see the order?"

"Yeah - why not." Carter got to his feet. "Which one do you want to see?"

John was shocked. "Do you mean to say that you stripped the lead off more than one building?"

"That's right. I done four buildings altogether including the main 'ouse and the stables. There was also the North and South lodges. I got the paperwork for 'em all together. 'Ere you are." He opened a drawer in the rusty filing cabinet, searched through for a moment, and drew out a large brown envelope. From its fatness John judged it represented quite a lot of work. Carter opened the envelope and pulled out a sheaf of papers. "'Ere you are."

One by one he extracted letters with the Stacey crest on the top. There were three of them - the last one, John noticed, was for Stacey Court and the stables together. They were spread over a period of approximately a year, culminating with the main house which had been done in the early spring of the previous year.

"'Ere's our quotations for the work, 'ere's the receipts for the lead wot we sold, and 'ere's our accounts enclosing the cheques. Lord Stacey got a copy of all this lot and our cheques was all cleared through the bank within a few days." He stood above the young man with his hands resting on his hips.

John was horrified at the figures. "From this it seems as though Sir Oswald got just over four thousand pounds after deducting your costs."

"That right," said Carter. "I can dig out the statements if you like."

John shook his head. "No. That isn't important at the moment. It seems an awful lot of money."

"Too right it was. There was bloody tons of the stuff, especially on the main house. There was acres of lead flats. We 'ad several lorry-loads to bring it all back." He leaned forward and retrieved the papers. "*An'* we got 'im a bloody good price, though I says it meself. Lead's in short supply at the moment an' industry wants a lot of it."

"Was it you who put pitch on the roofs of the houses to

replace the lead?" John accused.

But Carter wasn't at all embarrassed. "Yes, on the 'ips an' valleys. But not on the main flats. There we put felt on."

"Just one layer?"

"Yeah." Carter shrugged. "It was mineral-surfaced."

John shook his head. "But it was only one layer. How long do you expect that to last?"

"I dunno, mate." He shrugged again. "Maybe five years, maybe ten. Roofin' isn't really my line."

"You don't specialise in roofing?" John was mystified. "Yet Sir Oswald Stacey employed you to do this to his buildings. How did he get hold of you?"

"Oh, that was easy. 'E got in touch wiv a mate of mine what's a scrap metal merchant. One of the top boys in 'is field is Jimmy Abrams." Carter resumed his seat. "Lord Stacey wan'ed to sell his lead. Jimmy's willin' to sell it for ím, but 'e won't strip the stuff off 'imself. So 'e puts the old geezer in touch wiv me, like."

John shook his head again. "I just don't understand. You call yourself a builder and yet you let this old man nearly wreck his property for the sake of a few thousand pounds of short term gain. What were you thinking of?"

"Now, look 'ere, sonny." The man leaned forward and pointed a finger at him. "You button yer bloody lip. If I 'adn't told Lord bloody Stacey that 'e'd have a lot of trouble, 'e'd 'ave just chucked some tarpaulings over them roofs. 'E was the one what said 'e was desperate for money an' 'e'd got rid of jus' about everything else wot 'e could sell. So I told 'im 'e 'ad to do something to keep the rain out." John was satisfied to feel that at last he'd got under the man's skin. "It's none of my business if 'e wants to play silly buggers wiv 'is properties. So you just keep your allergations to yourself - all right?"

John stood up. He decided there was nothing to be gained from arguing with this character. "All right," he said, "I'll leave it at that for now. Can I borrow one of these letters from Sir Oswald Stacey?"

"No, you bloody can't," Carter shouted. "Think I'm some sort of bloody fool, do you? If you go round stirring up trouble, I'm goin' to need those, aren't I? Not that it'll do you any good," he added as an afterthought. "I know a bit more than you cocky young whippersnappers, when it comes to what the law says about these things." He jerked his head to one side. "So, you'd better bloody get out, before I chuck you out."

John did as he was told. He knew he wasn't going to get any further with Mr Carter. Now he had to go back and face Sir Oswald Stacey and tell him what the consequences were of his foolish action. But he knew he couldn't just walk in and tell him. He would have to find the right way of going about it.

58

John was in the office before eight the next morning, and was waiting when Bill Kingley turned up. He followed Bill into his little room and told him straight away about what he'd discovered from Mr Cavanagh and from Carter, the builder.

"God knows what sort of condition Stacey Court is in after that butcher's been up on the roof stripping off all the protection," John said. "But, at the same time, he's obviously made sure that *he* can't be held legally liable for what he has done. I'll be honest, Bill, I don't quite know what I ought to do next."

Bill didn't seem to be in one of his usual helpful moods. He sat at his desk and regarded the young man solemnly. "I think you ought to wait until Mr Grant gets back next Monday. Then you'd better tell him the whole story and let *him* decide what line to take with old Stacey. This business has got a bit too big for you to deal with on your own."

"I agree with that," admitted John, "but I *would* just like to see the big house, to see what sort of state it's in. If half of what this bloke Carter said is true, then it's Stacey who ought to be prosecuted for criminal negligence."

"I know you hate the old boy's guts for what he did to you." Bill grinned and shook his head. "But there's nothing *you* can do about it if he decides to let the house fall down. The man has the right to do what he wants with his own property."

"Well, there damn well ought to be some way of making him more responsible," said John hotly. "It's a splendid house. It goes back centuries. The local people like it more than they like its occupants. It's part of their heritage and he shouldn't be allowed to just let it go to rack and ruin. There ought to be a law to prevent it happening."

"My, my! You really are on your high horse." Bill was obviously amused. "And here are you, covering parts of our beautiful green countryside with little brick and tile houses."

John wouldn't accept that. "Ah, but we're providing people with homes in the countryside. As long as we make them as nice as possible and retain some of the best features of their surroundings, we're actually enhancing the environment and also giving people a chance to enjoy living there, instead of being stuck in inadequate housing in the middle of some dreary town."

"Well, I don't disagree with that. Just make sure you don't forget that principle when you're designing your estates in future." Bill tapped him on the arm to accentuate his point. "That means - don't try and squeeze in as many houses as possible so that you can get the maximum profit out of a site."

"In future?" John was interested. "It sounds as though you've got more plans than we have?"

The older man nodded seriously. "Don't you forget it, young John. Some of us are watching you very carefully, because we think *you* might turn out to be the future for all of us."

"Actually," John looked at him, considering, "I wanted to talk to you about that. Now that the first houses are nearing completion, we have got to decide the best way of selling them. For obvious reasons, we can't simply hand the marketing to Grants. And, as Sarah says, Reggie would be absolutely furious if he found out later that we had given the job to one of his competitors. So we're thinking that we want to try and sell the houses direct to the public ourselves. That's why we have prepared a show house before any of the other houses are nearing completion." He paused.

Bill grinned. "Why are you saying this to me, John?"

"I want your advice. You've got much more experience than me in selling houses. I reckon you sell most of the stuff which passes through Grants. How do *you* think we should go about it?"

"Well," Bill considered. "If you're not selling through an agent, you're going to have to advertise. Have you got a signboard up at the entrance to the site?"

John nodded. "Yes, but it's not very informative. I think we need a new one."

"In any case," said his superior, "the site is on a minor road, so not many people are likely to see it. You'll have to get the word out to more people than that. You'll have to advertise in the local papers. I would suggest you spend quite a bit of money on a big spread that lots of people will see. You might even consider a half-page in the Western Morning News. In fact they might be prepared to do an article for you, if you spent a bit on advertising with them. You probably realise they have a day each week when they specialise in property sales."

"That's a good idea," John agreed. "Would you be willing to give us some advice on that sort of thing? Obviously we'd pay you."

"Well, I'd have to be careful that I didn't do anything which might get back to old man Grant, but I'll give you a hand as long as my name's kept out of it." He leaned back in his chair and put his hands behind his head. "Mind you, you're going to need to take on sales staff to show people round and talk to them about prices, if you're not employing an estate agent. You'll need a sales office on site with a phone, and somewhere for prospective purchasers to come and park their cars while they're looking at the details and viewing what's available. You said there are several different house types, didn't you?"

"Yes." John corrected himself. "Well, five actually. The next problem, once we've got the people to come, is to find someone who can do the selling for us. We want a person who knows what they're talking about."

Bill pulled a face. "It seems to me, young John, that now is the time for you to stand up and be counted. You are obviously the one to do it. It would be a much better idea for you to give in your notice to Reggie Grant and move to the new company, before he finds out what you're doing. He'll probably sack you then anyway. If you've already left, you'll save all the bad odour that comes with getting the push."

"Yes, I suppose you're right." John smiled ruefully. "I guess I've been hesitating, because there's some risk involved. If the business doesn't take off and the houses don't sell, then I'll have burned my boats in two ways at once."

"But," Bill pointed out, "you've also got the fitted furniture business which is taking off fast. I'm sure these houses will sell like hot cakes, but you *have* got something to fall back on if they don't."

John reflected for a while before replying. "You're right, of course. Now's the time to take the plunge."

"Don't think I'm trying to persuade you to go for my own purposes. Personally, I'll be sorry to lose you. You're the best trainee I've ever had. You've proved to be a real help to me." He shrugged. "But that's the way of life. I'll just have to start off with someone new. Or maybe young Jimmy Perkins will have seen enough of the way you've got on, to get off his backside and try to do something."

"It'd be no good me talking to him. He hardly acknowledges me now." John grinned wryly.

Jimmy Perkins had watched John's progress in Grants with undisguised envy, regularly passing half-heard comments about "arsehole creeping" and "using family connections" to other members of the staff. John hadn't bothered to correct him. He reckoned he got on well with the others, none of whom thought much of Jimmy anyway.

"Well," said Bill, "I can give you some advice and some useful contacts if you decide to take the plunge."

"That'd be appreciated, Bill."

His superior smiled slightly. "Who knows," he said, "if things go well for you, I could be looking for something myself in a few months."

"If this thing takes off," said John, "I'll be beating a path to your door. And I promise you the pay would be a lot better than what you've got here."

"Let's see what happens." Bill had a tolerant grin on his face. "You'll need to get yourself sorted out first."

"I'll discuss it with Sarah and let you know in a few days." He paused. "Anyway, that's decided me. I'm going to look at the roof of Stacey Court and see just what sort of a state it's in. I've got nothing to lose now, have I?"

The shop door clicked, and he peered through the door into the outer office.

"We'd better stop now. Here's Miss Brain already." John left Bill's office and went back to his desk.

"Hello, Miss Brain," he greeted her. "Lovely morning, isn't it?"

But his thoughts were elsewhere.

59

John was careful to tell Alison the truth when he rang her. "You know that Grant's have been retained by your father to advise him about the Stacey Estates until he gets a new estates manager?"

"Yes." Her voice was slightly breathless, as though she was trying to talk to him without being heard by someone close to her. He found it rather attractive.

"He asked me to look at the roof to the North Lodge," he explained. "They'd been complaining about leaks."

"There are lots of complaints . . ."

"This one was justified," said John impatiently. "When I went to check it, I found leaks all round the roof. A lot of water was getting in. The house is a health hazard for anyone living in it. In a couple of years, it will have deteriorated to the point where it will have to be pulled down."

He paused, waiting for her reply. Was she going to avoid any involvement? Was she going to censure him?

At last she said quietly, "That's dreadful. What needs to be done about it?"

"Well," said John, "the cause of the problem is that somebody stripped all the lead off the roof and replaced it with an inferior material which is already breaking up and letting in rainwater through the cracks. The lead will have to be reinstated if the building is to be saved."

"Will that cost a lot of money?" He was surprised at how hesitant she was.

"I'm afraid it will." Carefully he raised the next point. "I told your father all about it the other day. I asked him who took the lead, and I told him he might be able to claim the cost of replacement from whoever did it."

"What did he say?"

John had the strangest feeling that she already knew what he was going to tell her next.

"He told me he didn't know who did it, but he would sort it out. He said I shouldn't do any more until he instructed me."

"You didn't let him browbeat you like that." It was more of a statement than a question.

"Well," said John, "I thought that first I ought to talk to the former Estates Manager, Mr Cavanagh. But, when I did that, Cavanagh said the lead had been removed before he started the job. But he did know who the contractor was." John decided he wouldn't say anything about getting his information from Susie Partridge.

"What did the contractor say?"

"I went to see the man on Tuesday," he told her. "I'm not very happy with what he told me. He showed me written instructions from your father. Worst than what he did to North Lodge, he also said that he'd stripped the lead off the roof of the main house."

"What?" she gasped. "Stacey Court?"

"That's why I'm ringing you," said John. "I want to check it out myself before I say anything to your father or to Mr Grant. I don't want to look a fool."

He paused for a second, but she didn't reply.

"The question is, Alison, would you be willing to show me up onto the roof of the main house one day when your father isn't there, so that I can carry out a check on what this bloke said?" He paused. "Would you do that?"

"Of course." She seemed much less suspicious than he'd expected her to be.

"You know how to get up there, do you?" asked John.

She laughed musically and that made him realise that he wanted to see her again. "Of course I do. We used to play up there when we were kids. I think I know where I can still find a key to the roof door. I expect I'm the only one who knows it's there."

"That's great," said John. "When would be a good time for me to come?"

"Actually this afternoon would be very suitable. Daddy has been taken to a meeting today by some old friends. They won't be bringing him back till late. Cook's gone shopping and there's only Susie Partridge and me in the house."

"That's all right. I know Susie."

"I know you do." Alison chuckled again. "We've talked

about you."

John wondered what they'd discussed about him, but he didn't have the cheek to ask. Instead he said, "What time shall I come?"

"About two?"

"OK." He rang off, still wondering what on earth Susie and Alison could find to talk about which involved him.

60

Promptly at two Alison opened the front door to him. There was no sign of Susie. She held up her hand and showed him the key for a mortice lock.

"I found it, you see," she said triumphantly. "I went straight to it."

John put on a serious expression. "I never doubted for one moment that you would."

"No, I really don't think you did." She put her head on one side and observed him carefully. "You're not like Ambrose and his friends. They automatically assume that, because I'm a girl, I'm totally useless at everything." She smiled. "You're not like that."

"It's more likely to be the other way round," said John. "You were pretty doubtful about me as a sailor."

"That was only because you'd never done it before. In any case you proved me wrong, didn't you?" She turned and led the way up the wide main staircase. "Come on then."

At the half landing John noticed a niche in the wall containing a tall vase with a collection of rather tired-looking feathery grasses in it. "It looks as though there ought to be a statue in there," he observed.

Alison clapped her hand over her mouth. "Goodness, there used to be. I hadn't even noticed it had gone. I suppose that's because I was so used to it always being there. I wonder when that went. I must ask Annie. There are two more on the main landing. We must check if they've gone as well."

Sure enough both niches were empty. There weren't even vases of grass standing in those.

"I suppose Daddy's sold the statues," said Alison philosophically. "He's always carrying on about how broke he is."

"Some of the paintings have gone as well." John indicated the blank patches on the walls which showed where paintings had once hung. Now there were only three left.

"Yes, in Mummy's day there used to be dozens of paintings

all around the main staircase. They've nearly all gone now."

"When did your mother die?" The question seemed to be out of his mouth before he had thought. "I'm sorry. Perhaps you don't want to talk about it."

She shook her head. "I don't mind. It was a long time ago. I suppose it must have been more than fifteen years." She looked into the distance. "I was quite little. I can't remember very much about her. I'm told she was a beautiful, rich American. She was still quite young when she died. I *can* remember her coming in to say goodnight to me in her lovely ball-gowns before they went out for the evening. Daddy adored her. I don't think he ever recovered from her death."

"What did she die from?"

"Oh, some sort of cancer, I think." She took a breath. "We're not allowed to talk about it when he's around. In fact, I do believe this is the first time I've actually discussed her since I was a little girl."

John tried to imagine what it would be like growing up without a mother, especially if you were a young girl in a great barn of a place like Stacey Court and with a father like Sir Oswald. His respect for Alison was improving somewhat.

She was still thinking about her mother. "Of course, he originally married her for her money. And Mummy's family thought it was super for her to marry into the English aristocracy - poor fools. But I do believe the two of them genuinely loved each other. I suppose you'd say that Daddy was really the fool, because Mummy's family tied up the money so that he couldn't get his hands on it for himself. As a result of her dying young, he's been struggling to make ends meet ever since. In fact, he got so bitter about it, that he hasn't spoken to any of our American relatives for years."

"Perhaps the shortage of money explains what he has done to the roof."

John followed Alison as she shook off her memories and continued up the stairs. When they got to the top, underneath the great circular skylight which lit the staircase, he was silenced by the dreadful condition of the place. At one time the whole area had been whitewashed, but now there were great, green damp stains trailing down the walls. They started walking down the corridor to the left. When he looked into various rooms he noticed the whole floor seemed to be unfurnished. Most of the rooms were empty except for occasional piles of rubbish and other detritus.

John was quite overcome by the dereliction. “It looks as though nobody’s been up here for years.”

“When we were children, we used to have our bedrooms and the nursery and playrooms up here. They were at the front of the house. But they were closed down when we went away to school.”

“What age were you when you went to school?” he asked, wondering.

Alison looked at him with some surprise. “I was ten. I think Ambrose was eight when he went. So I was alone here, being tutored, for five years.”

John noticed that she showed no apparent self-pity. The thought of a girl being sent away to school from the age of ten seemed awful to him.

“Quite a few of the in-house staff used to live in the rooms on this floor at the back of the house. Now we have no-one but Annie.” Alison led him into a large room at the corner of the house which had windows on two sides. Here, as everywhere else, there were trailing cobwebs and damp stains on the walls. A piece of ceiling had partly come down above the side window. “This was our playroom. This door in the corner leads to the stairs which go up to one of the roof pavilions. There’s another one on the other corner but I don’t know where the key is for that.”

She opened the door and led him up a circular staircase. They emerged into a small room which was lit by a single oval window. On the opposite wall was a door. She put the key in the lock and tried to turn it.

“I’m afraid it’s got a bit stiff. I may have to ask you to have a go.” But the next second it gave way and she opened the door from the little airless room on to the roof. John stepped out behind her into the refreshing sunshine and looked round.

He saw that there were in fact four of these dome-roofed pavilions, one at each corner of the main roof. In the centre was the large circular skylight above the main staircase. Elsewhere the roof was nearly flat, gently sloping from the skylight to a wide, shallow gutter which ran round the edge of the whole roof behind the balustraded parapet.

"This has changed since I was last up here," said Alison. "It used to be all grey metal with little ridges in it."

John nodded. "That's right. That was the lead. It's the best and most expensive material for flat roofs. It lasts for centuries. As far as I can tell, your dad sold it and had this cheaper material laid in its place."

Indeed, the whole of the flat area was covered by green roofing felt which had been roughly turned up against the walls. He inspected the balustraded parapet round the outside of the roof. There was no lead on the copings.

"This parapet will be in danger now that the water can soak in and soften the stone," he told her. "Make sure you don´t lean against it because it may collapse."

He looked over the parapet and saw that the lead had also been stripped off the tops of the cornices and the copings. Nothing had been put on top of the projecting stonework to protect it from the weather.

He pointed it out to Alison. "Do you see this bare stone cornice? The winter rains will soak into the stone. Then it will freeze in the frosts and expand and begin to blow it apart. In a couple of years the stone will start to spall and crumble. After five years it will fall off the building and even more rain will start to leak into the house. Your father was very badly advised when he decided to do this - if he took any advice at all. Within a few years this house is going to have very serious problems."

"What?" she demanded. "Do you mean Stacey Court? The whole building?"

John nodded. "I certainly do. The top floor will probably become uninhabitable within a year or two. The roof timbers and floor joists will rot. The whole building will have to be abandoned in a few years if something serious isn't done to restore it."

"But that's dreadful." She was gazing at him, horrified. "How can it have got like this so quickly?"

"I told you I inspected the North Gatehouse just over a week ago. I would say *that* building needs work to be carried out on it before next winter. If not, the occupants should move out. I assume the South Gatehouse is likely to be in a similar state. The stables and the main house may last a bit longer, but a lot of money needs to be spent on all the buildings to save them. If your father doesn't have the money himself, can he approach your rich American relatives to see if they will bear the cost?"

She shook her head. "I don't know. I'll have to ask him."

"Ah," said John, aware that he was on dangerous ground. "I think perhaps you ought to wait a few days before you speak to him. I'm actually exceeding my authority in getting you to show me round like this. What I need to do is talk to Mr Grant and tell him about the problems. Then he should approach your father. After that, you can speak to him and suggest he goes to his in-laws. Is that all right?"

"Will you do it quickly?"

John nodded. "Monday morning - as soon as Mr Grant gets back."

"All right. I'll wait until after that to speak to him."

They were standing by the front balustrade just to the right of the central pediment. Looking down, John could see the circular sweep of the gravel drive as it approached the steps to the front door. Away to the left was the grassed area where the carnival floats had been burned last autumn. To the South, behind the house were the formal terraced gardens where previous Staceys had enjoyed their luxurious leisure. They were now very over-grown. On the right was the entrance to the stable block. Even from here he could see the bare stone copings and the pitch-covered hips to the roof. Somewhere there, probably pushed to the back of one of the storage rooms, may be the remains of a canvas covered dragon.

Her next remark betrayed that Alison had been thinking the same thing. "It would be a laugh, wouldn't it, if we'd gone to all the trouble to rescue that old dragon, only to have the stables fall down on top of it." But she wasn't laughing at all. She turned to face him. Her eyes were troubled. "This place is important, John. We've got to do something to save it."

"We?" He felt the anger rise in him again at her casual presumption that he'd do whatever she wanted to help save her house, which her father was quite happy to pillage for his day to day extravagances.

She laid a hand on his arm. “I need your help, John. I know I haven’t always been very nice to you and I’m sorry for that.”

“Why do you need *my* help? Why not somebody else, like Ambrose? He’s got much better contacts than I have.”

“Oh, Ambrose.” She dismissed him with irritation. “He can’t apply himself to anything. He’d find it difficult to stir himself to put on the brakes if he was in a runaway car rushing down a steep hill. But *you* know about these things. Will you help me?”

“Well - of course I’ll do my best,” he said reluctantly.

“There’s something else I wanted to ask you.” Alison spoke hesitantly. “I’ve been invited to a ball at Henley next Friday and I haven’t got an escort. I was going to ask if you’re willing to take me.”

John was astonished. “Me? This will be some sort of posh society event, won’t it?”

“I suppose you could call it posh,” she smiled. “It will be dinner jackets. But you can hire one, can’t you?”

“But I’d never be welcome in a place like that.”

She tossed her head in annoyance. “What do you mean? It’s only a dance with a buffet supper. It’ll be in a marquee beside the river. There’s nothing to be frightened of. Royalty won’t be there.”

“Just ordinary upper classes having fun,” John sneered. “Will Ambrose and his chums be there?”

“I don’t know. I expect they will. But so what? Ambrose hasn’t got anything against you. In fact, I think he rather likes you. He was the one who made me realise that I was wrong in the way I had behaved towards you.” There was a pause while he digested that comment. “Well,” she demanded, “will you take me, or are you too clever to mix with the pleasure-seeking upper classes.”

He didn’t know why, but suddenly John decided he liked the idea of escorting Alison to something like that - to show her off. He could imagine she would be worth showing off. He wasn’t proud of himself, but he decided to accept the invitation. “We’ll have to stay somewhere overnight, won’t we? Do you know someone who could put us up?”

"I'll stay with my friend Camilla. I'll ring her and ask her to arrange a hotel room for you."

He was thoughtful. "I'll need to take next Friday off so that we can drive up during the day."

"Do I take it that constitutes a "yes"?" asked Alison.

John nodded, aware that they were circling round each other like wary boxers.

"Well, hallelujah," she exclaimed. "I don't think I've ever had such difficulty persuading a man to take me out."

"Sorry." He grinned.

She shrugged. "That's all right. I won't even ask you to be polite to my friends."

And on that hopeful note they parted.

61

It was just after eight when Ambrose got back from London. He went straight to his father's study, tapped on the door, and entered. The old man was sitting in his usual chair behind the desk. It seemed to Ambrose that he had hardly been anywhere else in the last few months.

Sir Oswald blinked at him like an awakened owl. "You're late back."

"Traffic's awful." Ambrose noticed the newly broached bottle of gin by the old man's left hand. That would be the second of the day. He didn't seem to be taking water with it any longer.

His father broke the silence. "Did you talk to this fellow Maeterlink?"

"Yes."

"I mean – did you speak to him about what we need?" Stacey was leaning forward with the hint of a dribble escaping from his loose, heavy jowls. His red-rimmed eyes were fastened on his son.

"It's about what *you* need, father. Don't include *me* in this."

"Well," the old man demanded, "what did he say?"

Ambrose turned away and looked out of the window at the beautiful parklands dropping gently towards the river. The scene meant nothing to him. He had always found the country boring since the first time he had returned on holiday from school at the age of eight and a half. From that date he had only come alive when he was stimulated by the contact with others. School holidays in the country had been purgatory, relieved only by baiting his sister. He wanted nothing more than to escape from the country. Then he might be able to forget the blame he felt at not being at home when his mother died.

"Please, Ambrose." His father broke the silence. "This is important to me."

The bleating dragged his son back to the present. Ambrose turned and spoke quietly. "I told you, father - there's no chance. I knew there wouldn't be. No bank is going to be interested in helping you."

"But why not?" The wheedling tone was back in his voice.

"Because they want to see the prospect of a *return* for their money. That's what they always look for." He spread his hands. "What can you *offer*?"

"What about a mortgage on the house?" A note of desperation had crept into Stacey's voice. "After all, the old place has got to be worth something."

Ambrose swung round to face him. "Who to, father? Who's going to be interested in a run-down old mansion of forty rooms, half of which are no longer inhabitable?"

"Well - I don't know." The old man looked down at his desk and mumbled almost to himself. "I'd have thought that all this land, all these buildings -"

"All what land, father?" Ambrose interrupted. "You admit the farms are all let on long, low-rental leases. The home park isn't big enough to farm as an economic unit. And even I know enough to recognize that the buildings are crumbling away through lack of maintenance. There's no value in any of it. There's no return for a bank to get hold of."

Sir Oswald Stacey took another gulp of gin and slumped back in his chair. "I don't believe that," he mumbled. "It *has* to be worth something. They could advance me well below the market value." He gestured feebly. "Just anything to keep the wolf from the door for a few more years."

Impatiently Ambrose strode over to the desk and leaned on it, facing his father. The whiff of alcohol assailed his nostrils, setting the gastric juices working in his own stomach. "And what would you do *then*, father? That's what worries the bank. You have very little income. You admitted to me the other day that all your shares and other investments have been sold. If the bank made you a loan, how would you make your repayments? The income from rents on the farms and the cottages wouldn't bring you in enough." He stood up again and stepped back. "Henri pointed out that you could only make repayments out of the money loaned to you. That would mean you would run through the loan even faster. Nobody's going to lend you money on that basis. In order to repay a loan you need be receiving sufficient income."

Sir Oswald raised his moist, bloodshot eyes and looked into his son's face. He raised his hands in a helpless gesture. "Then what am I to do? Where am I to turn?"

Ambrose turned away in revulsion. He couldn't face the look of surrender and self-pity which he saw on his father's face. He walked back to the window. "I discussed all the possible options at some length with Henri. When it comes down to it, he thinks you really only have one option. You must sell up for the best deal you can get. You will then have to invest the proceeds so as to bring in an annual income. And you will have to move somewhere where you can live within that income."

"What do you mean?" The old man seemed unable to grasp the full meaning. "Are we to leave Stacey Court? The family have lived here for over two hundred years."

The young man took a deep breath. "I'm sorry, pater. Neither I nor Henri Maeterlink could see any alternative."

"But who would buy the place?" Stacey gestured feebly. "Would they let me remain in one wing - in a few rooms even?"

"Well, they might," Ambrose admitted. "Obviously it would devalue the market price of the property. But you might find a purchaser willing to do that."

"Does this Maeterlink fellow know anybody who might be interested in such a proposal?" Sir Oswald seemed to be trying to recover some shred of dignity.

Ambrose shook his head. "It's not his field. He suggested you try the Vanderplatts. He seemed to think they might have some interest in preventing the estate from being broken up."

"No!" There was a burst of anger from the old man. His eyes suddenly recovered the sparkle. "I will not go back to your mother's family again. I have never been so humiliated as the last time I asked them for some help. My God, when I think that I even flew over to America to see if I could persuade them to lend us some cash. You can't imagine how dreadful it was."

"I know," said Ambrose softly. "I heard about it afterwards."

"Since your grandfather died, there has been nobody who

shows any respect or even any *liking* for the Staceys. Your American uncles would do anything in their power to stop any part of their fortune crossing the Atlantic." Sir Oswald shook his head. "There is no way that I would bring myself to ask them again."

"Of course," murmured his son, "I understand. But it does reduce the prospects considerably. You need to find an investor who may have a future use for the place. Henri seemed to think some sort of country club might be a possibility. You know - the sort of place where you have tennis courts, maybe a golf course, perhaps turn the house into an up-market hotel." He let the idea hang in the air for the old man to pick up.

Stacey turned his bloodshot eyes back on his son. "Do you know anyone who would buy it for that purpose?"

"*I* don't, but there *are* such organisations around. Henri said that apparently the best idea is to get planning permission for the conversion first, and then offer it on the open market, with the plans already drawn up. Of course, you'd have some special problems here, because of the state of the roof -." Too late he stopped himself.

The old man was suddenly alert. "What do you mean?"

Ambrose tried to make light of the matter. "Oh, Alison mentioned it last evening - something about the lead has been stripped off the buildings. She says that means they will start to deteriorate as soon as the weather turns bad. She said a lot of money will have to be spent on the place soon to prevent it from falling apart."

"Alison told you *this*?" Sir Oswald was sitting erect. "Where did she get it from?"

He shrugged. "She has her sources. You'd better ask *her*."

"I'm asking you."

Ambrose was astonished by the sudden, steely edge in his voice. With a slight grimace he capitulated. Why should he save John Tucker's bacon?

"Apparently young Tucker came to look around yesterday. She showed him up to the roof and he pointed out what the problems are." Ambrose watched with astonishment as a look of demoniacal fury rose on his father's face. "I thought it was you who had appointed him to look at the place," he said weakly.

"Young Tucker!" Stacey burst out. "I appointed *Grants* to look at the problems at the North Gatehouse. I presume the young whippersnapper works for them. I certainly gave no permission for him to break into my house and start telling me what's wrong with the place."

Ambrose smiled ingratiatingly. "God, it looks as though I've opened my big trap too far. The thing is, father, it's no good you trying to pretend that there isn't a problem when there clearly *is* one - especially if you're thinking of selling the place."

"That has nothing to do with it." Sir Oswald was working himself into a fine old temper. "The fellow has no right to take this responsibility upon himself. I shall telephone Grant straight away and tear him off a strip. I doubt if the young fool will keep his job after I've given Grant a piece of my mind."

"Is that a good idea?" asked Ambrose.

"First thing in the morning I shall get on the telephone to him."

"Tomorrow is Saturday, father."

"Never mind. Young Susan will be in. She'll be able to find Grant´s number for me somewhere. Just wait until I have made my displeasure known to him."

Stacey seemed to have focused all his frustration and anger on John Tucker. The chap was obviously a suitable target, not being strong enough to fight back. Ambrose found it difficult to like the old man when he was behaving in this way. He made his excuses and left his father to his childish rage.

He went down to the kitchen to see if Annie had anything left over from dinner for him to eat.

62

John was surprised to find that Reggie Grant was already in the office when he arrived at eight-thirty on Monday morning. Bill appeared briefly at his office door.

"The boss wants you to go in to see him straight away." And he disappeared back into his own room.

With a sinking heart John went and tapped on Mr Grant's door.

"Come."

He opened the door and went in.

Grant looked up. "Ah, Tucker. Come in and close the door behind you."

John did as he was instructed and crossed to stand in front of the boss's desk.

Grant began quite mildly. "How is your survey going on the North Gatehouse at Stacey Court? Have you any proposals to make to me?"

"I was waiting for your return to discuss the whole problem with you, Mr Grant," said John. "I have prepared a report with all the details. I believe there is quite a major problem which needs to be sorted out."

"Yes." Grant leaned back in his chair and surveyed his trainee. He indulged in his favourite activity of inserting his thumbs under his braces and stretching them away from his chest. "You *do* seem to have a bit of a problem. I had a telephone call from Sir Oswald Stacey yesterday evening at my home – on a *Sunday* evening, Tucker." He shook his head. "Stacey was not a happy man."

John's heart sank further. It sounded as though Alison hadn't been able to keep his visit to herself.

"In fact," continued Grant, "he was in a towering rage. It appears that you have grossly exceeded your instructions. Not only have you looked at the North Gatehouse. You have apparently also been to see the contractor for the alterations - in London, of all places - I hope you aren't going to claim expenses for driving up there, since you did it on your own authority."

"Of course not."

"Furthermore," said Grant heavily, "I understand you have also tricked Sir Oswald's daughter into showing you around Stacey Court and inspecting the roof of the main house - which is totally outside your brief. Sir Oswald is furious about it."

"I didn't trick her. I just asked and she agreed. I told her what it was about."

His boss shook his head. "Going to London and interviewing some builder fellow was much worse."

"How did he know I'd been to London?" demanded John.

Grant waved a dismissive hand. "Apparently the fellow rang Sir Oswald and complained. Even went so far as to threaten legal action if you weren't called off." He leaned forward and regarded the young man. "You'd better tell me now. Is there anybody else you've been and upset?"

"But the important fact, Mr Grant, is that those buildings are at serious risk." John felt he had to get across to his boss the necessity of taking some urgent action. "I needed to find out the facts. Unfortunately you weren't here, and I didn't feel I could burden Bill . . ."

"I have already told *Mr* Kingley how seriously displeased I am with the way things have been allowed to get out of hand while I was away for a couple of weeks."

"It's not his fault," said John hurriedly. "I acted entirely on my own initiative."

"I'm aware of that." Mr Grant took a deep breath. "And *you* must bear the responsibility. Sir Oswald Stacey has asked for you to be dismissed. What have you to say to that, eh?"

John shook his head. "Well, that's for you to decide, Mr Grant."

"Stacey is a very important client to this firm. He is an influential person in the area. We collect all his rents for him." The boss pulled a face. "Only recently we finally got ourselves appointed to carry out estate management duties for the Stacey Estates." He leaned back in his seat again. "Now your behaviour has endangered all that. At the very least I will have to remove you from anything to do with that business."

"But surely," said John, "we have a duty to expose what has

been happening to the buildings at Stacey Court. Surely you're not going to let him sweep it under the carpet."

A degree of irritation crept into Grant's voice. "It is not a question of sweeping things under the carpet, Tucker. It was never part of our brief to report to him about the roof at Stacey Court and we will not do so."

"But it won't do Grant's reputation any good," John insisted, "if it is believed that we hid the true state of the building from our client for whatever reason. As my final duty I will also give you a written report of my findings at Stacey Court for you to take whatever action you wish."

"Final duty?" demanded his boss. "What are you talking about?"

"You've already told me that Stacey has instructed you to dismiss me and that you daren't refuse in case he takes his business elsewhere."

"Ahem." Grant cleared his throat and looked even more pompous than usual. "I think we can find a way around this. If you provide Sir Oswald with a written apology, I will then explain that you are young and a little over-enthusiastic and that I'm removing you from all work connected with Stacey Estates. I'm sure that he will accept that a sharp dressing-down is sufficient punishment to atone for this first black mark on your character."

"But that wouldn't be acceptable to me, Mr Grant." John felt absolutely furious at the attempt which was being made to make him back down. "My report will make it clear that I believe Sir Oswald Stacey has been guilty of extreme negligence, in the way he has plundered his estate for the purpose of short-term financial gain. I'm not sure whether he has done it with a purpose of defrauding the company which insures his buildings - only time will tell. But it's certainly not something which Grants should allow themselves to support or condone in any way."

Reggie Grant's eyebrows almost disappeared under his hairpiece. "You -, you -," he spluttered. "You can't talk about Sir Oswald like that."

"Mr Grant," said John calmly, "I have been to a builder in London who has shown me written instructions from Sir

Oswald Stacey to remove all the lead from the roofs and gutters of the buildings at Stacey Court and to sell the lead and send the money to him personally. At the very least, I should have thought he is liable to be taxed on his income from selling the stuff."

Grant was horrified. "But you can't make information like that public."

"I shan't do that," said John. "That is up to you. I will make my report to you and I will keep a copy to protect myself, in case the matter ever becomes public from another source. It will then be up to you to decide what to do with it. I shan't be employed here any longer."

"But what are you going to *do*?" Grant wagged a finger at him. "It's not so easy to find new jobs these days, you know. And I'm afraid I would find it difficult to give you a good reference, if you left us under a cloud."

John smiled. "Don't worry about me. I've already got something else lined up. So I won't need a reference."

"And what is that?"

"I'm going to become a salesman for a development company."

Grant snorted. "You won't get a professional qualification doing something like that."

"I know." John nodded. "But I've come round to the view in the last year that a professional qualification isn't as valuable as all that. I'll just write out my report in its final form and then I'll tidy my desk. I assume you won't want me to work out my notice under the circumstances."

He turned and left the office. He had the satisfaction of seeing Mr Grant for the first time with his mouth wide open. But he wasn't going to leave the matter in limbo. John decided it was about time that Sir Oswald bloody Stacey faced up to the consequence of his actions.

63

John arrived at Barker's yard the next day at just after six. Sammie had requested that they had this meeting. John had an uncomfortable feeling that he was going to have some problems with Sammie. However, if that was the case, he would just have to face them. He took a deep breath, walked in through the open door and up the stairs.

The offices were situated in a row above the joinery shop with a link corridor at the back. The first door on the right was Sammie's office. His partner liked to have a view of everything that was going on in the yard below. John tapped on the door out of courtesy, opened it and went in.

Sammie got up from his desk to greet him. "Hello, John. Thanks for coming over this evening."

John noticed he wasn't smiling. "I'm sorry I'm too busy to see much of you these days," he said. "How's the fitted furniture side of the business going?"

"Very well. You'll know that from the monthly figures. Those big jobs that we're getting from Ambrose Stacey's introductions are particularly profitable, even after we've allowed for the extra cost of the new van which we needed to make the deliveries and all the travelling costs."

"Those people can afford it. In any case we're saving them money over what they'd pay to one of the big London companies." John crossed to the window and looked out at the sleeping factory. "How is young Jimmy coping with the surveying?"

"He's brilliant - a very fast learner. That was a good idea of yours."

"I *thought* he'd probably be a success," said John. "After all, there's no way I could have done all those surveys for you, what with the other things on my plate."

Sammie pulled a face. "I suppose we'll have to think about a new workshop soon. I've already had to go on to shift-working to get everything out on schedule, what with that stuff and Forrester's and our own work at Pound Lane."

That made John laugh. "What a turn up for the book. I never thought I'd hear Sammie Joslin actually talking about new premises."

His friend scratched his head. "Well, you know I was worried about this new housing development. I thought we were biting off more than we could chew. But I've got to admit that you seem to be coping with it successfully, at least at present."

"It'll be better from next Monday, when I'm up there full time," said John. "You won't feel that you need to go up so often to check on Angus. You can just turn up from time to time and I'll show you what progress we're making."

"Yes. That'll be a big help." Sammie paused. "Er - that reminds me, John. Something funny happened the other day when I was on site. Mrs Grant was there, and she was very off-hand with me. In fact, she was acting as if she owned the place. Angus told me she's up there several times a week, which I thought was odd. Is there something I ought to know about her?"

John took a deep breath and continued to survey the yard. So this was the problem. He'd been feeling bad about keeping his partner in the dark. Things like this didn't bode well for future relations between them. Yet at the same time he couldn't tell him the whole story.

"All right, Sammie," he nodded. "I think it's time you were told about it. Sarah Grant is the person with the money behind Landscale Developments. The reason for the secrecy is that she was left a lot of cash when her father died last year. She bought the field and came to me to arrange for the building work to be done. Now - the point is that she hasn't told her husband anything about this money of hers. Apparently she's worried he'd grab it for himself, or something like that. So she insisted that nobody should be told about her involvement - and she made a point of telling me that included you, because I specifically asked her about that."

"I see. So that's what it is?" It was clear that his partner wasn't at all pleased about it.

"I'm sorry, Sammie. I've felt a bit awkward about it myself. But I'm afraid that was her wish. However, I'll tell her now, that by her own actions, she has obviously made you suspicious. Of course, I'll have to ask you not to tell anyone else. Is that all right?"

Sammie swung round to look out the window. "I don't *want* to tell anyone else. It all sounds so damned sordid. Really John, I'm surprised you let yourself get mixed up in it."

John raised his eyebrows. "That's a bit of an over-reaction, Sammie. As far as I'm concerned, it's a business transaction. We stand to make a good profit out of building these houses. We've been able to find the men and the machinery to do the work economically, the money is there up front, and we know that we're going to get paid. That's a good enough reason to 'get mixed up in it' as you call it. If the client asks for confidentiality, I don't think that should be a problem for us."

"How do you know the money's there?" demanded Sammie. "How do you know she's not going to drop us in it, halfway through the contract?"

"Well, let's just say I trust her. She´s paid for everything I´ve asked for so far." John sighed. "Look at it logically, Sammie. She knows nothing about building. She could be taken to the cleaners by some builders and there would be nothing she could do about it. Then she'd look a right fool in front of her husband. So she relies more on us, than we do on her."

Sammie still wasn't convinced. "I must say, I don't like the way you've got involved with her without her husband knowing. There's something about her that makes me feel uncomfortable."

"Well," said John, refusing to answer the main object of Sammie's criticism, "we can't guarantee to like all our clients. All we can do is trust them, and I trust Sarah Grant."

"Rosemary doesn't trust her." Sammie looked defiant. "She thinks that you've got yourself involved with the woman and that she's using you."

"Oh, yes? How come you and Rosie are discussing my relationship with one of our clients? When does all this cosy chat go on?"

Sammie turned a bit pink. He shook his head in dismissal. "She just comes in here from time to time to find out how things are going and to ask what's happening to you. I gather you and she haven't been seeing much of each other recently."

"That's not my fault. Whenever we meet, she seems to fly into a tantrum because I'm not giving her enough attention." John was starting to get angry himself now. "It seems that she's found an alternative way of fuelling her jealous little rages, aided and abetted by my partner."

Sammie's eyes glinted. "That's not fair, John. We've both of us been worried about you for our different reasons. You've been taking on far too much recently. And Rosemary can see that you're apparently spending a lot of your time with Mrs Grant. You can't expect us not to discuss ways of trying to sort things out. We used to be a happy little group before Sarah Grant came along."

"Well - now you know the reason for her presence. Of course you can't tell Rosie anything about it. When you have your next cosy little tête-à-tête, you'll just have to tell her that I've explained it all to your satisfaction." John found he was walking up and down by the window as he talked. He deliberately made himself stop and relax. He lifted a pile of samples from the other chair in the office, placed them on the corner of the desk and sat down. "Now look, Sammie. I don't want *us* to row. We never used to. As far as I am concerned, you're welcome to have your chats with Rosie. And there's nothing to worry about in my contact with Sarah Grant. Now that I'm leaving her husband's company, I'm going to have more time to spare for my friends. If you like, we'll get together at least once a week to check up on each other's activities and find out what's going on. Will that make you happy? And I won't object to Rosie sitting in from time to time if she wants to."

"You know she's off to London to start her new job on Monday?"

John grinned ironically. "She hadn't told me *when* it was happening. But I'm not going to get steamed up about it. I think she's doing the right thing. She needs to learn to stand on her own feet for a while."

"I don't think she really wants to go," said Sammie. "She'd stay here if you asked her to."

"Well, I'm not going to." John leaned forward. "You know my philosophy, Sammie. People have got to make their own decisions. Rosie must decide what she wants and go for it."

Sammie tried to smile but failed. "Not everyone's as tough as you are, John. Rosie needs some guidance. She wants to know what *you* think about it."

"Well, she doesn't seem to want to ask me." He laughed. "It seems as though she's spending more time discussing it with you."

"You know that's not fair, John. She wants to know how you're thinking. Rosie has only turned to me because you seem to have shut her out."

"I've done nothing of the sort. If anything, it's the other way round."

"Well," said Sammie, "you'll have a chance of rectifying that in a minute, because she's calling in. She told me she's got tickets for the theatre. I think she's hoping that you'll go with her, since it will be one of her last evenings down here. Maybe that'll give you a chance to have a chat."

"Why the hell didn't she ring *me* to make the arrangement, instead of telling you?" John was on his feet again, annoyed at the attempts by Rosie and Sammie to organize his life. "I've already got an appointment that I can't break. You'll have to go instead. Perhaps that's what you've been hoping for all along."

"Don't be stupid, John," said Sammie wearily. "Rosemary doesn't even know I exist when you're around. But I can tell you that someone's going to come along one day and snap her up when you're not looking, unless you start treating her properly."

John leaned forward and rested his hands on the edge of the desk. "Look Sammie, let me make it clear to you. Rosie and I have grown apart. She knows it. I know it. We've hardly seen each other since she's been back from Sheffield." He spread his hands wide. "I accept that I have no rights over Rosie - where she goes, what she does, who she spends her time with. Anybody else (and that includes you) is entitled to make their play for her if they want to. Is that clear?"

Sammie swallowed and nodded dumbly.

"Good. Now then, I'm not going to hang around to get

miserable looks and sighs when she turns up." He stood upright. "I'll leave *you* to sort out who goes to the theatre with her. All right?"

"OK."

"So I'll be off," said John. "Shall we meet again for a progress meeting next Monday at six?"

Sammie smiled weakly. "If you like."

"How about if you come to the Pound Lane site," asked John. "We can alternate between the two locations if you think that would be a good idea."

"I suppose it would," said Sammie.

"I want to show you the advert I´m putting in the Western Morning News on Friday week. I´ve also written an article about the development, which they´ve promised to publish alongside the advert." John´s enthusiasm surfaced again. We should also have the new sign-board up at the entrance to the site and I´ll show you my plans for the sales office where I´ll be working."

"That´ll be interesting."

"Right. See you Monday."

John went out, leaving his friend sitting there, trying to think of something to say to Rosemary when she turned up.

64

The music swirled and washed around the marquee. The dancers swayed and spiralled across the floor. Henri held Alison in his arms and danced with her expertly and smoothly. As usual his conversation was deft and humorous and now slightly romantic.

"I am looking forward to our dinner date next Wednesday, Alison."

"So am I, Henri," she said. "I don't get up to town very often, and almost never in the evening."

"I've booked us a table on the roof garden of the Grosvenor overlooking the park. We'll have to hope for nice weather." He beamed up at her.

She smiled back. "It sounds lovely. I'll have difficulty in remembering to leave in time to catch the last train back."

"Ah," he said, a shade hesitantly. "I hope you don't mind, but I thought it seemed such a pity to spoil the evening by bringing it to an early end."

"Pardon?" She looked at him a shade suspiciously.

"So I took the liberty of booking you into a room for the night." He rushed on, "The Grosvenor is a very nice hotel."

Alison gulped. "I know it is. It is one of the best in London. A room there must cost a fortune."

"Oh, it won't cost *you* a penny," he assured her. "This is *my* present."

She shook her head. "But you shouldn't spend so much on me. We're only friends, after all."

"I have no intention of taking advantage of the position." He hastened to put her mind at rest. "Naturally I hope that our friendship will continue to grow. But I don't intend to put any pressure on you."

"Oh, dear Henri." She smiled at him. "You're such a gentleman."

Much more of a gentleman, she thought to herself, than John Tucker, who was lost in the crowd somewhere around the edge of the floor. Why was it that people like John were so much more interesting than the true gentlemen of this world?

"I thought I might join you for breakfast on the Thursday morning," said Henri. "My flat is just across the park from the hotel. Then I could take you round a few of the sights. I could get you into the Commons, if you like, to watch old Winston tearing into the opposition."

"That would be nice."

"I don't think that fellow Atlee's going to last much longer," he said. "He's not popular in the party. *Now* we're starting to get the country back on an even keel again."

Oh, god! Not politics on the dance floor, thought Alison, as they swooped in a statuesque turn into the corner of the floor where Camilla and her friends were sitting. Millie gave her a cheerful little wave and turned back to the crowd.

Where was John? He should have been there. She'd been dancing with Henri for less than five minutes and he was only the second other man she'd danced with. Surely he hadn't lost his temper with her friends' inanities and stormed off without her. That would be so like him. She sighed and turned back to listen to Henri's waffle.

It was several more minutes before the music came to an end and she could escape back to the group in the corner.

It was a beautiful summer evening. The sun had gone down and a misty darkness was rolling off the river and across the meadows. John had no doubt the woods were alive with the evensong of birds, but the sound was blotted out by the noisy music coming from the marquee behind him. He was alone in this other world outside.

He realised now that he had made a mistake in agreeing to come to the ball with Alison. This type of event and the life it represented were foreign to him. It wasn't that she and her friends hadn't tried to be friendly to him. They had all been very polite.

"Oh hello. Are you an old friend of the Staceys?"

"Tucker? Are you related to the Yorkshire Tuckers? Big name in Harrogate?"

"Were you at the palace on Wednesday? There were so many there that I didn't know more than half of them."

"What do you do? Are you something in the city?"

"Don't you think Philip's a darling?"

But he just didn't know what to say in reply. He recognized, when he was in the middle of this happy, self-confident throng, that he could never let himself become, or aspire to become, a member of the English upper class.

Alison had been swept away from him in a whirl of chattering friends, all comparing their experiences and conquests of the season. To watch them made John breathless. It was a sparkling kaleidoscope of bare shoulders, low *décolletés*, revealing cleavages. There were ball-gowns of every conceivable fabric and pattern, hairstyles of every shape and colour he could think of.

He had danced with Alison on three occasions and with a number of her friends - bold looks, intimate touches, overpowering fragrances. But he found it hugely tiring to discuss the weather and the little he knew of the great in the land when his mind was wanting to talk about the shape and the feel of his partner of the moment. He decided that his too frank conversations with Sarah had made him even less socially acceptable than he had been before.

They had eaten splendidly from a magnificent buffet of canapés and petit fou*rs* and vol-au-vents, caviar and smoked salmon, cold roast sucking pig and pheasant in aspic, all washed down with ice-cold champagne. There was no sign of rationing or food shortages among these people. However nobody else had been in the least excited, or even polite, about the food. Obviously it was so normal to them as to not merit a comment.

Finally, he had decided that he could take no more and had slid surreptitiously outside to witness the death of the day. Once there, out of the sweltering heat in the marquee, he removed his tight dinner jacket to cool off. He loosened his bow tie and eased one wing of his stiff dress shirt off the front collar stud. The relief was enormous. He was astonished that there weren't dozens of men outside, all doing the same thing. It seemed to him that these evening dress suits had been designed to impart an exquisite agony to the body. But such pain was probably surpassed by the suffering of the officers in their military dress. They bore the discomfort with such fortitude that it was not surprising their wearers were so insensitive to the day-to-day distresses of their men, or of the lower classes in general.

He began to stroll gently towards the river. He could feel every little twig and stone through the thin soles of the patent leather shoes. The glistening toes, hardly smudged by the various evening sandals with which they'd come into contact while he was dancing, were collecting beads of icy cold dew on them. It occurred to John that he would have to make sure he cleaned them thoroughly before they were returned to the hirers.

At the river bank he paused by a tree-stump. He would have liked to sit for a while, but he suspected the tight trousers might well split up the backside if they were subjected to such stress. The water moved languidly past, occasionally punctuated by the movement of some aquatic creature breaking the surface, which sent out widening circular ripples to set the bank-side reeds and grasses waving gently in their wake. He took in a deep breath of the exquisite peace.

He wondered why Alison had brought him to this event. It seemed to him that escorts were hardly a standard requirement. Many of the young ladies had come in twos and threes, as had the gentlemen. Was there some deeper purpose? Was she trying to soften him up for some reason which suited the Stacey family? He must try and find out.

He turned and looked back at the marquee, all lit up, the centre of the night. He supposed he should go back to the noise and the dancing before he was missed. How long was he expected to stay? Obviously as long as Alison wanted to continue chatting and flirting with her friends. With a sinking heart he decided it would probably be at least another four hours - longer than had already passed. And he couldn't even get drunk, since he was driving his own car. He started the slow stroll back in the near-darkness.

Outside the marquee he paused to put on his jacket and do up his collar stud and adjust his bow tie. But try as he would, he couldn't get the damn stud done up. He was still wrestling with it when a girl appeared at the doorway. She was wearing a black cocktail dress with little puff shoulders and a very low décolleté which revealed the tops of her splendid breasts.

Alison saw him at once and hurried over. "John, where have you been? I've been looking for you for ages."

"Sorry," he said. "I decided I needed a breath of fresh air."

"Well, you might have told me." She came close. "Perhaps I would have wanted to come with you."

He grinned apologetically. "I thought you were too busy with your friends. I didn't want to break up the fun." He thought to himself of the comments, the knowing smiles which would have been exchanged behind their backs.

"What are you doing?" Alison peered at him with his half-undone shirt collar.

"Well," confessed John, pink with embarrassment, "the collar-stud was pressing into my throat. It was agony. So I decided to give myself some relief while I was outside by partly undoing it. Now I can't do it up again."

She giggled. "Oh, John. At least you admit to being human. Here - let me see if I can do it."

John looked quickly round but there was nobody else watching. So he submitted to her efforts. He felt her cool, capable fingers slide inside the tight collar of his shirt. Her slim figure was pressed against his. He was very conscious of the scent of her soft, dark hair close to his face as she fiddled with the collar stud.

After a minute or so she said, "Who invented these silly devices? I can get the top buttonhole of the shirt on, but I can't also get the collar to fit. Here, take your bow tie off."

John was having acute difficulty in breathing. "Let go for a minute," he gasped. "I'll do it."

She stood back and watched as he undid the stud again and took a welcome lungful of night air. "Now you've undone it again."

"But I couldn't breathe," he gasped.

"You got it on all right before you came out?"

"Yes. I think my neck must have swelled up with the heat."

"Take your tie off," she ordered. "That'll give you a bit more room."

"But if I do that, I'll never get it back under the stiff collar, will I?"

Alison considered carefully. "I suppose not. Well, let me have one more go with the silly thing." She grasped both ends of the collar and pulled them together with her strong fingers.

John howled and twisted out of her grip.

"What do you mean by wriggling," she demanded. "I nearly had it then."

"And you almost cut my windpipe in half," he gasped.

Alison started to laugh. "Oh John, you do look funny, with one end of your collar stuck up in the air. Tell me, why do men have to wear such stupid items of clothing?"

"I don't know." John thought he ought to have felt aggrieved by her laughter, but he couldn't help chuckling as well. "I've never worn one before. I suppose I should have had a shirt a couple of sizes bigger. Then there would have been room for expansion."

"And until you warmed up, you'd have looked like an ostrich with its head protruding out of a rubber ring." Alison fell against his chest, almost weeping with laughter.

John hugged her to him, feeling her slim body through the thin fabric of her dress. "But what am I going to do now?"

"I don't know." She looked up at him and shook her head. There were tears of laughter in her eyes. "You can't go back in there looking like this."

"You're too right, I can't."

"Never mind," she said. "I'll go in and make apologies for us both. Then we'll go back to your hotel and you can change."

"But that'll spoil the evening for you."

She shook her head. "No, it won't. I've had enough of this lot anyway. I came to look for you to tell you that I was feeling bored and to ask you dance with me. You'll be giving me a good excuse to get away early. Can you lend me your handkerchief to dry my eyes?"

"OK. If you don't mind." He handed it to her and she mopped at her eyes' leaving smears of mascara on her cheeks.

"Thank you." She gave it back and erupted again in giggles. "Will you take that silly collar and tie off while I'm gone? I can't take you seriously while you're wearing that."

Then she disappeared before he could tell her about the

smudges in her mascara.

65

The private hotel into which John had been booked was located in a wooded road outside the town. He parked the car on the gravel forecourt and turned to Alison. “Want to come in?”

“Well, I’m certainly not staying out here with all those trees swaying and whispering in the dark.”

The front door was locked although it was still before midnight. But John had warned them he would be late and had been given a key. A low wattage night light burned in Reception. The bar and restaurant were closed and dark.

“It’s not the entertainment centre of Henley, is it?” he asked.

She grabbed his arm. “I think it’s a bit creepy. You read about hotels like this in mystery novels. All sorts of things seem to happen in these places.”

“You’ll have to come upstairs with me then.” John felt his pulse quickening.

“I certainly will.” Alison seemed unworried by the suggestiveness in his voice. “Which way do we go?”

“Up here.” He shepherded her up the stairs.

At the top she stopped. “Which way now?”

He came up behind her and rested his hands on her hips. “Let me show you. My room’s the third on the left.”

She giggled and moved close against him as they went down the darkened corridor. Outside the door to his room he stopped her. His left hand was round her waist and her right buttock was tucked into his groin as he put the key in the lock and turned. He opened the door quietly and they went in. He turned away from her to search for the switch.

“Don’t put the light on.” She had crossed to the window and was looking down into the car park.

So instead John slid the bolt across on the door and put the keys back in his pocket. He took off his jacket and tossed it on the chair.

Alison turned to face him as he walked towards her. “I hope you’re going to take that silly shirt off at last,” she said.

She started to unbutton it for him, and John took her in his arms and kissed her. He could tell she was ready for him by the way she responded. There was no surprise and no resistance. He almost had the feeling that he was being tried out. It was a strange sensation, as though she was going to report back to someone about his performance.

He decided to try some of the techniques that Sarah had taught him. He slid his lips off her face into the nape of her neck. Then he ran his knuckle round the bottom of her rib cage. It got the usual shuddering response.

"Agh." Her body stiffened against him. He returned his lips to her face and this time he was rewarded with a kiss of real passion. He slid his hand up towards her breast, squashed into the stiffly boned basque just beneath the neckline of her dress. She pulled back from him.

"I want to take that stupid shirt off." She was pulling at the buttons again.

"In that case," said John, "I ought to be able to take off something of yours. What can it be?"

She giggled. "That's up to you."

It was then that he knew for sure that she was available to him. He felt a surge of excitement. He was going to make love to a member of the aristocracy, to one of the upper classes. He promised himself he would do his best to really make it something for her to tell to her friends, when they gossiped about him.

Then he remembered. "Sod it," he cursed.

"What's the matter?"

"I've left my packet of Durex down in the car."

She smiled. "Don't worry. I'm already prepared. They teach you all about that sort of thing at St Teresa's."

"What?" he laughed. "Do you mean the Catholic nuns at your convent have been teaching you about birth-control?"

"Oh, they didn't tell us about it themselves. They brought a doctor in to explain to us about good health in all things. They probably didn't even realise that he was teaching us the ways of the devil." She shook her head. "But I'm sure he was doing what the parents wanted. At the end of his talk we were all issued with our little contraceptive kits."

"What does that mean?"

"We had to buy them, of course. There were a couple of dutch caps – they're the things that fit over the entrance to the womb. Also there was a tube of spermicidal cream to rub over them. The doctor showed us how to fit them and we had to practice until we got it right."

"How romantic."

She looked at him. "Seriously, it all makes sense." She shrugged. "Then, because the things can come loose, especially if the man is a bit too big or a bit rough, we were given some pills that we could take the next morning. But we were warned to only take those in an extreme situation because they can be dangerous."

John nodded. "Of course, we've got to get our priorities right. We don't want any little semi-aristocratic bastards around, do we?"

"We were taught it was never wise to rely on the man for this sort of thing. They always forget them or they break or something." She smiled sweetly. "So it's all right. You can have your pleasure in complete safety."

"You mean you put one of these dutch cap things in before you came out this evening? Just in case?"

"Well, it´s wise to be ready. I decided I shouldn´t refuse you if you asked for it. After all, I felt I sort of owed it to you."

"You make it sound like a business transaction."

"Don´t be silly. It's not like that at all. If I like a man and he likes me, I don't have to play the distressed maiden and say, 'Sorry, I'm keeping myself for my wedding night.'"

"So how often do you do this?"

She looked at him coolly. "I think that's my affair, don't you?"

"So you're telling me this is my chance to be admitted to the favoured inner circle without any risk of an unfortunate outcome."

"Don't be so bloody plebeian."

John turned away and looked out of the window. He found that now he had lost any urge to make love to the woman. He was aware that he was a hypocrite, but Alison's practical attitude to sex had destroyed his wish to make love to her any more. "I'm sorry," he said, "I've sort of gone off the boil. I think we'll forget it for tonight."

She was quiet for a time. Then she said, "I suppose what I said spoiled it for you."

"It's my fault. As you say, I'm too much of a pleb to treat sex as something served up on a plate."

"It's a pity. I think you might probably be a good lover." She laid a hand on his arm and went on more hesitantly. "I can tell from what your hands were doing when you kissed me, it's not the first time you've made love to a woman either, is it?"

He shook his head. "Nor you."

She didn't reply to that. "You've had a good teacher," she said. "Don't tell me it was young Rosemary Williams."

He had the grace to grin. "Now *you* mind your own affairs." He turned to look at her so that she wouldn't be angry. "I'm afraid I'm not at liberty to say."

"Don't worry. I shan't press you. But I can guess who it is."

John said nothing.

Alison started to tidy her hair. "Will you drive me back to Millie's?"

"Of course." He sat on the bed and watched her, doing up his shirt as he did so.

She smiled at him. "What a pity it all came to nothing. Never mind. Perhaps there'll be another opportunity."

"Perhaps there will," said John, but somehow he didn't think there would be.

66

Ambrose sat at his desk and wrestled with his sales report. He reflected that this new job with the bank wasn't all fun by any means. For a start, they seemed to expect him to provide both verbal and written reports once a fortnight. They sat down with him and discussed his strategy and his approach to potential clients, and they set out an expected timetable for bringing in contacts.

Furthermore they had made it quite clear to him that they expected a lot more from him than he'd brought in so far. Ambrose sighed as he surveyed the blank sheet of paper. He had to admit that he'd shown them very little to date. In fact, he'd only been at the bank for three weeks, and already the whole thing was turning into quite a bore.

He was so busy concentrating on the best way of presenting the little he had to offer, that for a few seconds he didn't notice the young secretary standing by his desk. His head jerked up as she cleared her throat. But he quickly relaxed again. He felt a foolish pride in being caught concentrating on his job.

"Hello, my dear," he murmured, "what can I do for you?"

"There's a lady to see you, Mr Stacey." She was a smart little girl, a little flat-chested perhaps, but worth turning on the charm for.

"A lady, eh? What sort of a lady would that be?" Ambrose liked to bring in a little humour from time to time.

She blushed slightly and looked down at the card in her hand. "She's a Mrs Grant. Mrs Sarah Grant."

Ambrose put his brain cells in gear. The name had a familiar ring, but he couldn't put a face to it. "Mrs Grant? Well, if she's anxious to see me, I think she ought to be put out of her misery as soon as possible, don't you? Is there an interview room available?"

"I've already put her in number three."

"OK." He nodded approval. "Give her a cup of tea and tell her I won't be long. Oh - and Charlotte?"

"Yes, Mr Stacey?"

"What time do you finish, my dear?"

The girl went pink. "Five-thirty, Mr Stacey."

"Five-thirty. Right. I'll remember that." He smiled after her as she turned and hurried back to reception.

It took him about five minutes to struggle to the end of the first paragraph of his report. Then, acutely dissatisfied with the contents, he rose and made his way to interview room three. Sarah Grant was standing by the window looking down into the grey, cluttered city street. As she turned to face him, he realised immediately who she was. He was sure he'd seen her around in Devon on a number of occasions, although he'd never had the pleasure of closer contact with her. That was something to regret, since he could see that she had a splendid figure. Her shape looked even better in the well-cut costume she was wearing, which showed off more than a hint of cleavage.

Now the lady advanced towards him with her hand out. "It's so kind of you to see me without an appointment."

"My dear Mrs Grant, I'm delighted to be available when you need me. Please sit down." He ushered her toward the low, comfortable chair reserved for clients and went behind the table to the efficient, upright chair where he was able to command a good view of her assets. "Now, what can I do for you, Mrs – er - Grant."

"Please call me Sarah." She settled back in her chair and crossed her legs, displaying quite a lot of well-rounded thigh.

"Of course I will. I'm Ambrose." He leaned back and surveyed her with satisfaction. "So - how can I help you, Sarah?"

She paused for a moment, appearing to weigh in her mind exactly what she should reveal to him. "Firstly, Ambrose, I should like to make it clear that what we're about to discuss is confidential outside the bank. I particularly do not want any of it discussed with anybody back in Devon.

"Oh, let me assure you of that," he promised. "Coming to a merchant bank ensures complete confidentiality."

"Good." She took a breath. "Now - I was recommended to come and see you by John Tucker. I understand he shared rooms with you at Cambridge. He was the one who told me that you had recently joined Schuberts."

"Well, I'm blowed." Ambrose couldn't prevent his surprise showing.

"You are probably not aware that John and I are business partners in a housing development which has just started in Pound Lane, a mile or so from Stacey Court."

"What - those little boxes in the valley -." He stopped himself lest he should give offence.

But Sarah seemed not in the least put out. "Precisely. Those little boxes. You will of course be aware that John Tucker, though a very clever young man, has no personal wealth to speak of. The funding for the project has come from my side. He provides the know-how."

"I'm sure he has plenty of that."

"Now," she said, ignoring the innuendo, "this development is going very well, and a lot of interest is being shown by prospective purchasers. When the houses go on the market at the end of the month, we expect we will have no problem with selling them at the asking price. In fact, demand looks set to substantially outstrip supply in the area." Sarah leaned forward earnestly, providing him with a magnificent view down the front of her costume. "The reason for me coming to see the bank, Ambrose, is that an opportunity has arisen for us to capitalise on our successful start. However, the next stage of development will overstretch my own resources, and I am looking for an investing partner." She relaxed and leaned back again in her chair. "I am hoping, when we have shown you all the figures, that Schuberts will be interested in coming in with us."

Ambrose tried to prevent the disappointment from showing on his face, at having the wonderful view that she presented, snatched away from him. "What precisely do you have in mind?" he asked.

"In a nutshell - the development which we're doing at the moment is on a single eight-acre field I bought from Mr Fisher at Pound Farm. He now wants to retire and sell me the other hundred and forty acres, keeping only the farmhouse and a few acres of paddock and orchard for his own use." Ambrose noticed how business-like she sounded. "So the bank would have security for the money it loaned us in the form of land and houses under construction." She slid sideways in her chair and showed a bit more leg. "Do you think you would be interested?"

"Absolutely," he breathed. "Er - what I mean is that the bank would most certainly be interested in looking at your proposals in detail. This is just the sort of need that we exist to satisfy. I presume you can give us figures to show that the investment would be a profitable one."

"Of course we can. I must say I hoped that would be your reaction." Sarah's smile was just like a cat who has been offered a bowl of rich cream. "The prospect only arose a couple of days ago, so nothing has been worked out yet in detail. But I was in town and I suddenly thought - why not call in and see what sort of reception I get. I must say it's a great pleasure to receive such a warm welcome."

When she smiled at him like that, Ambrose felt the hairs stand up on the back of his neck. He told himself that he was going to make damn sure that this one didn't get away. "Nonsense, Sarah. The pleasure's mine. What I need to do next is get together somewhere quiet with you, so that we can go through your proposals in detail. When could you fit that in?"

"Oh," she shook her head, "I'll leave that to John to sort out with you. I'm no good at figures. But he's brilliant at that sort of thing. I'll get him to work it all out and give you a call in a week or two. Now, I'll have to rush, or I'll miss my train."

Ambrose rose as she did, and came round to her side of the desk, trying to hide his disappointment. "Very well," he smiled. "Tell him to ring me when he's ready. I'm here most days at present. But I must say I'm sorry I shan't be able to deal with you personally."

"Don't worry." Sarah laid a hand on his arm and smiled up at him in a way that turned his stomach over. "We'll have a celebration together when everything's signed and sealed."

She turned her back on him and minced out, hips swaying.

"I'll hold you to that," he said, almost to himself.

Then he returned to his desk. All of a sudden, his weekly report had become less of a chore.

67

Alison had to wait until after nine before Ambrose arrived. She didn't feel able to confront her father on her own without her brother's support. A whole lifetime of filial loyalty made this task one which she dreaded, but she had decided it was vital that somebody made Sir Oswald face up to the truth before he was totally destroyed. It should have been Ambrose who spoke to him, but he wouldn't do it by himself. So she insisted that her brother was at least going to be present when she tackled the old man.

She was sitting on her own in the morning room when he turned up, announcing his arrival by the ostentatious way his car roared up the drive and skidded to a halt on the gravel area. She got up to open the door. There had probably been a time when her father would have behaved in just such a puerile manner. She wondered whether either man would ever mature.

Ambrose came up the steps with a degree of hesitation. "Where is he?"

"In his study, of course."

"Is he sloshed yet? He won't be any good if he's sloshed."

Alison was a little shocked. "He doesn't get sloshed. He's always in control of himself." She looked at her brother closely. "What about you?"

"What do you mean?" He sounded aggressive enough to have been drinking.

"Have you had anything to eat?"

"I grabbed a sandwich before I left." He grinned a bit defensively. "I wouldn't mind a whisky before we go in to see him though. It'd even up the score a bit, if you know what I mean."

She shrugged. "OK. What's another five minutes?"

While he poured himself a double, Alison went over her proposed arguments again with him. Ambrose knew roughly what she was going to say. She'd told him the story on the phone. Now the part of her that she'd inherited from her mother wanted to get the whole thing over as soon as possible.

"Are you ready, Ambrose?"

He downed the rest of his drink. "Yes. We'd better get on with it. You're going to do the talking though. He'd never take it from me."

"Just make sure you back me up if I ask you. That's all."

Without waiting for his reply Alison stood up and walked through the main reception room to the library door. She tapped on it and went in. Ambrose followed her more slowly. Sir Oswald was sitting in his usual place at his desk. He was gazing at a glass about one third full of clear gin. He didn't raise his head when they walked in.

"Father." Alison received no reply, so she continued. "It is very important that Ambrose and I talk to you." She paused - again without response from the old man. "I have to tell you, that yesterday morning, when Susie Partridge had driven you to the hunter trials, I received a visit from a - er - from a man. He said he was a bailiff, and he had a court order empowering him to seize and sell all your goods and property."

Now she had her father's attention. "What? What did you tell him?"

Alison drew herself up to her full height. "I lied to him. I told him you were negotiating to sell the estate and would be able to discharge the debt when you had completed the sale. I told him to contact your solicitor about the details."

"What?" The old man's bloodhound eyes lifted to look at her for the first time. "You did that all by yourself? My God, I do believe you have some of your mother's fire in you."

"The only thing is," said Alison, "that I don't know whether the sale of the estate would bring in anything like enough money."

"What do you mean?"

"The bailiff was acting on behalf of a gambling club in London who say you owe them a hundred and forty-eight thousand pounds." She shook her head. "I just can't understand how much money that is. It's more than I've ever come across before. The man said it was definitely much more than they'd get for everything here on a forced sale basis - whatever that means."

"Huh, I can guess," interjected Ambrose.

Alison ignored him. She surprised herself with her own icy calm. “This news did not come as a complete shock to me,” she said, “although the horrifying size of the debt was something for which I was *not* ready.”

Sir Oswald just gazed at her, his eyes gripped by the sheer strength of personality of this twenty-one-year-old girl. How had he managed to father someone like this?

However Alison now felt completely in control. “You may want to know why I suspected that you had problems, and I’ll tell you. In addition to your increased drinking over the last year or two, I had also found out from Ambrose that you wanted him to try and borrow some money for you from the bank he has just joined. But more than that, you may recall that I returned from an evening out a couple of months ago to find you had taken an overdose of aspirin. I had to ask my escort, John Tucker, to help bring you round.”

Her father grimaced. “I don’t want him involved. Ghastly fellow. Don’t know what you see in him.”

“Well, after you’d been put to bed and everyone had gone, I happened to notice the letters on your desk. Then I found one in your waste-paper basket which said that a legal judgement had been made against you for debt - fortunately in a London court.” She leaned forward. “That was why you took the overdose, wasn’t it, father?”

The old man hesitated. Then he nodded. He seemed to shrink under her gaze. Alison had the ridiculous feeling that it was she who was the adult and he the irresponsible minor.

“You also know that more recently I invited that same ′ghastly fellow′ John Tucker round here to look at the state of the house. He revealed to me that you have stripped the lead from the roofs and sold it to get money.” She paused then suddenly accused him. “*Money to finance your gambling*.”

Sir Oswald managed to summon up some energy to protest. “You should never have let him in. He had no right -”

“He had every right, father. Am I not allowed to ask friends of mine into the house? Can’t I ask their views on things that I’m worried about? I understand that you’ve since used your influence to get him sacked from his job, because he was doing it too well. It disgusts me that you can be so petty and vindictive."

"Well, I - I -" His mouth opened and shut ineffectively.

"You've also sold almost all the valuable possessions which have been handed down in the family over centuries. You've thrown away the history and the pride of the Staceys." Alison was almost shouting now. "And you've just sat here and swallowed more and more gin and done nothing about these things, so that now you're utterly and irrevocably in REALLY DEEP SHIT. Isn't that right, Father?"

He just sat and gazed open-mouthed at her. He didn't even attempt to protest at her language - a sure sign that he was in shock.

"So," she demanded, "what are we going to do about it? Some of us still have pride in the Stacey name. I have discussed this with Ambrose, who agrees with me. You have built up vast debts and we must clear those. We cannot allow you to be made bankrupt and perhaps even be jailed for fraud. We see no alternative but to sell the one asset you have left, Stacey Estates, in order to settle the debt. The only question is whether we can bring in enough money to clear the account and leave you a little to live on. Do *you* know how to do that?"

Sir Oswald shook his head.

She turned to her brother. "Do you know, Ambrose?"

The young Stacey took up an exaggerated pose. "Well, actually," he said, "I think perhaps I do. I was thinking about it in the car on the way down."

There was a stunned silence for a moment, then Alison said, a shade sceptically, "Come on then. Tell us what your plan is."

"It's simple really." He regarded his sister with a lazy insolence. "We do what the English aristocracy always do when they're deep in the shit, as you so sweetly put it. It's what father tried to do twenty-five years ago, only it didn't work out that time. We marry some money into the family."

"Who do you have in mind with loads of money who would be willing to marry you?" She regarded him suspiciously, already half-knowing what his reply would be.

Ambrose blanched. "Not me, little sister. I don't give a damn about Stacey Court. The whole bloody place can go under the hammer tomorrow, as far as I'm concerned. It's you and father who want to save it. It's you who worry about the tradition of the Staceys. So – it is *you* who will have to make the sacrifice."

"What do you mean?" asked his father impatiently. "Stop talking in riddles."

He sniggered. "What I mean, father dear, is that it is *Alison* who must marry to get the money to save your bacon. I've even got the perfect chap lined up. He's my boss, Henri Maeterlink."

"Don't be stupid," she said. "I'm not interested in Henri - not in that way. And how do you know he's interested in me?"

"I've been keeping an eye on him, little sister. I believe he's potty about you. He's got plenty of cash. And I've no doubt that he'd like to be installed as the local squire down here at the weekends as a bonus. All *you* have to do is give him the idea and he'll come rushing. I can more or less guarantee it."

There was a long silence. Alison went over and sat in the old leather armchair. She leaned back and studied the moulded plasterwork of the ceiling. Stacey watched her furtively from beneath his beetling brows.

"Ambrose does have a certain point," he ventured. "We do have to do something pretty extreme to get out of trouble this time."

"Trouble which *you've* got us into, father," she reminded him acidly. "Why should I have to give up my independence to get you out of trouble? That's even supposing that Ambrose is right, and that Henri is interested in throwing away a big chunk of his wealth in order to acquire me and this place."

"What independence?" asked her brother. "It's no sort of independence to be out in the big world without an income or a means of earning one. Your loving daddy isn't going to be able to afford to keep giving you handouts if he's gone spectacularly bust. He won't even have enough to keep himself."

There was another silence while the others absorbed this truth.

Stacey said softly, "Your brother has an unfortunate knack of putting his finger on the spot."

"This is ridiculous." Alison shook her head. "Are you

seriously suggesting that I waltz up to Henri and say to him, 'Daddy's in trouble. He owes a hundred and fifty thousand pounds. I suggest you pay off his debts in return for acquiring the Stacey Estates and me as your wife'. Be sensible, Ambrose."

"It won't be like that at all," said her brother. "Henri already knows that father's deep in the mire. He just doesn't know exactly *how* bad it is. So, what I suggest is that I go back to Henri and say that father wants to sell the estate in order to find a hundred and fifty thousand pounds to pay off his debts and get an income for life. I can ask his advice on how he should go about it. Meanwhile you ought to be able to engineer an invitation out of him to meet somewhere."

She sighed. "He's taking me to dinner at the Grosvenor next Wednesday."

"That's perfect," said Ambrose. "You know what to do. Wear a sexy dress. Show plenty of cleavage. Douse yourself in perfume. Play the part of the poor little abandoned princess. And make sure you get him to bundle you into bed."

"Please don't be so crude," protested Stacey.

But his son ignored the interruption. "Next morning you tell him what a wonderful night it's been, and you can't wait for the next time. Take it from me - he'll have proposed within a week. Then all you have to do is work out the details of how the money gets paid across."

"You *are* revolting, Ambrose," she leaped to her feet. "You make me sound like a whore."

"Rubbish. It's the same thing that's been going on for generations." He grinned smugly.

"Well, not with me, it hasn't," she blazed at him. "Henri's a nice person. Why should we take advantage of him like this?"

Ambrose spread his arms in supplication. "It won't be taking advantage of him. I've already told you he's potty about you. This will be the culmination of everything he's planned and worked for."

"And what about me?" she demanded. "I don't want to get married. I'm only twenty-one, for God's sake. I want to see a bit more of life before I commit myself permanently to being a housewife and a mother."

"There was a time," Sir Oswald muttered, "when young people did what their parents wanted. After all, it's not as though we're asking you to marry some scruffy character like young Tucker."

Alison rounded on him. "Why can't you leave John alone, Father? He is *not* a scruffy character. He's just too independently minded to suit your old-fashioned ideas of the upper classes and the respect owed to them."

Stacey was outraged. "Are you saying that you would prefer to ally yourself with that fellow?"

"I don't want to marry anyone, Father." Her chin jutted out and her eyes blazed.

"Anyway he wouldn't be any good," said Ambrose lazily. "He just hasn't got enough money. It'll be another five years before you can think seriously about jumping into bed with him."

"I am not thinking of jumping into bed with *anyone*." Alison held her head in her hands. "How many times do I have to tell you that I am not ready for marriage?"

It was suddenly quiet. Ambrose walked across to the uncurtained window and looked out at the gathering darkness.

Sir Oswald Stacey rose to his feet slowly. "Very well," he said quietly. "You have made the position clear to me. I will decide what action I must take. You can leave me now."

"What do you mean, Father?" she demanded.

"Look father," said Ambrose, turning back from the window, "you won't solve any problems by blowing your brains out, or anything foolish like that. The estate will just be broken up and sold off in bits to the highest bidder. Alison will have nothing. She won't even have a good name. Who would want to marry the daughter of somebody who'd committed suicide rather than face his creditors?"

Stacey sank back into his chair. "Then what are we to do?" he asked pathetically.

"I don't know." His son shrugged. "I've made *my* suggestion. If Alison refuses to play along with it, she'll have to come up with something better." He turned to her. "The only thing is, you'd better be quick. These bailiffs, who you've put off with this story, will be back in a week or two expecting an answer."

She nodded. "Very well. I suppose I´m going to have to think about it."

"Talk to lover-boy, if you like," said Ambrose. "But don't spend too long making up your mind."

"I won't," she said. "I will let you know in a few days."

She turned and went up to her bedroom to think in isolation.

68

John started his new job on Monday morning. He was at the site at Pound Lane before eight but Angus was there before him. And somebody else was there as well. Alison Stacey's horse was tied to a post just outside the site gate and she was waiting for him in the new sales office which had been finished over the weekend.

She stood up as he walked in. He thought how attractive she looked in her jodhpurs and dark riding jacket, nipped in at the waist and open at the front to reveal a plain white silk shirt. Her long, dark hair was piled up on her head and tied with a wispy scarf.

"Hello," said John, not quite sure of his reception after their last parting. "This *is* a surprise. To what do I owe the honour of this visit?"

Alison had spent the whole of yesterday preparing her approach carefully in her mind. "Well," she said, "firstly I have come to apologise for the way that father reacted to your inspection of the roof at Stacey Court. I didn't know about it when you took me to the dance at Henley. I have told him that his behaviour was petty and vindictive."

"You *have*?" John couldn't keep the surprise out of his voice.

"I told him he had no right to react as he did. I told him that it was me who invited you to look at the place." She smiled apologetically. "Of course, I realise that won't be much compensation to you at this stage."

He shook his head. "Actually the incident didn't do me any harm. It forced me to come to a decision I should have reached before."

"Nevertheless, I wanted to apologise personally for being the unwitting cause of your being sacked from your first job." She looked down at the floor, remembering that she had also been the cause of him having to get the job in the first place. "I'm sorry for that."

John was quite touched to have such an apology from

someone to whom he knew humility did not come easily. "Forget about it," he said. "By coincidence you're here on the very day that I start work on my new job." He grinned at her. "Do I seem depressed about it?"

She looked up at him and smiled that heart-stopping smile of hers. "No. I must say you seem quite happy. What exactly are you going to do here?"

"I'm building and selling houses. I've been supervising the start of the work over the last three or four months. Now we're actually ready to put them on the market. Adverts will appear in the local and national papers in the next few days, and we've already got a list of nearly thirty people who are interested. We open the show-house today, and I shall be ringing round, inviting anyone who might want to see it, to visit for an inspection. Meanwhile we'll have the first houses ready for occupation within a month and we expect that quite a few people will have moved in before Christmas."

Alison was infected by his enthusiasm. "I'd like to look round this show-house of yours."

"Would you really?" John felt a shade suspicious. "They're not your type of house at all. They're quite small. They are built with the concept of carefully planned and well fitted-out space. They'll seem minute to you."

"That's why I'd like to see one, to see -" She paused, aware that she'd nearly blundered.

"To see how the other half lives." He supplied the finish bitterly.

"John, why do you have to be so prickly about this?" She laid her hand on his arm. "Please will you let me have a look at this show-house?"

Suddenly he grinned, forgetting his anger. "All right. Why not? You can perform the opening ceremony since we have nothing else planned. We'll go down now." He looked at her shiny black riding boots. "They should be all right as long as you wipe them on the mat."

"Cheek!" She followed him as he went into the next-door office.

"Morning, Angus," he said to the foreman, "I'll see you later to go through plans for the week. Is the show-house open?"

"Not yet, Mr Tucker. The key's here." He took it from his drawer, stood up and gave it to him.

"I'm taking Miss Stacey to look at it, if anyone wants me."

"Mrs Grant rang just ´afore you arrived, to say 'er'll be over in about an hour."

"Thanks."

John led Alison across the site, explaining as they went, about the progress they were making - which houses would be ready first, where the children's play area was going to be, what their plans were. "If our sales go well," he said, "we hope to complete the whole estate some time next summer."

"What will you do when they're all finished and sold?"

"Sit back and count the profits of course." He grinned engagingly. "No, not really. We've already got plans for another, bigger estate which will start at the beginning of next year."

"Did you say "we"?"

"I and my backers." He spread his arms wide. "You didn't think I'd have the money to finance all this, did you?"

Alison decided that now was not the right time to ask him who his backers were. Instead she asked, "Do you like doing this sort of job?"

"Of course I do. A lot of it is outdoor work and I can see the place growing as I planned it. Surely it's the sort of thing that anybody would like to do. *And* I feel as though I'm giving ordinary people nicer places to live in than the little two-up and two-down that many of them have been used to." He pointed to the house in front of them. "Here you are. This is the show house. You can judge for yourself."

He led her up the neat concrete path to the brightly painted front door. He unlocked it and stood back to usher her in. "Do you mind brushing your boots on the mat outside?" he asked. "We want to try and keep the carpets clean for as long as possible."

Alison did as she was told with hardly any hesitation. She stepped into the narrow hallway with the stairs going up to the right.

"The sitting room is on the left," he said.

She went in to what seemed a very small room to her. “Why, it’s all furnished.”

“Yes,” he explained. “This is the show house, furnished to give potential purchasers an idea of what the place might look like when it’s occupied. Of course, we don’t include the carpets and loose furniture in the house price. If someone wants to buy the place complete with furniture, they´d have to pay extra.”

“Is that what they might do?”

“I believe it often happens if the prospective purchasers are living in rented furnished accommodation. It would save them money in setting up their new house and they could probably get some of it paid by the mortgage company.”

“That´s a clever idea.” Perhaps she was thinking of her father.

He took a breath. “To carry on, you can see that there’s a fireplace with a back-boiler to heat the water, which is included in all the houses, and there’s room to get a three-piece suite in, which is what modern families are usually looking for. The dining room has a serving hatch through to the kitchen and a full-height back door to the garden. Come and have a look at the kitchen.”

He led her through the hall and into the room at the back. “You will see there are worktops all round the walls with cupboards under them and wall cabinets to put the crockery in. This is fairly unusual in new houses at present, but I think that everyone will be doing it soon.”

“Yes, I like it.” She turned to him. “But I suppose any woman would like a properly fitted-out place like this. I think you’re very clever, John Tucker. You know how to get the women on your side.”

“Well, we’ve advertised this as one of our special advantages and there’s been a lot of interest in it. Actually it allows us to slightly reduce the size of the kitchen so that it fits under the bathroom and saves on structural costs. There isn’t a separate larder but we leave space for a refrigerator, as you can see. Also there’s a ventilated cupboard under the stairs which is reached from the hall and can be used for storage.”

John continued to talk about the special advantages of the house as they walked round. Alison was impressed by his expertise. When he had finished, she felt ready to broach the subject which she had really come to discuss with him. She paused at the foot of the stairs.

"There's something I want to ask your views about, John."

"OK." He pointed to a door. "Do you want to come and sit in the lounge?"

"That's a good idea." She preceded him into the front room and sat down in one of the armchairs. It was a bit too small and upright for her liking. When he was sitting opposite her, she launched into her prepared subject. "You know when you came round and looked at the roof of Stacey Court? You found that you'd stumbled on something my father had done which suggested he was desperate for money." She paused, waiting for his comment.

"Of course I had no idea of the reasons why he had taken such drastic action."

"Maybe not. But I decided to find out some more." Alison took in a deep breath. "The fact is that I've uncovered an absolutely horrifying situation. All in all Daddy owes something like a hundred and fifty thousand pounds."

"My God, how did he manage to get into that situation?"

She shook her head. "I don't know. I think all sorts of things entered into it. But mainly it was gambling in one of the private London clubs. I just don't understand myself how he could let himself get into such a position."

"I presume this is much more than he can repay from his normal annual income." John was thinking that he would have expected himself to be gloating over the financial ruin of the old man, whom he had long regarded as a personal enemy. But recent events had subtly affected his feelings towards the Stacey family, and he could only feel sorry for the daughter who had to try to pick up the pieces.

Alison was looking at him. "Well, I don't know how much he gets, but I'm sure it's no more than a thousand or two a year. He's sold all the shares and other investments he used to have, so he'll mainly be relying on rents from the farms and the estate cottages and that won't bring in nearly enough to pay for the normal expenses of running the house and things like that, ignoring his personal debts." She shook her head. "Ambrose and I had a straight talk with him on Friday night. We told him he has no alternative but to sell the estate to clear his debts and we hope there will be enough surplus to give him an income."

John got up and walked to the window. He felt more able to think clearly on his feet. "What does that mean for *you*?"

"I don't know yet. Of course Ambrose has his job in London," she answered obliquely. "In any case he says *he* wouldn't want to inherit the house. He prefers city life."

"What I asked," he persisted, "was how would *you* feel if you had to move out of Stacey Court?"

She was quiet for a time, looking down at the patterned carpet, before she answered his question. This was what she had been thinking about all over the weekend. "Actually I have been offered a solution which would mean that perhaps I could stay in the place."

"Really?" He turned and looked at her oddly. "What is that exactly?"

Alison looked up at him. There seemed to be a plea in her eyes. "My father and Ambrose have suggested that I should marry a rich man who would buy Stacey Court and install himself and me there, allowing my father to live in a flat on the property."

"What! That's a bit feudal, isn't it?"

"It's been done plenty of times before in the history of the English aristocracy," she said defensively. "Even my father tried to marry into American money. Unfortunately for him, my mother died before she inherited enough wealth to save Stacey Court."

John could only look at her - horrified.

Alison plunged on, her eyes glued to his face. "Ambrose says that he believes he can arrange the right man for me, with sufficient wealth to save the place. He's going to speak to him today or tomorrow and I will meet him on Wednesday evening."

"Who's that?" He felt the words dragged out of him without his own volition.

"He's a banker called Henri Maeterlink." She tried to keep her voice expressionless. "I believe you met him at the ball the other day."

John swallowed. Why did he suddenly feel this was important to him? "I know who you mean. But why are you telling *me* this, Alison?"

"I don't know exactly." She shrugged. "It's a big step for me and I don't have any disinterested people I can turn to for advice." She smiled a lop-sided smile. "I suppose I value your opinion. I hope you'll actually tell me what you really think about it." She put her head on one side. "What *do* you think about the idea?"

"What do *I* think?" he burst out. "I think it's bloody awful. Whatever you decide in the next few days, is going to be with you for the rest of your life. Do you love the bloke?"

Alison shook her head. "I don't know really. I don't know him well enough to decide."

"I must say that it seemed as though he was quite fond of you at the ball."

She thought to herself that at least he had noticed.

"But the question is," continued John, "how do *you* feel about *him*?"

She took a deep, shaking breath before she answered. "I have been reminded by my father that such marriages were once commonplace." She paused. "Henri is a nice man. I imagine we could build a satisfactory life together."

"OK," he said. For some reason he felt furious with her. "If you've decided you can manufacture a satisfactory life together, you'd better go ahead. There's obviously no need for love in your life."

"That's unfair, John." Now he could see there were tears in her eyes. "What alternative do I have, if I'm to save Daddy and Stacey Court?"

"The alternative you have," he said, "is to live your own life - to do what *you* want to do, and not what suits your bloody father."

"But you haven't thought it through, John," she jumped up. "As Ambrose pointed out - without Stacey Court, I have no home and no income." Her tone was becoming anxious. "I haven't been trained to do a job. I haven't any money of my own, to buy a place where I can live. I'm reliant on other people for my standard of living." Now she almost shouting.

"What else can I actually *do* with my life? Just tell me that."

John felt stunned by her vehemence. He looked down at the carpet to avoid her blazing eyes. "I don't know," he mumbled, aware that he had failed her, just as he seemed to have failed Rosemary. He looked up at her. "I'm sorry, Alison."

She sighed. "Oh, that's all right," she said quietly. "You've only confirmed to me that I really have no other choice."

She turned and went out of the pleasant little house, leaving the front door open. She strode up the road towards the site office without a backward glance. John watched her go through the window. He felt deeply dissatisfied with himself. Ought he to be doing something to prevent Alison from walking into a future like that? He shook his head. But what on earth *could* he do?

He was still standing in the middle of the room, trying to find an answer, when he saw the Sunbeam Talbot pull up outside.

69

Sarah climbed out of her car and looked up at the house for a minute or so. Then she slammed the door and walked up the path. John went to the front door to let her in. As he met her, he felt his gloom lifting. He couldn't be downcast for long when Sarah was around. It flitted across his mind, just how much she gave to him - the wealth of support and guidance. With a positive effort he pushed Alison to the back of his mind and concentrated on his partner.

"Hello," she smiled. "Isn't it lovely this morning?"

John thought she was looking very pretty today, wearing a loose white cotton blouse with a drawstring neck which just rested on her shoulders. A pale blue skirt licked around her calves as she walked. She was carrying a dark blue cardigan and her hair had been combed out. It now hung in corn-coloured waves about her head. It made her look younger and somehow a little vulnerable.

"It's turned brighter since you arrived," he admitted.

She contrived to do a little curtsey. "Thank you, sir." She laughed up at him. "Well, John, it's the start of a new life for you. I think Reggie was foolish to let you go. But his loss is my gain."

"It's also the beginning of our sales campaign." he said. "This morning I'll be starting to ring up the people who've already shown an interest. I'll be inviting them to come and inspect the show-house."

"That's why *I'm* here." She took his elbow. "I want to be the first person that you show round our lovely show house."

John laughed. "I'm afraid you're already too late for that. I had Alison Stacey here before eight o'clock."

"Alison Stacey? What on earth does she want with one of these? I'm aware that the Staceys are no longer the power they once were, but I can't believe that they're reduced to buying one of our houses." She laid her hand on his arm placatingly. "And that is no reflection on the excellent standard of your building."

"You're right, of course," he said. "She was here on another matter." Briefly John gave her a summary of what Alison had told him.

Sarah didn't interrupt him as he spoke. By the time he had finished she was looking thoughtful. She shook her head. "Silly girl," she said. "I'm not at all sure she's doing the right thing." She looked up at him. "What do you think about it?"

"I told her it was feudal." He shrugged. "But when it came down to it, I couldn't think of anything better to suggest."

"Hmm. I don't think she should agree to Ambrose's idea too easily." She took his arm and shepherded him into the house. "Now, what about our own plans? Have you got your calculations ready for the bank?"

"Nearly," said John. "They will be complete by the time we go up on Friday."

She stepped back and looked at him. "You don't think the idea of buying Fisher's Farm is too ambitious?"

"Well, we've got to have all the figures together before we decide." He grinned at her. "So far the calculations are looking very good – far better than I expect this first development will turn out - and that's going to be good enough. Perhaps we'll find that the bigger the development, the more profitable it is, because the unit costs are reduced. For example, there's a big saving on roads and services."

Sarah turned away. "Don't worry me with detailed figures, John. I don't want to know how you arrive at them. I just want to see the end results. Then I can judge."

"There's faith for you." He laughed. "I don't think I'll have any problems in convincing them about the sales and the costs, because I've based it on the actual recorded figures we've got to date on this site. Of course, there *is* the little question of whether the bank will lend us about two hundred thousand pounds or whether they'll think we're over-reaching ourselves."

"How could we be over-reaching ourselves?" asked Sarah, "as long as we're only building at the same speed that we can sell the houses?"

John pulled a face. "One thing we don't know yet is how many houses in total the local authority is going to let us build in this area. That's something you could try and find out with your contacts in the council offices. We don't want to hear that another fifteen hundred houses on this side of the city are likely to be regarded as an over-development."

"Oh, my God!" Sarah shuddered. "That means I've got to expose myself to that lecherous little James man again."

"Dressed like that," said John, "you're enough to make any man feel lecherous."

She smiled at him in a conspiratorial way. "Perhaps you'd better start showing me round the house if you feel like that. We'll start upstairs, shall we? And I suggest you lock the front door so that we're not interrupted."

John felt his excitement rising. "The double bedroom's at the front," he called after her as she went up the stairs.

He found her inspecting the bed. "It's a bit soft," she criticised.

"So are you." He came up behind her and reached over her shoulder. "What happens if I pull the end of this bow?"

She leaned her head back against him and her hair smelled of spring flowers. "If you do that, the blouse comes undone and ends up around my waist."

He pulled. "Ah. So it does." With a little help she was left wearing nothing but a strapless brassiere above her skirt.

"Did you make sure you locked that front door?" she asked.

"And the back one." He began to massage her shoulders.

She arched her back and pressed her buttocks into his groin. "Oh, that's nice, John." She laughed gutturally. "I may not be the first woman you've shown round the house, but I hope I'm to be the first one you've made love to on the bed."

"You certainly are." He undid her bra and removed it. Then he began to move his hands over her beautiful, voluptuous body - feeling it react to his touch - shivering, tensing, moving in undulations. They reached her waist and slid inside the elasticated belt of her skirt. He could feel the warmth of her body as his fingers moved towards her genitals. He felt a great urge begin to grip him. In one sudden movement he pushed her skirt and knickers down to her ankles.

"Quick," he urged, "kneel on the side of the bed with your back to me."

She had the foresight to pull the covers to one side as she obeyed him. With a desperate urgency he parted her legs and mounted her from behind. He grasped her breasts and pulled her body to him as he worked into her. Then, as he neared a climax, he remembered her feelings. He forced himself to stop.

"I'm sorry," he said, "I must think of you. It's just that I was desperate for you after recent events."

She chuckled. "Really? I think we must organize some more of those events. Now, shall we do it properly?"

So she rolled over and he made love to her slowly and lingeringly until they both reached an agonizing orgasm, made all the more excruciating by the suppression of his earlier rushing excitement.

But, as he relaxed on top of her, the memory of that last look in Alison's eyes seeped unbidden into his mind.

He didn′t know how much later it was that he became aware that Sarah was shaking him.

"John. There's someone knocking at the door." She jerked him into wakefulness.

"Blimey. I didn't realise I'd fallen asleep. What should we do?"

"It's probably someone to look round the show house. You'd better go and answer it."

"Me?"

"Well, I can't go, can I," she retorted. "I'm completely undressed. At least you've still got most of your clothes on."

John climbed off the bed. A further knocking at the door urged him to hurry. "Just a minute," he called out as he did himself up and slipped on his shoes.

"Don't let them come upstairs for a couple of minutes," she called after him as he went down to open the front door, straightening his clothes and tidying his hair as he went.

Outside the door Angus was standing with his hand raised, about to knock for the third time. Behind him were at least a dozen people of all ages. "Sorry to trouble you, Mr Tucker, but you had a sign up, saying that the show house would be open at nine o'clock this morning. These people," he indicated with a sweep of his hand, "have decided they want to be the first to look around."

"Of course." John gave them a little bow. "Welcome." He smiled politely. "I'm sorry to have kept you waiting. We were just putting the finishing touches to things upstairs and I didn't hear your first knock. OK, Angus. I'll take over. Send down anyone else who comes, and I'll see you later."

"Right you are, Mr Tucker." Angus set off back to the site office.

"Please come in. I hope you don't mind looking round together. Just ask me if you have any questions." John stood in front of the stairs, indicating that they should go into the ground floor rooms. In a loud voice he said, "Sarah has just about finished cleaning upstairs."

"It's all done now, me dear," said a broad voice from just behind him.

John spun round and Sarah was there, her blouse slipped down on one shoulder, a broad grin on her face. "'T'were smelling a bit stale up there, me dear, so I opened the windows to let in a bit o' fresh air. Now don' 'e forget to close 'em afore 'e goes 'ome tonight, will 'e."

"Er, no," said John hurriedly. "Of course I won't."

"That's lovely. Well, I'm off then. I 'opes you 'as a successful day." She called out to the people looking round, "And I 'opes you likes it. I think it's a lovely little 'ouse."

She gave John a wink and bustled down the path to the Sunbeam Talbot.

"Blimey," said a voice from the front room. "She's doing all right for a cleaner, isn't she, if she can afford a car like that."

John grinned at him. "Obviously we're paying her too much. Well, you can come upstairs to look round when you're ready."

He went up ahead of them to check if the heavy scent of their love-making had dispersed in the breeze coming through the open windows. He discovered Sarah had done a good job in tidying the bed. He looked out of the window and, for a second, caught her eye as she pulled away from the kerb. She gave him a thumbs-up sign and a little smile, and then she was gone.

70

It was a beautiful evening. Alison sat at a table near the edge of the roof terrace and watched the sun setting through the trees in Hyde Park. The noise and heat of the day was over. The light evening traffic swished along Park Lane. It was the perfect place to have dinner. She found herself wondering what John would have thought of such perfection, surrounded as they were by members of the upper classes at play.

Henri was a most attentive host. He had collected her by chauffeur-driven Daimler from Waterloo. He had brought her a spray of fresh flowers which he clipped to her left shoulder strap. She could still smell their freshness through her own liberal layer of perfume. He had waited in the hotel lounge while she went to bath and change in the room he had booked for her. She wondered why she resented the fact that he hadn't tried to go up to the room with her. She suspected that someone like John would have expected to be rewarded for his generosity.

A table had been reserved in one of the best positions on the roof-top restaurant, near the parapet with beautiful views across the park, but behind a glass screen to protect them from any cool evening breeze. Henri must know all the right people to be able to arrange that. Everything else had been perfect. The menu had been splendid, the wines magnificent, the service discreet but attentive. She had no doubt that a life spent with Henri Maeterlink would be full of such good things. It would be easy to have a happy marriage under such circumstances.

Now he was relaxing with a cigar and a brandy while she tried to clear her head with a black coffee. He leaned forward. "Have you enjoyed the meal, Alison?"

"Yes I have, Henri - very much," she said. "This must be one of the loveliest places to eat in London."

"It is one of my favourite places," he agreed. "I only allow myself to come here on very special occasions."

Alison forbore to ask him what constituted a special

occasion for him. She didn't wish to know such things. "It is very kind of you to lavish so much care and attention on me." She smiled. "I'm not sure that I deserve it."

"On the contrary," he assured her, "I could wish for no more delightful companion with whom to share such an evening." He reached out and placed his hand over hers, which lay waiting for just such an eventuality. "I should like the opportunity to lavish a lot more care and affection on you."

She leaned towards him. "Henri," she said softly, "you are a most generous and thoughtful man. I can't ask you for any more than you have already given me."

"On the contrary," he said. "Your brother Ambrose has been telling me about some of the problems you are facing at the moment." He looked straight into her eyes. "You must not hesitate to discuss any such problems with me. I hope you realise that I would do anything in my power to help lift these worries from your shoulders."

She turned away from him and looked out at the view of the park, now fading gently in the dying light. "I just don't know what to do, Henri." She shook her head slightly. "Daddy's problems are so huge. I don't know if Ambrose told you the figures involved. I find it difficult to conceive just how much he actually owes."

"Ambrose said something about a hundred and fifty thousand," he murmured.

"But what does that mean?" She turned back to look at him so that he should notice that her eyes were misty with the start of tears. "Ambrose says it could be more than the whole of Stacey Estates is worth if there was a forced sale."

"It *is* a huge amount of money," he confessed, his expression pained by the sight of her looking so sad. "But it does not have to be a complete disaster. You must get the very best advice before you rush into anything."

She shook her head again. "And if we do manage to sell, I don't know where we'll go. The Staceys have lived there for over two hundred years. I think it will kill father if he has to go and live in some little place in Exeter."

"And you?" asked Henri. "What will you do, Alison? None of this is in any way your fault, and yet you are going to suffer as much as he."

"Oh." The girl shrugged and put on a brave smile. "I am young. I expect I will be able to find something to keep me occupied. There must be something useful that I can do." She took a breath. "I'll have to find some kind of job. I won't be able to be kept as a spoilt little brat any longer." She looked down at the table. "But I shall miss my horses. I love horses." She looked up at him and smiled. "Do you like horses?"

He shook his head. "I regret that I have spent too much of my time in the cities of London and Zurich and Vienna - sitting in offices and making money. I have missed a lot of the things connected with the country."

"Oh, Henri." She was immediately all concern. "There is more to life than money. You should try and relax more. You can *do* that in the country. You enjoyed your visit to us last month, didn't you?"

"Yes, I did." He smiled. "Mind you, it was especially because *you* were there." Greatly daring, he squeezed her hand. "I think you would make *anywhere* nice to visit."

She smiled back at him. "What a lovely thing to say. I enjoyed having you, although your time with us was so brief. Even Daddy admitted you seemed a very nice person." She laughed musically. "He's a miserable old so-and-so, but I think he would take to you in time. You must come and have a longer stay with us before -." A shadow passed across her face and she dropped her eyes again. "- before we have to get out."

"Alison," said Henri urgently, "I don't see why it has to come to that." He pursed his lips. "Yes, I *do* see that something serious has to be done. Your father will probably have to lose control of the estate. Somebody else will have to make the decisions on investment and what to do with the land so as to maximise the returns." He squeezed her hand again. "But I would have thought we could construct a package that would allow you and your father to still live in at least a part of the house and enjoy the benefits of the estate and also receive a reasonable income as part of the package."

"Oh. Henri, if only we could." She gazed deep into his eyes. "But I don't understand how we could even *start* to go about arranging something like that. What do you mean exactly?"

"Well, as I said, we'll have to get some experts involved. I'm only a financier." He spread his hands wide and she thought, at the sight of the automatic movement, how her father would say that he looked just like a Jew. "I know nothing about managing estates. But we'll find out who the right people are. We'll get them to come and look at Stacey Court and the land all round it. I've asked Ambrose to get me all the details of the estate so that I can put these in front of the experts." He caught hold of her hand again. "But *you're* not to worry. Believe me - it's in safe hands now."

Alison felt herself relax a little. "Henri, you don't how much relief it is to hear you say that. But what about these - these bailiff people? How can we hold them off, while we sort things out?"

"Don't worry." He patted her hand. "Give me the details, and I'll get in touch with them." He nodded and grinned reassuringly. "I can assure you that sort of person takes a different attitude, when they find they're talking to a banker."

"I - I don't know what to say." She shook her head. "I'm really ever so grateful." She clasped his hand and lifted it quickly to her lips. "You're ever such a special person, Henri. You're so kind and so generous. I just don't know what I'd have done without you to take the load off my shoulders."

He pulled his chair close to hers and gazed into her eyes. "Alison, I'd like to think that you'll always come to me with your problems - no matter what they are. I could find no happier aim in my life than to prevent you from ever having to worry about things like this again."

"Henri -." She allowed a single small tear to escape from her troubled eye and trickle down her cheek.

Quick as a flash he had pulled the handkerchief from his top pocket and dabbed it away.

"Let's go somewhere more private where I can really tell you how much I appreciate what you are doing," she said, and rose from her seat.

She saw him gulp and his face flush as he realised what she meant. She turned and preceded him from the beautiful roof garden. Within three paces Henri had caught up with her and settled his protective hand proprietorially at her waist. Alison didn't object to that. She was of a generous nature and felt it only reasonable that he should be rewarded in a way which would clearly give him much pleasure. It might also be the first step down a path which would offer them both a comfortable future.

Then why was it, she asked herself, that an image of John Tucker swam before her eyes as she walked towards the lift which would take them to the floor where her room was located?

71

"What a pleasure it is to see you both." Henri Maeterlink ushered Sarah and John into comfortable seats in his palatial office. "Ambrose Stacey has, of course, given me a brief summary of your plans, but I've no doubt you're going to spell them out in detail for me."

John handed him a file containing the proposals and calculations for the Pound Lane Farm project. "Of course," he said, "Ambrose may have his own views about these proposals because the land lies partly along the borders of the Stacey Estate."

Henri nodded. "I understand what you mean. For that reason, I thought it best that he should not be present at this meeting." He paused as though trying to decide exactly what to say. "However I think I should declare, that it is likely that I may also have a personal interest in the Stacey Estates. That will not of course reduce my support for your proposals. Indeed, I can assure you that I intend to support you most strongly."

"Are you willing to tell us precisely what is your personal interest?" asked Sarah smoothly.

Maeterlink again paused, but there was no hesitation in the nature of his reply. "Certainly. In addition to the fact that Ambrose works for us, I have recently become a close friend of his sister, Alison. I can't put it any more strongly than that at present, because nothing is yet finalised, but I have hopes that she may one day consent to be my wife."

"Indeed?" Sarah looked at John and raised her eyebrows. He didn't respond. For some unknown reason he felt a sense of dismay at hearing the banker's declaration.

"Of course," Henri continued, "you will understand that I would wish you to keep this matter confidential between the three of us at present. However, I felt I should be honest with you, so that you should not later accuse me of having some hidden agenda. Nevertheless, I don't regard this as any sort of obstacle to us reaching a very satisfactory arrangement with you, if you agree."

"Of course." Sarah nodded. "Over to you then, John."

"Right." It was John's turn to pause now, as he tried to arrange his tumultuous thoughts. "Well, as you say, I've produced figures for the Pound Lane Farm project. They are set out in detail in the file. So I suggest that I just summarise the results now. Is that all right with you?"

Maeterlink nodded. "That's a good idea. I think I can trust my accountants to check your mathematics. I just want a general picture."

"Well, first of all," said John, "we'll have just over a hundred and forty acres to build on altogether. I decided not to cover the whole area with small houses. There's about twenty acres in a shallow valley surrounded by trees which I thought would deserve a higher standard of five-bedroomed houses on large plots which we could sell for about seven thousand pounds each. There would be fifty of those. The remainder of the land will take about twelve hundred and fifty smaller houses selling at about three thousand each. That will mean total sales of over four million pounds."

"Is there a market for the larger type of house in Devon?" asked Henri. "I'm aware that they would sell very readily in the London area. But is there enough wealth to support so many in that area?"

"I believe so. Exeter is becoming quite an executive centre. The university is expanding and moving to a new campus, there is a new County Hall planned, th~~e university is expanding and moving to a new campus~~, and several large insurance companies and other financial organisations have published plans to relocate there. In addition there is a general shortage of housing, and quite a few people are looking to upgrade their accommodation, now the war is well behind us."

"However," interposed Sarah, "as John says, we have agreed with the planners that we will be building a majority of the smaller houses at the same time, similar to the ones we are building at the present Pound Lane development. Those are selling like hot cakes. Didn't you say we'd had more than twenty offers already, John?"

"Nine people have put down deposits of fifty pounds and

want to move in before Christmas. Another twelve have indicated they are interested, and are talking to solicitors or trying to sell their own places."

Sarah sat back in her chair. "And we opened the show-house only ten days ago."

"Yes," agreed John. "New customers are turning up at the rate of two or three every day. In fact the big problem at the moment is to get enough houses finished to satisfy the demand for completion dates."

"So - when will you complete the - er -" Maeterlink looked at his notes, "- the first Pound Lane development?"

"We had planned for summer of next year, but it could be earlier."

"But won't you have started the new site before then?" Henri enquired.

"Yes, we will," said John. "I see what you're asking - won't we be competing with ourselves? The answer is no. The houses in the first Pound Lane project are very reasonable - right at the bottom of the market. They're terraced or semi-detached with quite small rooms, only two bedrooms with a small box-room as the third bedroom. What we are planning for Pound Lane Farm, as well as the more luxurious houses, are some middle of the range, detached dwellings with garages, costing between two and a half and three and a half thousand pounds. So, in that way, we could satisfy the whole market."

"That seems a reasonable concept. Now let's have a look." Maeterlink thumbed through the file of calculations. "I must say you seem to have done your homework well." He raised his eyes and nodded at John. "However, I have a few ideas of my own which I would like to put to you. Do you mind if I do that?"

John looked at him a little suspiciously, but Sarah said, "We will be pleased to listen to any suggestions which you might wish to make."

"Well now - where do I begin?" He cleared his throat. "The situation is this. I mentioned to you that I have hopes of a developing relationship between Alison Stacey and myself. A few days ago she and her brother asked me if I could assist them in solving the financial problems currently being suffered by the Stacey family."

"I know about the old man's gambling debts," said John. "You can speak about that without betraying any confidence."

Maeterlink's eyebrows rose. "Indeed? Well then, the fact is that the only asset the family has is the property. I have been making some enquiries of experts who know what they are talking about, and the unpalatable fact that I'm left with, is that the sale of the whole estate in one lot is unlikely to bring in enough to make Sir Oswald solvent - much less leave any surplus to give him and his daughter a living income."

John couldn't prevent a snort of derision which drew an enquiring glance from the banker.

"Until recently," explained Sarah, "Mr Tucker worked for my husband, Reggie Grant, who is a chartered surveyor. Grants had recently been employed as managers by Stacey Estates and John has a very good idea of the condition of the estate."

"Really?" Henri looked a little uncomfortable. "Perhaps you could fill me in with the details to set against the other professional opinions I have received."

"Very well." John took a breath. "The total area of the Estate is about fifteen hundred acres of which five hundred are dense woodland which hasn't been cropped for thirty years at least. That part is probably worth at least a hundred and fifty pounds an acre and I should think it would sell quite easily. Call it eighty thousand pounds," he said, noticing that Maeterlink was making notes.

John waited a second for him to finish writing. Then he continued. "About eight hundred acres of the remaining land is let out in three farms on long leases at low rents. The land is quite good and would probably fetch a hundred pounds an acre in a free sale. However, the way it is entailed would probably halve that price, and might make it less than that. I don't think you can put down more than fifty thousand pounds for the rest of the land."

"I see," murmured Henri, scribbling furiously.

"There are about fifty other houses and cottages on the estate," continued John. "Most of them are let on long leases at low rents by present-day standards. Quite a lot need maintenance work doing to them - some of it severe. I would think you cannot expect to get more than about three hundred pounds each for them on average in their present condition - say fifteen thousand altogether. There's nothing else of value on the estate. I would say the total value is less than a hundred and fifty thousand pounds."

"You haven't included the house and outbuildings," said Maeterlink.

John's look was almost insolent. "Have you inspected the house?"

"Not all over - no." Maeterlink felt at a disadvantage. "Alison says that it is in a run-down condition."

"It is worse than that," said John. "Sir Oswald arranged for a cowboy contractor to strip the lead from the roof of the main house and some of the other buildings. Damp is already endemic. They will be ruins in five years unless at least twenty thousand pounds is spent on them in the very near future."

There was a long silence. At last the banker said, "I had no idea it was so serious."

"Somebody needs to do some first aid work at the very least before winter sets in."

"What do you mean?" asked Henri.

"Tarpaulins need to be stretched across the roofs and over the parapets," said John. "The joints in the sheeting will need to be sealed. Temporary rainwater disposal will have to be arranged. And internal props will need to be inserted below the roof of the main building to carry the additional loads until the repairs are completed."

Maeterlink looked worried. "Can the Staceys remain in occupation while that is going on?"

"Yes." John grinned. "The place won't *look* very nice, but it will be quite safe. The top floor isn't occupied now anyway."

Maeterlink's eyes went back to his scribbles. John watched him work through the figures step by step, looking for something he had missed before. At last he said, "There is one discrepancy here. You said that the estate comprises a thousand acres of land, excluding the forest, and yet only eight hundred is let on long-term lease as farms. What about the other two hundred acres?"

"That is the home park," said John. "The gardens and open

parkland surrounding the house."

"What is that used for?" The banker blinked at him.

"Well - excluding the actual gardens, which are only a few acres - the remainder is let for grazing to two of the farms."

"Is that land entailed?" asked Henri. "I mean is it let on a long term basis, or can it be taken back by the owners?"

John could see what he was aiming at. "Oh, it could easily be repossessed. It is let on a casual basis. The farmers agree to pay so much a year depending on the number of cattle they have grazing it. The arrangement can be brought to an end at any time. But it only consists of about a hundred and ninety-five acres and there are no buildings on it except Stacey Court and outbuildings. It couldn't be economically let or sold as a farm."

"But could you get permission to use it for other purposes?" John was aware that the banker was watching him very closely. "For example, could you build houses on it - as you are proposing to do on Pound Lane Farm? I don't mean on the few acres around the main house," he said hurriedly, "But on the remaining hundred and ninety acres or so."

The audacity of the proposal almost took John's breath away. "I don't see anything technically against it," he said cautiously. "In fact it would be ideal building land - relatively level and well-drained. But Sarah would know whether there are likely to be problems with planning permission."

She shook her head. "I think the council would like it, providing the area immediately around the house was protected. They are planning a big expansion of the village and Stacey Park takes a substantial bite out of that."

"Of course," said John, "it would destroy our development at Pound Lane Farm if the Staceys were to get permission for this."

"Do not fear," said Henri hastily. "As customers of the bank, I regard you financially as highly as the Staceys. I'm certain that we - er, they - would want *you* to do the development and just buy the land off them. After all, you are the people who know about housing developments."

John thought about it some more. It was probable that the development could be made extremely pleasant. Most of the existing trees could be retained and the estate roads routed to pass close to them. He could see the advertising slogans already – 'Live in a beautiful house in a parkland setting.' He looked back at the banker. "Did you have a price in mind for the land?"

"I thought a thousand pounds an acre," said Henri smoothly. "That would solve the problem for the Staceys and give you a large chunk of prime land near the centre of the village."

"It's a lot more than we're proposing to pay for Pound Lane Farm." Now it was John's turn to scribble figures down furiously.

Maeterlink grinned. "But you would be getting land which was more suitable for building in a superior setting. Looking at your figures for Pound Lane Farm, the cost of the land is a small part of your overall costs. I think you could easily afford a thousand pounds an acre."

John nodded, still immersed in his figures.

"What would Sir Oswald think of being surrounded by a housing estate?" asked Sarah. "I can't imagine that he'd like it."

Maeterlink repeated his bland smile. "Sir Oswald is in no position to raise objections. We will be saving his bacon. The alternative for him is complete disaster."

"And what about financing the scheme?" said Sarah cannily. "We would need a lot of financial backing."

"Ah," said Henri. "I can assure you there will be no problem there. As long as you present me with a set of detailed costed proposals, and they show comparable figures to these for Pound Lane Farm (which I don't doubt they will) I can guarantee the funding. I will also advance the money to you at a quarter percent lower rate than I would lend it to you on the other development." He saw that John had finished his scribbled figures. "Well," he asked, "what is the bottom line?"

John showed the page to Sarah. "Of course, I need to check the figures in much more detail, before we're sure," he said.

Sarah's eyebrows raised. "It shows a profit of over one and a quarter million," she breathed.

Henri nodded casually. "I thought it would be something like that." He smiled. "How much funding do you think you will need?"

"Er - well this is provisional." John ran his pencil down the sheet of figures. There's the purchase price of the land of course - that's a hundred and ninety thousand. Putting in roads and main services would be a similar amount. Then I guess we'd possibly want funding for the first fifty houses at say two and a half thousand each - say a hundred and twenty five thousand."

"So - just over half a million." Henri raised his eyebrows. "It's a lot, but that is not important. What sort of period do you envisage for repayment?"

John smiled to himself. Now came the crunch. "Actually," he said, "I was going to suggest we might have the money in the form of an overdraft facility to be reviewed after five years. This would reduce our debit interest of course, because we would hope to pay it back more quickly than that. But it would also give us the funds to take on further developments as this one began to pay off."

"Ah." Henri grinned. "I understand what you have in mind, and I think it's very clever. You'll understand, of course, that we're not the usual type of bank with branches and cheque books."

"No," said John, "but we can presumably make an arrangement with our present bank for them to receive transfers from you as we need it. We don't want the distraction of having to manage a huge credit balance when we are trying to concentrate on building and selling houses. You're much better at that than we are."

"Very well. And for an interest rate - shall we say one and a half percent above base rate?" Henri looked down his nose at him. "Normally we would charge one and three-quarters to two percent for this type of arrangement."

John sensed that he was being asked to give away a bit too much. "For such a big sum I would have thought a lower figure - maybe one percent?"

Henri grinned and shook his head. "Even the big blue chip companies can't get us down to that. But I'll split it with you and say one and a quarter." He poked his finger at John. "That's a good rate, let me tell you." He leaned back in his chair and took in a breath. “Well, now - you’ll understand that this is too big a sum for me to give you an answer straightaway. In any case, you’ve got to give me your finalised figures. How long is that likely to take you?”

“Give me three or four days,” said John.

“OK. I’ll bring it up at the directors’ morning meeting in a week’s time, with my recommendation that we sanction the go-ahead on the basis we have discussed.”

John heard Sarah let out a big sigh. “Thank you very much,” he said.

“I know that it is important for Sir Oswald Stacey that we go ahead as soon as possible. How do you see the time scale?”

“The delay,” John pointed out, “is likely to be with Planning. We can have our outline proposals drawn up quite quickly. But it’s likely to be two or three months before we get the go-ahead from them.”

“But you would expect to be successful on that front?”

“I think I can guarantee it.” Sarah’s expression held a world of meaning.

Henri smiled. “Well, I think that would be enough for us to make temporary assistance available to Sir Oswald until the final agreement is in place. Can you have your lawyers ready to move quickly?”

“We have a meeting with them on Monday afternoon,” said Sarah.

“Good.” Henri rose to his feet. “It’s been a pleasure meeting you. I hope our association continues to be as pleasant and also proves to be profitable.” He held out his hand to Sarah. “Are you staying in town tonight?”

“I’m meeting my husband at his club.” Sarah held his hand in one of her long, suggestive handshakes.

“And you, John?”

“No. I’ll catch the first suitable train back. There’s a lot going on at Pound Lane at the moment.”

“Of course,” Henri shepherded them towards reception, still feeling the warm softness of Sarah’s touch on his hand.

72

Contrary to what he had told Henri and Sarah, John didn't immediately catch the first train back to Exeter. He turned his back on Schubert's offices when he left, and walked along the pavement, jostled on all sides by the crowds who were starting to come out of the shops and the great office blocks and make their way home at the end of the day. He had a great deal to think about. He didn't feel like going back to the country just yet. He wanted to lose himself in the anonymous multitude.

After a while he hopped on to a bus going west and climbed to the top deck. As the vehicle lurched and swayed, accelerated and braked its uneven way through the rush-hour traffic, he sat and watched the unfamiliar scene and waited for his enthusiasm to grow for the new project at Stacey Court. Now that the stimulus of the meeting with the banker was over, he felt tired and drained of emotion.

He also had to admit to himself that he had been disappointed to hear of Henri Maeterlink's plans to marry Alison. He liked the banker, but he didn't think the man was suitable for her. For a start, he was quite a bit older than she was.

He tried to think logically about his own feelings for her. In the last few weeks, somewhat to his surprise, he had begun to like her. With the exception of Sarah, she was the first woman he'd come across who seemed to have genuine views of her own, and who was willing to fight for them. He could see that she was behind a lot of this plan to redevelop the Stacey Estates. A woman like that would be a very stimulating contact in the future. But somehow he didn't think that friendship with her would be encouraged, if she was married to Henri Maeterlink. She would become a socially very acceptable housewife, spending her time bringing up children and entertaining her husband's friends and clients, but never making any contribution of her own to any business decisions which were taken. It seemed such a waste of a good brain.

He gave himself a shake. He realised that he was feeling

lonely for the first time since he went up to Cambridge, more than four years before. And even then he had known that there was Rosemary and the others to return to in the holidays. Now there was no-one to meet up with when he got home. He couldn't confide in Sammie, who already believed he was over-stretching the business by taking on these new projects. In fact it was more than likely his friend would refuse to have anything to do with this huge new development if it went ahead. Of course, Sarah was available on Wednesday evenings, but he wanted someone less closely involved with his plans to whom he could talk.

While he was musing, the bus had left the City behind and was passing through the West End. Green Park opened up to his left. Ahead was Hyde Park Corner. This looked a good place to walk. When the bus next came to a halt, John went downstairs and got off. He started to walk through the park. Suddenly he found himself opposite Buckingham Palace, the centre of inherited status and wealth in the nation. With a dismissive shrug of the shoulders, he turned and followed the high wall round the most exclusive and expensive garden in the country. What a laugh it would be, he thought, to build houses all over that – *and* what a crime, even though the ordinary public never had a chance of even glimpsing the beautiful grounds.

Immersed in his thoughts, he suddenly found he had arrived at Hyde Park Corner. He crossed the road, dodging the creeping, bustling traffic and entered the posh shopping area of Knightsbridge. He continued through this area and along the Brompton Road. Almost without realising it, he found he was outside the Victoria and Albert Museum.

It wasn't quite six and the museum was still open. He stood on the steps, hesitating about whether to go in. At that moment his mind was made up for him, because through the swing doors came Rosemary. Her coat was hanging open, revealing a large, fluffy grey sweater above dark slacks. Her hair was pulled back behind her head in a little pony-tail and she looked pale and very young.

She saw him at once. "My goodness, John. What on earth brings *you* here?"

"Hello, Rosie." He felt like an awkward schoolboy. Would she think he'd been hanging around, trying to see her? "I had to come to London to meet the bank about a new development project we're planning. So I thought I'd come along and see where you do your work. How are you settling in?"

"Oh, I´m fine." She sounded light-hearted. "The work's very interesting. I'm so lucky to have got this job." But despite her comments, he had a feeling she wasn't very happy.

"Have you got time for a drink before you go home?"

She smiled and he thought again how young she looked. "I'd love to have a coffee."

They went to a little cafe nearby. At this time the place was empty, and they took their coffees to a corner near the window to chat. Outside, the dull autumn day was declining into a drizzly early night.

"What exactly do you do in the museum?" he asked. "You never got around to telling me."

"We never had enough time together to even talk about it," she reminded him. She paused but John refused to apologise, so she continued. "I work in the documents section. That covers books and any other type of written works - for example on papyrus - but not carvings, although our senior researchers are often called in to advise on inscriptions. The museum has an absolute mass of documents stored away in the basements."

"What's the point of that?"

"Well, most of them aren't of sufficient interest to the general public to be put on display, but they're used for research. We get a lot of students from all around the world who are doing papers on various subjects. There are five of us in the English Language section whose job is to read and catalogue the documents which are in modern English (That's about the last seven hundred years) and then try to help give answers to queries that come in. It's really exciting at times - almost like old-fashioned detective work. Our senior reader is absolutely brilliant. Of course, he's been doing it for over thirty years. He's completely steeped in it. But we all have our moments."

"I begin to see why I'm not post-graduate material." He hurried on when she raised an eyebrow. "But it's great that you're enjoying it so much. How is your social life? Have you made friends up here?"

She pulled a bit of a face. "That's side of things is not so good. I've got myself a bedsit about half a mile away and I think that was a mistake. There seems to be no opportunity to meet anyone. The whole house is split up into individual bedsits, with a shared bathroom on each floor. Quite a few of the people are middle-aged and nobody seems to talk to anyone else. If you pass people on the stairs, it's as though they haven't seen you. I've never felt so cut off before. Being a girl, I feel a bit awkward about going out on my own in the evening to a pub or a cafe." She took another sip of her coffee. "It's really quite lonely at night."

"What about the West End theatres and cinemas?"

"I've been a couple of times." She looked down at her cup. "But the second time I had a nasty experience with a dirty old man who tried to pick me up. I've not had enough confidence to try again since. It's rather dark and forbidding round my flat. I don't like going out on my own after dark."

"You make it sound as though you're imprisoned in the evenings."

She nodded. "Yes. It feels like that at times."

"Poor old Rosie." He reached out and patted her hand. "On the edge of the most lively place in the country, and you can't go out and enjoy it."

Suddenly she was in tears. The little touch of kindness had broken through her defences. "I'm sorry," she sobbed. "I don't mean to be so stupid."

He reached out and grasped both her hands firmly. "You're not being stupid. You're obviously lonely, when you're away from work." He suddenly grinned. "Here - will you come to the theatre with *me*? Are you free tonight?"

"Of course I am," she said bitterly. "But you don't need to take pity on me. I can cope on my own."

"I wasn't taking pity on you, silly. I'd been trying to work up the cheek to ask you out. What you've just told me has given me the confidence to do it." He felt as though they needed each other at that moment.

She laughed through her tears. "I never imagined you would

lack confidence, John." She shook her head. "And I should know. After all you used to be my boyfriend."

"It's the 'used to be' that causes the confidence problems."

"Yes." She looked down at the table again. "I know what you mean."

John consulted his watch. "Well, then. It's a quarter past six now. We'll need to be at the theatre in just over an hour. Have we got time for a quick meal?"

"I've got to change if we're going to the theatre."

"Forget about putting on special clothes. Aren't you hungry?"

She smiled, her tears forgotten. "Not really. But I bet you are. We can be back at my bedsit in ten minutes. I'll rustle up something to keep you going and you can eat that while I'm getting ready."

"Have you got a phone so that I can book us seats?"

"There's a pay-phone downstairs in the hall."

They drained their coffee cups and set off for her lodgings.

It was eleven-thirty when the taxi dropped them outside the darkened building where her bed-sit was located. The street lights seemed rather feeble. John had to admit the place would be quite daunting for a young woman to come back to. He could see why Rosemary didn′t go out much on her own at night.

Freed for a night from her urban prison, she had blossomed more than he had ever remembered. After the theatre they went for a meal in a Lyons Corner House. She had a few drinks with the meal, in addition to the glass of wine in the interval at the play. Her cheeks had regained the pretty flush he remembered from their days together in Devon.

John paid off the taxi-driver and came up behind her as she fumbled in her bag for the keys. He put his arm round her waist, and she leaned her head against his shoulder. He could smell the freshness of her hair, which she had insisted on shampooing before they went out.

"John," she said in a conspiratorial whisper, "you've let the taxi go. You'll never catch the last train now."

"Nor will I," he agreed. "I suppose I shall have to sleep on the platform in the cold with all the tramps, and wait to catch the milk train in the morning."

She looked up at him. "You're *not* serious?"

"I hope not." Her face was very close and he couldn't stop himself any longer from kissing her soft lips.

When they stopped, she sighed. "I suppose you're going to have to stay here for the night."

"That's what I've been angling for all evening," he admitted.

"But your mum? Won't she be worried when you don't get back tonight?"

He shook his head. "I rang her after I'd booked the theatre to say I was staying in London overnight."

She poked him in the ribs. "You cheeky thing. You just assumed I'd take pity on you."

"I didn't assume anything. I only hoped." He jogged her elbow. "If you don't find that key soon, we'll both be frozen before we get upstairs."

She held it up triumphantly. "It's all right. I had it before you kissed me. Then I sort of forgot about it. Now - be quiet going upstairs, or you'll get me a bad reputation."

Rosemary's bed-sitting room was on the third floor. With exaggerated care, John tiptoed up the stairs behind her. Inside her door she turned to face him. "Oh, John, I *have* enjoyed this evening. I can't remember when I last had such fun." Her smile shaded. "It will be that much more difficult tomorrow evening."

"Can I relieve you of your coat?" That meant he was able to look at her again in her plain pink blouse and black velvet skirt, with the broad belt accentuating her slim waist and jutting breasts.

She lowered her eyes under his gaze. "Anyway, I wanted to thank you," she mumbled.

"There's a charge. I want another kiss. I liked that last one."

"So did I," she admitted. "I've been waiting for it all night."

The second kiss lasted longer than the previous one. By the time it had come to an end her blouse was undone to the waist, her hair was untidy and they were both breathing heavily.

"Oh, Rosie," he murmured, "it *is* nice having you in my

arms again."

"I still feel the same about you as I've always felt, John."

He made a decision. "I'm going to come up to London once a week and take you out for the evening . . ." He left the ending hanging in the air.

"And then stay the night," she whispered, and she was in his arms again.

When they made love on the single bed at the back of her room it was more tender and gentle than he had expected. He knew it was probably the first time for her. So he didn't hurry her, despite his urgency for physical love. It gave him a special pleasure to feel her opening up to him little by little. In the end it was she who was urging him to hurry, to bring her to her first excited orgasm. He had always known it would be very easy to make love to Rosemary.

Afterwards he pulled some bedclothes over them and they lay intertwined until half their limbs had lost their circulation. They separated but close for their first night together.

73

Rosemary and John′s relationship blossomed anew in her little bed-sit in Kensington. They both agreed that his arrival each Friday night was now the most important event in their lives, which they both looked forward to all week. Their love was now so much more physically intimate than it had been before, and he was allowing himself to luxuriate in the feeling that they were gradually moving towards the situation where he would feel confident enough to ask her to share the rest of her life with him. On the third Friday he drove up in the afternoon and brought her home for the weekend to stay with her parents.

"I've got a surprise to show you this weekend," he told her in the car on the way back.

"What is it?"

"I don't want to *tell* you about it," he said. "I want to show it to you. And it's not something you can see properly in the dark. So I want you to come round tomorrow morning, and I'll take you to see it then."

"Oh, John," she protested, "you *are* a pest. Now I'll have to wait until tomorrow, wondering what on earth it is that you're going to show me. I hope I'm going to like it after all this build-up."

He grinned to himself in the dark. "I hope you are too. It's going to make quite a difference to us in the future."

"Now that's even worse." Rosemary twisted in her seat to stare at his face, reflected in the lights from the instrument panel. "You've *got* to tell me now."

But he steadfastly refused to give her any more information. It was late when they got to her parents′ house and he carried her bag in, kissed her goodnight and left,

At home, his mother welcomed him with the news that Sammie Joslin had been trying to get hold of him all day.

"I'll ring him in the morning," he said, "before I take you and Rosemary to show you the surprise I've got planned for you." Then he went to bed.

Sammie was on the phone at seven-thirty next morning. John was beginning to regret that he'd had these phones installed everywhere.

"John. Something urgent has come up. Can you come round to the yard as soon as possible?"

"How urgent?"

"We need to talk about it this morning," said Sammie.

"Blimey." John was intrigued. "What on earth is it?"

Sammie was a bit coy about telling him on the phone. "I'd rather we discussed it face to face."

"All right. Just let me get washed and dressed and have a bite to eat and then I'll come straight round. I should be there between eight and eight-thirty."

"Thanks, John." Sammie rang off.

In fact it was nearly nine, by the time that John finally got there. The yard was a hive of activity, even on a Saturday morning. He knew from their weekly meetings that the fitted furniture business was continuing to expand rapidly, and the men had to work extra hours to cope with the demand.

He went up the stairs and into Sammie's office. "Still plenty happening, I'm pleased to see."

"Yes." Sammie got to his feet. He looked distinctly embarrassed.

"What's the matter?" said John. "You look as if you've got a problem."

His friend shook his head. "I'm sorry, John," he said, "but I think it's you who's going to have the problem."

"Come on then. Spit it out."

"In a nutshell," said Sammie, "I've had my call-up papers for national service."

"Oh, heck." There was a long silence while John thought about it. "When is this likely to happen?"

"First of January."

"Isn't there any way you can get some extra deferment? Otherwise you're not going to be much use to us for the next two years. You might even get sent abroad."

Sammie shook his head. "I haven't told you everything, John. In fact I was called along to my medical two weeks ago. When I was there, I had interviews with officers from all three services. I had a really long chat with a major in the Royal Engineers and we got on really well. The long and the short of it is that he's virtually guaranteed me the rank of corporal at the end of my trade training, if I sign on for five years."

"Five years?" John's mouth fell open. "Sammie - you *didn't* sign on for *five* years!"

"The pay and conditions are a lot better."

"Come off it, Sammie. Your pay and conditions and your overall prospects are a hell of a lot better here than they are as an NCO in the bloody army." John felt himself starting to get angry. "You've not signed up for five years for the pay and conditions, *have* you?"

"Not for that – no." Sammie shook his head miserably. "The fact is, John, I just don't like this business any longer. It has all got much too big for me. I've tried to talk to you from time to time to get you to slow down, but I don't seem to be able to get through to you." He raised his head and looked his partner in the eye. "To be honest, John, I decided a few months back that I was going to resign. I just didn't know how to do it. Now this call-up business has shown me the way."

"You can't just resign!" John was shattered by the suddenness of Sammie's decision. "You're a partner in the business. You've got responsibilities. And you're also worth quite a lot of money. You're entitled to half of what the business is worth."

"I don't want it." Sammie shook his head again. "You can take my share. You can pay me for it later, when you can afford it."

John walked over to the window and looked out at the bustle down below. "Oh no, Sammie," he said. "If you're going to go, it's got to be done properly and legally. What would happen, for example, if you turned up again in five years and wanted your half of the business back? It might be worth hundreds of thousands by then."

"You can rely on me, just as I do on you," said Sammie. "Our friendship goes back a long way."

"So much for relying on friendship -" John turned back to him furiously, "- when you go off behind my back and fix yourself up with a five-year posting to the Royal Engineers. No

- I'll get an accountant to value the business. Then a lawyer will draw up an agreement next week for me to buy you out. It may take me a few months to pay you off. But that's how we'll do it. I take it that you are willing to work up until Christmas to make the handover a bit easier."

Sammie nodded. "Of course I am." He had never seen John like this before. It was as though his friend was consumed by a cold rage. It made him seem quite frightening.

"OK," said John. "I'll come over some time next week, so that I can find out the up-to-date situation on the various jobs. I want to sort out a few other things before I get involved in that. I'll give you a ring." He gave Sammie a brief smile and walked out of the office.

By the time he got back to the cottage he had already more or less decided how he was going to re-organise the business following Sammie's departure. He found Rosemary was already waiting for him, desperate to find out what the secret was that he had been keeping from her. They met in the cosy parlour.

"I'm glad to see you've got a warm jumper on," said John. "You too, Mum. *You're* coming with us as well."

"I'm not walking miles with you," protested his mother. "I've got my shopping to do before lunch."

"It's not far," he promised. "We'll be back in an hour."

"Do you know what it is? - this surprise of his?" Rosemary asked his mother as they set off.

"I haven't the least idea," she replied. "All I know is that he's been full of some new plans for the last few weeks."

When they reached the High Street, they turned left towards the river. They continued along the Strand. It was a dull day with a cold wind coming off the river, and they walked quickly to avoid being chilled.

"I remember walking all the way back along here every day with my basket full of shopping when we lived at Riversmeet," said his mother. "It was *such* a relief when we moved to the cottage and I could just pop round the corner to the shops whenever I liked."

John ignored her. When they reached the end of the Strand,

he stopped, with his hand on the gate. "Well, here we are," he said.

"This is Riversmeet House." Rosemary gazed up at the grey stone facade. "It's in a bit of a state, isn't it? I don't think anybody's lived here since you moved out."

"No, they haven't," said John. "There's still quite a lot of our old furniture left in the place. It's never even been thrown away."

His mother hung back. "I don't want to go any further, John. I'll go home now and do my shopping. You take Rosemary in and show her."

"But Mum," he said. "I own it now. I've bought the place. I got it very cheap. I'm going to do it up and we'll move back in."

"No." She shook her head violently. "I don't want to move back into it. I want to stay in my little cottage. I like it there."

"Just let me explain, Mum -"

She backed away. Her voice seemed almost hysterical. "No, John. I will not go back in there. The place has too many bad memories for me. Once upon a time - yes - it was a happy place. But the last few years have ruined it for me." She turned to face him. "*You* can live there if you want to. But I will never sleep there again. I'll leave you now to show Rosemary round and tell her all about your plans. I'll see you at lunch." She turned and almost ran back up the road.

John gazed after her, speechless. Rosemary kept a tactful silence.

At last he said, "I thought she'd be pleased to move back into a decent, large house."

"You've got to see her point of view," said Rosemary. "She's nice and comfortable in the cottage. It's warm and cosy and convenient. And this great barn of a place has so many bad memories for her." She took his arm. "Tell me what you've got planned for the place. It's going to need a lot of work to get it into proper shape."

They climbed the three steps into the front garden, went up the stone paved path, and then stood on the wide step outside the front door while John unlocked the door.

"It's going to need repainting all over." Rosemary pointed to the peeling front door. "And some of the glass will need re-puttying."

"It needs a lot doing everywhere," he agreed. "I pointed that out to the people who were selling it. That's one reason why I got it so cheap. But I can send men up from Pound Lane when the sales are a bit quiet there. I'll soon get it done at a fraction of the normal cost."

They walked across the empty, echoing hall and went through to the kitchen at the back. "I'm going to put a great big range along that wall," said John. "It will do the cooking, run the central heating and provide hot water. The flue will run up the chimney. Then I'll put in a raised timber floor with lino finish and there will be kitchen units all round the walls. It will be the sort of cosy centre of the house."

He led her through into the living room. "There will be radiators here to give background heating, but we'll have roaring log fires on winter evenings and there will be warm velvet curtains across the windows and nice antique furniture." He looked at her. "All right. Let's go upstairs." He was disappointed that Rosemary didn't seem to be showing much enthusiasm.

The first bedroom they went into at the front was still half-furnished, with a large double bed against one wall.

"Was this your parents' room?" she asked.

He thought for a minute. "It might have been once, but I can only remember them sleeping in the room behind this. This room was hardly used at all - just occasionally when we had guests. Of course, in later years my father's bed was in the back sitting room. That's when he was ill."

Rosemary kept quiet.

"What do you think of this for a view?" John shook his head to clear the memories and led the way to the tall windows which looked across the estuary, now bare of life in the autumn wind. A fine drizzle was starting to drift in from the sea.

"It's a bit bleak, isn't it?"

"You see the most beautiful sunsets on warm summer evenings," he promised her.

"But they'll be much the same as you'd see from the top of Church Steps," she pointed out. "And it's more interesting there because you've got all the boats to look at as well."

"I like the privacy and the sense of isolation that you get here," he said.

Rosemary turned to face him. "That's what worries me about you, John. You've always been a loner. Even at school you held yourself a bit aloof at times."

"I like my privacy. That's all," he said defensively.

"No." She shook her head. "It's more than that."

John didn't feel like entering into a deep psychological discussion. He turned away. "What I'm planning is that this will be the main bedroom. Then I'll knock a doorway through to the room at the back and turn that into a second, private bathroom - just for this room. That means the other two bedrooms on this floor will share the other bathroom. Actually," he chuckled, "I thought that later we could knock a doorway through the partition wall and turn the middle bedroom into a nursery. Everything would be together then, wouldn't it?"

"What's all this about 'we', John Tucker?" she asked innocently.

He shrugged. "Well, I thought, that if you liked the place -"

"Actually, I don't."

He was quiet for a minute. Then he asked her softly, "What did you say?"

"I don't like this house, John." She shook her head. "It gives me the creeps. It's not just that it's cold and damp and the weather outside is miserable. I can feel a strange sense of mystery about the place, as though all sorts of unpleasant things have happened here in the past. I don't like that. I like modern, fresh places. I'm sure that the new houses that you are building at Pound Lane are much nicer than this."

He had turned to look at her as she talked. But his eyes weren't really in contact with hers. Now he had the feeling that she was separating herself from him. It seemed that his plans, in which he had thought she would want to be included, were unimportant to her.

"Besides," said Rosemary, "I'm starting to enjoy my life in London. I get to see you every week - which is more often than I've seen you at home for the last four years. I've also joined the social club at the V & A. They've said they'll arrange for someone to come and pick me up and drop me home in the evenings. They arrange visits to shows and things like that. And they tell me that on summer Sundays they go for walks on the North Downs. I feel as though I'm starting to make friends now."

"I see." He smiled a little bleakly. "Then - as far as Riversmeet House is concerned - I'm on my own."

She moved forward and took his arm. "Oh, John. You said before that we weren't ready to plan a future like this together. Nothing has changed." She put her head on one side. "Maybe one day - but not yet. We′re being careful with our love-making. Until the right time comes, can't we just be loving friends?"

"OK," he agreed, even though he was disappointed. "As long as we understand each other. But this place is important to me, Rosie. It will always be a part of me."

"I understand," she said, "but you can't expect me to feel like you do about it - not at the moment, anyway." She smiled and stood back from him. "I've got lots to do, so I'll leave you to do your planning in peace. Will I see you later?"

"Of course," he agreed. "Shall we go to the dance at the Imperial tonight?"

"That'd be lovely."

"I'll pick you up at seven-thirty then, and we can have a drink on the way."

"OK." She gave him a quick peck on the cheek before she left him.

He listened to her shoes clattering down the uncarpeted stairs, followed by the squeak of the unoiled hinges on the big front door. He turned and watched her through the window as she hurried down the path, pulled the gate closed behind her, and set off up the Strand. He couldn't avoid the feeling that everyone seemed to be deserting him.

He raised his eyes and looked out again at the view. The far side of the river was now almost obliterated by the developing drizzle, blown in billowing gusts by the strengthening wind. It was going to be a miserable, wet day to be left alone here with his plans. In fact, everything seemed to be turning against him, with Sammie running away to the army, his mother wanting to stay in her little cottage and Rosie going back to London on Sunday.

As he stood there in silence, his thoughts were nearly as bleak as the view.

"Damn them all," he muttered to himself. "I'm going to make this place into just what I'd like a home to be, even if I have to stay here all by myself."

74

"Daddy." Alison swept unannounced into the library. "Henri has solved your financial problems. He's found a way to pay off your debts and have some money left over and still keep Stacey Court. Isn't that splendid?"

Sir Oswald raised his half-befuddled eyes from their contemplation of the desk-blotter and gazed at her. "How -?" He began again. "How'd he do that?"

"I'll let him tell you the details." She gestured towards the door where Henri stood, hesitantly peering in, his shiny domed forehead glistening in the lights. "But before he does that, I must tell you that there are a few facts which *you've* got to accept, daddy. You will keep Stacey Court and the stables and the out-buildings and a few acres around the house - the formal gardens and the walled kitchen garden and the circular driveway in front of the house. You will also keep the freehold of the farms and the estate cottages which will give you an annual income in the future. But you are going to lose the rest."

Stacey shook his head, seemingly unable to grasp what she was saying. "What do you mean?"

"Henri is going to use the money that comes in from selling the home park and the forest to settle your debts and to repair the buildings and bring them back to life again. Whatever is left over will be invested in a trust and the income from that will be paid to you for as long as you live. After that it will go equally to Ambrose and to me. Do you understand?"

"Why is it being sold?" The old man still looked confused.

"Oh - you explain it to him, Henri." Alison grabbed his elbow and drew him to the desk.

The banker blinked. His normal self-possession seemed to have deserted him. "Well, it's like this, Sir Oswald. Nobody will lend you the sort of money which you need to clear your debts. Your income isn't enough to cover the interest on the loan. You need to be receiving an annual income of at least a third of the amount which you want to borrow."

"I know." Stacey waved a dismissing hand. "Ambrose told

me about that."

"Yes. Well, the only alternative is to sell at least a part of the estate. Alison tells me that Stacey Estates is your only remaining asset."

Sir Oswald cleared his throat and seemed to clear his mind a little at the same time. "That is correct."

"Alison did of course mention to me about your American in-laws - the Vanderplatts. But I did not consider them."

"They are *not* to be approached." Stacey's voice was suddenly sharp and clear.

The banker swallowed. "Yes. That's what Alison said. In any case I think they would be unlikely to be willing to help."

"They would see me dead before they raised a finger." The old man's voice rose in tone.

"Well, that leaves us with just the one option - the sale of all or part of the estate." Henri glanced at Alison. "Now - I approached a number of people, and the fact is that the estate, as it is presently constituted, is worth a great deal less than the total of your debts."

"I don't understand," said Stacey. "I thought it was to be arranged that *you* were going to take it over."

There was a long, tense silence. Henri looked again at Alison and she felt her cheeks burn with embarrassment. She contrived an awkward shrug.

He turned back to the old man. "Er - I'm afraid that I don't personally have that sort of money to hand."

"They said you were worth millions," said Sir Oswald accusingly.

"Oh, no." Henri shook his head. "Nearly all my money is tied up in the bank. I have to receive the agreement of the other directors before I can personally hazard large sums like that." He pulled a face. "I know they would not consent to my putting a large portion of our joint personal wealth into a project which has no prospect of an adequate return." He spread his hands. "You must understand that we are bankers, not property developers."

"I never believed them anyway." Stacey turned his head away. "I thought you were nothing more than charm and hot air."

"Father," gasped Alison, starting forward. "You mustn't be so rude to Henri. He is really doing his best to help you."

The banker laid a restraining hand on her arm. "Don't worry, my dear. I understand that your father is under a lot of strain at present." He took a breath and turned back to the old man. "The point is, Sir Oswald, that I *have* been able to find one property developer who has seen a way to put a part of the estate to profitable use and save the rest for your future ownership."

"Who is this developer?" Stacey looked suspicious.

"It is a company called Landscale Developments. They are house builders."

"House builders?" Sir Oswald rose unsteadily to his feet. "Are they going to build houses on my land?"

Henri nodded. "On a hundred and ninety acres of home park."

"A hundred and ninety acres? That's nearly all of it." The old man's eyes seemed about to pop out of his head.

"It is the whole area of the home park except for the few acres which Alison mentioned surrounding the house," Maeterlink agreed.

Stacey's eyes narrowed. "How many houses will that be?"

"Er - I think about fifteen hundred altogether."

"Impossible." Sir Oswald sat down again abruptly. "I will not have thousands of little boxes crowded all round my house where my guests can see them - where their noise will interrupt my peace."

"Don't be stupid, father," interrupted his daughter. "When do you ever have any guests? When are you sufficiently sober to notice any outside noises?"

"I will not have it," he repeated, almost to himself.

Alison suddenly lost her temper. She strode forward and hammered on the desk. "Father, when *will* you understand that you have no choice? What Henri has arranged is going to save your bacon." She took a sharp breath. "If you refuse to accept this, it will be the end for you and for the whole family, including me."

He flinched away from her anger. "We're going to live in the middle of a housing estate," he complained. "Is this what the Staceys have been brought to after two hundred years?"

"That's right! The Staceys have been brought to the brink of bankruptcy. It is *you* and your stupid gambling who has brought them to it, and you'd better accept that fact."

"What is happening to us?" He gazed up at her mournfully.

"It's *you* that's happened to us, father," she shouted. "It's all due to your stupid, self-indulgent drinking and gambling. I don't understand how you could have let yourself get into a state like this. You have let us all down."

The old man stared at her. He hardly seemed to have taken in what she was saying. "Then what do I have to do?" he asked.

"Henri is having an agreement drawn up to sell the hundred and ninety acres to the development company. All *you* have to do is sign the agreement and the money will be paid to your creditors within a few days. The rest will be put in trust."

"That's right," said the banker. "I am also having a trust agreement drawn up. It will be called the Stacey Trust. You will need to sign that as well. In effect it will place the whole of the remainder of the estate in a trust, so that no-one can get at it in future. The trust will use the money from selling the building land and the forest to pay off your debts and to put Stacey Court and the other buildings in order. Any balance will be invested in gilts. All the income from the estate will go to the Trust. The Trust will grant you or your heirs the right to live in Stacey Court rent-free. And you (or your heirs) will be able to receive as much as you require of the annual surplus which the Trust earns from its rents and its investments, after deducting the maintenance costs of the estate."

"That means, father," said Alison, "You will never again be able to put Stacey Court at risk. The worst you can do is throw away your annual income on more of your foolish gambling."

The old man ignored her barbed comments. "So," he mumbled, "I've got to give my land away to some faceless city financiers who won't give a damn what happens to it."

"No." Henri shook his head. "These people aren't faceless. They live locally and have an interest in producing a nice-looking landscape. They've already discussed their plans with me. They plan to keep most of the mature trees. And the main roads will wind through the estate. It's not going to be straight rows of houses."

"Who are these people?"

"Yes," agreed Alison, "you haven't told *me* who they are, Henri."

Henri took a breath. "Well, I don't see any problem in telling you now. Landscale Developments is owned by Sarah Grant and John Tucker, both local people who you know. But you must keep Sarah's involvement confidential. Her husband doesn't know about it yet."

"John Tucker? Did you say John Tucker?"

They both turned to look at the old man. Alison was astonished to see his face was distorted with rage and hatred.

"I will not have that man anywhere near my land," he hissed through clenched teeth. "You can tell them that the deal is off. I will *not* sign any agreement with John Tucker. You will have to find another property developer if you want to build houses all over my land."

"Father - why on earth shouldn't it be John Tucker who builds here?" demanded Alison. "We're likely to get much more consideration from him than from somebody we don't know. As long as I talk to him nicely, I'm confident he'll do his best to maintain the character of Stacey Court. After all, it was him who brought to our attention what a dreadful state it had got into."

"That's right. Once again it was a member of that family which got us into this dreadful mess," said the old man acidly.

She shook her head. "Oh no, it wasn't. It was *you*, father, who got us into the mess. It was John Tucker who made us face up to it. That's why you don't like him," she said accusingly. "*He's* not afraid of you. He's the only person you've ever come across who will tell you what he thinks of you. And you don't like that."

"I will not speak to him," said Stacey determinedly.

"This is foolishness," said Henri. "Landscale are ready to sign a deal with you, Sir Oswald, which will rescue you from the bailiffs. I cannot hold your creditors off for much longer."

Stacey turned on him. "Well - you will have to. I tell you finally that I will not make a deal with any organisation which contains John Tucker. You will have to find another developer."

Maeterlink took a deep breath. "Well, I'll try. But I don't think I will have any luck. And time is not on our side. If I tell your creditors that there will be a delay while we look for another developer, I don't know what they'll say. They will lose a lot of confidence in our ability to put a package together which will pay them out in full."

"You are a banker," said the old man. "Use your influence on them."

Henri smiled weakly. "Believe me, I and my colleagues at Schubert's have been doing that for the last few weeks. I don't know how long we can continue to keep it up."

"Why are you so foolish, father?" Alison's voice took on a pleading note. "What have you got against John which makes you behave like this?"

Stacey was on his feet again. "What have I got against him? The Tuckers have been the bane of the Staceys' existence for two generations. Don't talk to me about the Tuckers." He turned and stormed out of the room leaving the other two staring open-mouthed at each other.

"I wonder what John Tucker has done to upset your father so much," said the banker after a pause.

Alison shook her head. "I don't know. Well, the only thing I can do is ask him. Let's see if he can spread some light on the subject."

"And meanwhile, what am I to do?" asked Henri. "I don't know anyone else who I can go to, or who would be interested in investing a lot of money in this part of the country. The trouble is that I am not the best man to persuade property developers of the potential for new house sales in the provinces. Landscale are the only people I know who are doing this sort of thing. And I wasn't dissembling when I told your father that I wouldn't be able to hold off the bailiffs much longer."

"I know." Alison patted his arm. "I'll speak to John as soon as I can. When I understand why the old man is so set against him, I'll ring you, and we can plan our next step." She looked grimly determined. "I don't intend to let father destroy this plan after all the work that you've done on it."

"Well," said Henri, "all I can do is wish you luck."

"Thank you." She thought to herself that she was going to need it.

75

A few days later John had moved most of his clothes to Riversmeet House. He had found enough furniture to make one bedroom comfortable, had aired the bed and decorated the room. There were curtains at the windows and a fire in the grate. The rest of the house was untouched, but he had to start somewhere. Despite the prospect that he would be living in the place on his own, he refused to admit to a sense of loneliness.

He had just begun decorating the hall one evening, when there came a knock at the door. He went to open it and was surprised to find Alison Stacey standing there. She was wrapped up in a big, light-coloured fur coat with a black scarf wrapped around her head. Her cheeks were pink from the wind and her eyes were bright. He thought she looked absolutely delightful.

John was rooted to the spot. He couldn't think of anything to say. He was aware that he smelled of paint and dust and sweaty work-clothes.

"Can I come in?"

He stood aside and she walked into the hall. She looked around.

"Your mother said I would find you here," she said. "I couldn't understand it. Why are you in this house again?"

"I′ve bought it."

"Bought it? Who from?" She loosened the scarf from round her head and it fell over her shoulder. Her hair was coiled up on top of her head and held in place with a clip which had a flower decoration on it. John thought how pretty it looked.

"I bought it from the people who owned it - the people who your father sold it to after we were evicted - after Dad died." He made no attempt to keep the bitterness out of his voice.

"I've said I was sorry about that," she told him. "I thought you'd agreed to forgive and forget."

"Yes," he admitted, "but it's difficult sometimes."

"Those people you bought it from," Alison said wonderingly, "They never actually lived in the place, did they?

I wonder why not."

"They told me they didn't like the cold and the damp and the isolation," said John. "As a result they let it go very cheaply."

"So *you* don't object to this cold and damp and isolation?" she asked.

He shook his head. "I'm going to change it. I've got the specialists coming to damp-proof the basement next week. After that I'll have central heating installed. I'll put heavy, warm curtains at the windows and have new double windows to keep out the draughts."

"And what about the isolation?" She said it very quietly.

"It's only a hundred yards from the end of the village. I have never felt isolated here." He took a breath. "I like the lonely views, even in the middle of winter - especially in the middle of winter."

She looked towards the sitting-room door. "Is there somewhere we can talk?"

"The only room I've made habitable is the main bedroom," he said. "If you don't mind going up there, I can offer you an arm-chair. I can heat a kettle on the fire, if you want a cup of tea."

"That sounds all right," she smiled.

He followed her up the stairs. "Turn left and it's the last one on the right," he directed.

"Gosh, it's warm in here," she said as she went through the door into the bedroom.

"That'll be the log fire." He helped her off with her coat and scarf and hung them behind the door. "Here you are. You have the armchair and I'll sit on the bed." He couldn't fail to notice the loose, white woollen jumper she was wearing under her coat, which completely failed to disguise the curves of her figure, and the straight skirt which slid part-way up her thighs when she sat down. He tried to turn his mind away from the nearness of her, as he balanced the old kettle on the side of the fire and put the tea-pot near the flames to warm.

"You've made it quite cosy in here," said Alison. "Do you cook for yourself?"

He shook his head. "I still go to Mum's for my evening

meal. That's a big help. It leaves me free to work here in the evenings."

"I understand your wish to be alone at times," she said. "This place suits you. I think you have found your home."

"Really?" He looked at her face, surprised by her perception. Then his cynicism resurfaced. "In fact it *was* my home for more than twenty years."

She didn′t allow his bitterness to deflect her. "I've been trying to contact you on an urgent matter. You seem to be a difficult person to track down."

"I'm sorry," he said. "I've had a lot on my plate recently."

She looked up at him. "On Thursday evening of last week, Henri and I presented my father with the scheme which you and he had worked out for buying the Home Park for enough money to save the rest of Stacey Estates. Father didn't like it. But I think we could have got him to agree, until he found out that *you* were one of the directors of Landscale Developments."

"Ah," said John, "I wondered about that."

Alison gazed into the heart of the fire. "When I asked him what he could possibly have against you, he wouldn't tell me."

John watched her closely. He noticed the play of firelight across the fine features of her face. He saw the steely determination in her eyes. This was a woman one could admire for her resolve as well as her beauty.

"It is important for *all* of us that this land deal goes through." She turned to look at him. "I do not intend that my father should destroy it all over some ancient enmity between your family and ours. Do you understand what I am saying?"

He nodded. Although she was speaking quietly, he could discern the same unshakeable determination to achieve her goal, which he had noticed about her before. He knew what her next question was going to be.

"Can you tell me what it is that makes my father hate you so much? When I understand that, maybe I shall be able to do something about it."

"I only wish I knew," said John. "Didn't your father give you any clue as to what it was about?"

She shook her head. "I was hoping you might know."

"The only thing he's got against *me*," said John, "is that I persuaded you to let me look at the roof of Stacey Court and then I tracked down the builder who had stripped the lead off the place. If that is the cause of his refusing to sell to Landscale, it seems a bit of an over-reaction."

"I'm sure it isn't that." She pursed her lips. "I think it's something that happened a long time ago."

The kettle began to boil, and John busied himself with making the tea.

Alison changed the direction of the conversation. "Is your mother pleased that you have bought Riversmeet House?"

"Not in the least." He grinned lopsidedly. "She says that she won't come back to the place even if I pay her to. She much prefers her little cottage. I suppose I'll have to see if I can buy it for her from the trustees." He shrugged. "Rosemary doesn't like this place either. It looks as though I'll be living here in splendid isolation. Perhaps you'll visit me from time to time."

She shook her head but didn't answer him. He poured her mug of tea and put it on the small table beside her chair. He waited for her to speak.

She looked up at him and said, "You know they want me to marry Henri Maeterlink?"

"You told me."

"What do *you* think I should do?" She looked up at him.

He wanted to tell her that he hated the idea, but instead he said, "I suppose he'd be able to give you the sort of life you've been brought up to expect."

"Yes." She nodded at the fire. "I think he is very generous."

John swallowed. "He's been working hard to solve your father's problems."

"He's put himself out an awful lot," she agreed.

"It would be a way of rewarding him for his help and support."

"Yes."

"I think he would be a very safe and reliable husband."

"I'm sure he would."

"He would lavish lots of care and attention on you."

She nodded.

"Married to Henri, you'll become a famous London hostess," said John. "I'll read about you in the gossip columns.

You'll wear splendid, expensive clothes and everyone will envy your wealth and your happiness."

"I don't want to think about that."

"People will worship you and adore you from afar." He goaded her, "and I'll be able to say to friends – 'I knew her once.' - and they'll be most impressed . . ."

"Please stop it, John." She looked up and he was astonished to see there were tears running down her face.

"What on earth -?"

Alison shook her head. "I don't know what´s the matter with me. I haven't cried since I was ten." She took a breath. "It's the thought that everything's going to change, I suppose."

"Don't be silly. It's going to be great." He bent forward and kissed her salty cheek. "I envy Henri - having enough money to get you."

She looked into his eyes. "You never need to envy Henri, John."

It was then that he knew for sure that she wanted him. He bent forward and kissed her - this time, very gently on the lips. She gasped and opened her mouth wide, allowing her head to fall back. He began to kiss her excitedly and his free hand started to stroke her shoulder. He broke off at last for breath.

"It's so hot in here," she complained.

"Come away from the fire and take your clothes off." He stood up, taking her hand and drawing her with him to the far side of the bed, where they were shielded from the direct heat of the burning logs. He went to the door and switched the light off, leaving them standing only in the glow of the firelight. He walked back to her slowly, looking into her eyes as she waited for him. He knew that at last he was going to make love to this beautiful woman who had often haunted his dreams. He promised himself that he was going to make sure that she enjoyed the experience.

"Turn round," he ordered. "I want to let your hair down."

Slightly to his surprise, she obeyed him. He moved close behind her, inhaling the scent of her. He pulled out the clip with the pretty flower decoration which held her hair coiled on top of her head. There were another couple of clips which he removed, and the hair came cascading down over her shoulders. The light of the fire made it look like a halo about her head. He ran his fingers through it to comb it out into gentle waves.

With the heels of his hands, he began to massage the muscles in her shoulders, working them until he felt that she was beginning to relax. Then he transferred his interest to her neck, rubbing his fingertips around the knobs of her spine. Her head dropped and her back arched. His fingers worked slowly down her spine until they reached her bra-strap. There were two hooks to be undone and then her back was bare under the thin, slightly knobbly fabric of her jumper.

His hands continued until they reached the waistband of her skirt. There was one button to undo in the middle at the back and then the zip, which peeled open across her rounded bottom. A little help caused the skirt to fall to the floor, revealing that she had no other clothes on than a pair of bikini pants and the high-heeled, shiny black shoes on her feet.

He returned his hands to massaging her shoulders but now they were underneath her jumper.

"You have lovely warm hands." She wriggled appreciatively as they explored the muscles of her back. He was surprised by how willingly she was letting them ramble over her body. He pulled her jumper and her loosened bra up over her head and dropped them to the floor. She shook out the long tresses of her hair. Then, bending forward, he kissed her softly on the back of her neck.

"Oh," she said, "I like that."

His massaging hands worked down her back again, then slid round beneath her ribcage from both sides. She gasped and arched her back against his chest. Looking over her shoulder he could see her firm young breasts jutting out into the firelight, almost without any sag to them. He slid his hands up to cup them gently. His thumbs just touched the hardened nipples. He could tell how sensitive they were from the way she flinched. But she didn't stop him. Instead her own hands reached behind her, searching for a way to release the lump in his trousers.

"I'm sorry if I smell all dusty in my work-clothes," he murmured.

She chuckled throatily. "I rather like it. I have never been possessed by a working man before."

Instead of annoying him, this time her comment excited him. Quickly he undid his shirt and tossed it aside. Then he moved her towards the bed, undoing his trousers as he went. She stepped out of the little heap of her skirt and kicked off her shoes. Now she had nothing on but her silky pants. He thought they were very sexy. Her hair brushed her shoulders. He'd never seen her wear it long before. It softened her and gave her a more feminine appearance.

He pulled off his shoes and socks with his trousers. She lay down on the bed and covered her breasts with her hands and for a moment he had the feeling that she was going to refuse him at this late stage. But when he knelt beside her and lifted her right hand there was no resistance. He kissed the palm of her hand and the wrist and inside the elbow and on the shoulder. Then very slowly his lips approached her nipple, enticing her. Her body arched, raising it towards him as he did so. He touched it very gently with his dry, closed lips. Then the tip of his tongue came out and moistened round it. He began to lick her gently and gradually, more strongly as the nipple and its surround grew large and rigid and the whole breast seemed to become firm. As he moved to her other breast her hands went to hold his hair and pull his head against her. He knew she was starting to want him.

Sarah had taught him what to do. His gently exploring hand slid across her stomach and eased under the top of her pants. His fingers softly worked through the fine hair of her genitals until he found the moist hollow of her labia and began to softly stimulate it. When he touched the tiny bump of her clitoris it brought another gasp from her. His fingertip rubbed round it, making it grow, making her body stiffen and squirm. Her back arched again. Her buttocks tightened. Her knees rose and her legs parted.

"For Christ's sake do it, John," she urged.

His own erection was enormous now, thrusting against the restraint of his underpants. He pushed them down and climbed on top of her. He pulled her silken panties to one side and entered her. She was so ready for him that, with one or two gentle thrusts, he penetrated deep into the centre of her. She gasped and writhed beneath his onslaught. But she was trapped on the bed by him, like a live butterfly pinned to its velvet board.

"Oh, my God," she gasped.

"Am I hurting you?" His lips sought hers.

"No," she groaned as she kissed him. "Please hurry up."

He reached behind her and clasped her tight little buttocks through the silkiness of her knickers. The sensation excited him and he began to push more violently, ignoring her gasps as he thrust into her. Quickly they rose to a combined, gasping climax and he collapsed on top of her.

"Oh, John," she sighed. "That was good. That was *the* best."

"My darling," he murmured, when his breath returned. "I have often dreamed of making love to you, but the experience was better than the dreams."

"We should have done it before," she said drowsily, and then, "this heat is sending me to sleep."

He reached down and pulled the covers across them. "You're not in a hurry, are you?"

"No."

"Then let's sleep together. I'd like that."

It was an hour before either of them moved again. For some reason, John didn´t feel guilty about making love to Alison. It was the first time he had slept with a lover at Riversmeet.

76

John met Bill Kingley in a pub near his home on the outskirts of Exeter. Bill had got there before him, and was sitting at a table in the corner with a pint of beer in front of him. John noticed his hair seemed to have got even thinner in the three months since they last met, but the guy was just as cheerful. Bill rose to greet him with a smile.

"Hello, John. Long time no see. What will you have?"

"A pint of bitter, please." He accompanied his short, plump, former boss to the bar. "How has life been treating you?"

"Things have changed a bit. Reggie now seems to be spending almost all of his time down at the Cranford - most of it drinking with his friends in the club-house." He shrugged. "It´s the way he runs his business these days."

"Leaving you to do all the work."

Bill looked at him. "You said it. I´m trying to train up young Jimmy to take your place, but I´m not having much success with him. As a result, I´m turning down most of the pure survey work that we´re offered. We mostly just sell houses now."

"Selling houses is where the future is, Bill."

"I accept that. We can´t go wrong with that sort of business. Everybody seems to want to become an owner-occupier nowadays." He looked at the young man. "You´re doing all right yourself, aren´t you?"

"That´s what I want to talk to you about."

Kingley looked at him sharply. "Is that so?" He turned to pay for the drinks before he led the way back to their corner.

John followed him and they sat down. "I´d better fill you in on the set-up first," he said. "I´m not sure how much you actually know." He took a slurp of his beer. "I´ll start at the beginning. I think you know that one of my old school friends, Sammie Joslin, has been an apprentice for the last six years with Jim Barker, our local builder. But in his spare time he has used his skills in the evenings and at weekends to do carpentry work in people´s houses – fitted kitchens and wardrobes, porches, conservatories, replacing rotten windows and doors – that sort of thing."

"Yes, I knew all about that. And I know you´ve been helping him in your spare time."

"That´s right. But it soon became more than we could cope with as a part-time job. So, first of all, Sammie took on a young trainee who Barker didn´t need any longer. The lad was working in the shed Sammie had built at the end of his back garden. Then during the summer, it really took off. Sammie realised he had to concentrate full-time on the fitted furniture business. Old man Barker was starting to run down the building company and they came to a sort of agreement that Sammie and the young lad could take over the joinery workshop and use Barker´s machine tools in return for occasional back-handers." John paused to take another drink.

"Soon after that Barker decided it was the time for him to retire completely. He apparently put the business on the market, but he didn´t get any response. So he offered the whole company to Sammie, in return for being paid an annual rental for the premises of about a thousand a year and a pension of a hundred pounds a month."

"I suppose the old guy´s doing all right out of that," said Bill. "And he still owns the freehold of the premises."

"Yes." John took another drink. "Well, Sammie isn´t interested in the administrative side of running a business, so he said he´d only take it on if I went in with him on a fifty/fifty basis. At almost the same time I was approached by Sarah Grant. Now, this next bit is still confidential at present, so I must ask you not to spread it round, especially in the office."

Bill was leaning forward, clearly very interested in John´s story. "Of course I´ll keep it to myself."

"Well, apparently Sarah´s father died a year or so ago. He had obviously saved up a bit and owned a bit of property. Sarah was an only child and her mother had already died. So she inherited the lot and it amounted to over thirty thousand pounds."

"My goodness!"

"Yes. Well, she told me she wanted to keep this from Reggie, who might want to use it for his own ends. She decided to invest it in property development instead. You know about the field that you and I surveyed back in May. That side of the business seems to be working out well. But she still hasn´t told Reggie about it. That´s why it´s confidential. I think she´ll have to tell him in the near future, then it will all be out in the open."

"I´d like to see Reggie´s face when she tells him that she´s making more money than he is."

John grinned. "Maybe. Of course, this development business fitted in well with Jim Barker´s offer. Sarah didn´t want to be involved with the actual construction of the houses. She was only interested in selling them. So I agreed to go in with Sammie on the basis that I would help him half of my time with running the fitted furniture side, and with the other half I would be organising the building side. He wasn´t interested in that kind of work." He took a breath. "Well, Barker had a good site agent, who I took on to run the site at Pound Lane. As you know, soon after that I left Grants and set myself up on site selling the houses for Landscale and running the building business, arranging supplies of materials, labour and plant. Sammie and I met up once a week to discuss how the fitted furniture business was going." He took another swig of his beer. "It all seemed to be working out very well."

"You seem to be building quite an empire, John."

"Well, it was all going fine until Sammie got his call-up papers to go for national service. He only told me about it a couple of weeks ago, after he´d already been for the medical and the interviews."

Bill stared at him. "He´s been called up? What are you going to do about that? When does he go?"

"It´s worse than that, Bill. He´s gone and signed on for five years in the army. When I had it out with him, it turned out that he hadn´t been happy with our rapid expansion, particularly into housing. He´s decided to pack the whole business in."

"Bloody hell!"

"That´s why I asked you to meet me here today, but before that, I must tell you I´ve decided to reorganise the whole business, which has been sort of cobbled together up until now." John took a swig of his beer. "First of all, I want to separate the fitted furniture side completely from the building company. It's grown so big that Barkers yard is bursting at the seams, and there's no room for all the stuff connected with the building activities. So I'm renting a modern factory on the Marsh Barton Trading Estate. They're offering them at cheap rents to encourage new industry in the area. And I'm going to move the whole fitted furniture business over there - lock, stock and barrel. I'm advertising for a manager and I've got interviews next week. But of course it will take up quite a bit of my time while I'm getting it sorted out." He paused for another drink before he continued.

"It means I'll have less time to do the selling at Pound Lane. I've already picked up a bright school-leaver to help me with that. However, all the other activities mean that I'm not going to be able to spare enough time to run the building side on my own and I'm looking for someone to manage that." He paused for breath. "So I wondered if you'd be willing to take it on. I think you're under-valued for what you do at Grants, and I reckon you would make a great job of this, with me just lending a hand as and when I was needed."

"So that's it." Bill smiled. "What exactly did you have in mind?"

"My idea is, that you'd be installed in the office at Barker's yard. You'd be responsible for seeing the housing and the other building work would be carried out to programme, controlling the supplies of materials, hiring or purchasing the plant and equipment, and recruiting and organising the labour, so that the building work ran as smoothly as possible, We'd agree the sequence of work together and I would help where necessary with finding the resources we need. I think we worked well together at Grants and I don't see why we couldn't make a success of it."

Bill looked down at the table, obviously thinking hard.

"I'd make the move worth your while," said John. "To start with I'd pay you fifty percent more than you're getting at Grants. Then I'd give you a twenty-five percent share in the building business. It looks as though our turnover in the first year should exceed two hundred thousand pounds, and the agreement with Sarah is that we will receive ten percent gross profit on costs on all the work we carry out for Landscale. We should also earn a couple of thousand a year from the other work we get, mainly from clients who used to give work to old man Barker."

"Does that mean I´ll get a quarter of something over twenty thousand pounds on top of my salary?"

"No. The admin costs have to come out of that."

"And what are they?"

"I told you we pay Jim Barker a thousand a year for rent plus a hundred a month pension. Then there´s electricity and rates. There´s your salary and a secretary and probably a young trainee to help out. There´s a van and a trailer for deliveries and you can have a car if you want one. With some costs for repairs and maintenance, I think the annual overheads will come to somewhere between six and seven thousand."

"What about your salary?"

"I get paid by Landscale. Of course, I might want to take some of the profits from the business in due course. If I did, I would expect to agree with you to take whatever the business could afford. It would be up for discussion if either of us thought we genuinely needed it. But I have to say that I want to build a healthy business over the first few years with sufficient financial reserves, in case we hit any unforeseen problems, and I don´t intend to take much out to start with." John had a thought. "Oh, we´re thinking of building some more up-market five bedroomed houses with double garages on the next development and you could have one of those at cost if you want."

"What´s this about the next development?"

"We´re in negotiations to get the land to start a much bigger project, which will follow on from Pound Lane. The plans haven´t been finalised yet. I´ll let you know when that one is in the bag." He gazed at his friend. "Well, Bill, are you prepared to think about it?"

Bill grinned back. "I don´t have to think about it, John. I´d be a fool to turn down an offer like that. I can tell you now that I accept."

"That´s great, Bill." John leaned across the table with his hand held out and they shook hands firmly. "When would you be able to start?"

"Well, I´ll have to give Reggie a month´s notice and we´re already well into November. So I guess the beginning of January is the earliest I´ll be free."

"OK. First of January it is. I´ll get the confirmation offer typed up and send it to you in the next few days. Then you can tell old man Grant that he´ll have to find someone else to run the place."

"Oh, he won´t need to replace me. He can forget most of the survey work. The details of the new houses are all prepared by the architects and most of the town stuff has already gone through their books in the past. He can use a local photographer and just take on a salesman to deal with customers. Estate agency isn´t what it used to be." Bill paused. "Now what about another beer to celebrate?"

"This one´s on me," said John, rising and grabbing his friend´s glass.

77

A few hectic weeks later John had a phone call from Susie. It was early on a Friday morning before he left for work.

"John, can I talk to you?"

"Of course you can. What's the problem?"

There was a brief pause. "I would prefer for us to meet somewhere private."

"All right. Where are you?"

"I'm at home at the moment."

"Are you alone?" He was aware that Lionel Plowright was usually away during the week. "Do you want me to come round?"

"Er –." There was another pause. "Would you mind picking me up from the bus stop just round the corner from the end of our road."

John grinned. "This all sounds very mysterious, Susie."

"I know." She took a deep breath. "I'm sorry, but I need to talk to someone and – well, I don't want any tongues wagging about my meeting a strange man."

"All right." He chuckled as he thought about the time he had seen her at the Cranford with a man who certainly wasn't her husband. "When do you want to be picked up?"

"Well – er – can you do it now?"

John thought quickly. He had no immediate appointments this morning. "OK. My car's parked at the yard, but I should be able to get to your place in about a quarter of an hour."

"I'll be waiting at the bus stop."

He saw Susie was there as he came round the bend approaching her estate. He pulled up and she scrambled in with a quick look round to see that she wasn't observed. He noticed she was smartly dressed in a grey woollen coat and carrying a black shiny handbag which matched her shoes. Underneath she was wearing a grey linen blouse which was buttoned up to the neck. She was carefully made up, but her cheeks were pink from the December wind or from embarrassment. John thought again that he could easily fancy the lady.

"Good morning," he greeted her. "Where do you want to go?"

"Can we talk as we drive? I have to be at work at nine."

John checked his watch. "It's ten past eight. If we go up on Woodbury Common, it'll only take us a quarter of an hour each way, and that will leave twenty minutes up there. Does that suit you?"

"That's a good idea."

There was long period of silence as he drove. At last John said, "OK, Susie. When are you going to start?"

"I was wondering how to put it," she began. "I – er - I used to know a gentleman." She glanced at him with a gleam of a smile. "That was before I met my husband."

"Susie, I've promised not to ask about him and I won't."

"I know, but he's part of what I've got to tell you. Actually I haven't seen him or spoken to him for a long time – not since you saw us together that afternoon. Then last night he rang me up."

"What did Lionel say about that?"

"He doesn't know. He's away at the moment."

"Are you telling me that this man is making trouble for you?"

She shook her head. "Oh, no! It was nothing like that. He rang me to tell me to pass on a warning."

"A warning?" Even as he asked the question, he began to guess what was coming.

"Yes. You see – er – this gentleman knows a lot of people in London." She paused. "Somehow he had found out that I was working for Sir Oswald Stacey. He told me that it was well known in the clubs in London that Sir Oswald had very big gambling debts."

"I suppose it's difficult to keep that sort of thing quiet."

"Yes, but it was more important than that. He said that somebody had contacted the people who Sir Oswald owed the money to. He said this person was – what do you call it? – a sort of go-between."

"Do you mean an intermediary?"

“Yes. I think that’s right. An intermediary.”

“So, what about him?”

“Well, apparently this intermediary had told these people that he owed the money to, that they couldn’t claim the money back legally, because gambling debts aren’t recognised by the courts. I think that’s what he said.” She paused. “But this man said that his – was it his principals?”

“That sounds right.”

“Well, his principals were prepared to offer a part of the money on condition that this was accepted as full payment of the debt but that was all they would get. Well,” she rushed on, “my friend said these people were very angry about this, and they have threatened to take it out on Sir Oswald and his family, and my friend says they are not nice people at all, and that I should warn Sir Oswald about it.” She turned to face John. “The trouble is I don’t feel I know him well enough to talk to him about it, and he might get angry with me and tell me I was talking rubbish and perhaps he might even decide he didn’t want me to work for him any longer. So I – I thought you might be able to help me.”

They had just reached the car park at Woodbury Castle. John pulled off the road on to the rough track which led to a place where the view was across the broad sweep of the estuary to the Haldon Hills beyond. There was no-one else there at this early time of the day. He switched off the engine and leaned back in his seat with a sigh.

“Do you think you can help me?” asked Susie anxiously.

He shook his head and turned to face her. “As far as I’m aware, I am Sir Oswald’s most hated man at the moment. He hasn’t forgiven me for exposing the state of the roof at Stacey Court. But I think it’s much more than that. There seems to be some old feud between his family and mine that I don´t understand. So I don’t think I am the right person to talk to him about this.”

“But I can’t think of anyone else.”

“What about Ambrose?” But, even as he asked, he knew the chap wouldn’t be much help.

“He’s away in London. I don’t know how to get hold of him.”

"So what about Stacey′s daughter? What about Alison? You say that you and she talk to each other and I think she has enough courage to confront her father and make him see sense."

Susie shook her head. "She's gone back to St Theresa's in Geneva. It′s her final term. I don't know when she'll be back."

"Can you contact her?"

She thought for a moment. "Perhaps I can find out her phone number. I've seen some correspondence from the convent. But international calls are difficult and expensive. Sir Oswald might catch me. He would be furious if he found me talking to Alison behind his back."

"Well," said John, "I'll phone her from the office if you give me the number."

"Oh, would you?" She turned to him with a smile. "I'd be ever so grateful."

"But first, Susie, I need to know all the details. What is the name of this gentleman of yours?"

She paused for a moment, biting her lip. "Yes, of course. I – I think his name is Mr Barrington."

"You think?"

She blushed. "He told me his name was Richard Barrington."

"And how did he find out about Stacey's gambling debts?"

"I don't know." She shook her head. "He didn't tell me that. But he hears about all sorts of things. He knows a lot of people."

"It sounds as though he's a bit of a shady character."

She thought a bit more before she responded. "I suppose perhaps he is."

"Is he likely to be somebody that Stacey knows? Or perhaps Alison knows him."

"I don't know about that."

John gazed across the cold, bleak car parking area, trying to get an idea of what might have been happening. "This intermediary – the go-between chap – who is he?"

"I'm sorry, John, but Richard – er – Mr Barrington didn't say and I didn't think to ask him."

"And did he say who the man was representing – the people who were offering to pay part of the debt?"

She shook her head again. "He didn't say that either."

"Would it perhaps be some bankers?" He turned to face her. "They are the only people I can think of who might have enough money to even partly clear debts that big." And, he thought, there would only be one banker who would be interested in settling Stacey's debts. That probably meant that Alison already knew about it. He would have to be careful how he put the information to her.

John continued to question Susie for a few more minutes without getting any further useful information. So he drove her to Stacey Court and waited while she went in and found St Theresa's telephone number in Geneva. There was no sign of Sir Oswald this early. He didn't normally rise for his breakfast until well after nine.

It took three phone calls and a testing of John's rudimentary French before he managed to get Alison to the phone. When she finally spoke to him she sounded a little breathless.

"Oh, hello John. I was wanting to talk to you."

"It's important that I talk to *you*, Alison. I was contacted by Susie Plowright this morning. She had a strange story to tell." He proceeded to give her an edited version of what the secretary had told him.

"Oh, my goodness," she said, when he paused. "What *is* happening?"

"Do you know what is going on?"

"I – er – I don't think so."

"Do you know this fellow Barrington?"

"I've never heard of him."

"What about the people offering the money? Do you think Henri would have anything to do with this?"

"I suppose he might." She paused. "I suppose I ought to talk to him."

"I think that would be a very good idea. And Alison," John tried to stress the next point, "if it is him, I think you should tell him that it's not a good idea to try and short-change your father's creditors. They sound a very unpleasant bunch of characters."

"Yes, I agree." There was another, longer pause. "I think I´m going to have to come back. I can't sort this out over the telephone. Besides, John, I want to talk to you as well." She sighed. "In any case there's not much point in my staying here any longer. Term finishes in two weeks and I think it is more important that I should be back in England."

"That sounds like a good idea," agreed John.

"I will be there in two or three days. I will try to get to the bottom of this business and then I will contact you."

"OK. I'll see you in a few days."

"Yes, please. 'Bye."

"Cheerio."

He hung up, deep in thought. Did she know more than she had let on?

78

Three days later Sarah picked him up from Riversmeet in her sleek Sunbeam Talbot. She smiled at him as he opened the door and got in. “Isn’t it a beautiful day?”

“Is it?” It was true that the weak December sun was starting to disperse the clammy mist which hung above the river. But John had had enough of mists in the last couple of months. “I’d forgotten how damp it is down here by the river,” he said. “Perhaps that’s why nobody else but me wants to live here.”

“How are you getting on with the renovations?”

“Well enough. I’m not in a hurry. I want to do it properly and that´s obviously going to take some time. In any case, everything is pretty hectic, now that I’m having to prepare for Sammie’s departure.”

Sarah looked at him. “I don’t think you’ll regret him going in the long run.”

“It´s costing nearly nine thousand pounds to pay him off.” He shook his head. “Even though you let me take two thousand of my sales bonuses for the houses, it has virtually cleaned Barkers out of cash.”

“I think Sammie was always going to hold you back,” she said. “I´m sure he wouldn´t have agreed to you taking on this big new development, and he would have prevented you from achieving your full potential.”

“I´m not going to argue with you about that, but all the extra work means I haven´t got much time for renovating Riversmeet.”

She smiled sideways at him. “When are you going to invite me to inspect the work you’re doing?”

“I wondered about having our next Wednesday meeting there.” He chuckled. “At least we wouldn’t need to worry about Reggie suddenly turning up.”

“It was only the once, John.”

“True.”

“However I agree that it *would* be a good idea.” She nodded. “I accept your invitation.”

“I look forward to it,” he said. “That will turn Wednesday into a special day.”

“I think,” said Sarah, as she reversed into the turning bay, “that actually today is also going to turn out to be a special sort of a day.”

“We could do with some decent weather.” He stretched out in the comfortable seat. “It seems to have been at least six weeks since we saw the sun.”

She chuckled. “That’s just about as long as we’ve been waiting for Sir Oswald to make up his mind. You’ve got to hand it to young Alison - anyone else would have given up and let him go bust weeks ago.”

“There must be a reason why she wants to see us now.”

Sarah turned up the High Street away from the riverside. “I don′t know why she contacted me. She was quite mysterious - talked about something new having come up.” She looked at him. “I suppose you haven’t any idea?”

John didn’t feel he should discuss the subject of his recent meeting with Susie. “She seems to have been keeping out of my way since she got back from Switzerland,” he said bitterly, “just as everyone else has.”

“There now.” She patted his knee. “I haven’t been keeping away from you. If anything, it seems to have been the other way round.”

“I’m sorry about that,” he said. “It′s only that I’ve been frantically busy, having to reorganise the furniture side, on top of everything else.”

“Have you got a manager for the fitted furniture business?”

He nodded. “I’m hopeful. I’ve got the final interviews on Friday and there are two applicants that I’m especially interested in.”

“And then there′s Bill Kingley?” She laughed. “Reggie was furious that you’d poached him for the building company.”

“Not furious enough to make the chap a better offer to stay. I′m giving him a twenty-five percent share in Barkers as well as a much better salary.” He pursed his lips. “But Bill doesn’t start until January. I must say I could do with him now. I’ve got quite a problem getting all these houses ready, in addition to the other jobs.”

"It really is marvellous." Sarah changed down as she turned into Station Road. "In my wildest dreams, I never expected the sales to go through the roof like that. How many have moved in so far?"

"We've got fourteen completions and all but three have moved in. There's another five completing before Christmas. And we've got eleven deposits from people hoping to move in during January." He grinned at her. "At this rate we'll have completed the development by midsummer."

"So we really must have a decision on Stacey Court before Christmas." Sarah amused John by the way she gesticulated while she was driving. "Otherwise we won't have anything to move on to, when we've completed Pound Lane."

"I think," he said, "we should make it clear to them today. We must have a firm date from the Staceys, or we will be going ahead with the Pound Lane Farm development next week. It's just not fair on old Fisher to keep him hanging on for a decision like this."

Sarah nodded. "I agree." She swung through the gates into the home park and took the winding drive at speed. "But I must say that this would make a beautiful setting for a well-planned housing estate. I see in your plans that there are plenty of green areas and, because you're retaining the big trees, I think it will look lovely."

"We can't let that influence our decision." John watched as Stacey Court came into view round the bend in the road. "We'll just have to do our best on the other site if we can't get any joy today. Personally, I'd rather have a positive target to aim at, than carry on messing around in this way."

"That's because you're a man of action," she said and patted him on the knee. "It's one of the things I find most attractive and exciting about you." She coasted on to the gravel turning circle and pulled up just before the main steps. "Well, in the next hour we should find out."

They were met at the front door by Annie who showed them into the sitting-room to the left of the hall. "Miss Alison will be down in a minute," was all the cook said, as she left them on their own.

They didn't have long to wait. Alison hurried in through the door. John could see there was the light of battle in her eyes. But she also seemed to be avoiding looking at him. He wondered what had come out of her talk to Henri Maeterlink.

"I'm going to take you in to see my father," she said without greeting or preamble. "I think that it's important that you are here with me when I talk to him. I believe it's my last opportunity to convince him to change his mind. But before we go in, I want to explain something to you, John."

"Why is Sir Oswald so opposed to John?" asked Sarah. "We've been trying to recall anything that he might have said or done in the past. But the worst thing anyone can come up with is that he discovered about the lead which had been stripped from the roofs the estate buildings. The facts of that have not been publicised, and I can hardly imagine that a reasonable man would hold the perhaps over-scrupulous performance of his duties against John for any length of time."

"I just don't know." Alison raised her hands. "All I *do* know is that there is nothing reasonable about this. He has an almost fanatical objection to John being involved in anything to do with Stacey Court."

"There is a perfectly good reason," said a voice from the door, "and I suppose I shall have to give it to you."

Everyone spun round to look at the old man as he advanced towards them. To John's eyes he appeared quite alert this morning, and free from the influence of alcohol. Perhaps it was too early in the day for him to have had his first drink.

"What *do* you mean, Father?" Alison asked.

"I mean, that I shall tell you why no member of the Tucker family should ever be permitted to get their hands on any part of Stacey Court." He pulled himself erect. "It is time that your generation understood what has happened in the past."

"So it has nothing to do with John," said Sarah.

"Not directly," said the old man. "He is just another example of how the Tucker breed has destroyed the Staceys." He turned to John. "But tell me first, young man, what you thought of me, when Mr Grant gave you the sack because I had insisted on it?"

John looked him straight in the eye. "Actually I resigned before I sent in my report about the condition of this place. I didn't want to be involved with a business that runs on lies and hypocrisy. Apparently that is what you expect of the people you employ."

"That is the sort of answer I would have expected to get from your father," sighed Sir Oswald. It was as though he was speaking half to himself.

"Why did you say that?" John stared at the old man.

There was a ghost of a smile hovering around Sir Oswald's features as he gazed at the youngster. "You remind me almost exactly of your father thirty years ago - so clever, so self-confident." His eyes hardened. "So totally unforgiving of anybody whose standards were less exacting than his own." The smile was now fixed mirthlessly across his face. There was no sentiment in his voice.

"How did you know my father thirty years ago?" asked John.

"Did he never tell you? Did he *really* never tell you?" Sir Oswald raised his gaze and stared unseeingly over John's head into the distance. "Didn't he tell you why a mere employee of the estate should be living in such a grand house and doing so little for the privilege?"

"My mother said something about what he did for Sir Bertram in the Great Depression -"

Stacey snorted. "What he did for Sir Bertram? It would be more correct to ask what my father did for *him*. The truth is that he should never have been treated as he was. That was what caused the later problems. The man got above himself." He shook his head. "But *I* had no say in what was arranged. I just had to live with the consequences."

"I don't understand." John moved forward, but the old man held up his hand to stop him. "What are you trying to tell me? As far as I knew, my father was a good and efficient estate manager. He served you and your father loyally and well. Everybody I have talked to speaks well of him."

"Oh," Sir Oswald made a dismissive gesture, "he was all of those things. He was certainly a good estate manager. Your father was a man who would have been good at anything he put his hand to." He paused. "But we could just as easily have employed somebody much less expensive to do the job. Why do you think we employed your father, of all people?"

John put his hands on his hips, looking at the older man with undisguised animosity. "I don't know. Perhaps you'd better tell me."

"We employed him because," the old man bent forward and hissed at him, "because he was my cousin. That's why!"

"Your cousin?" He hesitated. "Does that mean - ?"

"Exactly. He was the son of Bertram's younger sister. She married a small but reasonably successful businessman from London. They decided to go to America where they thought the opportunities for his class were greater. They chose to travel on the maiden voyage of the ship which became infamous. The ship was the Titanic, and they were both drowned in the disaster. Your father, who was then ten or so years old, had been left in the care of Bertram until they had settled in the United States, when he would be sent to join them. After the disaster, he was brought here to live. He was treated as though he was my younger brother."

"What? My father lived in this house as a child?"

"That's right. He went to a local school while I was away at Eton. When he finished his schooling, he was given the job as assistant to the then estate manager. He was given a good training." Sir Oswald lapsed into silence, gazing into the distance, immersed in his own thoughts.

"And what happened then?" prompted Sarah.

"Then?" The old man looked back at John. "Then came the real disaster." He felt for a chair and Alison helped him to find it and seat himself. "Your grandfather on your father's side had a brother, who had gone to the United States in the early part of the century and had made good. In the end he had become a banker on Wall Street in New York. It was he whom your grandparents had been going to join when they were drowned."

He paused again, as if assembling his thoughts to get them in the right order. "Your father's uncle wrote and invited him to go to Wall Street and learn the trade of banking. Your father decided that was a good idea. He was then in his early twenties. He decided to turn his back on estate management. At the same time, my father - the man you know as Sir Bertram - wanted me to learn a trade. He proposed that George Tucker should train us both for a fee, and the man agreed. The long and the short of it was that we sailed to America together. That was in the summer of nineteen twenty-eight." He looked at John piercingly. "We were never close, you understand. Our age difference was more than ten years. But we didn't dislike each other. We just went our own separate ways."

Stacey paused for a long time, looking down at the pattern on the carpet. John wondered whether he was going to deny him the rest of the story. But at last the old man resumed, his voice a deep, slow rumble of reminiscence.

"Life in New York was very different for the two of us. Your father was just a young man learning a trade and being paid a modest salary while he was learning. I was paid nothing, but I had a comfortable allowance from my father." The ghost of a smile crossed his face. "The Staceys were well off then."

"Did you live together?" ventured John.

He shook his head. "No. I stayed with friends of the family. David - he -. After the first couple of weeks living with his uncle's family, he found a flat in some unsavoury district of the city. It was all he could afford. He worked a lot, and I didn't see all that much of him outside the bank."

"You didn't spend much time together?"

"Certainly not." Stacey threw his shoulders back with an attempt at a swagger. "I was the son of an English lord, you see, and I was welcome in all sorts of houses where your father wouldn't be allowed across the threshold." He looked at John. "Don't let anyone tell you that the Americans aren't class conscious." He shook his head. "But that doesn't matter. I had a splendid time in New York. Your father - well, he just worked there."

He balled his fists. "And then it happened."

"What?"

"I met Arabella."

"Who?"

"That was Mummy," explained Alison breathlessly.

Stacey looked up at John, but he had the strange sensation that the man was looking past him at his long dead wife. "Arabella was the most beautiful and magnificent woman I have ever seen, before or since." He took a breath. "From the first minute I saw her, I worshipped her. I wanted her."

He slumped back in the chair, breathing unevenly. Alison started forward, worried that he was making himself ill, but Sir Oswald straightened up and put out his hand to push her away.

"To start with, she had little interest in me. But I persevered, and gradually I believe I began to mean something to her. And then -." He glared at John with such a look of evil that the young man recoiled. "And then she met your father. I forget how it came about, but they were thrown together in some way."

John swallowed. Half of him wanted to bring this story to an end. He had a horrible feeling he was going to wish that he had never heard it. But the other half hung to on every word that fell in the clumsy torrent from the old man's lips.

"I don't know how it happened or why it happened," Stacey said, "but Arabella fell in love with your father. They had a secret affair. Neither I nor anyone else knew anything about it until she found out that she -" he paused, then his voice went on in a high-pitched tone, " - that she was to have a baby."

"Oh, my god," broke from Alison's lips.

"There was hell to pay when she confessed it to her family. They were one of the highest and most splendid in New York. They refused absolutely to sanction her union with your father, even though she protested that she loved him. In those days, daughters did what their parents told them. She was forbidden to see your father again." He sniffed disdainfully. "In any case, he was on his way back to England within two days. His visa was cancelled on the spot. The Vanderplatts had that sort of power. If he had tried to go back, he would have been stopped at immigration and thrown out again." He paused. "But the fellow had the luck of the devil. He should have been ruined. Two weeks after he left New York the stock market crashed on Wall Street."

Stacey looked around for a drink. Alison poured him a glass of water from the carafe that stood on a side table.

"In England there was great fear and indecision. David found he had a very powerful weapon called information. He had been close to the action on Wall Street and he didn't scruple to make himself useful to anyone here who wanted this information. My father naturally was pleased to benefit from his advice. As a consequence, Sir Bertram allowed him to resume his old duties on the estate."

"So *you* married Arabella instead?" asked Sarah wonderingly.

He nodded. "Her family knew I loved her beyond all reason. I was from the right sort of family. I was prepared to accept paternity of someone else's child, as long as it meant I would be with her. We were quickly married and sent to live in a house which her family owned in San Francisco. We stayed there for some time after Ambrose had been born." He sighed. "Those three years were the happiest of my life. I put all my efforts into winning Arabella's affections, and I believe I made her happy." There was something like a contented smile on his face.

Alison put her hand to her face. "So Ambrose and John are - ." She couldn't finish.

"- half brothers," supplied Sarah.

"But it couldn't last." Stacey shook his head. "Sir Bertram became ill. He died in nineteen thirty-two. Then I had to return to take over the estate. In the meantime, your father had married, and you had been born. Of course I was dreadfully afraid that your father and Arabella would try to renew their love affair. But they seemed to keep out of each other's way. As far as I am aware, they never met or spoke to each other again. By then your father ran the complete estate from Riversmeet House and from an office at one of the farms. He met me once a month at the office to report about on progress on the estate and to receive any instructions I might wish to give him."

"What a story," breathed Sarah.

Sir Oswald looked sharply at her. "Alison was born a little more than a year after we returned from the States. And Arabella died when the girl was nearly eight." He paused, his mind wandering across the old scenes. "For some reason, although they were only too pleased to marry me to their daughter, the Vanderplatts never took to me. They were happy to let me marry their daughter, but they seemed to blame me, in some peculiar way, for your father's actions, although it was me who actually pulled their irons out of the fire. They would never trust me with any money. It was all paid to Arabella. But still -." He shrugged and said no more.

John took a huge breath to release some of the tension which had been building up inside him as he listened to the incredible story. He turned and walked across to look out of one of the tall windows and stretch his legs.

Stacey's eyes followed him. "Now you know why I feel as I do about your family," he said. "There has been too much misery brought to us by the Tuckers already."

"That is stupid, father." Alison came forward. "You have reacted in entirely the wrong way to what has happened. Can't you see that the future of the Staceys and the Tuckers are inextricably linked together? Even your own actions have helped to bring this about."

The old man looked up at her. "I don't understand. What are you talking about? What do you mean?"

"I mean just this," she said, standing upright. "On their own, the Staceys are lost. They will soon have nothing and be worth nothing. But together with the Tuckers they can recover. We must not be too proud to bring new blood into the family. That is how the English aristocracy have survived for hundreds of years."

They all watched her, trying to understand the meaning behind her words. Sarah said quietly, "There's something else that you have to tell us, isn't there Alison?"

"Yes." She turned and looked at the young man. "I'm sorry, John. I wanted to talk to you first, before I told my father. But I didn't have the chance."

"What is it?" His eyes were glued on her face.

"Yesterday evening I went to see Doctor Morton. He told me what I had suspected for a few days." She took a deep breath and let it out again. "I am pregnant."

John advanced towards her. "Who -?"

"*You* are the father, John. It was that night at Riversmeet House about two months ago."

There was a kind of a sigh from her father and he seemed to slump in his chair, but John and Alison ignored him completely. They were locked in their own confrontation.

"But you told me you always had your own protection," said John.

She lowered her gaze. "That night I didn't use it."

"On purpose?" he asked.

She nodded.

In four violent strides he crossed to her and gripped her arm. "You mean you did it on purpose to get pregnant? Your only purpose was to make your father change his mind? You used me to try and get him to sign the agreement?"

"No," she protested. "It wasn't only that. Please John, can we go into the library and I'll try to explain to you."

"How can you *explain*," he spat at her. "You used me to try and rescue the Staceys from the depths to which this pathetic old reprobate had dragged them."

"It wasn't like that -"

"Wasn't it?" he demanded. "Why then did you just suddenly happen to turn up that evening? Why did you willingly come up to my bedroom? You had obviously planned it all."

"Wait a minute, John," Sarah interrupted. "Are you trying to say it was all Alison's fault? Did she fall on her knees and beg you to make love to her? Can you honestly say she trapped you into it?" She approached him, shaking her head. "I know you, John Tucker. I think I understand you as well as anyone - better probably than your own mother. I know what crossed your mind. You said to yourself, 'Aah, here's a chance for me to shag one of the aristocracy - someone I've fancied for a long time. And she's offering it to me on a plate. I'd be a fool to turn it down.' Isn't that the truth, John?"

He turned away, shaking his head. "It wasn't like that for me. I'd begun to realise that . . ." He stopped.

"That what?" asked Sarah. "That you´d begun to realise you were falling in love with the girl? Is that it?"

He nodded but said nothing more.

"And how do you think Alison feels? She didn't have to offer herself to you. She's a beautiful young woman, daughter of one of the oldest aristocratic families in the country. She could have had her pick of the sons of the nobility. We know that Henri Maeterlink was trying to win her hand. And she was willing to throw it all away for you. I happen to think she made the right decision. Don't you dare go and ruin it now." She paused, breathing heavily.

Neither Alison nor John said a word.

"And what about the child?" Sarah spoke defiantly. "Is it to be born a bastard? Or even worse - do you want the child aborted - this little body which is half Stacey and half Tucker?" She waved at him violently. "Of course - if you decide you want to do that, I can help you. I know a very good man in Harley Street. You can easily afford the thousand pounds. He'll do it in the next few days before anyone even suspects she's pregnant."

"Oh. Please - no," cried Alison.

"What about you, John?" asked Sarah. "You say she tricked you into it. But it can all be solved by an abortion. You think she owes you *that*, doesn't she? Then you can walk away from it and forget that the two of you even knew each other. Is that what you want?"

He turned to face her. "You know it isn't."

"Then put your arms round her and tell her you understand why she gave herself to you, and beg her to marry you." Sarah was leaning forward, almost hectoring him. "Go on," she said, when he still hesitated.

She watched them for a moment as they came together and clung to each other. Then she turned on Sir Oswald.

"And as for you," she said to him, "can't you see that it's your foolish attitude that has caused all this heartache. What happened between John's father and your wife is thirty years in the past. You said yourself that they had never even met again after you were married. Hadn't your wife always been faithful to you since you married?"

The old man looked up at her, transfixed by her standing over him like an avenging Valkyrie. He nodded almost imperceptibly.

Sarah took a breath. "What husband can ask for more than that? David Tucker never tried to seduce her back from you. He never approached Ambrose, or told anyone else about the son who everyone thought was yours, but who was genetically his. He left you and your two children to have a happy and peaceful family life." She paused to clear her throat. "It was no fault of his that Arabella died young. If she had lived, I believe that she would have blessed this joining together of the Tucker and Stacey families. She would have regarded it as a strange kind of justice. Don't you agree with me?"

"Er, well -" Stacey hesitated. The telling of his long-hidden story seemed to have purged the anger from him. "Perhaps she was always more tolerant than I was. Americans are, you know."

"Exactly." Sarah took a step backwards. "I only hope that you realise that your inflexible attitude came very close to causing a major tragedy to both these young people, as well as bringing economic disaster to yourself. I hope you will now try to help them to achieve as great a success as possible, in the life that they have ahead of them."

Sir Oswald pulled himself to his feet. "Do you know, Mrs Grant, I think you're a very remarkable woman. Arabella was also remarkable in a different way. I only wish she had been permitted to stay with me until now. I think she would have wanted me to shake your hand."

He reached out and they shook hands firmly.

"So that's settled," said Sarah. "Now – we need to get those agreements for you to sign?"

THE END

Also by **Michael Hillier**:-

The Secret of the Cathars

The Legacy of the Templars

The Treasure of the Visigoth

The Discovery of Franco´s Bankroll

The Eighth Child

Go to his website (https://mikehillier.com) for details.

Printed in Great Britain
by Amazon

63849638R00270